The Relic

A Novel

José Maria de Eça de Queirós

Translated from the Portuguese by AUBREY F. G. BELL

Preface by HAROLD BLOOM

Tagus Press at UMass Dartmouth Dartmouth, Massachusetts

Adamastor Series 7

Tagus Press at UMass Dartmouth.
www.portstudies.umassd.edu
© 1925, renewed 1953 Alfred A. Knopf, Inc.
Preface by Harold Bloom © 2012 Tagus Press at UMass Dartmouth
All rights reserved.
Manufactured in the United States of America
General Editor: Frank F. Sousa. Managing Editor: Mario Pereira
Designed by Richard Hendel
Typeset in Joanna and Estilo by Tseng Information Systems, Inc.

Tagus Press books are produced and distributed for Tagus Press by University Press
of New England, which is a member of the Green Press Initiative. The paper used
in this book meets their minimum requirement for recycled paper.

For all inquiries, please contact:
Tagus Press at UMass Dartmouth
Center for Portuguese Studies and Culture
285 Old Westport Road, North Dartmouth MA 02747-2300
Tel. 508-999-8255   Fax 508-999-9272
www.portstudies.umassd.edu

Published by arrangement with Alfred A. Knopf, an imprint of
The Knopf Doubleday Publishing Group, a division of Random House, Inc.

Published with the generous support of the Luso-American Foundation.

Library of Congress Cataloguing-in-Publication Data
Queirós, Eça de, 1845–1900.
[Relíquia. English]
The relic: a novel / Jose Maria de Eça de Queirós; translated from the Portuguese
by Aubrey F. G. Bell; preface by Harold Bloom.
     p. cm.—(Adamastor series ; 7)
ISBN 978-1-933227-35-1 (pbk. : alk. paper)— ISBN 978-1-933227-38-2 (ebook)
I. Bell, Aubrey F. G. (Aubrey Fitz Gerald), 1882–1950. II. Title.
PQ9261.E3R413 2012   869.3′3—dc23   2011049956

5 4 3 2 1

The Relic A Novel

Over the stark nakedness of truth—

the diaphanous cloak of fantasy.

Contents

Preface

Eça de Queirós (1845–1900) remains the subtlest and most gifted novelist that Portugal has brought forth. *The Relic*, superbly rendered by Aubrey F. G. Bell, may not be Eça's masterwork, yet it is a delight, by any standards, and should be widely read and appreciated by discerning American readers. Its startling fusion of comedy and authentic spirituality is virtually unique, in any national literature of the Western world. Eça, who by residence was nearly as familiar with Paris and London as with Lisbon, shared perspectives both with Gustave Flaubert and with Robert Louis Stevenson, an unlikely combination, yet curiously prophetic both of Borges and of Saramago. I tend to think of Balzac as Eça's authentic precursor, since the interpenetration of societal realism and of fantasy distinguishes the fiction of both.

The *Relic* is narrated in the first person by the sublimely outrageous Teodorico, who at first is honest only with himself, and with the reader. A marvelous scamp, orphaned early, he is taken at the age of seven to Lisbon to be raised by a wealthy and pious maiden aunt, a monster, wonderfully comic to the reader but a monster nevertheless. To survive, and to remain her heir, Teodorico grows up a complex hypocrite, always involved in a double life:

> My aunt gave me a prayer on a piece of paper which I was to pray daily to St. Luis Gonzaga, patron of studious youth, that he might preserve my body fresh and clean and my soul in the fear of the Lord. . . . I disliked [my theology tutor] Dr. Roxo from the first. In his house I endured a hard cloistral life, and it was a tremendous joy when in my first year of studying Law the disagreeable priest died miserably of an anthrax. I then went to the pleasant lodging-house of the Pimentas, and forthwith without moderation made the acquaintance of the great delights of life

in full independence. I never again prayed the insipid prayer to St. Luis Gonzaga; nor bowed my manly knee to any holy aureoled image; I became gloriously drunk in the tavern of the Camellas; I proved my strength by knocking out a marker of the Café Trony; I drank my fill of love in the Terreiro da Erva; I sauntered singing ballads by moonlight; I carried a stout stick; and as my beard began to grow strong and thick I accepted with pride the nickname of Raposão. Every fortnight, however, I wrote to Auntie in my good handwriting a humble pious letter, in which I told her of the severity of my studies, the austerity of my habits, my many prayers and stern fasting, the sermons that were my daily food, the sweet atonement to the Heart of Jesus of an afternoon in the Cathedral, and the special services that consoled my spirit at Santa Cruz in the leisure of holy days.

After completing his studies, our hero must dwell in his aunt's house, while solacing himself, with secret evening visits to the passionate Adelia:

My precautions were now therefore such that in order to prevent the delicious scent of Adelia from remaining on my clothes or skin I carried in my pocket loose pieces of incense. Before going up the gloomy steps of the house I would go furtively into the deserted stables at the further end of the courtyard and on the lid of a barrel burn a piece of the holy resin, and remained there bathing in its purifying odor the lapels of my coat and my manly beard. Then I went up and had the satisfaction of hearing Auntie sniff delightedly and say: "Heavens, what a good smell of church"; and with a modest sigh I would murmur: "It is I, Auntie."

Auntie loves God, but cannot forgive nature for having created two sexes. Our Teodorico has the accurate fear that he may be disinherited in favor of the Church and so he augments his devotion in the presence of his benefactress. Betrayed by Adelia, he then re-

ceives the further ill news that he is to make a pilgrimage to the Holy
Land, on Auntie's behalf and at her insistence, to bring back a sacred
relic to comfort her, and to cure all her ills. Already lively, The Relic
vaults into greater exuberance throughout Teodorico's quest.

✳ Eça's great metaphor for Portugal's long decline is incest, which
haunts much of his fictive achievement. Its absence from The Relic
testifies to the novelist's romp, the freedom bestowed upon him by
this book's essential wildness. Amidst so many charming ironies,
the most intricate is that the picaroon's search for an appropriate
relic turns out to be both Teodorico's undoing and his ultimate
emancipation from the tyranny of false piety.

In Alexandria, en route to holiness, the hero passionately disports
himself with Mary, a voluptuous blue-eyed English blonde, who
gives him, as a precious relic of their marvelous nights together, her
long lace night-dress. Carrying this elegant parcel, he departs for
Palestine, dominion of the Blood and Sepulchre. There he contemplates the Tree of Thorns, source of his intended relic for Auntie,
and invokes it with a delicious admonition, presage of an ironical
reversal he cannot anticipate:

> Walking round the Tree of Thorns, I therefore questioned it
> with hoarse and gloomy words: "Come, monster, tell me, are
> you a divine relic with supernatural powers? Or are you merely
> a grotesque shrub with a Latin name, duly classified by Lin-
> næus? Speak! Have you, as He whose head you crowned in
> mockery, the gift of healing? Consider well: if I take you with
> me to a pretty Portuguese oratory, delivering you from the tor-
> ture of solitude and the cheerless dark, and give you the com-
> forts of an altar, the living incense of roses, the flattering flame
> of candles, the respect of hands joined in supplication, and all
> the sweetness of prayer, it is not in order that you should in-
> dulgently prolong a cumbersome existence and so deprive me
> of a speedy inheritance and of the pleasures due to my youth.
> Consider: if your contact with the Gospel has imbued you with

puerile inclinations to charity and mercy and you go with the
intention of curing Auntie, then you shall remain here among
these rocks, lashed by the dust of the desert, defiled by birds of
prey, wearied by the unbroken silence. But if you promise to
remain deaf to Auntie's prayers and behave as a poor withered
bough without influence and do not interrupt the desired decay of her body, then you shall have in Lisbon the comfortable
softness of a chapel lined with damask, the warmth of devout
kisses and all the pleasures of an idol: I will surround you with
so much adoration that you will feel no envy towards the God
whom your thorns wounded. Speak, monster."

Here, as throughout, the feckless Teodorico all but effortlessly
charms the reader. Unfortunately, the bough of thorns is packed in
such a way by a companion of the quest that it is indistinguishable
from the parcel containing Mary's night-dress. We are given the surprising visionary episode of the Passion of Jesus Christ, pretty much
in the barbaric, anti-Jewish version of the Gospel of John (shall we
say now the Gospel of Mel Gibson?). Eça, who could have known no
better, is blameless in the absurd notion he follows, that the wicked
Pharisees were responsible. But Eça's Passion, however unacceptable
it now should be found, is marvelously well narrated, and tells us
much about the essential goodness of Teodorico, whose name after
all means God's gift. The vision is a champagne-induced dream of
our quester, yet it may tell us more about Eça than he himself knew.
    Realizing that he cannot risk bringing into Auntie's house the
dangerous night-dress parcel, Teodorico charitably gives it away to a
weeping Palestinian woman, before his departure for the long voyage back to Portugal. In Alexandria, he discovers that Mary has not
been amorously idle during his absence. Steaming home, he seriously contemplates an on-board seduction of a nun, but she is saved
by his seasickness. His dealings with the wicked night-dress are,
however, less fortunate. In an ironic twist worthy of *Monty Python and
the Holy Grail*, there then emerges the grand comic triumph of Eça's
art. Expelled from Auntie's house forever, but endowed with sub-

lime resilience, he survives by selling various minor relics brought back from Jerusalem until finally he is rescued from destruction by an old school friend. Teodorico's final epiphany occurs when he recognizes that the wicked night-dress, while not the Crown of Thorns, is indeed a relic.

We are almost beyond irony, as the hero blames himself for this failing in audacity. Instead, we hear a new voice in Teodorico, as the novel concludes:

> Because for an instant I had lacked that shameless heroism of affirmation which stamps its foot vigorously on the earth or gently raises its eyes to heaven, and amid the universal illusion founds new sciences and religions.

It is Eça's rhetorical triumph that this is wistful and not sardonic. Exquisitely comic (except for its Passion sequence), *The Relic* ends upon a note it shares with the Brazilian novelist Machado de Assis, disciple of Laurence Sterne's *Tristram Shandy*. Both Eça and Machado evade mere satire, as does Sterne, but they do not cultivate Sternean nuances of apparent sentimentality. Instead they are humane nihilists, doubtless as reflectors of the long waning of Portuguese culture throughout the nineteenth century.

Harold Bloom

The Relic

Prologue

I decided in the leisure of this summer, in my country-house, the Mosteiro, ancestral home of the Counts of Lindoso, to compose the recollections of my life, which in an age so exhausted by intellectual doubts and troubled by the craze for money, contains, as I and my brother-in-law Crispim think, a clear and strong lesson. In the year 1875, on the Eve of St. Anthony, a terribly bitter disillusion upset my existence; at that time my Aunt Dona Patrocinio das Neves sent me from the Campo de Sant' Anna, where we lived, on a pilgrimage to Jerusalem; within those sacred walls, on a broiling day of the month of Nizzam, when Pontius Pilate was Governor of Judea and Elius Lamma the imperial legate in Syria and J. Kaiapha the High Priest, I witnessed miraculously scandalous events; then I returned, and a great change occurred in my material and moral existence. It is these events, standing out clearly in my commonplace life as branching oaks filled with sunshine and rustling murmurs in a field of mown grass, that I wish to relate, soberly and sincerely, while the swallows are flying along my roof and the clumps of red carnations fill my orchard with their scent.

This journey to the land of Egypt and Palestine will always be the chief glory of my career, and I could wish that a fine and solid monument of it should remain in literature for posterity. Yet, writing as I do from purely spiritual motives, I resolve that the intimate pages in which I tell of this journey should not resemble a Picturesque Guide to the East. Therefore, despite the prompting of vanity, I have suppressed in the manuscript full and splendid descriptions of ruins and of customs.

But indeed that land of the Gospel which has such fascination for men of feeling, is far less interesting than my dry native Alentejo; nor do I think that countries favored by the presence of a

1

Messiah ever gain in charm or splendor. It has not been my privilege to travel through the Holy Places of India in which the Buddha lived: the woods of Migadaia, the hills of Velluvana or that fair valley of Rajagaha, which the adorable eyes of the perfect Master were contemplating when a fire broke out among the reeds, and he taught in a simple parable that ignorance is a fire which devours man and is nourished by the deceitful sensations of life received by the senses from the deceitful appearances of the world. I have not visited the cave of Hira nor the sacred sands between Mecca and Medina so often traversed by Mahomet, the excellent prophet, slowly and pensively riding on his camel. But from the fig-trees of Bethany to the sleeping waters of Galilee I am well acquainted with the places where dwelt another divine Mediator, full of tenderness and dreams, whom we call Our Lord Jesus; and I found in them nothing but ugliness, drought, dirt, desolation and rubbish.

Jerusalem is a Turkish town of sordid narrow streets, crushed between walls of the color of mud and stinking in the sun as the bells ring out mournfully. The Jordan is a muddy shrivelled thread of water crawling through the sand and cannot be compared with the transparent gentle Lima which there below on the edge of the estate bathes the roots of my elms; and yet these peaceful Portuguese waters have never flowed between the knees of a Messiah, they have never been brushed by the wings of angels in shining armor carrying from Heaven to Earth the threats of the Almighty.

Nevertheless since there are insatiable spirits who in reading about a journey through the lands of Scripture long to know everything, from the size of the stones to the price of beer, I recommend the full and luminous work of my companion on this pilgrimage, the German Topsius, Doctor of the University of Bonn and a member of the Imperial Institute of Historical Excavations. It consists of seven quarto volumes of close print published at Leipzig and bearing the delicate and profound title, "Jerusalem Seen and Described." On every page of this substantial itinerary the learned Topsius speaks of me with admiration and regret. He always refers to me as the illustrious Portuguese nobleman: the noble rank of his companion, to which he assigns a remote antiquity, evidently fills the learned plebeian with a delicious pride. Besides this, the enlightened Topsius makes use of me in these exhaustive volumes to hang fictitiously upon my lips or my mind sayings and opinions of devoutly absurd credulity, which he then refutes and overthrows sagaciously and eloquently.

Thus, for instance: "Before this ruin, of the time of the Crusade of Godefroi, the illustrious Portuguese nobleman pretended that Our Lord, as He went one day with St. Veronica. . . ." And then follows a tremendous passage full of turgid arguments by which I am annihilated. Since, however, the speeches which he attributes to me are not inferior to those of Bossuet in substantial wisdom and theological arrogance, I did not denounce in my note to the *Kölnische Gazette* by what tortuous methods the sharp reason of Germany decks itself with triumphs over the obtuse faith of the South. There is, however, one point in "Jerusalem Seen" which I cannot allow to pass without an energetic protest. I refer to the passage in which the most learned Topsius speaks of two paper parcels which accompanied me on my pilgrimage from the narrow streets of Alexandria to the hills of Carmel. In that full style which marks his academic eloquence, Dr. Topsius says: "The illustrious Portuguese nobleman was carrying in these the bones of his ancestors which he had gathered together, before leaving the sacred soil of his native land, in his ancient castle." A singularly false and blameworthy way of writing; since it caused learned Germany to suppose that I was travelling through the land of the Gospel with the bones of my ancestors wrapped in a brown paper parcel! No other charge could possibly be so disagreeable to me; not because it denounces me to the Church as thoughtlessly profaning the graves of the dead, since the fulminations of the Church have less weight for me, a knight and a proprietor, than the dry leaves which from time to time fall on my sunshade from a dead branch, nor indeed does the Church, when it has pocketed its fees for burying a bundle of bones, care whether they lie for ever in the uninterrupted peace of a marble tomb or knock together in the soft folds of brown paper.

No, Topsius' statement discredits me in the eyes of the Liberal bourgeoisie, and it is only from this ubiquitous and omnipotent bourgeoisie in this Semitic and capitalist age that one can obtain the good things of life, from a post in a bank to the Order of the Conception. I have sons, I have ambitions. Now the Liberal bourgeoisie values, accepts and assimilates with alacrity a gentleman who possesses ancestors and estates, as a precious old wine which tempers that which is too crude and new; but it has reason to hate the gentleman with a degree who passes before it in rigid vanity, his hands full of the bones of his ancestors, as if in mute sarcasm towards the ancestors and bones which the bourgeoisie lacks. That is why I invite my learned Topsius, who through his keen spectacles saw the contents of my parcels in the land of Egypt and in the land of Canaan, in the second edition of "Jerusalem Seen," to cast aside his academic scruples and his narrow philosophical disdain and tell scientific and sentimental Germany exactly what was in these brown paper parcels, as frankly as I unfold it to my fellow-citizens in these restful holiday pages, in which reality lives, now halting and hampered by the heavy robes of history, now leaping free under the gay mask of farce.

One

y grandfather was Padre Rufino da Conceição, Licentiate in Theology, author of a devout "Life of St. Filomena" and parish priest of Amendoeirinha. My father, confined to the protection of Our Lady of the Assumption, was called Rufino da Assunção Raposo, and lived at Evora with my grandmother, Filomena Raposo, nicknamed the Repolhuda, a confectioner in the street of the Lagar dos Dizimos.

My father was employed at the post office and amused himself by writing in the *Farol do Alentejo*. In 1853 an illustrious ecclesiastic, D. Gaspar de Lorena, Bishop of Chorazin (in Galilee), came to spend the season of St. John at Evora, at the house of Canon Pitta, where my father used often to go of an evening to play on the violoncello. Out of courtesy to the two priests, my father published in the *Farol* an article laboriously gleaned from the Preacher's Manual, congratulating Evora on its good fortune in sheltering within its walls the eminent prelate D. Gaspar, brilliant light of the Church and a shining tower of holiness. The Bishop of Chorazin cut out this article from the *Farol* in order to place it in the pages of his breviary; and everything in my father began to meet with his approval, from his clean linen to the melancholy charm with which, accompanying himself on the 'cello, he sang the ballad of Count Ordonho.

But when he learnt that this Rufino da Assunção, so charming and attractive, was the true son of his old fellow-student Rufino da Conceição in the good seminary of St. Joseph and the theological paths of the University, his affection for my father knew no bounds. Before leaving Evora he gave him a silver watch, and through his influence my father, after serving an idle apprenticeship in the Oporto custom-house, was scandalously appointed Director of the custom-house, at Viana.

The apple-trees were aflower when my father arrived in the pleasant valleys of Entre Minho e Lima; and in the same year, in July, he made the acquaintance of a gentleman from Lisbon, the Co-mendador G. Godinho, who was spending the summer with two nieces near the river, in a country-house called the Mosteiro, ancestral home of the Counts of Lindoso. The eldest of these ladies, D. Maria do Patrocinio, wore dark spectacles and came every morning into the town on a donkey accompanied by a servant in livery, to hear Mass in the church of St. Anna. The other, Dona Rosa, stout and dark-complexioned, played the harp, knew by heart the verses of "Love and Melancholy," and spent hours at the edge of the river in the shade of the elm-trees, her white dress trailing over the grass as she gathered nosegays of wild flowers.

My father began to pay frequent visits to the Mosteiro. A subordinate official of the Customs carried his 'cello, and while the Comendador and another friend of the house, the magistrate Margaride, were deeply engaged in a game of backgammon and Dona Maria do Patrocinio was engaged in prayer upstairs, my father on the veranda by the side of Dona Rosa, beneath the round white moon over the river, made his 'cello moan in the silence as he sang the sad tale of the Count Ordonho. Sometimes it was he who played at backgammon, and then Dona Rosa would sit near her uncle, a flower in her hair and a book fallen on her lap; and my father as he rattled the dice would feel the flattering caress of her long-lashed eyes.

They married. I was born on a Good Friday afternoon, and my mother died as Easter morning broke merrily. She lies under flowering stocks in the Viana cemetery, in a path near the wall, damp under the shade of willows, where she liked to walk on summer afternoons dressed in white and accompanied by her little long-haired dog called Traviata. The Comendador and Dona Maria did not return to the Mosteiro. I grew up, and had measles; my father grew stout, and his 'cello slept forgotten in a corner of the drawing-room in a sack of green baize. One very hot July my servant Gervasia dressed me in a heavy suit of black velvet; my father put a band on his straw hat: it was in mourning for the Comendador Godinho, whom my father used often to call between his teeth a knave.

Later, one Carnival night, my father died suddenly as he went down the steps of our house dressed up as a bear, on his way to the dance of the Senhoras Macedo. I was then seven years old, and I remember next day to have seen a tall stout lady in a rich mantilla of black lace sobbing in the court of our house in front of the traces of his fall which no one had washed away. At the door an old woman was waiting, praying, wrapped in a cloak of kersey. The front windows of the house were closed; in the dark passage a brass lamp on a bench threw a murky gloom, as in a chapel. It was a day of wind and rain. Through the kitchen window, while Mariana, weeping, blew the fire, I saw a man pass through the Square of A Senhora da Agonia carrying on his back my father's coffin. On the cold height the chapel of Our Lady, with its black cross, seemed even sadder than usual, bare and white among the pine-trees, almost lost in mist; and in front among the rocks a great winter sea ceaselessly rolled and moaned.

When night came, my servant Gervasia in the ironing-room set me on the floor, wrapped in a cloak. From time to time the boots of John, the custom-house porter, creaked in the passage as he disinfected the place with scented herbs. The cook brought me a slice of gingerbread. I went to sleep, and found myself walking by the side of a transparent stream, where the ancient poplars seemed to possess a soul and sighed; and at my side went a naked man with two wounds in his feet and two wounds in his hands who was Jesus Our Lord.

Some days later I was awakened on a morning early when the window of my room shone marvelously in the sun as though to announce some holy thing. By the side of my bed a stout smiling man was gently tickling my feet and calling me a young scamp. Gervasia told me that it was Senhor Matias, who was going to take me far away, to the house of my Aunt Patrocinio; and Senhor Matias paused as he took snuff in astonishment at the torn stockings which Gervasia had given me to wear.

They wrapped me in the grey cloak belonging to my father; John, of the custom-house, carried me to the door, where a litter with oilcloth curtains was waiting. We began to journey over long roads. Half asleep, I could hear the slow bells of the mules, and Senhor Matias, seated opposite me, would from time to time pat my face and say: "Here we are on the way."

One afternoon at dusk we suddenly stopped in a deserted place in a rut full of mud; the driver was cursing furiously, brandishing his flaring torch. Around us, black and sad, murmured the pine-trees. Senhor Matias, fearfully, pulled his watch from his pocket and hid it in his boot.

One night we passed through a city where the street lamps shed a bright cheerful radiance such as I had never seen, of the shape of an open tulip. At the inn where we stopped, the servant, whose name was Gonçalves, knew Senhor Matias, and after bringing us our beefsteaks remained familiarly by the table, his napkin on his shoulder, telling us about the baron and the Englishwoman. As we were retiring to rest, lit by Gonçalves, a large white lady suddenly passed us in the passage with a great rustling of silk and a scent of musk. It was the Englishwoman. In my iron bed, kept awake by the noise of the carriages, I thought of her as I prayed my Ave Marias. I had never come near anyone so beautiful, of a scent so penetrating; certainly she was full of grace and the Lord was with her, and she passed, blessed among women, with a rustling of silken skirts.

We left in a carriage which bore the arms of the King and rolled along the smooth road to the heavy trot of four strong horses. Senhor Matias, taking snuff and in slippers, told me occasionally the name of some village clustered round an ancient church in a cool valley. At evening sometimes the windows of a quiet dwelling on a hill would gleam with a radiance of fresh gold. The coach passed on, the house remained asleep among its trees, and through the clouded windows I saw Venus begin to shine. During the night a horn would sound and we thundered down the paved street of a sleepy town. Flickering lanterns moved silently in front of the inn doorway; up-stairs, in a comfortable room, on a table laid for many persons, the soup was steaming; the weary travellers yawned as they pulled off their thick woolen gloves, and I ate my chicken broth tired out and without appetite, by the side of Senhor Matias, who always knew one of the servants, inquired after the local judge and asked how the works of the town council were going on.

At last one rainy Sunday morning we arrived at a large house in a square full of mud. Senhor Matias told me that this was Lisbon, and, wrapping me up in the cloak, set me on a bench at the end of a damp room which contained luggage and large scales of iron. A bell was ringing slowly for Mass; a company of soldiers passed the door, with their rifles under their oilskin capes. A man took our trunks on his back, we got into a carriage and I fell asleep on Senhor Matias' shoulder. When he placed me on the ground we were in a gloomy court paved with small stones, with seats painted black; and on the stairs a stout girl was whispering to a man in a scarlet cloak from whose neck hung the money-box of the Souls. This was my Aunt Patrocinio's servant Vicencia. Senhor Matias went up the steps conversing with her and leading me gently by the hand.

In a room walled with dark paper we found a very tall, very thin lady dressed in black, with a gold chain on her breast; a red kerchief, tied beneath her chin, fell in prim gloom over her forehead, and in the depths of its shadow the glasses of darkened spectacles gleamed blackly. Behind her on the wall an image of Our Lady of Sorrows was looking at me, her breast pierced with swords. "This is Auntie," said Senhor Matias; "you must always be very fond of Auntie; you must always say yes to Auntie." Slowly, with difficulty, she lowered her green and withered countenance. I felt a vague kiss, cold as stone; and she at once drew back in disgust. "Good Heavens, Vicencia, how horrible! I believe they have put oil on his hair." Frightened, with trembling lips, I raised my eyes to her and murmured: "Yes, Auntie." Senhor Matias then praised my intelligence, my good behavior in the litter and the clean way I ate my soup at the inns. "It is well," muttered my aunt dryly; "it only remained for him to behave ill, knowing as he does what I am doing for him. Go, Vicencia, take him and wash that shock of hair; see if he knows how to make the sign of the Cross." Senhor Matias kissed me twice rapidly and Vicencia took me into the kitchen.

In the evening they dressed me in my suit of velvet, and Vicencia solemnly, in a clean apron, led me by the hand to a room hung with curtains of crimson damask, the tables in which had gilt legs like the columns of an altar. My aunt was seated in the middle of the sofa, dressed in black silk, a kerchief of black lace on her head and her fingers glittering with rings. Near her, on chairs likewise gilt, two priests were conversing. One of them, stout and smiling, with curly white hair, opened his arms to me paternally. The other, sad and dark-complexioned, merely muttered: "Good evening." And from the table, where he was looking at a book of pictures, a little man of shaven face and enormous collar, greeted me nervously, letting his glasses fall off his nose. Each of them vaguely kissed me. The sad priest asked me my name, which I pronounced Tedrico. The other kindly, showing his excellent teeth, advised me to separate the syllables and say Te-o-do-ri-co. Then they said that I was like my mother, the same eyes. My aunt sighed. She gave thanks to the Lord that I had nothing of the Raposos. The man in the huge collar closed his book and his eye-glasses and asked me timidly if I was sorry to leave Viana. And I murmured in confusion: "Yes, Auntie." Then the old stout priest took me on his knees and recommended me to fear God, be quiet in the house and always obey Auntie. "Teodorico has no one but Auntie. He must always say yes to Auntie." And I repeated timidly: "Yes, Auntie." My Aunt ordered me severely to take my finger out of my mouth, and then bade me return to the kitchen, to Vicencia, straight on along the passage. "And when you pass the oratory, where there is a light and a green curtain, kneel down and make the sign of the Cross."

I did not make the sign of the Cross, but I opened the curtain, and my aunt's oratory impressed me tremendously. It was all lined with red silk, with flowered patterns round panels which related tenderly the sufferings of the Lord; the lace of the altar-cloth fell over the carpet on the floor; the saints of wood and ivory with shining aureoles dwelt in a wood of violets and red camellias; in the light of the wax candles two noble plates of silver standing restfully against the wall gleamed like the shields of holiness. High on a cross of black wood under a canopy Our Lord Jesus Christ shone all in gold. I went up slowly to the cushion of green velvet before the altar, hollowed out by the devout knees of Auntie. I raised my black eyes to Jesus Crucified. And I considered that in the sky the angels, the saints, Our Lady and the Father of all must be like that, of gold, perhaps with precious stones; their radiance made the daylight, and the stars were the brightest points in the gold, shining through the dark veils in which the devout love of men wrapped them asleep of nights.

After tea, Vicencia put me to bed in a little room off hers. She made me kneel down in my shirt, join my hands and raise my face to the sky; and then she said for me the paternosters which I must pray for Auntie's health, for the repose of mamma and for the soul of a very good, very saintly and very rich Comendador of the name of Godinho.

As soon as I was nine my Aunt ordered shirts for me and a suit of black cloth and placed me as a boarder in the College of the Isidoros, then at St. Isabel. In the very first weeks I made a strong friendship with a boy called Crispim, taller than I, son of the firm Telles, Crispim and Co., who owned a linen factory at Pampulha. Crispim helped at the celebration of Mass on Sundays and, as he knelt, with his long fair hair resembled an angel. Sometimes in the passage he would eagerly kiss my soft face; and at nights, in the schoolroom, as we turned over the pages of our sleepy dictionaries, he would send me notes written in pencil promising me boxes of steel nibs.

Thursday was the unpleasant day on which we had to wash our feet; and thrice a week greasy Padre Soares, toothpick in mouth, would examine us on the Catechism and tell us of the life of Our Lord. "Then they took Him and dragged Him to the house of Caiaphas." "You at the end of the bench, who was Caiaphas? Wrong. You further on. Wrong again. You dolts! He was a Jew and one of the worst. Now they say that in a very ugly part of Judea there is a tree all thorns, a terrible tree."

The recreation bell sounded and we all at the same moment

noisily closed our text-books. The playground, covered with gravel, was gloomy and ill-smelling; and the delight of the older boys was to smoke a cigarette on the sly in an earth-paved room where on Sundays the dance-master, smart in evening shoes, taught us mazurkas.

Once a month Vicencia, in a cape and kerchief, came to fetch me after Mass to spend a Sunday with Auntie. Isidoro Junior, before I went, would examine my ears and nails; often in his own basin he would give me a furious soaping and call me a dirty pig. Then he would take me to the door, caress me, call me his dear little friend and send his respects by Vicencia to Dona Patrocinio das Neves.

We lived in the Campo de Sant'Anna. As we went down the Chiado I would stop at a picture shop in front of a languid picture of a fair-haired woman with naked breasts lying on a tiger-skin, and holding in her fingers, more delicate than those of Crispim, a heavy pearl necklace. The whiteness of her made me think of the Baron's Englishwoman; and the scent which had overcome me in the passage of the inn came to me again in this street full of sun, from the skirts of the ladies going up, grave and solemn, to hear Mass in the Loretto church.

At home Auntie gave me her hand to kiss, and I spent the whole morning turning over the pages of the *Panorama Universal* in the room which contained a striped sofa, a fine cupboard of black wood, and colored lithographs with affecting passages from the blameless life of my aunt's favorite saint, the patriarch St. Joseph. Auntie, with a red kerchief on her head, seated behind the window-panes, her feet wrapped in a rug, carefully examined a large account-book. At three o'clock she would put away the account-book, and from the shadow of the kerchief begin to ask me questions regarding the Catechism. And as with lowered eyes I said the Creed and the Commandments, an acrid, sickly sweet smell of snuff and ants came from her.

On Sundays the two priests came to dine with us. The one with the curly hair was Padre Casimiro, my aunt's agent; he would fondle me cheerfully and make me decline *arbor* and *currus*, and proclaimed me affectionately a great talent. The other priest would praise the

College of the Isidoros, a beautiful establishment such as even Belgium could not boast. His name was Padre Pinheiro. He seemed to me to become ever sadder and more sallow. Whenever he passed a looking-glass he would put out his tongue and unconsciously remain there examining it in fear and dismay. At dinner Padre Casimiro rejoiced in my appetite. Another mouthful of roast veal? he would say; boys should be gay and have good appetites. And Padre Pinheiro would rub his stomach and murmur: Ah, happy age, in which one takes two helpings of veal. Then he and Auntie would talk of their complaints; Padre Casimiro, red in the face, his napkin tied beneath his chin, his plate full, his glass full, smiled beatifically.

When the gas-lamps began to shine in the square among the trees, Vicencia would don her old check shawl and take me back to the college. At that hour on Sundays the man of the shaven face and huge collar arrived. He was Senhor José Justino, secretary of the Association of St. Joseph and my aunt's solicitor, with his office in the district of St. Paul. In the court, as he took off his overcoat, he would pat his chin and inquire of Vicencia as to the health of Dona Patrocinio. Then he went upstairs and we closed the heavy door; whereupon I breathed happily, for that great house threw a gloom over me with its red damask and its innumerable saints and its smell of chapel.

On the way Vicencia would talk to me of Auntie, who had taken her six years ago from the Misericordia. Thus I learnt that she was ill of the liver; that she always had much gold in a purse of green silk; and that the Comendador Godinho, her and my mother's uncle, had left her forty thousand pounds in houses, investments and the Mosteiro estate near Viana, and in silver and porcelain of India. How rich Auntie was! I must be good and always be grateful to Auntie. At the door of the college Vicencia said: "Good-bye, my love," and gave me a great kiss. Often at night as I lay in bed I would think of Vicencia, and of Vicencia's plump arms white as milk. And gradually in my heart arose a tender passion for Vicencia.

One day a tall youth called me a worm. I challenged him to fight, and spoilt his face with a great blow. I became feared. I smoked cigarettes. Crispim had left the college. My ambition was to learn how to fence; and my love for Vicencia disappeared one day insensibly, as a flower dropped in the street.

The years went by. When Christmas came a brazier was lit in the dining-room, and I put on my coat lined with silk and having an astrakhan collar: later the swallows made their appearance on the eaves of our roof, and in Auntie's oratory instead of camellias came armfuls of the first red carnations to perfume the golden feet of Jesus. Later came the season of sea-bathing, and Padre Casimiro sent Auntie a basket of grapes from his Torres country-house.

I began to study rhetoric. One day our good agent told me that I was not to return to the Isidoros but would finish my preparatory studies at Coimbra, in the house of Dr. Roxo, professor of theology. They provided me with linen. My aunt gave me a prayer on a piece of paper which I was to pray daily to St. Luis Gonzaga, patron of studious youth, that he might preserve my body fresh and clean and my soul in the fear of the Lord. Padre Casimiro accompanied me to the fair city where Minerva slumbers. I disliked Dr. Roxo from the first. In his house I endured a hard cloistral life, and it was a tremendous joy when in my first year of studying Law the disagreeable priest died miserably of an anthrax. I then went to the pleasant lodging-house of the Pimentas, and forthwith without moderation made the acquaintance of the great delights of life in full independence. I never again prayed the insipid prayer to St. Luis Gonzaga; nor bowed my manly knee to any holy aureoled image; I became gloriously drunk in the tavern of the Camellas; I proved my strength by knocking out a marker of the Café Trony; I drank my fill of love in the Terreiro da Erva; I sauntered singing ballads by moonlight; I carried a stout stick; and as my beard began to grow strong and thick I accepted with pride the nickname of Raposão. Every fortnight, however, I wrote to Auntie in my good handwriting a humble pious letter, in which I told her of the severity of my studies, the austerity of my habits, my many prayers and stern fasting, the sermons that were my daily food, the sweet atonement to the Heart of Jesus of an afternoon in the Cathedral, and the special services that consoled my spirit at Santa Cruz in the leisure of holy days.

The summer months in Lisbon were a painful contrast. Not to be able to go out, even to get my hair cut, without servilely asking Auntie's permission. I did not even dare smoke in the cafés. I must return home religiously at dusk, and before retiring to bed I must pray a long litany with the old lady in the oratory. It was I myself who had brought down this detestable penance on my head. You are accustomed during your studies to pray your litany? my aunt had dryly asked me. And I, smiling abjectly, had answered: Why, of course. I cannot positively sleep without having prayed my dear litany.

The Sunday dinners continued. Padre Pinheiro, sadder than ever, now complained of his heart and sometimes of the bladder. And there was a new guest, an old friend of Comendador Godinho, Margaride, formerly public prosecutor at Viana, then judge at Mangualde. Enriched by the death of his brother Abel, secretary on the Patriarch's staff, he had retired, having had enough of trials, and now lived at leisure, reading the newspapers, in a house that he owned in the Praça da Figueira. He was stout and pompous, already bald, with a white face in which the bushy eyebrows stood out black as coal. As he had known my father and often gone with him to the Mosteiro, he at once treated me with familiar authority. He rarely entered my aunt's drawing-room without shouting from the door some fearful piece of news. "Have you not heard: a terrible fire in the lower part of the town?" This meant a chimney on fire. But the good Margaride as a young man in a gloomy imaginative mood had composed two tragedies; and had ever since had a morbid pleasure in exaggerating and in impressing people. No one like me, he said, can appreciate the grand. And whenever he had alarmed my aunt and the priest, he would gravely take a pinch of snuff.

I liked Dr. Margaride. As companion of my father at Viana, he had often heard him sing to the 'cello the ballad of Count Ordonho. He had spent whole afternoons with him wandering poetically by the edge of the river while my mother gathered her bunches of wild flowers beneath the elms. And the very evening of the Good Friday on which I was born he sent his congratulations. Moreover, even in my presence he would frankly praise before my aunt my intelligence and modest behavior. "Our Teodorico, Dona Patrocinio, is a youth to delight an aunt's heart. Your Excellency has in him a true Telemachus." I blushed modestly.

It was when I was walking with him one August day in the Rossio that I made the acquaintance of a distant relation, a cousin of Comendador Godinho. Dr. Margaride introduced him, merely saying: "Xavier, your cousin, a young man of great gifts." He was a man of sordid aspect, with a light moustache, who had recklessly squandered six thousand pounds inherited from his father, the owner of a boot factory at Alcantara. The Comendador Godinho, a few months before his death of pneumonia, had out of charity obtained for him a post in the Ministry of Justice, bringing in four pounds a month. Xavier now lived with a Spanish woman called Carmen and their three children in a poor house of the Rua da Fé. I went there one Sunday. There was scarcely any furniture. The only basin was stuck in the broken straw seat of a chair. Xavier had been spitting blood all the morning, and Carmen, disheveled and in slippers, with her cotton dressing-gown stained with wine, was walking sadly to and fro rocking a child wrapped in rags and with its head covered with sores. Xavier at once familiarly spoke to me of Aunt Patrocinio. That servant of the Lord and owner of so many houses could not let a relation, a Godinho, die in that miserable house without sheets, without tobacco, with his children half naked and crying for bread. Could she not give him, as the State had formerly done, a monthly allowance of four pounds? "You ought to speak to her, Teodorico; you ought to tell her. Look at those children: they have not even stockings. Come here, Rodrigo, and tell your Uncle Teodorico what you had for luncheon. A piece of stale bread, without butter, without anything. And that is our life, Teodorico. It is very hard." In my pity I promised to speak to Auntie. To speak to Auntie! I would not dare even tell her that I knew Xavier or that I had gone to the house where lived the Spanish woman worn out with sin. And that they might not perceive my ignoble terror of Auntie, I did not return to the Rua da Fé.

In the middle of September, on the day of the Birth of the Virgin, I heard from Dr. Barroso that my cousin Xavier, almost at death's door, wished to speak to me in secret. I went there against my will in the afternoon. There was a smell of fever on the stairs. Carmen, sobbing in the kitchen, was speaking to another Spaniard: a thin woman with a black mantilla and a sordid bodice of cherry-red satin. The children on the floor were scraping a bowl that had contained soup. In the bedroom, Xavier, wrapped in a rug, with the basin at his side, was torn with coughing. "Is it you, young fellow?" "What is the matter, Xavier?" He said with an oath that he was done for. And turning round, with a dry light in his eyes, he at once began to speak of Auntie. He had written her a beautiful, most affecting letter, and the cruel woman had not answered; and now he was going to send an advertisement to the *Jornal de Notícias*, asking for alms and signing himself Xavier Godinho, cousin of the rich Comendador Godinho. He would see if Dona Patrocinio das Neves would let a relation, a Godinho, beg publicly in the columns of a newspaper.

"But you must help me; you must soften her. When she reads this advertisement, tell her of our misery, appeal to her pride, say that it is a disgrace to allow a relation, a Godinho, to die of neglect. Tell her that people are beginning to talk. Consider that if today I had some soup it was because that girl there, Lolita, who lives in the house of Benta Bexigosa, brought us four crowns. See to what I have come."

I rose full of pity: "You may count on me, Xavier." "If you have half a crown that you do not want, give it to Carmen." I gave it to him, and went out swearing that I was going to speak solemnly to Auntie in the name of the Godinhos and in the name of Christ.

Next day after luncheon, Auntie, toothpick in mouth, slowly unfolded the *Jornal de Notícias*. She must have come at once on Xavier's advertisement, for she remained a long time gazing at the corner of the third page in which it stood in black letters, sad, shameful, horrible. Then I seemed to see fixed on me from the bare darkness of that poor house the sad eyes of Xavier; I saw the face of Carmen, bathed in tears, and the poor thin little hands of the children asking for a crust of bread. All those wretched beings hung on the words which I was about to speak to Auntie, strong touching words which would be their salvation and give them their first piece of meat that miserable summer. But already Auntie, lying back in her chair, had begun to mutter with a ferocious smile: "He must put up with it. That is what comes of consorting with drunken women. He should not have spent all his money in dissolute living. In my eyes a man who once goes after women is done for. He cannot expect the forgiveness of God nor mine. Let him suffer, let him suffer, since Our Lord Jesus Christ also suffered." I bent my head and murmured: "And we do not suffer enough; Auntie is right. He should not have run after the women."

She rose and said grace. I went to my room and locked the door, trembling, still hearing the cold threatening words of Auntie, for whom a man who had anything to do with women ceased to exist. I too had run after women, at Coimbra, in the Terreiro da Erva. There in my trunk were the proofs of my sin, a photograph of Theresa, a silk ribbon, and a charming letter from her in which she called me her only love and asked me for ten shillings. I had sown these relics into the lining of a waistcoat in fear of my aunt's continual meddling among my clothes. But they were there, in the trunk of which she kept the key, inside the waistcoat, making a hardness of cardboard which might any day attract the attention of her distrustful fingers. And then I should cease to exist for Auntie.

Slowly I opened the trunk, undid the lining and took out Theresa's delicious letter, the ribbon which preserved her scent, and her photograph wearing a mantilla. On the stone floor of the balcony I ruthlessly burnt everything, phrases and words of endearment, and desperately scattered over the court below the ashes of my affections.

That week I did not dare return to the Rua da Fé. One rainy day later I went there at dusk, buried under my umbrella. A neighbor, seeing me looking from a distance at the dead black windows of the house, told me that poor Senhor Godinho had been carried away to the hospital. I went sadly down the steps, and in the wet evening, as I brushed suddenly against another umbrella, I heard my Coimbra name uttered joyously: O Raposão! It was Silverio, called Rinchão, my fellow student and comrade in the house of the Pimentas. He had been spending a month in Alentejo with his uncle, the rich and illustrious Baron de Alconchel. And now he was going to visit Ernestina, a fair-haired girl who lived in the Salitre quarter, in a rose-colored house, with roses on the balcony. "Will you come for a bit, Raposão? There is another pretty girl, Adelia. Do you not know Adelia? Well, come and see Adelia. She is no end of a woman."

It was a Sunday, the night of Auntie's dinner-party. I ought to be back punctually at eight. I stroked my chin doubtfully. Rinchão spoke of the white arms of Adelia, and I began to walk beside him, drawing on my black gloves. Furnished with a packet of cakes and a bottle of Madeira, we found Ernestina sewing an elastic on her felt boots. Adelia, lying on a sofa in dressing-gown and white skirt, her slippers fallen on the carpet, was slowly smoking a cigarette. I sat down beside her in silent embarrassment, my umbrella between my knees. It was only when Silverio and Ernestina ran into the kitchen together to look for glasses for the Madeira that I plucked up heart to ask her, reddening: From what part of the country do you come?

She was from Lamego. And I in my shyness could only stammer that that rainy weather was very cheerless. She politely offered me a cigarette, calling me the "gentleman." I was attracted by her courtesy; and the wide sleeves of her dressing-gown falling back displayed soft white arms between which death itself would be delightful. It was I who handed her the plate on which Ernestina had placed the cakes. She asked me my name. She had a nephew of the same name, she said; and this was as a strong and subtle thread which came from her heart to twine itself round mine.

"Why does the gentleman not put his umbrella in a corner?" she asked laughing. The piquant gleam of her tiny teeth gave birth to a flower of poetry in my mind: Because I would not go even for an instant from your side. She slowly tickled my neck; and I, speechless with joy, drank the wine which she had left in her glass. Poetical Ernestina, singing a ballad, was seated on Rinchão's knees; and Adelia, slowly turning round, pulled my face towards her, and our lips met in the most profound and earnest kiss that I had ever experienced.

In this sweet instant a horrible clock, with a face like the face of a full moon, which seemed to be watching me from its place on the marble top of a mahogany table between two jars of flowers, slowly, ironically, metallically began to strike ten. Heavens, it was the hour of tea at Auntie's! In terror I hurried, without even opening my umbrella, through the dark and interminable streets which lead to the Campo de Sant'Anna. When I arrived I did not stay even to take off my muddy boots, but crept into the drawing-room. At its further end, on the damask sofa, I saw at once the dark spectacles of Auntie gleaming angrily in wait for me. I only had time to murmur Auntie, but she was already shouting, green with rage and shaking her fists: "Dissolute ways in my house I will not admit. He who wishes to live here must keep the hours I say. Wickedness and debauchery, not while I live. And if you do not like it you may go."

Under the hurricane of Dona Patrocinio's indignation, Padre Pinheiro and the lawyer Justino had bowed their heads in embarrassment. Dr. Margaride, in order scrupulously to measure my sin, had pulled out his heavy gold watch. And it was the good Casimiro who as priest and agent intervened, softly influential: "Dona Patrocinio is right, very right indeed, in wishing to have order in the house. But perhaps Teodorico stayed a little too late in the Café Martinho, talking of studies and text-books." "Not even that, Padre Casimiro," I exclaimed bitterly, "I was not even in the Café Martinho. Do you know where I was? In the Convent of the Incarnation. Yes, I met a fellow student, who was going to fetch his sister. Today was a holiday, and his sister had gone to spend the day with an aunt, a Comendaderia. We waited for her, walking up and down the court. His sister is going to be married, and he was telling me of her fiancé and of the trousseau, and of how greatly she is in love. I was dying to come away, but did not like to offend him, for he is a nephew of the Baron de Alconchel; and he went on and on, talking of his sister and the courtship and the letters. . . ."

Aunt Patrocinio howled with rage: "What a conversation, what a disgusting conversation, what an indecent conversation for the court of a religious house! Be silent, you lost soul, you ought to be ashamed of yourself. And understand once for all. Another time you come at this hour, you will not enter the house, you will remain in the street like a dog." Then Dr. Margaride peacefully and solemnly stretched out his hand: "Everything is explained. Our Teodorico was imprudent, but the place in which he was is respectable. And I know the Baron de Alconchel. He is a gentleman of the gravest character, and one of the richest men in Alentejo. Perhaps one of the richest men in Portugal. The richest, I might say. Even outside Portugal few fortunes can exceed, can even be compared with his. Only in pigs! Only in cork! Thousands of pounds. Hundreds of thousands!"

He had risen, and his powerful voice reverberated, rolling down mountains of gold. And the good Casimiro at my side murmured gently: "Take your tea, Teodorico, take your tea, and be assured that your aunt only desires your good."

I drew my tea-cup towards me with trembling hand, and as I timidly stirred the sugar, thought of leaving for ever the house of the horrible old woman who thus insulted me in the presence of the Bench and the Church without any regard for my beard which was beginning to grow strong, black and respectable. But on Sundays tea was served in the silver plate of the late Comendador Godinho. There it was, solid and gleaming before my eyes: the great tea-pot with a spout shaped like a duck's beak, the sugar-basin with a handle formed by an angry snake, and a charming stand for toothpicks in the shape of a horse trotting under its saddle-bags. And all belonged to Auntie. How rich Auntie was! It was necessary to be good, and always grateful to Auntie. Therefore later when she came into the oratory to pray the rosary, I was already there prostrate, groaning, beating my breast, and praying the gold Christ to forgive me for having offended Auntie.

At last one day I arrived in Lisbon with my degree of doctor in its tin case. Auntie examined it reverently, finding an ecclesiastical savor in the lines of Latin and the gaudy red ribbons and the solemn seal. "It is well," she said; "you are a doctor. To Our Lord God you owe it: see that you are not ungrateful." I ran to the oratory, with the case in my hand, to thank the golden Christ for my glorious degree. On the following morning, as I was trimming my beard, now black and thick, before the looking-glass, Padre Casimiro came into my room, joyfully rubbing his hands. "I have good news for you, Dr. Teodorico." And after giving me some gentle taps on the back in his usual affectionate way, he revealed to me that my aunt, being satisfied with me, had decided to buy me a horse in order that I might take rides in Lisbon and enjoy myself honestly. "O Padre Casimiro, a horse!" Yes, a horse; and, moreover, not wishing that her nephew, with his beard and his degree, should have the unpleasant experience of not being able to place a coin in the plate of Our Lady of the Rosary, she was going to give me a monthly allowance of three pounds. I embraced Padre Casimiro warmly, and I asked him if it was Auntie's loving intention that I should have nothing to do except ride about Lisbon and throw sixpences into the plate of Our Lady. "I think, Teodorico," he said, "that your aunt wishes you to have no further occupation but to fear God. What I do say is that you are going to have a very good time. And now go in and thank her and say something affectionate."

In the drawing-room, where the pious story of the Patriarch St. Joseph shone from the walls, Auntie was sitting on a corner of the striped sofa knitting, with a Tonking shawl over her shoulders. "Auntie," I murmured timidly, "I have come to thank you." "It is well. You may go with God." Then devoutly I kissed the fringe of her shawl. Auntie was pleased, and I went with God.

Then began my comfortable existence as nephew of Dona Patrocinio das Neves. At eight o'clock punctually, dressed in black, I went with her to the church of Santa Anna to hear the Mass said by Padre Pinheiro. After luncheon, having asked Auntie's permission and prayed three *Gloria Patri* against temptation, I went out riding in light-colored breeches. Almost always Auntie gave me some devout commission: to pass by St. Domingos and say a prayer for the three saints and martyrs of Japan; to enter the church of the Conceição Velha and make an act of atonement to the Sacred Heart of Jesus. And I was so afraid of displeasing her that I never forgot to fulfill her commissioned prayers in the house of the Lord. But it was the most disagreeable moment of my day; sometimes as I came secretly out of a church I would meet some Coimbra fellow-student, one of those Republicans who on afternoons of procession would join me in mocking at the Lord of the Green Reed. "O Raposão, you too;" and I denied in annoyance: "What an idea! The last thing likely to happen, I am fed up with piety. It was on account of a girl that I went into the church. Good-bye, my mare is waiting." I mounted, and in black gloves, legs glued to the saddle and a camellia bud in my buttonhole, went ambling in leisurely state to the Loreto.

Sometimes I would leave the mare in the Arco da Bandeira and spend a happy morning playing billiards at the Café Montanha. Before dinner, in slippers, in the oratory with Auntie, I said prayers to St. Joseph, tutor of Jesus, guardian of Mary and most loving patriarch. At dinner, at the table adorned merely with saucers of jam round a tray of pastry, I would tell Auntie of my ride and of the churches that had delighted me and what altars were illuminated. Vicencia would listen with devotion, rigidly in her accustomed place between the two windows, where the portrait of our Holy Father Pio Nono filled the whole interval of green wall, and under it hung by a chain a telescope, a relic of Comendador Godinho.

After coffee Auntie would slowly fold her arms, and her face would sink heavily asleep in the shade of the red handkerchief. I went to put on my boots, and, having her permission now to remain out till half past nine, hastened at length to the Rua da Madalena, near the Largo dos Caldas. There cautiously, with my coat collar up, clinging to the wall, as though the gas lamp there was Auntie's implacable eye, I went hurriedly up Adelia's stairs. Yes, Adelia, for ever since Rinchão took me that night to the Salitre, I had been unable to forget the slow white kiss that she gave me on the sofa. At Coimbra I even attempted to write poems to her, and during my last year at the University, when I was studying Canon Law, that love flowered within my breast like a wonderful lily scenting my life unseen.

No sooner had Auntie given me my allowance than I hurried triumphantly to the Salitre; the roses were in the balcony, but Adelia had gone. And it was the friendly Rinchão who told me of this story near the Largo dos Caldas where she lived under the protection of Eleuterio Serra, of the firm of Serra, Brito & Co., with a dressmaker's shop in the Conceição Velha. I sent her a serious fervent letter, beginning with "*Minha Senhora*." She answered with dignity: "The gentleman can call here at midday." I took her a box of chocolates tied with a ribbon of blue silk. As not without emotion I trod the new carpet, the stiff white curtains seemed to tell of the freshness of her skirts, and the careful order of the furniture told of the rectitude of her mind. She came in, with a slight cold, a red shawl over her shoulders. She at once recognized Rinchão's friend, and spoke of Ernestina with asperity, calling her a dirty pig. And her hoarse voice, her cold, made me wish to cure her in my arms, on a long sleepy day, in the soft shadows of her room.

She inquired if I had a business or employment, and I told her proudly of the wealth of Auntie, of her houses, and her silver. I said to her, as I held her large hands in mine: "If Auntie were to die now, it is I who would find a nice house for you." She murmured, as she bathed me in the dark softness of her eyes: "If the gentleman got the money, he would not think of me again." I knelt trembling on the mat, pressing my breast against her knees, and offered myself to her without reserve. She opened her shawl and mercifully accepted the offering.

And now the radiant bliss of my life centered in Adelia's room of an evening, while Eleuterio was playing cards in a club in the Rua Nova do Almada. I had taken a pair of slippers there, I was the elect of her heart. At half past nine, disheveled and wrapped hurriedly in a flannel dressing-gown, she accompanied me down the backstairs, taking at each step from my lips a long and passionate kiss. "Good-

bye, Delinha." "Take care of yourself, my precious one." And I returned slowly to the Campo de Sant'Anna, pondering on my bliss.

The summer went by languidly. The first winds of autumn had
carried off the leaves and the swallows from the Campo de Sant'Anna,
and suddenly in October my life became more easy and free. Auntie
had ordered a dress-suit for me and with her permission I wore it
for the first time at the opera at S. Carlos, going to see *Polyeucte*, which
Dr. Margaride had recommended as being full of religious senti-
ment and lofty instruction. I went with him, wearing white gloves
and carefully groomed.

Next day at luncheon I told Auntie about the plot, the overthrown
idols, the hymns, the noble ladies in the boxes and the fine velvet
dress of the Queen. "And do you know who came to speak to me,
Auntie? The rich Baron de Alconchel, uncle of my fellow-student.
He came to shake hands with me and remained with me a short
time in the stalls; he treated me with great consideration." That consideration pleased Auntie. Afterwards sadly, like a pained moralist
I complained of the excessively *décolleté* dress of an immodest lady
with bare arms and breast, displaying a splendid and impious ex-
panse of flesh, which is the sorrow of the just man and the vexation of the Church: "Most disagreeable indeed; believe me, Auntie,
I was disgusted." That disgust pleased Auntie. And some days later
after coffee, as I was going in slippers to make a brief prayer to the
wounds of the gold Christ, my aunt, sleepily with folded arms said
to me from the shadow of her kerchief: "It is well; if you wish, you
may return tonight to the opera; and when you like, don't be afraid,
you have my permission to go and enjoy a little music. Now that
you are a man and seem to have character, I do not object to your
remaining out till eleven or half past. In any case, at that hour I wish
to have the door locked and everything ready to say the litany." She
could not see the triumphant gleam in my eyes. I murmured, bending forward in joyful devotion: "The litany, Auntie, my dear litany
I would not lose for the greatest enjoyment; not if the King invited
me to have tea with him in the palace!"

I ran in mad delight to don my evening coat; and that was the beginning of my longed-for liberty which I had conquered so laboriously by bowing before Auntie and beating my breast before the
Lord. Liberty twice blest, now that Eleuterio had left for Paris in
order to replenish his stock and Adelia had remained alone, free and
beautiful, more spirited and merry.

Yes, I had certainly won Auntie's confidence by my punctual,
prudent, servile, devout ways. But what had really induced her thus
generously to extend my hours of honest entertainment was, as
she in confidence told Padre Casimiro, the certainty that I behaved
religiously and did not run after the women. For Aunt Patrocinio
all human action outside the doors of the churches consisted in
running after men or running after women, and to her both these
pleasant natural impulses were equally odious.

This old maid, withered as a vine-twig, whose livid skin had only
been touched by the grey paternal moustache of Comendador Godinho, and who muttered incessantly melancholy prayers of divine
love before the naked Christ, had gradually become permeated with
an envious bitter rancor towards every form and charm of human
love. It was not enough for her to condemn love as a thing profane:
Dona Patrocinio das Neves made a gesture of disgust and brushed it
aside as so much dirt. A serious young man seriously in love was vile
in her sight; and if she heard that a lady had had a child she would
mutter: How disgusting.

She almost considered Nature obscene for having created two
sexes. Rich and fond of comfort, she would never have a manservant
in the house, so that the two sexes should not meet in kitchen and
passage; and although Vicencia's hair was turning white and the
cook was a stammering decrepit old woman and the other servant,
Eusebia, a toothless crone, she was always fumbling desperately
among their trunks and even in the straw of their mattresses to see
if she could discover a photograph of a man, a letter of a man, any
trace or smell of man.

All the amusements of the young, a pleasant donkey-ride with
ladies, a dewy rosebud offered and accepted, a decorous dance on a

festive Easter day, and other even simpler pleasures were in Auntie's eyes perverse, disgusting and dissolute. In her presence the prudent friends of the house had learnt not to mention interesting stories read in the newspapers revealing a love motive, since they scandalized her like a naked offence. "Padre Pinheiro," she called out one day furiously with blazing eyes to the luckless priest, on hearing him tell of a servant girl in France who had thrown her child into a drain. "Padre Pinheiro, be good enough to respect me. It is not the drain, it is the child that disgusts me."

Yet it was she who was always alluding to the sins and wickedness of the flesh, to lash them with her hatred: she would set her ball of wool on the table and dig at it furiously with her knitting-needles, as though she was thus piercing and rendering cold for ever the vast and restless heart of man. And almost every day, she would repeat, showing her teeth and alluding to me, that if a person of her blood or who fed at her table were to run after women or abandon himself to dissolute ways, he would go into the street, swept out like a dog.

My precautions were now therefore such that in order to prevent the delicious scent of Adelia from remaining on my clothes or skin I carried in my pocket loose pieces of incense. Before going up the gloomy steps of the house I would go furtively into the deserted stables at the further end of the courtyard and on the lid of a barrel burn a piece of the holy resin, and remain there bathing in its purifying odor the lapels of my coat and my manly beard. Then I went up and had the satisfaction of hearing Auntie sniff delightedly and say: "Heavens, what a good smell of church"; and with a modest sigh I would murmur: "It is I, Auntie."

Moreover, in order better to persuade her of my indifference towards women, I placed one day on the floor of the passage as if it had been dropped, a stamped letter, certain that the religious lady, my aunt Dona Patrocinio, would at once open and read it greedily. It was directed to a fellow-student at Arrayolos, and in a fine hand said the following edifying things: You must know that I have quarrelled with Simes, the student of philosophy, for having invited me to go to a house of ill fame. I do not admit such behavior. You will remember at Coimbra how I hated such ways; and he seems to me a most senseless brute who for the sake of one minute's pleasure runs the risk of suffering for ever and ever amen, in the fires of Satan. Such folly is utterly foreign to your affectionate friend Raposo.

Auntie read and was pleased. And now I put on my dress clothes, told her that I was going to hear Norma, kissed her bony fingers, and ran to the Largo dos Caldas, to Adelia's room, to abandon myself to the delights of sin. There, in the half-light coming through the glass door from the paraffin lamp in the drawing-room, the cambric curtains and hanging skirts seemed to have a celestial whiteness of clouds, the face-powder excelled in sweetness the scent of mystic jonquils, and I was in heaven, I was St. Theodoric, and on the bare shoulders of my love fell the plaits of her black hair, coarse and strong as the tail of a war-horse.

One of those nights I was coming out of the cake-shop in the Rossio where I had been buying some sweetened eggs for my Adelia, when I met Dr. Margaride, who after a paternal embrace told me that he was on his way to the opera to see "The Prophet." "And I see you are in evening dress, probably you are coming too." Great was my dismay. I had indeed dressed for the evening and told Auntie that I was going to see "The Prophet," an opera as religious as sacred music. And now I had in very truth to endure "The Prophet," seated in a stall, knee to knee with the learned magistrate, instead of lying lazily on a mattress lovingly watching my goddess eat her sweetened eggs. "Yes, I was indeed going to see 'The Prophet,'" I murmured in my despair. "Its music is said to be very devout. Auntie was very pleased that I should come." And with my useless packet of sugar-plums I sadly went up the Rua Nova do Carmo with Dr. Margaride.

We took our places. In the gleaming theatre, white, with tints of gold, I was thinking longingly of the dark room of Adelia and her hanging skirts, when I became aware that in a box at the side a fair-haired elderly lady, an autumnal Ceres dressed in straw-colored silk, was turning upon me her clear and serious eyes as the violins played softly. I at once asked Dr. Margaride if he knew that lady whom I often saw on a Friday in the Graça church visiting the Senhor dos Passos with devotion and fervor. "The man behind now talking is the Visconde Souto Santos. She is either his wife, the Viscondessa Souto Santos, or his sister-in-law, the Viscondessa de Villar o Velho."

As we went out, the Viscondessa of Souto Santos or Villar o Velho remained for an instant by the door waiting for her carriage, wrapped in a white cloak delicately edged with fur; her head seemed to me proudly incapable of lolling foolishly on love's pillow, the train of her straw-colored dress trailed on the pavements; she was magnificent, she was a viscountess; and once more her clear grave eyes pierced me through. It was a starry night, and as I went down the Chiado in silence with Dr. Margaride I thought that when all Auntie's gold lent me new glamor I might know a Viscondessa de Souto Santos or Villar o Velho not in her box but in my own room, without her great white cloak and straw-colored silken skirts, small, white and gleaming in my arms. Ah, when would the happy hour of Auntie's death arrive?

"Will you come and have tea in the Café Martinho?" asked Dr. Margaride as we came into the Rossio. "I don't know if you are acquainted with the toast at the Martinho. The best toast in Lisbon."

In the Café Martinho, now silent, the gas was going to sleep amid the dim mirrors; and there was but one melancholy youth at a table at the further end, with his head buried in his hands, in front of a glass of syrup. Dr. Margaride ordered the tea, and, seeing me look anxiously at the hands of the clock, assured me that I would arrive home in plenty of time for my touching litany with Auntie.

"Auntie," I said, "does not mind now my being out later. Auntie now, thank God, has greater trust in me."

"And you deserve it. You obey her wishes, you are prudent; and gradually, so Padre Casimiro tells me, she has become fond of you." This reminded me of the old friendship between Dr. Margaride and Padre Casimiro, my aunt's agent and zealous confessor. And, seizing the opportunity, I sighed slightly and opened my heart to the magistrate unreservedly, as to a father: "It is true, Auntie is fond of me; yet believe me, Dr. Margaride, my future sometimes disquiets me.

I have even thought of competing for a legal post. I have even inquired if it would be difficult to obtain a post in the Customs. For
though my aunt is rich, very rich, and I am her nephew, her only
relation, her only heir. . . ." And I looked anxiously at Dr. Margaride,
who perhaps through the talkative Padre Casimiro knew Auntie's
will. The grave silence that he maintained, with his hands crossed
on the table, seemed to me of bad omen; and at that instant the
waiter brought the tea-tray, smiling and congratulating the magistrate because his cold was better.

"Delicious toast," murmured the Doctor.

"Excellent toast," I sighed politely.

From time to time Dr. Margaride would pick his teeth, then he
would wipe his lips and his fingers, then he would begin again to
munch slowly, delicately, religiously.

I ventured to remark again, timidly: "It is true that Auntie is fond
of me. . . ."

"Auntie is fond of you," interrupted the magistrate with his
mouth full, "and you are her only relation. But that is not the question, Teodorico; the fact is, you have a rival."

"I will do for him," I cried on the spur of the moment with flaming eyes, bringing my fist down on the marble table. The melancholy youth at the further end of the room raised his face from his
drink, and Dr. Margaride severely reprimanded me for such vio-
lence.

"Such an expression is unworthy of a gentleman and of a well-
behaved young man. Generally speaking, one does not 'do for' anyone. And, besides that, your rival, Teodorico, is none other than Our
Lord Jesus Christ."

Our Lord Jesus Christ! I only understood when the distinguished
lawyer, having now calmed down, informed me that even in my last
year at the University it was Auntie's intention to leave her fortune,
houses and estates, to sisterhoods in which she was interested and
to priests of her special devotion. "I am lost," I murmured; and my
eyes chanced to fall on the melancholy youth in front of his glass of
syrup. And he seemed to me to resemble me as a brother, he seemed

to be myself, Teodorico, disinherited, dingy, with worn boots, come there at night to meditate on my sorrows over a glass of syrup. But Dr. Margaride had finished his toast, and, happily stretching his legs, consoled me, toothpick in mouth, with clear-sighted affability. "All is not lost, Teodorico. I do not think that all is lost. It may be that your aunt has changed her mind. You behave well, you enliven her, you read out the paper to her, you pray the litany with her. And all that tells. At the same time, one must own that your rival is strong."

"Tremendous," I moaned.

"Is strong; and, I must add, worthy of all respect. Christ suffered for us, He is the religion of the State, one can only bow one's head. But if you would like to have my opinion, here it is, frank and undisguised: You will inherit everything if your Aunt Dona Patrocinio is convinced that to leave her fortune to you is the same as to leave it to Holy Mother Church."

The magistrate nobly paid for the tea, and afterwards in the street, wrapped in his overcoat, he said in a low voice: Frankly now how did you like the toast? — There is no better toast in Lisbon, Dr. Margaride. He affectionately shook my hand, and we parted as the old Carmo clock struck midnight.

As I hurried along the Rua Nova da Palma, I saw clearly and bitterly how mistaken had been my life. Yes, mistaken. Till now the complicated devotion with which I had sought to please Auntie and her gold had been steady but never ardent. What was the use of correctly murmuring the litany before Our Lady of the Rosary? Before Our Lady in every shape, in order to impress Auntie, I should openly and skillfully display a soul burning in flames of sacred love and a body bruised and wounded in a penitent hairshirt. So far Auntie could say with approval: He is excellent. In order to become her heir, she must say with open mouth and clasped hands: He is a saint!

Yes, I must identify myself to such an extent with ecclesiastical things, so bury myself in them, that gradually my aunt would be unable to separate me clearly from the ancient medley of crosses, images, prayer-books, chasubles, candles, scapularies, palm-branches and processions which for her spelt religion and Heaven; she must mistake my voice for the holy muttering of the Mass, and my overcoat must seem to her sprinkled with stars, and shining as a tunic of the blest. Then evidently she would make a will in my favor, certain that in doing so she was making it in favor of Christ and her dear Mother Church. For I was perfectly decided not to allow the Son of Mary to have the pleasant fortune of Comendador Godinho. What, were not His countless treasures sufficient: the dark marble cathedrals which cover the earth with their gloom; the interests and investments which human piety is constantly piling up in His name; the heaps of gold which the State lays at His feet pierced with nails; the vestments and chalices, the diamond shirt-links in use in the Graça church? Must He still turn voracious eyes from the cross to a silver tea-pot and some poor Lisbon houses? Well, we will dispute these wretched fleeting possessions, you, O son of the carpenter, showing Auntie the wound that You received for her one afternoon in a barbarous city of Asia, and I adoring that wound noisily, splendidly, so that Auntie will be unable to decide whether the merit is in you who died for us through loving us too much, or in me who wish to die because I cannot love you enough.

These were my thoughts as I looked askance at the sky in the silence of the Rua de S. Lazaro. When I reached home I saw that Auntie was alone, in the oratory, wrapped in prayer. I went secretly to my room, took off my boots, took off my coat, disheveled my hair, flung myself on my knees on the floor, and went on my knees along the passage groaning, weeping, beating my breast, calling desperately on the name of the Lord. When Auntie heard these mournful moans of penitence sounding through the silent house, she came to the door of the oratory in a fright: "What is it, Teodorico, my dear, what is the matter?" I fell sobbing on the floor, fainting under my divine sorrow. "Excuse me, Auntie. I was at the theatre with Dr. Margaride; we had tea together and were speaking of Auntie; and suddenly, on my way home, in the Rua Nova da Palma I began to think that I must die, and of the salvation of my soul and of all that Our

Lord suffered for us; and I had a wish to cry. So, Auntie, please, leave me for a little alone here in the oratory, that I may seek comfort."

Impressed and silent, she reverently lit one by one all the candles of the altar. She placed the image of her favorite St. Joseph on the edge that it might be the first to receive the fervent storm of prayer which was about to burst from my burdened and sorrowful heart. She let me come in on my knees, and then in silence disappeared, carefully closing the curtain behind her. And there I remained, seated on Auntie's cushion, rubbing my knees, sighing aloud, and thinking of the Viscondessa de Souto Santos or Villar o Velho and of the ardent kisses I would rain on her plump shoulders if I could have her alone for an instant, even if it were here in the oratory, at the golden feet of Christ my Savior.

My devotion now became more perfect. Considering that stock-fish on Fridays was not a sufficient mortification, on those days in Auntie's presence I ascetically drank a glass of water and ate a crust of bread: the stockfish I ate later, in the form of onion sauce and beefsteak in Adelia's house. My wardrobe that hard winter contained but one old overcoat, so indifferent I wished to appear to the wicked comforts of the flesh; but to cleanse my profane tweeds the red cloak of a brother of the Senhor dos Passos hung there and was my pride, as well as the pious grey habit of the Third Order of St. Francis. On a chest of drawers a lamp burnt perennially before a colored lithograph of Our Lady do Patrocinio, and every day I placed roses in a glass before it to scent the air around it; and Auntie, when she came to search among my things, remained gazing at her patroness in gratified vanity, without knowing whether it was to the Virgin or indirectly to herself that I offered this homage of light and scented praise.

On the walls I hung the images of the noblest saints, as a gallery of spiritual ancestors from whom I received a constant example in the difficult path of virtue. Indeed, there was no saint in heaven, however obscure, to whom I did not dedicate a scented offering of paternosters aflower. It was I who introduced to Auntie St. Telesforo, St. Secundina, the blessed Antony Estronconio, St. Restituta, St. Umbelina, sister of St. Bernard, and our beloved and charming countrywoman St. Basilissa, who is celebrated with St. Hypatius on the festal day of August when the penitents embark for Atalaya.

I was indeed of a prodigious activity in my devotions. I went to Matins, I went to Vespers. I was never absent from church or hermitage in which there was adoration of the Sacred Heart of Jesus. Wherever the Host was exposed, there was I on my knees. I joined patiently in every act of atonement to the Sacrament. The special services in which I took part are countless as the stars; and the Septenary of Sorrows was one of my special cares. There were days when without resting I ran breathlessly along the streets, to seven o'clock Mass at Sant'Anna, nine o'clock Mass at the church of St. Joseph, midday Mass in the hermitage of Oliveirinha. I took a moment's respite at a street corner, my prayer-book under my arm, hastily smoking a cigarette, and was off again to the reservation of the Host in the parish church of St. Engracia, to the litany in the convent of St. Joanna, to the blessing of the Sacrament in the chapel of Our Lady at the Picoas, to the service for the wounds of Christ, with the special music. Then I took a cab and hastily visited at random the Martyrs and St. Dominick, the church of the convent of the Atonement, and the church of the Visitation, the chapel of Monserrate and the Gloria, the Flamengas, the Albertas, the Pena, the Rato, the Cathedral.

In the evening in Adelia's house I was so worn out, so slack and listless in a corner of the sofa, that she would thump me on the shoulders, crying furiously: Wake up, simpleton. Alas, there came a day when Adelia instead of calling me simpleton as, wearied in the service of the Lord, I could scarcely help her to unfasten a button, began when my lips sought her neck to shove me away, to call me moonface. That was on the gay eve of St. Anthony, when the first marjoram appears, in the fifth month of my perfect devotion. Adelia began to appear absent and thoughtful, and sometimes when I was speaking she had a way of saying eh? with a vague and distant look which was a torment to my heart.

Then one day she ceased to give the caress that I most desired, the piercing delight of a kiss on the ear. She was still affectionate, she still carefully folded my overcoat, she still called me her precious one, she still accompanied me to the landing, and, after we had embraced at parting, gave that slow sigh which was to me the most precious proof of her passion, but she no longer kissed me on the ear. When I came in heatedly I would find her still undressed, her hair not done, dull and slack and with pits beneath her eyes. She would hold out her hand carelessly, yawn and listlessly take up her guitar, and while I in a corner, silently smoking cigarettes, waited for the glass door to open and let me into heaven, the inhuman Adelia, lying on the sofa, her slippers half off her feet, would strum on the guitar and hum with melancholy moans songs of strange sadness. In a moment of tenderness I would go and kneel by her side; and immediately would come the hard icy word: Be quiet, moonface. And she kept repelling me; she would say: I have indigestion, or she would say: I have a pain in my side. And I stretched my legs and returned to the Campo de Sant'Anna, frustrated, wretched, longing in the darkness of my soul for that delightful time when she still called me simpleton.

One July night, soft as black velvet and sprinkled with stars, I arrived at her house earlier than usual and found the door open. The paraffin lamp, set on the floor of the landing, lit up the stairs and I came on Adelia in a white skirt talking to a youth with a fair moustache, wrapped poorly in a Spanish cloak. She grew pale and he shrank away as I appeared, tall and bearded with my stick in my hand. Then Adelia, calmly smiling, with a true straightforward air, presented to me her nephew Adelino. He was the son of her sister Ricardina, who lived at Viseu, and brother of little Teodorico.

Taking off my hat, I pressed the shrinking fingers of Senhor Adelino in my large and loyal hand: Very glad to make your acquaintance. I hope your mother and brother are well? That night, Adelia, radiant, once more called me simpleton and kissed me on the ear; and the whole of that week was delicious as a honeymoon. It was in the height of summer and the devotion of St. Jehoakin had begun in

the church of the Conceição, Velha. I went out in that restful hour
when the streets are watered, and felt happier than the sparrows
chattering in the trees of the Campo de Sant'Anna. In the bright
drawing-room with its chairs covered in white fustian, I found
Adelia fresh and scented with eau-de-cologne and with beautiful
red carnations in her hair; and after the hot mornings nothing could
be more idyllically charming than our teas in the kitchen in the cool
of the window, from which we could see green glimpses of gardens
and humble clothes drying on cords.

On one of those charming afternoons she asked me for eight
pounds. Eight pounds! At night as I went down the Rua da Madalena, I considered who would lend them to me generously without interest. The good Casimiro was at Torres, the serviceable Rinchão was in Paris. I was thinking of Padre Pinheiro, with whose
complaints I sympathized not without effect, when I saw, escaping
secretly and timidly from one of those sordid streets in which mer-
cenary Venus trails her slippers, José Justino, our José Justino, the
pious secretary of the brotherhood of St. Joseph, Auntie's most virtuous solicitor. I at once called out: Good evening, Justino; and
went back to the Campo de Sant'Anna in happy anticipation of the
fervent kiss which Adelia would give me when I gaily held out in
my hand the eight pieces of gold.

Next morning early I hurried to Justino's office at St. Paulo, and
told him the sad story of a fellow-student lying miserably consumptive on a mattress in a sordid lodging-house near the Largo dos
Caldas: "A real misfortune, Justino. He has not even money to buy
a bowl of soup. I do my best, but really I haven't a penny. All I can
do is to go and sit with him and read out prayers and Exercises for
a Christian life. Last night I was coming from his house, and believe
me, Justino, I do not like to walk along those streets so late. Heavens,
what streets, how indecent, how immoral! Those narrow stairways,
eh? I could see yesterday that you were horrified, and so was I. And
this morning I was in my aunt's oratory, praying for my comrade
and asking the Lord to help him and send him some money, and
suddenly I seemed to hear a voice from the cross saying: Come to

an understanding with Justino, speak to our good Justino, let him give you eight pounds for the poor fellow. And I was so grateful to the Lord. So I have come, Justino, at His wish."

Justino listened to me white as his collar and sadly cracking the joints of his fingers; then in silence he handed to me one by one the eight gold coins. Thus was I able to satisfy Adelia. But my joy was short-lived. Some days later as I was in the Café Montanha comfortably enjoying an iced drink, the waiter came to inform me that a dark girl in a shawl, Senhora Mariana, was waiting for me at the corner. Heavens! Mariana was Adelia's servant; and I ran out trembling, certain that my love must be suffering from that hateful pain in her white side. I even thought of beginning the litany of the eighteen appearances of Our Lady of Lourdes, which Auntie considers most effective in the case of pain in the side or of runaway bulls.

"Anything wrong, Mariana?"

She led me into an evil-smelling court; and there with red eyes, and furiously twisting her shawl, her voice still hoarse from her quarrel with Adelia, she began to tell her disgraceful, sordid, execrable tale. Adelia was deceiving me. Senhor Adelino was not her nephew, he was her lover, her *chulo*. As soon as I went out he came in, and Adelia hung passionately on his neck; and they called me moonface, saint, goat and other blacker terms of abuse, spitting on my portrait. The eight pounds had been for Adelino to buy himself a summer suit, and there had been enough over for them to go to the Belem fair in an open carriage with a guitar. Adelia adored him with passionate devotion, and her impatient sighs when he was late recalled the roaring of the deer in the woods in the hot month of May. If I did not believe her and require a proof, I might go late at night, after one o'clock, and knock at Adelia's door.

Livid, leaning against the wall, I scarcely knew if the smell which overcame me was from the dark corner of the court or from the filthy words which flowed from Mariana's lips as from a burst drain-pipe. I wiped my brow and murmured faintly: "Very good, Mariana, thank you; I will see about it." I arrived home so sad and exhausted that my aunt asked me with a smile if I had fallen off the mare. The mare? No indeed, Auntie. I was in the Graça church. . . . "You seem so upset, with your legs failing under you. And was the Lord looking well today?" — "O Auntie, He was splendid; but I do not know why, He seemed to me so sad, so sad. I even said to Padre Eugenio: 'O Eugenio, the Lord today is looking vexed.' And he answered: 'What do you expect, my friend, with all the villainies that He sees in the world?' And he does indeed, Auntie; such ingratitude, such falseness and treachery."

I roared in my anger. I closed my fist as though to let it fall in fearful vengeance on the vast perfidity of mankind. But I restrained myself, slowly buttoned up my coat and choked down a sob. "As I was saying, Auntie, I was so impressed by that sadness of the Lord that I was a trifle upset. And besides I have had bad news: a comrade of mine is very ill, poor fellow, at the last gasp." And once more, as with Justino, profiting by my recollections of Xavier and the Rua da Fé, I extended the carcass of a fellow-student on a wretched mattress. I described him as consumptive, and unable to afford even a bowl of soup. What misery, Auntie, what misery! And a young man who had so much respect for holy things, and who wrote so well in the *Nação*.

"A sad case," murmured Aunt Patrocinio, plying her knitting-needles. "Sad indeed, Auntie; and as he has no family and the people of the house are careless, we his comrades are taking it in turn to sit up with him. Tonight is my turn, and I was going to ask Auntie if she would give me permission to stay out till nearly two o'clock. After that comes another youth, a very cultivated man, a member of Parliament."

She gave her permission, and even offered to pray the patriarch St. Joseph to prepare for my comrade an easy happy death. "That would be a great favor, Auntie. His name is Macieira, squint-eyed Macieira. I tell you so that St. Joseph may know." I wandered all night about the city, as it lay asleep in the soft moonlight of July. And in every street floating transparently before me went two forms, a woman and a man in a Spanish cloak, clasped together and kissing one another furiously, only separating their close-pressed lips to laugh aloud at me and call me "saint."

I arrived in the Rossio as the Carmo clock was striking one. I smoked a cigarette, still undecided beneath the trees; then slowly and afraid I turned my steps towards Adelia's house. A dim sleepy light shone in her window. I seized the great door-knocker, but hesitated in terror of the certainty I was coming to seek, final and irremediable. Perhaps, after all, Mariana to revenge herself had calumniated my Adelia. It was only the evening before that she had called me her precious one with such fervor. Would it not be more sensible and better to believe her, to wink at this passing passion for Senhor Adelino and continue egoistically to receive the kiss on the ear?

But then came the terrible thought that she also kissed Senhor Adelino on the ear and that he cried out in pleasure as I did, and with that thought came the fierce desire to kill her, disdainfully, with my fists, there on the steps which had so often witnessed the soft delight of our parting. And I beat on the door with a tremendous blow as though it were upon her fragile ungrateful breast. I heard the window-latch open roughly and she appeared in night attire, with disheveled hair.

"Who is the brute?"

"It is I. Open."

She recognized me and the light disappeared; the extinguishing of that lamp's wick seemed to leave my soul in darkness, cold and empty. I felt myself icily alone, a widower without home or occupation. From the middle of the street I kept looking at the darkened windows and murmuring: "Oh, it will be the death of me." Once more the form of Adelia appeared white at the window: "I cannot open, for I had supper late and am sleepy." "Open," I cried desperately, "open or I will never come again." "Do as you please, and my love to your aunt." "Good-bye, you drunken wretch." And having hurled that severe cry at her like a stone, I went off down the street very stiff and dignified.

But when I reached the corner my grief knocked me over and I remained in a doorway bitterly weeping, quite overcome. The slow melancholy summer days that followed weighed heavily on my heart. Having told Auntie that I was writing two articles piously intended for the 1878 Almanac of the Immaculate Conception, I shut myself all morning in my room, while the sun blazed on the stone of my balcony. There, dragging my slippers over the watered floor, I would sigh as I thought of Adelia, or before the glass gaze at the soft part of my ear that she was wont to kiss. Then I would hear a window being opened and her perfidious, outrageous cry: Go where you please. And, raging in despair, I would rain upon the mattress the blows which I could not inflict on the shallow chest of Senhor Adelino.

In the afternoon when it grew cooler I went to walk about the lower city; but every window open to the afternoon breeze, every starched muslin curtain, reminded me of the intimacy of Adelia's room; a simple pair of stockings in a shop-window recalled the perfection of her leg; anything shining reminded me of her eyes, and even a strawberry ice in the Café Martinho seemed to have the sweet and pleasant savor of her kisses.

At night after tea I took refuge in the oratory, as in a tower of holiness, and gazed at the golden body of Jesus nailed upon His fair cross of black wood. But gradually the golden gleam of the precious metal grew dim and assumed the white color of warm soft flesh, the thin bones of the sad Messiah became rounded into forms divinely full and fair, from between the thorns of His crown sprang wanton rings of black curly hair, and on the breast, above the two wounds, arose two firm and splendid rose-tipped breasts; and it was she, my Adelia, who was there on the cross, naked, superb, smiling, victorious, holding out to me her open arms. And I did not see in this the temptation of the devil but, rather, a favor of the Lord. I began even to mingle with the words of my prayer the complaints of my love. Perhaps Heaven is grateful, and those innumerable saints, on whom I had lavished so many services and prayers, would maybe wish to reward my attentions by restoring to me the caresses of which the man in the Spanish cloak had robbed me.

I placed more flowers on the chest of drawers in front of Our Lady do Patrocinio, I told her the sorrows of my heart. Behind the clear glass of her shrine, with her sad downcast eyes she was the confidante of my unrequited passion, and every night, half undressed, before going to bed I whispered to her fervently: "O my dear Senhora do Patrocinio, make little Adelia grow fond of me again." I also took advantage of Auntie's high favor with the saints, her friends: the loving and gracious St. Joseph and St. Luis de Gonzaga, so benevolent to youth. I begged her to make petition for a certain need of mine, secret and pure. She eagerly assented, and through the curtain of the oratory I had the pleasure of watching the severe old lady on her knees, her beads in her hand, praying the most holy patriarchs that Adelia might again kiss me on the ear.

Early one night I went to see if heaven had listened to prayers of such worth. I arrived at Adelia's door and, trembling all over, knocked humbly. Senhor Adelino appeared at the window in his shirt-sleeves.

"It is I, Senhor Adelino," I murmured abjectly, taking off my hat; "I wish to speak to Adelia."

He turned round and muttered my name, I even fancied he said "the saint;" and from within, from between the curtains, where I imagined her fair and disheveled, my Adelia cried furiously: "Throw the pail of dirty water over him." I fled.

At the end of September, Rinchão returned from Paris, and one Sunday evening, as, coming from the service at St. Caetano, I entered the Café Martinho, I found him in a group of young men noisily relating his daring adventures in Paris. Sadly I took a chair and remained to listen to Rinchão. With his ruby horseshoe tie-pin, his eyeglass hanging from a long cord, a yellow rose in his buttonhole, Rinchão was impressive as through the smoke of his cigar he gave us the outlines of his glory: "One night in the Café de la Paix, as I was supping with Cora, and the Valtesse and a very smart youth, a prince. . . ."

What had Rinchão not seen and enjoyed! An enthusiastic Italian countess related to the Pope and called Popotte had loved him and taken him to the Champs Élysées in her victoria with its ancient crest of two horns crossed. He had dined in restaurants lit by golden chandeliers, where the waiters, grave and slender, respectfully called him Monsieur le Comte. And the entertainments under the trees in the gas-light, and Pauline with bare arms singing "the Sausage of Marseilles," had revealed to him the truth and magnificence of civilization.

Did you see Victor Hugo? asked a youth in black spectacles, biting his nails.

"No, he was never among the smart set."

All that week the thought of seeing Paris shone constantly in my mind, with the tempting promise of many delights. And it was less from the desire for the joys of pride and the flesh with which Rinchão had sated himself than a longing to leave Lisbon, where the churches and the shops, the bright river and the bright sky, only reminded me of Adelia and the bitter man in the Spanish cloak and the kiss on the ear lost for ever. Ah, if Auntie would open her purse of green silk and let me plunge in my hands and take out gold and go to Paris! But in the eyes of Dona Patrocinio, Paris was a loathsome place full of lies and greed, where a people without saints, with its hands stained in the blood of archbishops, is ever, by sunlight and gaslight, living a dissolute existence. How could I dare reveal to Auntie my immodest wish to visit that place of dirt and moral darkness?

But on the very next Sunday, as we were dining with her chosen friends at Sant'Anna, the conversation happened to fall during one of the courses on a fellow-student of Padre Casimiro who had recently left the quiet of his cell in the convent of Varatojo to assume amid the firing of rockets his arduous duties as Bishop of Lamego. Our modest Casimiro could not understand this desire for a mitre set with false jewels: for him the culminating point of a priest's life was to be as he was at the age of sixty, healthy and happy, without regrets or fears, eating the baked rice of Dona Patrocinio das Neves. "For let me tell you, respected lady, that this rice of yours is quite excellent. And the wish always to have rice like this and friends to appreciate it seems to me the best and most legitimate ambition for the righteous."

And thus we came to discuss the proper ambitions which, without offending the Lord, one might nourish in one's heart.

That of the lawyer Justino was a small property in Minho, with rose-trees and vines, where he might spend his old age quietly in his shirt-sleeves. "But one thing, Justino, you would miss," said Auntie, "and that is your Mass in the Conceição Velha." "When one grows accustomed to a certain Mass, none other can satisfy. I know that if they took from me mine in Sant'Anna, my health would begin to fail." It was Padre Pinheiro who said it, and Auntie in her emotion placed on his plate another wing of chicken.

Then Padre Pinheiro also revealed his ambition, a saintly one. He wished to see the Pope restored to the strong and prosperous throne on which Leo X had shone. "If only he were treated with more charity!" exclaimed Auntie. "To think of the most holy Father, the Vicar of Our Lord, in a dungeon, in rags, on straw. They are real Caiaphases, Jews." She drank a little warm water and retired within the sanctuary of her soul, to pray the Ave Maria which she always offered for the health of the Pontiff and the end of his captivity.

Dr. Margaride comforted her. He did not believe that the Pope slept on straw. Enlightened travellers had assured him that the Holy Father might, if he so wished, even have a carriage. "It is not everything, it is far from being everything that is due to one who wears the tiara; but a carriage, my dear lady, is a very great convenience."

Then our Casimiro, smiling, wished to know, since all were telling their ambitions, what was that of the learned, the eminent Dr. Margaride. Tell us yours, Dr. Margaride, tell us yours, we all cried affectionately. He smiled gravely. "Let me first, Dona Patrocinio, help myself to this tongue which is advancing towards us and seems a real dainty." After being helped, the venerable magistrate confessed that he wished to be a peer of the realm. It was not for the sake of the honor or the dress, but in order to defend the sacred principle of authority. Only for that, he added energetically. "For I should like before I die to give, if you will permit me the expression, a knock-

out blow to atheism and anarchy. And I would too." We all declared
eagerly that Dr. Margaride deserved to attain this social pinnacle;
and he thanked us very gravely.

Then he turned his white majestic face to me. "And our Teodorico? Our Teodorico has not yet told us his ambition." I blushed,
and Paris at once shone in my desire, with its golden chandeliers,
its countesses related to the Pope, and the froth of its champagne,
fascinating, inebriating and annihilating every grief. But I lowered
my eyes and declared that my only wish was to say my prayers by
the side of Auntie well and peacefully.

But Dr. Margaride had put down his knife and fork and insisted.
It did not seem to him an offence to God nor ungrateful to Auntie
that I, an intelligent, healthy gentleman with a degree, should have
an honest ambition. "And I have," I said with decision, as one who
throws a weapon; "I have, Dr. Margaride: I should much like to see
Paris." "Gracious!" cried Dona Patrocinio, horrified. "To go to Paris!"
"To see the churches, Auntie." "It is not necessary to go so far to see
beautiful churches," she replied with asperity. "And in good organ
music and luxurious manifestation of the Host and a fine procession through the streets and good voices and reverence and images
adorned with good taste, no one beats us Portuguese." I remained
silent and defeated; and the enlightened Dr. Margaride applauded
Auntie's ecclesiastical patriotism: certainly it was not in a republic
without God that one would find magnificent services: "No, to enjoy the grandeurs of our religion, if I had leisure, it is not to Paris
that I would go. Do you know where I would go, Dona Maria do
Patrocinio?" "The Doctor," said Padre Pinheiro, "would go straight
to Rome." "Try again higher, Padre Pinheiro; higher, my dear lady."
"Higher?" Neither Auntie nor the good Pinheiro could believe that
there could be anything higher than the Rome of the Popes.

Dr. Margaride then solemnly raised his eyebrows, which were
thick and black as ebony! "I would go to the Holy Land, Dona Patrocinio! I would go to Palestine. I would go to see Jerusalem and Jordan. And I should like also to stand, like Chateaubriand, for a moment on Golgotha and gaze and meditate and say Salve! And I would

take notes and publish historic impressions. That is where I would go. I would go to Zion!" The roast pork had been handed round, and there was a moment of reverent silence over our plates at the thought of the Holy Land where the Lord suffered. I seemed to see far away in Arabia, after weary days of travel on a camel's back, a heap of ruins round a cross; a sinister stream flows by the side of the olive-trees, and the bowl of the sky is sad and silent as the roof of a tomb. That was how I imagined Jerusalem. "A fine journey," murmured our Casimiro thoughtfully. "Without counting," murmured Padre Pinheiro low as though whispering a prayer, "that Our Lord shows a great appreciation and gratitude for these visits to His holy sepulchre." "The traveller," said Justino, "even has his sins forgiven. Is it not so, Pinheiro? I read it in the *Panorama*. He returns entirely free from sin."

Padre Pinheiro, having sorrowfully refused the cauliflower, which he considered indigestible, explained. He who went on a devout pilgrimage to the Holy Land received on the marble of the holy sepulchre, from the hands of the Patriarch of Jerusalem, and after the payment of certain fees, a plenary indulgence. "And not only for himself, so I am told," continued the well-informed ecclesiastic, "but for any pious person of his family who is certified to have been unable to perform the journey; with payment, of course, of double fees."

"For instance," exclaimed Dr. Margaride in a moment of inspiration, slapping me violently on the back, "for a good, an adored auntie, who has been an angel to you, all virtue and generosity." "On payment, of course," insisted Padre Pinheiro, "of double fees." Auntie said nothing; her spectacles, turning from priest to magistrate, seemed to grow strangely larger and to shine as with the inner light of an idea; a tinge of red appeared in her sallow face. Vicencia handed round the sweet rice and we said grace.

Later as I undressed in my room I felt infinitely sad. Auntie would never allow me to visit the tainted land of France, and I should have to remain shut up in Lisbon, where everything was a torture to me and the noisiest streets only increased the desolation of my heart, and even the transparent clearness of the summer sky reminded

me of the foul treachery of her who had been my star and queen of
grace. And at dinner that day Auntie seemed to me more strong and
solid and lasting, mistress for many years to come of the green silk
purse and the houses and money of Comendador Godinho. Alas,
how long should I have to pray that tedious litany with the hateful
old woman, and kiss the foot of the Senhor dos Passos, soiled with
so many devout mouths, and attend services and wear out my knees
before the thin wounded body of the Lord? Oh, life most bitter; and
I no longer had the soft arms of Adelia to console me for the weari-
some service of the Lord.

Next morning, with my spurs on and the mare ready saddled, I
went to inquire if Auntie had any pious message for St. Roque, that
being his day of miracles. In the room devoted to the glory of St.
Joseph, Auntie on a corner of the sofa, her Tonkin shawl fallen from
her shoulders, was examining a large account-book open on her
knees; and silent in front of her, his hands crossed behind his back,
the good Casimiro was smiling thoughtfully at the flowers of the
carpet.

"Ah, come here, come here," said he as soon as I appeared, bowing; "listen to the news: you are a jewel and show respect for the old
and deserve everything from God and your aunt. Come and let me
embrace you."

I smiled uncertainly. Auntie closed her account-book.

"Teodorico," she said stiffly, crossing her arms, "I have been consulting with Padre Casimiro, and I have decided that someone who
belongs to me, someone of my blood, shall make on my behalf the
pilgrimage to the Holy Land." "Ah, happy man!" murmured the radiant Casimiro.

"Therefore," proceeded my aunt, "it is understood and settled that
you are going to Jerusalem and to all the holy places. You need not
express your gratitude: it is for my pleasure and order to honor the
tomb of Jesus Christ, since I cannot go myself. And since, thank the
Lord, I have no lack of means, you are to travel with every comfort.
To cut the matter short, and in order to make all haste to please the
Lord, you are to start this month. And now go, for I have to speak

to Padre Casimiro. Thank you, I have nothing for St. Roque; I have already come to an understanding with him."

I muttered: "Very many thanks, Auntie; good-bye Padre Casimiro," and went along the passage, feeling half stunned. In my room I ran to the looking-glass to contemplate the face and beard on which would soon be falling the dust of Jerusalem. Then I fell upon my bed. What a tremendous bore! Jerusalem! And where was Jerusalem? I went to the trunk which contained my text-books and old clothes, I pulled out an atlas, and, placing it open on the chest of drawers before the Senhora do Patrocinio, I began to look for Jerusalem in the land of the infidels, where wind the obscure caravans and a well of water is a precious gift of the Lord.

My wandering finger already felt the weariness of a long journey and paused by the sinuous line of a river which must be the sacred Jordan. It was the Danube. And suddenly the name Jerusalem appeared black in a great white solitude, without names or lines, all bare and sandy by the sea. There was Jerusalem. Heavens, how distant, desolate, and sad!

But then I remembered that in order to reach that penitential soil I must pass through lands of feminine charm and full of gaiety. First there was lovely Andalucía the land of María Santísima, all scented with orange-flower, where the women, simply by putting a couple of carnations in their hair and wearing a scarlet shawl, soften the sternest heart, *bendita sea su gracia*. Farther on there was Naples with its dark warm streets, like those of an evil-smelling house, with images of the Virgin. And farther still came Greece: since I studied Rhetoric, Greece had always appeared to me as a sacred wood of bay-trees in which the façades of temples gleam whitely, and in shaded places, where sounds the cooing of doves, Venus suddenly arises, of the color of light and roses, offering to lips of man or brute the charm of her immortal breasts.

Venus no longer lives in Greece, but its women have preserved the splendor of her form and the charm of her immodesty. Heavens, how I might enjoy myself! A light came into my spirit, and I shouted as I gave the atlas a blow which made the Lady of Patrocinio and all the stars in her crown tremble: *Caramba*, I shall have the devil of a time! Yes indeed, and in fear that Auntie, either out of avarice or from distrust of my piety, should change her mind about this pilgrimage which promised such delights, I determined to bind her to it by a divine command sent from on high. I went to the oratory, disarranged my hair, as though some divine breath had passed through it, and ran to Auntie's room as in a dream, my arms trembling in the air: "O Auntie, what do you think? I was in the oratory, praying in my satisfaction, and suddenly I seemed to hear the still small voice of the Lord saying to me: You do well, Teodorico, to go to visit my holy sepulchre; and I am very pleased with your aunt: your aunt is one of mine."

She joined her hands in a fervent transport of love: "Blessed be His most holy name. Did He say that? Ah, He might indeed, since Our Lord knows that it is to do Him honor that I am sending you. Blessed again be His most holy name! Blessed in heaven and earth! Go, my son, go and pray to Him; do not cease to pray to Him."

I went, murmuring an Ave Maria. She ran to the door in a fervor of affection: "And, Teodorico, about your linen: perhaps you require more underclothes. Order whatever you need, for, thanks to Our Lady of the Rosario, I have the money and I wish you to be dressed decently and respectably when you go to the tomb of God."

I did order, and, having bought a Guide to the East and a cork helmet, I inquired as to the pleasantest way to reach Jerusalem of Benjamin Sarrosa and Co., a sagacious Jew who went every year, wearing a turban, to buy oxen in Morocco. Benjamin marked out in detail on paper my splendid journey. I would embark on the *Malaga*, a steamer of the house of Jadley, which, touching at Gibraltar and Malta, would take me through seas perpetually blue to the ancient land of Egypt. There I would have a rest full of pleasure at gay Alexandria. In the Eastern packet which goes up the sacred coast of Syria, I would arrive at Jaffa of the green orchards, and from there, following a macadamized road, I would trot pleasantly on a mare until after a day and a night I should see the walls of Jerusalem appear dark in their gloomy hills.

"Good Lord, Benjamin, there seems a great deal of sea and steamer. Can't you give me a little bit of Spain? Consider that I want to have a good time."

"You have a good time at Alexandria. There, there is everything, billiards, cabs, gambling, women. Everything of the best; it is there that you will have a good time."

Meanwhile in the Café Montanha and Brito's tobacco-shop there was talk of my holy enterprise, and one morning, scarlet with pride, I read in the *Jornal das Novidades* these honorable words: "Our friend Teodorico, nephew of the wealthy proprietress and model of Christian virtue Dona Patrocinio das Neves, will soon leave on a visit to Jerusalem and all the holy places in which Our Lord suffered. Bon voyage." Filled with vanity, Auntie placed the paper under the stand of the image of St. Joseph in the oratory; and I rejoiced to think of the anger of Adelia, a constant reader of the *Jornal*, at seeing me go off so carelessly, well furnished with gold, to these Muslim lands in which at every step one comes upon a harem, silent and smelling of roses amid sycamores.

The eve of my departure, in the room hung with damask, was a lofty and solemn occasion. Justino gazed at me as one gazes at some historic figure. "Ah, our Teodorico! What a journey, and how it will be talked of!" Padre Pinheiro murmured unctuously: "It was an inspiration of the Lord. How it will benefit your health!"

I showed them my cork helmet. They all admired it; but our Casimiro, after thoughtfully stroking his chin, observed that perhaps a tall hat would look more respectable. Auntie approved sorrowfully: "That is what I told him! I consider it rather disrespectful for a city in which Our Lord died." "But, Auntie, I have already explained to you: this is only for the desert. In Jerusalem, of course, and all the holy places, I shall wear a topper." "It is more gentlemanly," remarked Dr. Margaride.

Padre Pinheiro was anxious to know if I went well provided against any internal complaint in those deserts of the Bible. "I have everything: Benjamin gave me a list. I have even linseed and arnica." The slow clock in the passage began to strike ten. I had to be up early. Dr. Margaride, not without emotion, was wrapping his silken scarf round his neck. Then, before the final embraces, I asked my loyal friends what memento they would wish me to bring them from those distant lands which had seen the Lord. Padre Pinheiro asked for a small bottle of the water of the Jordan. Justino, who at the window had already asked for a packet of Turkish tobacco, in Auntie's presence only wished for a branch of an olive-tree from the Mount of Olives. Dr. Margaride would be content with a good photograph of the holy sepulchre which he could have framed. With my note-book open, after entering these pious commissions, I turned to Auntie, smiling, humble, affectionate. "As to me," she said from the middle of the sofa, as from an altar, stiff in her Sunday satins, "I only wish that you should make the journey with all devotion, leaving no stone unkissed, no service unattended, and praying duly in every place. And I shall be glad if you keep in good health."

I was about to give her hand, which gleamed with rings, a most grateful kiss; but she restrained me, dry and unbending: "Up to now you have behaved well, you have not transgressed the precepts of religion nor led a dissolute life. But if I learnt that on this journey you had had evil thoughts or had behaved ill or run after the women, be certain that, in spite of being my only relation and of having visited Jerusalem and obtained indulgences, you would go into the street without a crust, like a dog."

I bowed my head in terror; and Auntie, after wiping her sunken lips with her lace handkerchief, continued with ever greater authority and a growing emotion which for the moment gave the resemblance of a human breast to her flat bodice: "And now I will only say one thing more for your guidance." Standing up reverently, we perceived that Auntie was about to utter the supreme sentence. In this hour of separation, surrounded by her priests and magistrates, Dona Patrocinio das Neves was certainly about to reveal her real reason in sending me, her nephew, as a pilgrim to the city of Jerusalem. I was about to learn, as clearly as if it were written on parchment, what was to be the dearest of my cares, sleeping and waking, in the lands of the Gospel.

"Listen," said my aunt; "If you consider that I deserve anything of you for all I have done for you since your mother's death, in educating you and clothing you and giving you a horse to ride and caring for your soul, then bring me from those holy places a holy relic, a miracle-working relic for me to keep ever by my side to comfort me in my afflictions and cure the ills of my body." And for the first time after a dryness of fifty years a small tear ran down Auntie's cheek, under the dark spectacles.

Dr. Margaride turned excitedly towards me: "How your aunt loves you, Teodorico! Examine those ruins, search among those graves, and bring back the relic for Auntie."

I cried enthusiastically: "Auntie, on the honor of a Raposo, I will bring you back a tremendous relic."

The touching emotion in our hearts overflowed noisily in the severe damask room; and I found the lips of Justino, still wet from eating buttered toast, pressed against my beard. Early on Sunday morning, the sixth of September, day of St. Libania, I went to knock at the door of Auntie, still asleep in her chaste bed. I heard the approach of her soft slippers over the carpet. Decorously she opened the door a very little and, no doubt still in her night-dress, held out to me through the crack her livid bony hand smelling of snuff. I felt inclined to bite it. I kissed it affectionately. Good-bye, child; remember me to the Lord, murmured Auntie.

I went down the steps wearing my helmet and carrying the Guide to the East. Behind me came Vicencia in tears. My new leather trunk and well-filled canvas bag took up most of the room in the cab. Belated swallows were twittering on the eave of our roof; the bell of the chapel of Sant'Anna was ringing to Mass; and a ray of the sun coming from the East, coming from Palestine to meet me, bathed my face as with a caress of welcome from the Lord. I shut the door of the cab, stretched out my legs, and bade the coachman drive on. So, a rich pilgrim, blowing the smoke of my cigarette upon the breeze, I left my aunt's door on the way to Jerusalem.

Two

It was on a Sunday, the day of St. Jerome, that my Latin feet at length, on the quay at Alexandria, trod the sensual religious land of the East. I rendered thanks to Our Lord of Fortunate Journeys; and my companion, the illustrious Topsius, a German and Doctor of the University of Bonn and member of the Imperial Institute of Historic Excavations, murmured gravely as an invocation, as he opened his huge green sunshade: "Egypt, Egypt, I salute thee, black Egypt! And may the god Phtah, god of letters, god of history, inspirer of works of art and truth, be propitious to me in this land!" Through this scientific murmur I felt myself, as in the warm air of a hothouse, enveloped softly by scents of rose and sandalwood.

On the gleaming quay, among bundles of wool, sprawled the dirty commonplace shed of the Customs; but beyond, the white doves flew round the white minarets and the sky was filled with light. Surrounded by severe palm-trees, a languid palace slept at the edge of the water, and the sands of ancient Libya lost themselves in the distance, glimmering beneath the warm moving cloud of dust of lion's hue.

I fell in love with this land of indolence, dreams and light. And, jumping into the carriage that was to take us to the Hotel of the Pyramids, I also invoked the divinities, like the learned Doctor of Bonn: "Egypt, Egypt, I salute thee! May Phtah be propitious." "No, to you may Isis, the lovelorn cow, be propitious, Dom Raposo," interrupted the most learned man, smiling, with his arms round my hatbox. I accepted the alteration without understanding it.

I had made the acquaintance of Topsius at Malta one cool morning, as I was buying violets from a flower-woman in whose large eyes I could discern something of a Muslim languor, while he was carefully measuring with his sunshade the martial and monastic

walls of the palace of the Grand Master. Persuaded that it must be
the spiritual duty of the educated, in these lands of the East so full
of history, to measure the monuments of antiquity, I took out my
handkerchief and gravely drew it along those austere walls, stiff as a
yard-measure. Topsius at once darted at me over his gold spectacles
a look of jealous distrust. But, his mind no doubt set at rest by my
jovial and materialistic face, by my musk-scented gloves and my
silly bunch of violets, he politely raised from his long lanky maize-
colored hair his little cap of black silk. I saluted with my cork helmet, and we entered into conversation.

I told him my name and country, and the holy motives that took
me to Jerusalem. He told me that he had been born in glorious Germany, and was also going to Judea, and thence to Galilee, on a scientific pilgrimage, to obtain notes for his great work, "The History
of the Herods." But he was to stop at Alexandria, to collect the heavy
material for another monumental volume, "The History of the Lagidae." For these two turbulent families, the Herods and the Lagidae,
were the historical property of the learned Topsius. "Then, since we
are going the same way, we might go together, Dr. Topsius." Long-
legged, very thin and stiff in his short shiny black tail-coat, stuffed
with manuscripts, he bowed pleasantly: "Let us go together, Dom
Raposo. It will be a delightful economy."

With his thin neck, lanky hair, sharp and thoughtful nose and
tight-fitting trousers, my learned friend reminded me of a stork,
lettered and ridiculous, with his gold spectacles on the tip of his
nose. But my animal nature already felt a respect for his intellectual nature, and we went together to drink beer. The learning of
this young man was hereditary. His maternal grandfather, the natu-
ralist Scholck, wrote a celebrated treatise in eight volumes on "The
Physiognomic Expression of Lizards" which astonished Germany;
and his uncle, the decrepit Topsius, the well-known Egyptologist, at
the age of seventy-seven from a couch to which he was tied by the
gout, dictated that work of natural genius, "The Monotheistic Syn-
thesis of the Egyptian Theogony, Considered in the Relations of the
God Phtah and the God Imhotep with the Triads of the Nomos."

The father of Topsius, unfortunately, in the mist of this high
family science, humbly played the trombone in a brass band at Mu-
nich, but my companion resuming the tradition, had at the age of
twenty-two, in nineteen articles published in the *Weekly Bulletin of
Historical Excavations*, thrown splendid light upon the question, vital to
our civilization, of the brick wall raised by King Pi-Sibkme, of the
twenty-first dynasty, round the temple of Rameses II in the legend-
ary city of Tanis. In the whole of scientific Germany the opinion of
Topsius today about this wall shines as clearly as the sun itself.

My recollections of Topsius are all lofty or pleasant ones. On the
rough waters of the sea of Tyre, in the dark streets of Jerusalem, as we
slept side by side in a tent near the ruins of Jericho or passed along
the green roads of Galilee, I found him ever instructive, serviceable,
patient and discreet. I could rarely understand what he said in sono-
rous well-turned sentences having something of the perfection of
gold medals; but as before the closed door of a sanctuary I received
them with respect, knowing that within, in the shade, shone the
pure essence of the Idea. Sometimes, too, Dr. Topsius would mutter
a profane curse, and then a pleasant fellow-feeling arose between
him and my simple mind, that of a mere Bachelor of Law. He still
owes me six pounds, but this insignificant sum disappears beneath
the copious wave of historical knowledge with which he bathed my
spirit.

One thing only, apart from his learned hoarseness, I did not like
in him, and that was his habit of using my toothbrush. His pride
in his native land was also intolerable. Ceaselessly would he lift up
his voice to praise Germany, the spiritual mother of all peoples,
or threaten me with his irresistible force of the German armies.
The omniscience of Germany! The omnipotence of Germany!
She reigned in a vast entrenched camp of folios in which Meta-
physics armed went its rounds and issued commands. I had spirit
enough not to like this boasting. Thus when in the Hotel of the
Pyramids they asked us to enter our names and countries in a book,
my learned friend wrote Topsius and proudly added underneath:
"from imperial Germany;" I snatched up the pen and, remembering

bearded João de Castro and Ormuz in flames, Adamastor, the chapel of St. Roque, the Tagus and other glories, wrote in large round letters swelling like the sails of galleons: Raposo, from Portugal and Portugal beyond the seas. Straightway from a corner a worn thin porter murmured, sighing sadly: "If you require anything, ask for Alpedrinha." A fellow-countryman!

He told me his melancholy story as he unstrapped my portmanteau. He was from Trancosco and unhappy. He had studied and even composed an obituary notice and learnt by heart all the more melancholy verses of "our Soares dos Passos." But after the death of his mother, having inherited some land, he rushed off to Lisbon to enjoy himself; in the Travessa da Conceição he made the acquaintance of a ravishing Spanish woman, of the sweet name of Dulce, and went with her on an idyllic journey to Madrid. There gambling impoverished him, Dulce betrayed him and a *chulo* stabbed him.

Weak after his recovery, he went to Marseilles and spent some years in indescribable hardships as a social outcast. He became a sacristan at Rome, a hairdresser at Athens. In Morea, in a hut beside a marsh, he had employed himself in the dreadful search for leeches, and in a turban, carrying black skins on his shoulder, he had been a water-crier in the narrow streets of Smyrna. Fruitful Egypt had always had an irresistible attraction for him, and there he was, sad as ever, a luggage porter in the Hotel of the Pyramids.

"And if the gentleman has brought a newspaper from our Lisbon I should be glad to read about the political situation." I generously gave him all the *Jornals das Notícias* that were wrapped round my boots.

The owner of the hotel was a Lacedaemonian Greek with a fierce moustache, who spoke a little Spanish. Respectfully he himself, stiff in his black coat adorned with a decoration, conducted us to the dining-room, "*la más preciosa, sin duda, de todo el Oriente, caballeros.*" A large half-withered bunch of scarlet flowers stood on the table; in the oil cruet dead flies floated familiarly; and the waiter's slippers kept brushing against an old copy, stained with wine, of the *Journal des Débats*, which had been lying there since the evening before, trodden on by other indolent slippers; while on the ceiling the rank smoke of the brass lamps had formed black clouds by the rose-colored clouds on which angels and swallows hovered.

Under the balcony a violin and a harp were playing. And while Topsius swilled his beer, I felt my love for this land of light and indolence increasing strangely. After coffee my most learned friend, his pencil ready to take notes in the pocket of his tailcoat, went off to hunt for antiquities and stones of the time of the Ptolemies. I lit a cigar, called for Alpedrinha, and confided to him that my immediate desires were to pray and love. The prayer was on behalf of Aunt Patrocinio, who had commissioned me to say a prayer to St. Joseph as soon as I trod the soil of Egypt, which, since the flight of the Holy Family on a donkey, had become as sacred as that of a cathedral. The love was a necessity of my restless fiery heart.

Alpedrinha in silence raised the outer blind and showed me a bright square, adorned in its center by a bronze hero mounted on a bronze charger; a warm wind raised slow eddies of dust above two dry ponds, and in the blue air around appeared tall houses, each flying the flag of its country, like rival fortresses in a conquered country. The sad Alpedrinha showed me at a corner, where an old woman was selling sugar-cane, the quiet Street of the Two Sisters. There, he murmured, I would find above the door of a discreet little shop a heavy, red, roughly wrought wooden hand, and above that a board painted black, with these inviting words in gold: "Miss Mary. Gloves and Wax Flowers." That was the refuge he advised for my heart. At the end of the street, near a fountain flowing under trees, there was a new chapel where my soul would find both consolation and coolness. "And tell Miss Mary that you come at the recommendation of the Hotel of the Pyramids."

I placed a rose in my buttonhole and went out triumphant. At the entrance of the Street of the Two Sisters I found the hermitage chastely asleep under plane-trees in the gentle rumor of the street. But the loving patriarch St. Joseph was certainly at that moment occupied in receiving more urgent prayers from nobler lips than mine, and I did not wish to be importunate; so that I stopped before the wooden hand painted red which seemed to be there waiting to seize my heart in its long open fingers.

I entered with emotion. Behind the varnished counter, near a bowl of roses and magnolias, she was seated reading the *Times*, with a white cat on her shoulder. What at once attracted me were her clear blue eyes, of a blue that one only sees in china, ingenuous, celestial, such as are not to be found in dark-hued Lisbon. But even more fascinating was her hair, fresh-dressed, like a shock of gold, so soft and delicate that one could wish to remain for ever touching it with trembling fingers; it cast an irresistible profane halo round her plump face, softly delicious, of a whiteness of milk in which crimson has been melted.

Smiling and demurely lowering her dark eyelashes, she asked me if I required kid or suède. I murmured, moving eagerly up to the counter: I bring you a message from Alpedrinha. She chose from the flowers a shy rosebud and gave it to me in the tips of her fingers. I bit it furiously. The fierceness of this caress must have pleased her, for a warmer color came into her face and in a low voice she called me "a wicked one." I forgot St. Joseph and his prayer, and our hands, touching as she put on my light-colored glove, became permanently locked during the weeks that I spent in the city of Lagidae, in gay Muslim delights.

She was from York, the heroic county of old England, where the women grow strong and well-developed as the roses in their splendid gardens. On account of her gentleness and her golden laughter when I tickled her, I gave her the gallant high-sounding name of Mollycharm. Topsius, who had a regard for her, called her our symbolical Cleopatra. She fell in love with my strong black beard, and so as not to be parted from her I renounced Cairo and the Nile and the eternal Sphinx, lying at the gate of the desert smiling at poor humanity. Dressed all in white like a lily, I spent delicious mornings leaning against Mary's counter and respectfully stroking the back of her cat. She was of few words, but her simple smile with open arms or her charming way of folding the *Times* filled my heart with light and joy. It was not necessary for her to call me her dear little valiant

Portuguese: it sufficed for her breast to rise languidly in soft longing for my kisses for me to have been willing to go not merely to Alexandria but on foot without resting farther afield, even to where the waters of the Nile flow white.

In the afternoon in the carriage with our most learned Topsius, we went for slow loving drives along the Mamoudieh canal. Under the shady trees, along the walls of the gardens of the seraglio, I drank in the delirious scent of magnolias and other warm perfumes unknown to me. Sometimes a frail red or white flower would fall in my lap; with a sigh my beard touched the soft face of my Mary, who shivered deliciously. In the water lay heavy boats which go up the sacred and fruitful Nile and anchor by the ruins of temples and coast along green islands where the crocodiles lie asleep. The evening fell gradually, and we drove slowly through the scented shade. Topsius murmured verses of Goethe. The palm-trees of the opposite bank stood out against the yellow sunset as though cut in bronze relief on a sheet of gold.

Mary always dined with us at the Hotel of the Pyramids, and for her Topsius unfolded flowers of pleasant erudition. He told us of the festal afternoons in the ancient Alexandria of the Ptolemies on the canal which went to Canopia: either bank gleamed with palaces and gardens; the boats, with silken awnings, were rowed to the sound of music; the priests of Osiris, arrayed in leopard skins, danced beneath the orange-trees; and on the terraces, drawing back their veils, the ladies of Alexandria drank to Venus from the chalice of a lotus-flower. A general voluptuousness softened the souls of men; even the philosophers were of love's train. And, added Topsius with a wink, in all Alexandria there was but one honest woman, who wrote a commentary on Homer and was aunt of Seneca.

Poor Mary sighed. How delightful to have lived in that Alexandria and sailed up the Canopus in a boat with an awning of silk! "Without me?" I cried jealously. But she swore that without her valiant little Portuguese she would be unwilling to live even in heaven. And I in my joy paid for the champagne.

So the days went by, light, soft and happy, filled with kisses, until

arrived the sad eve of the day of our departure for Jerusalem. That
morning Alpedrinha said to me, as he was blacking my boots, that
I should remain in Alexandria and enjoy myself. Ah, if I could! But
the commands of Auntie brooked no denial, and for the sake of her
gold I must go to this wretched Jerusalem and kneel among dry
olive-trees and say pious prayers by cold tombs. Do you know Jerusalem, Alpedrinha? I asked as I dressed disconsolately. — No, Sir, but
I have heard about it: it is worse than Braga. "Gracious Heavens!"

Our supper that night with Mary in my room was broken with
silences and sighs; the candles were melancholy as funeral torches
and the wine was heady as that which is drunk at funerals. Topsius
generously administered comfort: "Fair lady, fair lady, our Raposo
will come back. Indeed, I am sure that he will return from the
ardent land of Syria, the land of Venus, of the Bride of the Song of
Songs, with even more heat and youth afire in his heart." I bit my
lips, overcome with sadness: "Of course I shall; and we will again
take our drives through Mamoudieh; it is only a question of saying
a few paternosters on Calvary; it will do me good; I shall return
strong as a bull."

After coffee we went on to the balcony to watch in silence that
splendid night of Egypt. The stars were like a great dust of light
raised there above by the good God as He walked alone along the
ways of heaven. The silence had in it something solemn and holy.
On the dark terraces below, the slight movement of a white form
from time to time showed that other persons were there like us
silently drinking in the splendor of the stars; and in this general
piety, like that of a multitude gazing in wonder at the lights of a high
altar, I felt irresistibly rise to my lips the soft accents of an Ave Maria.

The sea lay asleep in the distance, and in the warm radiance of
the stars I could distinguish on a strip of sand, almost in the water,
a small deserted house, white and dreaming among the palms. It
occurred to me that as soon as Auntie died and I was master of her
gold I could buy that pleasant retreat and furnish it with beautiful
silks and live there with the glove-seller, dressed as a Turk, a charming serene existence free from all the disquiets of civilization. Acts

of atonement to the Sacred Heart of Jesus would be as indifferent to
me as the wars waged by one king on another. Of heaven my only
care would be the blue light of the sky over my window, and of the
earth only the flowers of my garden to scent my joy. And I would
spend my days in a soft Oriental laziness smoking pure Turkish tobacco, playing on a French viola and receiving perpetually the im-
pression of perfect felicity which Mary gave me merely by sighing
and calling me her valiant little Portuguese.

I pressed her against my breast in a desire to drink her up. I whispered in her ear, white as a white shell, names of ineffable charm.
I called her my darling, my precious. She shivered and raised her
sad eyes towards the dust of gold: "What a number of stars! May
Heaven send a calm sea tomorrow!" then at the thought that that
wide sea was to carry me to the harsh land of the Gospel so far
from my Mary, an infinite sorrow surged in my breast and irrepress-
ibly flowed from my lips in moans and melancholy strains of song.
Above the sleeping terraces of Muslim Alexandria sounded my sad
voice as I turned to the stars, and, strumming with my fingers on the
breast of my coat where the strings of the viola should have been,
with wailing laments I sighed forth a ballad filled with the sorrow
of Portugal:

Here with my soul thou remainest,
And I must go hence with my woe;
And everything tells me, my dearest,
That ne'ermore to see thee I go.

I paused, overcome with sorrow. The learned Topsius wished to
know if these verses were by Luis de Camões. In tears I told him
that I had heard them from Calcinhas at Dafundo. Topsius retired
to take a note of the great poet Calcinhas. I shut the window, and
after going into the passage to make a rapid sign of the cross, I returned to enjoy a last night with my pleasant love. Swift, grudgingly
swift, was that starry night of Egypt. Soon, bitterly soon, came the
Lacedaemonian Greek to tell me that the steamer, fiercely called the

Shark, which was to take me to the gloom of Israel, was showing smoke in the rough and windy bay. Señor Topsius, who rose early, was already downstairs quietly eating his breakfast of ham and eggs, with a huge mug of beer. I only swallowed a little coffee in my room on a corner of the chest of drawers, in my shirt-sleeves, with eyes red beneath a mist of tears. My solid leather trunk lay across the passage, locked and strapped; but Alpedrinha was still hurriedly fitting the soiled linen into the canvas bag.

Mary, seated disconsolately on the edge of the bed, her charming hat adorned with poppies, was contemplating, sunken-eyed, that packing as though pieces of her heart were being thrown into the bag to go away and nevermore return. "So much soiled linen, Teodorico!" "It shall be washed at Jerusalem with the help of the Lord." I placed my scapularies round my neck. At the moment Topsius appeared at the door smoking a pipe, his mighty sunshade under his arm, and wearing large galoshes on account of the dampness of the deck, with a Bible bulging in the pocket of his alpaca tail-coat.

Seeing me not yet dressed, he chid me for my loving delays. "But I understand, fair lady, I understand," he added courteously to Mary, with a stiff bow, his glasses on the tip of his nose, "it is painful to leave Cleopatra's arms. For them Antony lost Rome and the world. I myself, absorbed as I am in my mission to throw light on the dark places of history, take away pleasant recollections of these days at Alexandria. Most delicious were our drives through Mamoudieh. Permit me to pick up your glove, fair lady. And if I ever return to this land of the Ptolemies I shall not forget the Street of the Two Sisters. 'Miss Mary. Gloves and Wax Flowers.' Exactly. You will allow me to send you, when it is completed, my 'History of the Lagidae.' It contains very interesting details. When Cleopatra fell in love with Herod, King of Judea. . . ."

But Alpedrinha from the edge of the bed cried in dismay: More soiled linen here, sir. In his search among the blankets he had come upon a long lace night-dress, with ribbons of light-colored silk. He shook it out, and from it came a sweet and lovely scent of violets. Alas, it was Mary's night-dress, still warm from my arms. "That belongs to Dona Mary. It is your night-dress, my love," I groaned as I went on dressing. My little gloveseller rose white and trembling, and in a poetical passionate impulse rolled it up and threw it into my arms as ardently as if its folds contained her heart.

"I will give it to you, Teodorico. Take it, Teodorico. It is a memorial of our tenderness. Take it to keep it by your side. But wait, wait, my love. I will write some words of dedication."

She ran to the table, where were remains of the prim paper on which I had been writing to Auntie the edifying history of my fasts in Alexandria, and of my nights spent in living the Gospel story. And I, with the scented night-dress in my arms and two tears rolling down my beard, sought anxiously where to put this precious relic. The trunks were locked, the canvas bag was full. Topsius had impatiently pulled out his silver watch from the depths of his breast-pocket; and our Lacedaemonian at the door was muttering: "Don Teodorico, es tarde, es muy tarde."

But now my love was holding up the paper on which she had written in large letters, frank and impetuous as her love. "To my Teodorico, my fine little Portuguese, in remembrance of all our joy."

"O my precious one, and where I am to put it? I can't carry a night-dress thus openly and unpacked."

Already Alpedrinha on his knees was desperately unstrapping the bag, when Mary in a moment of delicate inspiration seized a piece of brown paper and picked up some red string from the floor. The gloveseller's deft fingers swiftly made up a round handy and elegant parcel which I placed under my arm, pressing it jealously, passionately, against my side. Then there was a hurried murmur of sobs and kisses and soft words. "Mary, dear angel." — "Teodorico, my love." — "Write to me at Jerusalem." — "Remember your pretty little one."

I went dully down the stairs. And the carriage, which had so often taken me to Mary's side through the scented woods of Mamoudieh, started at the trot of the white horses, taking me from a happiness which had struck roots in my heart, now torn and bleeding in my silent breast.

The learned Topsius under the awning of his green sunshade

began once more to murmur impassively sentences of ancient learning. Did I know where we were? On the noble road which the first of the Lagidae had built in order to communicate with the island of Pharos, praised in the verses of Homer.

I paid no heed to him as I lay back in the carriage waving my tear-stained handkerchief. Sweet Mary at the door of the hotel by the side of Alpedrinha, beautiful in her hat trimmed with poppies, was likewise waving a loving handkerchief; and for a moment those two pieces of white cambric brandished to and fro in the warm air the ardor of our hearts. Then I fell back like a dead body on to the seat of the carriage.

As soon as we were on board the *Shark*, I ran to hide my grief in my cabin, although Topsius caught hold of my sleeve in order to show me sites of the grandeur of the Ptolemies, the harbor of Eunotus, the marble quay where anchored the galleys of Cleopatra. I fled; as I went down, I almost dashed into a sister of charity who was coming up timidly, her beads in her hand. I muttered an "Excuse me, little saint." At last falling upon my berth, I wept long over the brown paper parcel, all that was left to me of that passion of incomparable splendor in the land of Egypt.

During two days and two nights the *Shark* heaved and rolled on the great waves of the sea of Tyre. Wrapped in a blanket, without for a moment losing hold of Mary's parcel, I rancorously refused the biscuits which the most humane Topsius brought me from time to time; and deaf to the learned things which he kept calmly telling me about those waters known to the Egyptians as the Great Green, I searched my memory for the words of a prayer which I had heard Auntie use to still the anger of the waves.

But one evening at dusk, as I had closed my eyes, I seemed to feel firm land under me, a land of rocks with a scent of rosemary; and I found myself strangely ascending a wild hill in the company of Adelia and the fair Mary, who had come out of the parcel fresh and clear, the very poppies of her hat uncrumpled. Then from behind a rock a huge naked and sun-baked man with horns followed us; his eyes gleamed red like round lanterns, and his immense tail made on the ground the sound of an angry snake creeping through dry leaves. Without saluting us, he impertinently began to walk at our side. I understood that it was the devil, but felt neither scruple nor fear. The insatiable Adelia was casting side glances at his strong muscles; and I said to her indignantly: "What, with the devil too?" Thus we came to the top of the mountain, where a palm-tree waved its branches over an abyss full of darkness and silence. In front of us, very distant, stretched the sky line like a vast piece of yellow cloth, and on that living background, colored like the yolk of an egg, stood a very black hill with three small crosses at its top delicately outlined in a row. The devil spat and murmured, placing a hand upon my sleeve: "The one in the middle is that of Jesus, the son of Joseph, who is also called Christ; and we have arrived in time to witness the Ascension."

And indeed the central cross, that of Christ, uprooted from the hill like a shrub torn by the wind, began to rise slowly and increase in size until it filled the sky. And straightway from every part of space came flying bands of angels to support it, flocking thick as doves to the scattered grain; some pulled it from above, having wound about it long cords of silk, others pushed it from below; and we could see the swelling effort of the blue-grey arms. Sometimes from the cross fell a drop of blood like a very ripe cherry; a seraph took it in his hands and placed it in the highest part of heaven, where it hung shining brightly as a star. An old man of great size, in a white tunic, whose features we could scarcely distinguish amid the growth of his disheveled hair and shock of snowy beard, standing upon the clouds directed the Ascension in a language resembling Latin and a voice powerful as the rolling of a hundred chariots of war.

Suddenly everything disappeared, and the devil, looking at me, said thoughtfully: "It is finished, my friend. Another God, and another religion! And this one will spread an indescribable tedium through earth and heaven." And as we went down the hill the devil began to describe to me with animation the cults and feasts and religions that flourished in his youth. All that coast of the Great Green then, from Byblos to Carthage, from Eleusis to Memphis, was crowded with gods. Some of them astonished men by their perfect beauty, others by their complicated ferocity; but all took part in the life of men, making it divine: they journeyed in triumphal cars, breathed the scent of flowers, drank wine, loved sleeping maidens. That is why they were loved with a love which will never return, and peoples emigrating might leave their flocks and forget the rivers at which they had drunk, but lovingly carried their gods with them in their arms.

"Has my friend," he asked, "never been in Babylonia?" There all the women, matrons and maidens, came on a certain day to love in the holy groves in honor of the goddess Millita. The rich women arrived in cars inlaid with silver, drawn by buffaloes and escorted by slaves; the poor came with a rope round their necks. Some, laying a carpet upon the grass, crouched there like patient animals; others, standing white and bare, their heads covered by black veils, were like splendid marble statues among the trunks of the elm-trees. And all waited until someone threw them a silver coin and murmured: "In the name of Venus." Him they would follow, were he a prince of Susa with a tiara of pearls or one of the merchants who descend the Euphrates in a leather boat; and all night long in the darkness of the branches sounded the frenzy of love's rites.

Then the devil told me of the human holocausts of Moloch, of the mysteries of the Good Goddess at which lilies were watered with blood, and of the fervent funeral rites of Adonis. He paused, smiling: "Has my friend ever been in Egypt?" I told him that I had and had made the acquaintance of Mary; and the devil said courteously: "It was not Mary but Isis." When the floods reached Memphis the water was covered with sacred boats; and a heroic joy, ascending to the stars, made men equal to gods. And Osiris, horned as a bull, loved Isis, and all down the Nile, amid the clamor of the harps of bronze, sounded the lowing of the divine cow in love.

Then the devil told me of the gentle, beautiful brilliance of the religion of Nature in Greece. There everything was white and polished, pure, luminous and serene; harmony sprang from the sculptured marble and from the constitution of the cities, from the elo-

quence of the academies and the skill of the athletes. Among the
islands of Ionia, which floated like baskets of flowers on the soft
silent sea, the Nereids hung upon the ships, listening to the tales of
those who voyaged in them; the Muses on foot sang in the valleys;
and the beauty of Venus concentrated in itself the beauty of Greece.

But this Carpenter of Galilee had appeared, and all was over.
Men's faces had become perpetually pale and mortified; a dark
cross, crushing the earth, withered the splendor of the roses and
robbed kisses of their sweetness; and the new god delighted in ugliness.

Thinking that Lucifer was in low spirits, I sought to comfort him:
"Never mind, there will always be plenty of pride and dissolution
and blood and fury in the world. Do not regret the holocausts of
Moloch. You shall have holocausts of Jews."

He answered in amazement: "I? What do I care about any of
them, Raposo? They pass and I remain."

Thus carelessly conversing with Satan, I found myself in the
Campo de Sant'Anna; and while he was disentangling his horns
from the branches of one of the trees, I heard a yell: "See Teodorico
with the Swine-Devil." I turned round. It was Auntie. And Auntie,
livid, terrible, raised her prayer-book to beat me with.

Bathed in sweat, I awoke. Topsius was shouting gaily from the
door of the cabin: "Get up, Raposo. We are in sight of Palestine."
The *Shark* had stopped, and in the silence I could hear the water
washing against her sides, gently murmuring a soft caress. Why had
I thus dreamed, when nearing Jerusalem, of the false gods and of
Jesus their conqueror, and of the devil, rebellious to all alike? What
supreme revelation had the Lord in store for me?

I extricated myself from my rug; and dull, dirty, without leaving
hold of Mary's precious parcel, I went on deck, wrapped in my
coat. A strong delicate air bathed me deliciously with a scent of
hills and orange-flower. The sea lay still and blue in the freshness of
the morning. Before my sinful eyes stretched the land of Palestine,
low and sandy, and a dark city surrounded by orchards was lit from
above by rays of sun like the splendid halo of a saint. "Jaffa!" cried

Topsius, brandishing his porcelain pipe. "There, Dom Raposo, you have the oldest city in Asia, the most ancient Jeppo, dating from before the Flood. Take off your hat and salute the ancient of time, filled with legend and history. This was where that drunkard Noah constructed the Ark."

I saluted in astonishment. "*Caramba*, one has hardly arrived and is already confronted by religious memories." And I remained bareheaded, for the *Shark*, on anchor off the Holy Land, had become hushed as a chapel, given up to piety and prayer. A Lazarist in a long cassock was walking up and down with lowered eyes studying his breviary. Two nuns, deep in their black hoods, ran their pale fingers over the beads of their rosaries. By the drenched water-way, pilgrims from Abyssinia, hairy Greek priests from Alexandria, gazed with amazement at the houses of Jaffa which lay aureoled by the sun like an illuminated shrine. And the bell on the stern tinkled in the soft breeze with the soft devotion of a sacring-bell.

Seeing a dark boat rowing towards the *Shark*, I went down hurriedly to my cabin to put on my cork helmet and black gloves so as to disembark decorously in the land of the Lord. On returning, well groomed, well perfumed, I found the tender full of people, and I was going down quickly behind a Franciscan monk when Mary's beloved parcel escaped from my affectionate arms and hopped down the ladder like a ball to the edge of the boat. It was about to disappear in the sea. I gave a yell. One of the nuns caught it deftly and mercifully.

"Thank you," I cried timidly, "it is a parcel of clothes. Thanks be to the sacred love of Mary."

She withdrew modestly into the shadow of her hood, and as I had taken my place at some distance, between Topsius and the bearded Franciscan who smelt of garlic, the saintly creature kept the parcel on her lap, and even placed the beads of her rosary upon it.

The master of the boat, taking the helm, shouted: "Great is Allah. Push off." The Arabs sang as they rowed. The sun rose behind Jaffa; and I, leaning on my umbrella, contemplated the chaste nun who was thus carrying in her arms Mary's night-dress to the Holy Land.

She was young, and in the gloomy black hood her oval face seemed of ivory and the long lashes shaded it with melancholy. Her lips, destined barrenly to kiss the reddened feet of the dead body of God, had lost all heat and color. Compared with Mary, the rose of York, wide open and scenting Alexandria, she seemed a lily withered in the bud in the dampness of a chapel. She must be going to some hospice in the Holy Land. Life for her would be a succession of wounds to be covered with bandages and dead faces to be covered with handkerchiefs. And her pallor was certainly inspired by fear of the Lord. "Foolish creature!" I murmured. "Poor barren creature!" Had she perhaps realized what the parcel contained? Had she felt come from it to her dark hood a strange relaxing scent of vanilla and love? Had the heat still lingering in the lace pierced the paper and gently warmed her knees? Who knows? For a moment I thought I saw a tinge of color rise to her pale face and that her breast, on which gleamed a cross, heaved a sigh; I even fancied that I saw between her lashes the light of a swift frightened glance towards my thick black beard. But it was only for an instant: once more her face under its hood resumed its coldness of white marble, and the jealous iron cross weighed down her submissive breast. At her side the other nun, plump and spectacled, looked smilingly at the green sea and smilingly at Topsius, a clear smile born of the peace of her heart and dimpling her chin.

As soon as we had landed on the sands of Palestine, I ran to thank her, helmet in hand, courteous and polite: "My sister, I am very much obliged. I would have much regretted the loss of the parcel. It is something my aunt is sending to Jerusalem. I must tell you about it. My aunt has a great respect for holy things, she is very devoted to charity."

Silent in the depths of her hood, she held out the parcel in the tips of her fingers, fragile and transparent as those of Our Lady of Sorrows. And the two black nuns disappeared from view behind gleaming walls new-whitewashed, in a narrow street of steps on which the carcass of a dog was rotting beneath a cloud of great flies. "Foolish creature!" I murmured again.

When I came back, Topsius, in the shade of his parasol, was talking to a serviceable man who was afterwards our guide through the lands of Scripture. He was young, dark and tall, with a long moustache floating in the wind. He wore a velveteen jacket and white riding-boots; his strongly built chest was heroically armed with two pistols inlaid with silver emerging from his sash of black wool; and wound round his head, with the ends falling at the back, he wore a brilliant yellow kerchief. His name was Paul Potte and he came from Montenegro. He was known in all the coast of Syria as the merry Potte. Heavens, what a merry companion! Gaiety sparkled in his clear blue eyes, gaiety sang in his incomparable teeth, gaiety trembled in his restless hands, gaiety sounded beneath his heels. From Ascalon to the bazaars of Damascus, from Carmel to the orchards of Engaddi, he was the merry Potte.

He generously offered me his pouch of scented tobacco. Topsius was astonished at his biblical knowledge. I digged him in the ribs, calling him familiar names. After great shaking of hands we went to the Hotel of Jehoshaphat to sign our contract and drink a vast amount of beer. The most merry Potte had soon organized our caravan for the city of the Lord. A mule carried the luggage; the muleteer, an Arab dressed in blue rags, was so fine and handsome that I was fascinated by the dark glance of his velvet eyes; as an Oriental luxury we were followed by an escort of a hoarse old Bedouin in a cloak of camel's hair striped with grey and a stout rusty lance adorned with tassels. I carefully placed Mary's dear parcel in one of the saddle-bags, and when we had mounted and the stirrups had been lengthened for the long-legged Topsius, the festive Potte, brandishing his whip, cried the ancient cry of the Crusades and of Richard Coeur de Lion: Forward to Jerusalem by the will of God. And, trotting with our cigars alight, we left Jaffa by the Gate of the Market at the hour when the bell of the Hospice of the Latin Fathers was softly ringing to Vespers.

In the soft luminous afternoon the road stretched away through gardens and orchards, orange-groves, palm-trees, a land of promise, pleasant and gleaming. The fleet sound of running water came from among the hedges of myrtle. The air, of an ineffable softness, as though for the chosen people of God to breathe more easily, was all filled with the scent of jasmine and lemon. The grave and peaceful creaking of the well-wheels was dying down after the day's watering of the fields amid the pomegranates in flower. High and serene in the blue sky flew a great eagle. Delighted, we stopped at a fountain of red and black marble sheltered in the shade of sycamores in which doves were cooing. At the side stood a tent with a carpet spread upon the grass and covered with grapes and bowls of milk, and the white-bearded man who owned it greeted us in the name of Allah, with the noble air of a patriarch. The beer had made me thirsty, and it was a girl fair as Rachel of old who gave me to drink from her jar of biblical shape, smiling, with bare breast and two long golden ear-rings beating against her brown face, and a tame white lamb attached to the end of her tunic.

The afternoon was waning, silent and golden, when we came to the plain of Sharon, which the Bible of yore filled with roses. The bells of a herd of black goats, tended by an Arab naked as St. John, tinkled in the silence. In the distance the sinister mountains of Judea, touched by the setting sun, seemed still fair, blue and filled with a vague softness like the illusions of sin. Then everything grew dark; two stars of an infinite splendor appeared and began to journey before us towards Jerusalem.

Our room in the Hotel of the Mediterranean in Jerusalem, with its arched ceiling of whitewash and its brick floor, resembled the austere cell of a primitive convent. But opposite the window a thin partition wall covered with a blue pattern divided our room from another, in which we could hear a fresh voice humming the Ballad of the King of Thule; and also, sign of comfort and civilization, there was a shining wardrobe of mahogany, which I opened as one opens a reliquary to place in it my sacred parcel.

The two small beds disappeared behind chaste curtains of white cambric, and in the center stood a table of pinewood, on which Topsius was studying a map of Palestine, while I in slippers walked up and down paring my nails. It was the holy Friday on which

Christendom commemorates with devotion the martyrs of Evora.
We had arrived that afternoon at the city of the Lord in a fine and
melancholy drizzle; and from time to time Topsius raised his eyes
from the roads of Galilee to contemplate me with his arms crossed
and murmur in friendly wise: Here is my friend Raposo in Jerusalem. Pausing before the glass, I glanced at my thick beard and sunburnt face and murmured likewise with satisfaction: Yes, here is the
handsome Raposo in Jerusalem. And with eager curiosity I turned
again to admire divine Zion through the dingy windows.

Opposite, in the melancholy rain, rose the white walls of a silent
convent, with green blinds down; and two enormous zinc gutters,
one at either side of the roof, were gushing forth water, one noisily
on to a deserted side street, the other on to the soft soil of a garden
planted with cabbages, in which an ass was braying. On that side
was an endless sea of terraced roofs, gloomy, of the color of mud,
with small brick cupolas shaped like ovens and long poles for the
drying of clothes; and nearly all were rickety, tumble-down, most
miserable buildings which seemed to be melting away in the slow,
drenching rain. On the other side rose a hill covered with sordid
huts and green gardens, vague and uncertain in a damp mist. Between them went up a steep street of steps, where met and passed
continually monks in sandals under their umbrellas and gloomy
sleek-haired Jews, or a slow Bedouin in his long cloak. Above all
hung the grey sky. So from my window appeared to me ancient
Zion, the well-built, the gleaming joy of the earth and most beautiful of earth's cities.

"This is horrible, Topsius. Alpedrinha was right. It is worse than
Braga. No drives, no billiards, no theatre, nothing. What a city for
Our Lord to live in!"

"Yes, in His time it was more amusing," muttered my learned
friend. And he at once proposed that next Sunday we should start
for the banks of Jordan, whither he was called by his studies on
the Herods. There I could have rural pleasures, bathe in the sacred
waters and shoot partridges among the palms of Jericho. I gladly
agreed, and we went down to the dining-room, summoned by a

conventual bell ringing funereally in the dark passage. The dining-room also was arched, and had a matting of esparto grass over its brick floor. We were alone, the learned investigator of the Herods and I, at the gloomy table, adorned with paper flowers in cracked jars. As I stirred the macaroni of the insipid soup I murmured dis-consolately: "Heavens, Topsius, what a tremendous bore!"

But a glass door opened slightly at the further end, and I at once exclaimed enthusiastically: "Caramba, Topsius, what a tremendous woman!" She was great indeed, solid and healthy as myself, white, of the whiteness of well-washed flax, and freckled; crowned with a burning mass of waving chestnut hair; dressed in blue serge which seemed to imprison her strong breasts. She came in spreading a fresh scent of Windsor soap and eau-de-Cologne, and lit up the whole dining-room with the splendor of her youth and beauty. The eloquent Topsius compared her to the goddess Cybele. Cybele took her place at the top of the table, proud and calm. At her side, making the chair groan beneath the weight of his ample limbs, sat a quiet bald Hercules with a thick grey beard, who in the very way he opened his napkin revealed the omnipotence of gold and the habit of command. A "yes" which she murmured told me that she was from Mary's country. I thought too of the Baron's Englishwoman. She had placed near her plate an open book which seemed to me to be a book of verse; the bearded man, munching with the majestic slowness of a lion, was turning over the pages of his Guide to the East in silence. I forgot my roast lamb in passionate contemplation of her face. Occasionally she raised the fringed curtain of her eye-lashes and I waited anxiously for the favor of that clear soft glance, but it wandered over the whitewashed walls and the paper flowers and fell with unfeeling coldness on the pages of her book.

After coffee she kissed the hairy hand of the greybeard and dis-appeared through the glass door, taking with her the scent and light and gaiety of Jerusalem. The Hercules slowly lit his pipe, told the waiter to send him Ibrahim the guide, and rose large-limbed and heavy. By the door he knocked over the umbrella of Topsius, the most respectable Topsius, glory of Germany and member of the Imperial Institute of Historical Excavations, and passed on without picking it up, without even lowering his haughty look.

"What a brute!" I muttered, bubbling over with fury. My learned friend, with the social cowardice of a disciplined German, picked up and dusted his umbrella, tremulously murmuring that perhaps the greybeard was a duke. "A duke! What do I care for dukes? I am a Raposo, of the Raposos of Alentejo. I could kick him."

But the afternoon was advancing and we were to pay our reverent visit to the tomb of our God. I ran to my room to put on my top-hat, as I had promised Auntie; and as I reached the passage I saw Cybele open the door next to ours and come out dressed in a grey cloak with a cap adorned with two white sea-gull's feathers. My heart beat wildly with a great hope. So it was she who sang the Ballad of the King of Thule. So our rooms were only separated by the thin fragile partition wall-papered with a blue pattern. Without putting on my black gloves, I went down excitedly, certain that I should find her at the tomb of Christ; and I was already planning to bore a hole in the wall so that I might delight my eyes in her beauty.

It was still raining mournfully. As soon as we began to splash through the torrent of the Via Dolorosa between walls of the color of mud, I called Potte under my umbrella and asked him if he had seen at the hotel the strong and freckled Cybele. The jocund Potte had already admired her; and through his dear colleague Ibrahim he knew that the greybeard was a Scottish cork merchant.

"You see, Topsius," I cried; "a cork merchant, no duke. He is a brute. I could kick him. In matters of dignity I am ferocious. I could kick him."

The daughter of the fair locks, according to Potte, had the gleaming name of a precious stone: Ruby. She was daring and loved horses; in Upper Galilee, which they had just left, she had shot a black eagle. . . . Here is the house of Pilate. . . . "Let the house of Pilate alone, man. What do I care about Pilate? What more did Ibrahim tell you? Out with it, Potte."

The Via Dolorosa there became narrower, arched over like a passage in the Catacombs. Two beggars covered with sores were gnaw-

ing pieces of melon rind, grunting and squatting in the mud. A dog
was howling. And the smiling Potte told me that Ibrahim had often
seen Miss Ruby charmed by the beauty of the men of Syria; and at
night, at the entrance to the tent, while her father drank beer, she re-
cited verses, and gazed at the twinkling stars. "She is mine," thought
I to myself. "Here we are at the Holy Sepulchre." I closed my umbrella. At the further end of a court unevenly paved rose the front
of a church, tumble-down, gloomy, miserable, with two arched
doorways; one was walled up with stone and mortar as being un-
necessary, the other was shyly, timidly half open. At either side of
this dark half-ruinous temple crouched two rickety buildings, one
of the Latin rite, the other of the Greek, like two timid daughters
frightened by death and taking refuge at their mother's breast, she
too half dead and cold. I here put on my black gloves. Immediately
an importunate group of sordid men surrounded us, offering us
relics, offering us rosaries, and crosses and scapularies, pieces of
plank planed by St. Joseph, medals, holy trinkets, small bottles of the
waters of the Jordan, candles, Agnus Dei, lithographs of the Passion,
paper flowers made in Nazareth, blest stones, olive-stones from the
Mount of Olives, and tunics resembling those worn by the Virgin
Mary. And at the very door of the Sepulchre of Christ, where Auntie
had recommended me to go in on all fours, groaning and praying,
I was obliged to give a blow to a knave, bearded like a hermit, who
had hung on to my tail-coat, famished, furious, shrieking entreaties
that we should buy mouthpieces made out of a piece of Noah's ark.

"*Caramba*, take your hands off, you animal." So with a curse I
dashed with my dripping umbrella into the sublime sanctuary in
which Christendom keeps the sepulchre of its Christ. But I paused
at once in surprise when I smelt a delicious fragrance of Syrian tobacco. On a wide bench turned into a sofa with rugs of Carmania
and old silk cushions, three Turks reclined, grave and bearded,
smoking their long pipes of cherrywood. They had hung up their
arms on the wall. The floor was black with their spitting. And before
them a ragged slave was waiting with a smoking cup of coffee in
the palm of either hand. I thought that Catholicism had providently

established drinks and brandy at the door of the holy place for the comfort of pilgrims, and said in a low voice to Potte: "An excellent idea: I think that I too will have a cup of coffee."

But the festive Potte explained to me that those serious men smoking their pipes were Muslim soldiers guarding the Christian altars to prevent the rival priests who celebrate their rival rites there from coming to blows round the mausoleum of Jesus: Catholics like Padre Pinheiro, orthodox Greeks for whom the cross has four arms, Abyssinians and Armenians, Copts descended from those who of yore worshipped Apis the bull at Memphis, Nestorians who come from Chaldea, Georgians who come from the Caspian Sea, Maronites who come from Lebanon, all Christians, all ferociously intolerant. Then I saluted in gratitude those soldiers of Mahomet who, in order to preserve peace and quiet round the dead Christ, kept armed watch, serenely smoking at the door.

At the entrance we stopped before a square stone set in the dark pavement, so polished and shining with so soft a gleam of mother of pearl that it seemed the quiet water of a pond reflecting the light of the lamps. Potte pulled me by the sleeve and reminded me that it was customary to kiss that piece of rock, the most sacred rock, that in the garden of Joseph of Arimathea. . . .

"Yes, I know, I know. Shall I kiss it, Topsius?"

"Yes, you had better kiss it; you won't catch any disease and it will please your aunt." I did not kiss it.

Silently in single file we entered a huge cupola so dark that the circle of round windows above shone palely like a line of pearls on a tiara; the columns that sustained it, slender and close together as window-bars, stood out in the darkness, each marked by the red glow of a lamp of bronze. In the center of the sounding pavement rose, white and gleaming, a marble mausoleum, with sculptured designs; an old damask cloth covered it as with an awning, embroidered in faded gold; and two wings of torches formed an avenue of funeral lights to the door, a narrow crack hidden by a curtain the color of blood. An Armenian priest, disappearing under his ample black cloak and lowered hood, was waving incense in sleepy silence.

Again Potte pulled me by the sleeve: The tomb. O my devout soul! O Auntie! Here, then, close to my lips was the tomb of the Lord. And straightway like a greyhound among the noisy crowd of monks and pilgrims I began to search for a plump and freckled face and a bonnet with seagull's feathers.

Long I wandered in confusion; now I would run against a Franciscan with a cord round his waist, or fall back before a Coptic priest advancing like a thin shadow preceded by attendant sounding the sacred timbrels of the time of Osiris. Sometimes I would come upon a heap of white clothes, lying on the pavement like a sack, but from which came groans of contrition; farther on was a naked Negro at the foot of a column sleeping placidly. Occasionally the sound of an organ rolled along the marble nave and died away with the hiss of a breaking wave; and farther away an Armenian chant, sad and tremulous, beat against the austere walls like the fluttering wings of an imprisoned bird striving to escape into the light.

Near the altar I separated two stout sacristans, a Greek and a Latin, who, with faces afire and smelling of garlic, were insulting one another, and I met a group of shaggy Russian pilgrims, evidently from the Caspian Sea, their weary feet wrapped in rags, who in their religious awe did not dare to move but kept on twirling their felt caps between their fingers, from which hung great rosaries of glass beads. Children in rags played in the shadow of the arcades; others were begging. The scent of incense was suffocating; the priests of rival cults pulled me by the coat-tail to show me rival relics, heroic or divine, the spurs of Godfrey or a piece of the Reed.

In my confusion I joined a procession of penitents amid whose black veils I thought I saw, proud and white, two seagull's feathers. A Carmelite at the head of the procession was muttering the litany, and making us pause at every step as we crowded together in devout amazement at the door of cavernous chapels dedicated to the Passion, that of the Iniquity, where the Lord was scourged, that of the Tunic, where the Lord was stripped.

Then with torches in our hands we went up a dark stair hollowed out of the rock; and suddenly the pious band fell forward on the ground, howling, weeping, groaning, beating their breasts, calling on the Lord in melancholy ravings. We were on the Stone of Calvary. The chapel which contains it shone with a sensual pagan luxury; on the blue-grey ceiling gleamed silver suns, signs of the Zodiac, stars, angels' wings, purple flowers, and amid this starry splendor hung from ropes of pearls the ancient symbols of fertility, ostrich eggs, the sacred eggs of Astarte and of golden Bacchus. Upon the altar stood a red cross with a Christ roughly painted in gold, which seemed to live and sparkle in the radiance of the clustered lights, the gleam of the ornaments and the smoke of aromatic herbs burning in bronzen bowls. Spherical mirrors on stands of ebony reflected the jewels of the shrines and the brilliance of the walls covered with jaspar and mother of pearl and agate.

On the ground, amid this brightness of precious stones and lights from the pavement of white marble, rose a piece of plain rough rock, with a crack polished and enlarged by long centuries of devout kisses and embraces. A Greek archdeacon with unkempt beard shouted: "On this rock was set the cross. The cross. The cross. *Miserere. Kyrie Eleison.* Christ. Christ."

The prayers redoubled in fervor, with many sobs. A plaintive chant accompanied the swaying of the censers. *Kyrie Eleison. Kyrie Eleison.* And the deacons passed swiftly, eagerly, with huge velvet sacks, and the offerings of the simple tinkled as they fell into their depths.

I fled in dull confusion. The learned historian of the Herods was walking to and fro in the court under his umbrella, breathing the damp air. Again we were attacked by the famished band of relic-sellers. I pushed them roughly aside and went out of the holy place as I had entered, cursing sinfully.

At the hotel, Topsius at once went to his room to note down his impressions of the Sepulchre of Jesus; I remained in the hall, drinking beer and smoking with the amiable Potte. When I went up late my learned friend was snoring, the candle still alight and an open book on his bed, a book of mine which I had brought from Lisbon to read in the land of the Gospel: its title was "The Man with the Three Pairs of Trousers." As I took off my boots, heavy with the venerable mud of the Via Dolorosa, I thought of my Cybele. In what most sacred ruins, under what trees, divine for having given shade to the Lord, had she spent this misty afternoon in Jerusalem? Was it in the valley of Cedron? Was it at the white tomb of Rachel? I sighed, in love but tired, and was just opening the sheets of my bed, yawning, when through the thin wall I heard the sound of water being poured into a bath. I listened eagerly, and in the black melancholy silence in which Jerusalem is perpetually merged, I heard the slight notice of a sponge thrown into the water. I ran and pressed my face against the wall of the blue pattern. Bare soft steps sounded on the mat which covered the brick floor; and there was a sound of water, as though a soft bare arm were testing its heat. Then came all the sounds of a long slow languid bath, the squeezing of the sponge, the gentle rubbing of a hand full of the lather of soap, the tired comfortable sigh of a body lying under the caressing warm water, with a few drops of scent in it.

My forehead beating with emotion, I searched the wall desperately for a hole or crack; I tried to bore a hole with the scissors, but its delicate points broke against the thick mortar. Again the water poured from the sponge, and I seemed to see it sprinkled slowly over that strong fair body. It was too much: half dressed as I was, I went out into the silent passage, and pressed my eye, burning with a fierce and piercing curiosity, upon the keyhole. I saw in a circle of light a towel fallen on the mat, a red dressing-gown, a corner of white bed-curtain.

Crouching there, with drops of sweat upon my neck, I waited to see her cross in all her splendor that narrow circle of light, when suddenly behind me I heard a door creak and the wall was bathed with light. It was the greybeard in his shirt-sleeves, his candlestick in his hand. And I, miserable Raposo, had no escape. There he towered at one side, and at the other the passage ended in a solid wall. Slowly, silently, methodically, the Hercules placed his candlestick on the floor, raised his double-soled boot, and belabored my thighs. I roared: "Brute;" he hissed: "Silence;" and once more, as he held me against the wall, his brutal boot, hard as bronze, descended tremendously upon thighs and shins and all my precious delicate body. Then quietly he took up his candlestick.

Livid, half dressed, I spoke to him with immense dignity: "Do you know what protects you, Mr. Beefsteak? The fact that we are near the tomb of the Lord and that I do not wish to make an uproar, on account of my aunt. But if we were in Lisbon, in the streets, in a place I know, I would eat your heart. You do not know what you have escaped. Enough that I would eat your heart." And, very dignified, limping, I returned to my room to rub myself patiently with arnica. Thus I spent my first night in Zion.

Next day early the profound Topsius went on a pilgrimage to the Mount of Olives, to the clear fountain of Siloe. Bruised and unable to ride, I remained on the sofa, with "The Man with the Three Pairs of Trousers." I even, so as to avoid the insolent greybeard, did not go down to the dining-room, under pretext of feeling slack and out of spirits.

But when the sun set in the Tyrian Sea I felt revived and lively, for Potte had prepared for us that night an hour of festive pleasure in the house of Fatme, an accessible matron who kept a sweet dovecote in the quarter of the Armenians; we were to go to contemplate the glorious dancer of Palestine, "The Flower of Jericho," twisting her body in the dance of the Bee, full of fire and temptation.

Fatme's discreet door stood in the corner of a dark wall near the Tower of David. Fatme was awaiting us, stout and majestic, dressed in a white veil, with bare arms and strings of coral in her hair; on each arm was the dark mark of a plague spot. She meekly took my hand, raised it to her oily head and to her scarlet painted lips, and conducted me solemnly towards a black curtain fringed with gold, like the cloth on a coffin. And I trembled as I penetrated at length into the wonderful secrets of a seraglio, silent and smelling of roses.

It was a hall freshly whitewashed, with a fringe of red cotton above the window-blind; along the wall stood a sofa covered with yellow silk, with patches of lighter silk; on a piece of Persian carpet stood a brazier of brass, containing a cold heap of ashes; a velvet slipper spangled with scales had been forgotten there. From the

ceiling of white woods, stained with damp, a paraffin lamp hung
by two chains adorned with tassels. The warm air was filled with a
soft sickly smell of mold and benzoin. On the brick floor, beneath
the window, there were cockroaches.

I sat down prudently by the side of the historian of the Herods.
A negress of Dongola, in a scarlet shirt, with silver bracelets tinkling on her arms, came to offer us fragrant coffee; and then Potte
appeared in dismay, saying that we should not be able to enjoy the
celebrated dance of the Bee: the Rose of Jericho had gone to dance
before a German prince arrived that morning in Zion to adorn the
tomb of the Lord. And Fatme pressed her hands humbly against her
heart and called on Allah and said that she was our slave. It was very
unfortunate. The Rose of Jericho had gone to a fair-haired prince
who had come with plumes and with horses from the land of the
Germans.

In my annoyance I said that he was not a prince, but that my
aunt possessed great wealth and the Raposos were of the ancient
nobility of Alentejo. If the Rose of Jericho was engaged to delight
my Catholic eyes, it was an insult to me to have yielded her to an
armed pilgrim from heretic Germany. The learned Topsius looked
up petulantly and muttered that Germany was the spiritual mother
of the peoples. "The gleam which comes from the German helmet,
Dom Raposo, is the guiding light of humanity." "A fig for your helmet. I submit to nobody's guidance. I am a Raposo, of the Raposos
of Alentejo. I submit only to the guidance of Our Lord Jesus Christ.
And in Portugal there are great men: Afonso Henriques, Herculano.
Do you hear?" I rose, tremendous, and the most learned Topsius
trembled before me. Potte intervened: Peace, friends and Christians,
peace. And Topsius and I sat down again on the sofa, after shaking
hands nobly and honorably.

Fatme meanwhile was swearing that Allah was great and that she
was our slave. If we would give her seven gold piasters, she offered
us a jewel of inestimable worth, a Circassian whiter than the full
moon, fairer than the lilies of Galgala. "Bring the Circassian," I cried
excitedly. "Caramba, I came to the holy places to have a good time.

Bring the Circassian. Give her the piastres, Potte. I want to enjoy myself."

Fatme went out facing us, and Potte leant back between us, opening his scented pouch of tobacco of Aleppo. Then a small white door sunk in the whitewashed wall creaked slightly in a corner of the room and a vague veiled misty figure entered. Ample Turkish trousers puffed out languidly from her flexible waist to her ankles, where they were bound down by rings of gold; her white feet scarce rested on her slippers of yellow leather, and through the gauze veil over her head and breast and arms shone scales of gold, flashes of jewels and the two black stars of her eyes. I stretched myself in a frenzy of expectation. Behind her, Fatme with the tips of her fingers slowly drew aside her veil, and from the cloud of gauze appeared an ugly clay-colored face, with sunken cheeks, long nose and squinting eyes and black teeth displayed in a slow foolish smile.

Potte leapt from the sofa, hurling insults at Fatme, who called on Allah and beat her breasts, which gave forth a sound as of half-filled wineskins. The two disappeared in a wave of fury; and the Circassian, coming wantonly with her putrid smile, held out her dirty hand, asking for presents in a hoarse voice thick with brandy. I repelled her with disgust. She stroked her arm, then her thigh; then, quietly taking up her veil, she went out, trailing her slippers.

"O Topsius," I muttered, "this seems to me most infamous."

The learned man made some remarks on the subject of voluptuousness. It is always deceptive; beneath a bright smile is a hollow tooth; human embraces leave only bitterness, and when the body is in ecstasy the soul grows sad.

"It isn't a question of soul, it is a question of their insulting us in this way. At Lisbon this Fatme would have been hit in the face for her pains." I felt ferocious, with a desire to smash the banjo. But Potte reappeared stroking his moustache and announcing that for another nine piastres Fatme consented to show us her hidden marvel, a maiden from the banks of the Nile, from upper Nubia, beautiful as the most beautiful Eastern night. And he had seen her, and could answer for her, she was worth the tribute of a fertile province.

Weak and liberal, I yielded. One by one, the nine gold piastres fell into Fatme's fat hand. Once more the whitewashed door creaked, and against its whiteness stood out, bronze-colored, a splendid female fashioned like Venus. For a moment she paused, dumb, frightened by the lights and the men, slowly rubbing her knees. A white cloth covered her strong and agile flanks. Her thick hair, shining with oil and interlaced with sequins of gold, fell down her back like a wild mane; a thread of beads of blue glass was wound round her neck and hung between her perfect ebon breasts. Suddenly she began convulsively to move her tongue in a mournful wail: Lu lu lu lu lu; she threw herself on the sofa, and, lying there like a sphinx, grave and motionless, darted upon us her great dark eyes. "Well?" said Potte, nudging me. "What a body! Look at her arms! Look at the curve of her backbone! She is a panther!" And Fatme, showing the white of her eyes, kissed her finger-tips, to express the transcendent delight of this Nubian's love.

Certain from the persistence of her gaze that she had been fascinated by my strong beard, I rose from the sofa and went slowly towards her as to a sure prey. Her eyes grew larger, flashing restlessly. Gently, calling her "my pretty one," I caressed her cold shoulder, and at the touch of my white skin the Nubian drew back, horrified, with the frightened cry of a wounded gazelle. I did not like this but I wished to be amiable and said to her paternally: "Ah, if you knew my country; and indeed I am capable of taking you there. Lisbon is the place. Drives to Dafundo, suppers at Silva's. This is a wilderness. And girls like you are well treated there, respected, spoken of in the newspapers; they even marry landed proprietors." Other sweet endearments I murmured; she did not understand my speech, and in her distant eyes floated a longing for her Nubian village, with the herds of buffaloes asleep in the shade of the tamarisks and the great river flowing ever in majestic course amid the ruins of religions and the tombs of dynasties.

Imagining that her heart's fire might light itself at mine, I pulled her towards me; she fled and crouched in a corner, trembling; then, putting her head between her hands, began to weep continuously.

"Oh, what a nuisance," I cried in vexation. And I took my helmet and went out, almost tearing the black gold-fringed cloth to pieces in my fury. We paused in a brick-paved ill-smelling room; and there a fierce quarrel arose between Potte and the fat matron as to the payment for that splendid Eastern entertainment. She demanded seven more piasters, and Potte, with bristling moustache, hurled insults at her in Arabic, rough and full-sounding like stones thrown into an abyss.

We left that charming place pursued by the cries of Fatme, who was foaming with rage, waving her plague-spotted arms and cursing us and our fathers and the bones of our ancestors and the land that had given us birth and the bread we ate and the shade that sheltered us. In the black street two dogs followed us for a long time, barking mournfully. I entered the Hotel of the Mediterranean full of longing for my own smiling land. The joys of which I was deprived in this dark hostile country made me wish fervently for those which easy amiable Lisbon would give me when Auntie died and I inherited her ringing purse of green silk. There in the silent passages I should encounter no severe and brutal boot; there no wild form would flee in tears from my caresses. Gilded with my aunt's money, my love would never be outraged nor my desire repulsed. Ah, if only by my holiness I could win Auntie! And straightway I went to the table and wrote the horrible old lady this most tender letter:

"Dear beloved Auntie, Every day I feel more virtuous. I attribute this to the Lord's pleasure at my visit to His holy tomb. Night and day I spend the time in meditating on His holy Passion and in thinking of Auntie. I have just come from the Via Dolorosa. Ah, how affecting it was! It is a street so blessed that I scarcely like to tread on it with my boots, and the other day I could not restrain myself but crouched down and kissed its precious stones. Nearly all this evening I spent in prayer to Our Lady of the Patrocinio, for whom everyone here has the greatest respect. She has a beautiful altar, although in this matter my Aunt was right, as she always is, when she said that there were none like the Portuguese for feasts and processions. This evening, when I knelt in her chapel, after repeating six salves, I turned to her beautiful image and said: 'Ah, how I long to know how my Aunt Patrocinio is.' And—will you believe it?—with her divine voice she spoke these very words, which I even wrote down on my shirt-cuff so as not to forget them: 'My dear daughter is well, Raposo, and hopes to make you happy.' And this is no extraordinary miracle, for the respectable families with whom I have tea tell me that the Virgin and her divine Son always speak a few pleasant words to those who visit them. I would have you know that I have already obtained certain relics, a straw from the manger, and a piece of plank planed by St. Joseph. My German companion, who, as I told you in my letter from Alexandria, is very devout and learned, consulted the books he carries with him and assured me that it was one of the planks which there is proof that St. Joseph was wont to plane in his leisure moments. As to the great relic, the one which I hope to bring you for the healing of all your ills and the salvation of your soul, so as to repay my debt to you, I hope to obtain it soon; but at present I can say no more than that. Remember me to my friends, who are often in my thoughts and for whom I have prayed constantly; especially our virtuous Casimiro. And give your blessing to your faithful nephew who is filled with respect for you and with sadness at being parted from you and who desires your health.

"P.S. O Auntie, how was I filled with disgust to-day at the house of Pilate! I even spat at it. I told St. Veronica that Auntie was very devoted to her, and she seemed very pleased. That is what I say to tell all the priests and patriarchs: 'You must know Auntie to know what virtue is.'"

Before undressing, I went to listen, my ear pressed against the patterned wall. The Englishwoman was sleeping serene and insensible. I shook my fist in her direction and muttered: "Brute." Then I opened the cupboard, took out Mary's beloved parcel, and gave it a grateful fervent kiss. Next morning, early, we left for the holy river Jordan.

Tiring and tedious was our journey among the hills of Judah. They are all livid, rounded like skulls, dry and bare beneath the accursed wind; only occasionally on their sides appears a thin growth of whin, which from a distance in the fierce shimmering light seems a mold produced by age and neglect. The lime-colored soil glitters, and the radiant silence is melancholy as that of a tomb.

In the hard brightness of the sky, slowly a black vulture circled above us. At sunset we set our tents upon the ruins of Jericho. Pleasant then was our rest in the soft grass, as we slowly sipped lemonade in the soft afternoon air. A gay stream which ran chattering near our camp among wild shrubs mingled its freshness with the scent of their flowers, yellow as those of broom; in front lay a green meadow of tall grass streaked with white gleams of pompous languid lilies, and by the water the storks went thoughtfully in pairs. Towards Judah stood a dark gloomy mountain, the mountain of eternal penitence; and in the direction of Moab, the ancient sacred land of Canaan, an ashen-grey desolate sandy waste, stretched as far as the eye could see, even to the solitude of the Dead Sea.

At dawn, with well-furnished saddle-bags, we continued our pious pilgrimage. The month was December, in the clear soft winter of Syria; and the learned Topsius, as he trotted at my side over the fine sand, told me that formerly this plain of Canaan was covered with the sound of cities, and white roads between vines and irrigated fields, cool along the walls of the threshing-floors; the women, crowned with anemones, sang as they trod out the grapes; the scent of the gardens rose to heaven more pleasing even than incense; the caravans which came up the valley in the direction of Segor found here the rich abundance of Egypt and declared that it was in truth the orchard of the Lord. Later, added Topsius, smiling with infinite sarcasm, one day the Almighty grew tired and blotted it all out. "But why? Why?" "In a whim of fierceness and ill humor."

Our horses neighed as they felt the presence of the accursed waters; and soon they appeared, extending as far as the mountains of Moab, dumb, noiseless, glittering solitarily under the solitary sky. Marvelous is their sadness; and one understands that the anger of the Lord is upon them when one considers that they have lain there so many centuries without having any pleasant town such as Cascaes on their shore, without rows of tents, without fishing or regattas or gentle ladies in galoshes poetically collecting shells on the sand; without the sound of violins in a festive crowd in the gas-light under the stars: they lie there dead, buried between two mountain ranges as between the sides of a tomb.

"Yonder stood the fortress of Makeros," gravely said the learned Topsius, rising in his stirrups and pointing his sunshade towards the blue coast-line; "there lived one of my Herods, Antipas, Tetrarch of Galilee, son of Herod the Great; it was there, Raposo, that John the Baptist was beheaded." And as we rode slowly along the Jordan, while the merry Potte was making us cigarettes of the good tobacco of Aleppo, Topsius told me the lamentable story.

Makeros, the proudest fortress of Asia, rose from tremendous rocks of basalt. Its walls were a hundred and fifty yards high; the eagles scarcely flew as high as the tops of its towers. Outside it was dark and gloomy, but, within, it gleamed with marble and jasper and alabaster, and on the deep ceilings of cedar-wood hung shields of gold, like stars in a summer sky. In the heart of the mountain, in a subterranean chamber, lived Herod's two hundred mares, the fairest on earth, milk-white, with manes black as ebony; they were fed on honey-cakes, and they were so fleet that they could speed over meadows of lilies without spoiling their bloom. Lower still, in a dungeon, lay Jokanan, whom the Church calls the Baptist.

"But, my learned friend, what was the reason for this?"

"This is the story, Dom Raposo. My Herod had in Rome made the acquaintance of Herodias, his niece and wife of his brother Philip, who lived indolently in Italy, forgetful of Judea, enjoying Latin luxury. The beauty of Herodias was dark and splendid. Antipas carried her off in a galley to Syria; divorced his wife, a noble Moabite, daughter of King Aretas, who ruled over the desert and the caravans; and shut himself up incestuously in this fortress of Makeros. Anger ran through Judea at this outrage against the law of the Lord; and the wily Herod sent for John the Baptist who was preaching by Jordan."

"But why, Topsius?"

"The reason was this, Dom Raposo; to see if the rough prophet, flattered and caressed, softened by praises and the good wine of Sichem, would approve that wicked love and by the persuasion of his voice, which prevailed throughout Judea and Galilee, turn it pure as the snow on Carmel in the eyes of the faithful. But unfortunately, Dom Raposo, the Baptist lacked originality. He was respectable, certainly, but not original; in everything the Baptist servilely copied the great prophet Elijah; he dwelt in a cave like Elijah, he clothed himself with skins of wild beasts like Elijah, he lived on locusts like Elijah, he repeated Elijah's classic imprecations; and as Elijah had cried against the incest of Achab, so the Baptist thundered against the incest of Herodias. Mere imitations, Dom Raposo."

"So they silenced him in the dungeon."

"Indeed they did nothing of the kind: he shouted all the louder, terribly so; and Herodias must hide her head in her cloak so as not to hear his cries and curses coming from the depths of the mountain."

I murmured with tears in my eyes: "And Herod ordered our good St. John to be beheaded."

"No, Herod was weak and undecided. Very sensual, Dom Raposo, infinitely sensual, Dom Raposo, but how irresolute! Moreover, like all the Galileans, he had a secret weakness, an irresistible sympathy for prophets. And he feared the vengeance of Elijah, friend and supporter of Jokanan. For Elijah is not dead, Dom Raposo; he lives in heaven very much alive, still dressed in rags, implacable, shouting terribly. . . ."

"Save us," I murmured fearfully.

"Well, there he is. Jokanan continued alive and roaring. But intricate and subtle is a woman's hate, Dom Raposo. In the month of Schebat was Herod's birthday. There was a great feast at which Vitellius, who happened to be travelling in Syria, was present. You remember the stout Vitellius, Dom Raposo, who was afterwards lord of the world. Well, at the hour at which, according to the ceremony observed by the tributary provinces, the health of Caesar and Rome was being drunk, a marvelous maiden suddenly came into the hall to the sound of tambourines and dancing after the fashion of Babylonia. It was Salome, the daughter of Herodias and her husband Philip, whom she had been brought up secretly at Caesarea, in a wood near the Temple of Hercules. Salome danced, bare and lovely; and Antipas, inflamed and maddened with desire, promised her whatever she should ask in return for one kiss of her lips. She took up a golden salver and, after a look at her mother, asked for the Baptist's head. Antipas in dismay offered her the city of Tiberias, treasures and a hundred villages of Gennesaret. She smiled and looked at her mother, and again, stammering uncertainly, she asked for the head of Jokanan. Then the guests, Sadducees, scribes, wealthy men of Decapola, even Vitellius and the Romans, cried merrily: 'You promised, O Tetrarch; on your oath, O Tetrarch.' A few minutes later, Dom Raposo, a Negro of Idumea entered, a sword in one hand and in the other the prophet's head hanging by the hair."

As we rode slowly, listening attentively to these ancient things, we saw afar off in the gleaming sand a line of dull green and bronze. Potte shouted: "The Jordan, the Jordan," and we dashed forward at a gallop towards the river of the Scriptures. The festive Potte knew by the margin of the baptismal stream a most delightful spot for a Christian to spend the afternoon in; and there we passed the hot hours, lying on a carpet, languidly drinking our beer after it had been well cooled in the water of the sacred river. It here forms a quiet transparent backwater, resting after its slow hot journey through the desert from the Lake of Galilee and before it plunges for ever into the bitter waters of the Dead Sea; here it lies idly upon the fine sand, singing a low crystal song and rolling along the polished pebbles of its bed, or sleeps in the cool places, motionless and green in the shade of the tamarisks.

Above our heads murmured the leaves of the tall poplars of Persia; in the grass waved unknown flowers, such as formerly brushed against the tresses of the virgins of Canaan on mornings of vintage; and in the soft gloom of the branches, where the dread voice of Jehovah no longer came to frighten them, the finches sang peacefully. In front, blue and immaculate, as though carved from a single block of precious stone, rose the mountains of Moab. The white dumb dreaming sky seemed to be reposing deliciously after the fierce disorder that disturbed it amid prayers and tumults when the gloomy People of God dwelt here, and where constantly beat the wings of Seraphim, or floated the robes of prophets snatched up to heaven by the Almighty, it was peaceful to see now only a flight of wild pigeons flying towards the orchards of Engaddi.

In obedience to Auntie's command I stripped and bathed myself in the waters of the Baptist. At first in my devout emotion I stepped reverently upon the sand as if it were an altar-cloth, and naked, with folded arms, as the slow current beat about my knees, I thought of St. John and murmured a paternoster. Then I laughed and made good use of that idyllic bath among the trees; Potte threw me my sponge and I soaped myself in the sacred waters, humming Adelia's favorite tune.

In the cool of the evening, as we mounted our horses, a troop of Bedouins, descending from the hills of Galgala, brought their herds of camels to drink in Jordan; the young ones, white and long haired, ran about bleating, and the herdsmen, with long spears, galloped shouting war-cries, their cloaks flying wide in the wind. It was as if in the splendor of the evening a pastoral of the time of the Bible, when Agar was a girl, had come to life again in this valley. Upright in my saddle, the reins tight in my hand, I felt for a moment an heroic impulse; I wished for a sword, and for a law and a God for whom to fight.

Slowly a dreaming silence had fallen upon the plain, and the highest peak of Moab took on a rare gleam of the hue of roses and gold, as though once more for an instant only it had reflected the countenance of the Lord. Topsius raised his wise hand: "That illuminated peak, Dom Raposo, is the mountain on which Moses died." At these words a divine breath from those hills and water entered into me and I felt strong, even as one of the men of Exodus. I seemed to be actually one of them, one who had spoken with Jehovah and arrived from wicked Egypt with his sandals in his hand. The wind's sigh of relief was that of tribes of Israel as they emerged from the wilderness; beyond, down the hill-side, followed by an escort of angels, came the golden ark swaying on the shoulders of the Levites robed in linen and singing. Once more in the dry sand the Land of Promise decked itself with green, Jericho gleamed white among the crops, and through the thick palm groves sounded the trumpets of Joshua on the march. Unable to contain myself, I threw up my helmet and shouted over Canaan this pious cry: Long life to Our Lord and all the court of Heaven!

Early next day, a Sunday, the tireless Topsius, well supplied with pencils and carrying his sunshade, left to study the ruins of Jericho, the ancient city of the palm-trees which Herod had covered with warm baths and temples and gardens and statues and where he had loved Cleopatra in such strange wise. I, at the door of the tent, seated on a packing-case, stayed to drink my coffee and watch our peaceful camp. The cook was plucking chickens; the gloomy Bedouin was cleaning his peaceful sword by the water's edge; and our handsome muleteer was forgetting to give the mares their fodder as he followed on the sapphire sky the white flight of storks in pairs towards Samaria.

Then I put on my helmet and wandered off in the soft morning, hands in pockets, humming a pleasant ballad. My thoughts turned to Adelia and Senhor Adelino. Perhaps in her room, as they kissed furiously, they were calling me the "saint" while I was walking here in the Scripture places. At that hour Auntie, in her black mantilla, with her prayer-book, was going to Mass at Sant'Anna; the waiters at the Café Montanha, whistling, with disheveled hair, were brushing the billiard tables; and Dr. Margaride, at his window in the Praça da Figueira, was putting on his spectacles and unfolding the *Diário das Notícias*. O my cherished Lisbon! But even nearer, in green Egypt beyond the wilderness of Geza, my Mary was at that moment filling the bowl on her counter with magnolias and roses; her cat lay asleep in the velvet chair, and she was sighing for her valiant little Portuguese. I also sighed, and the ballad I sang became more melancholy on my lips. And I suddenly realized that I had wandered into a very lonely place.

It was far from the stream and the scented shrubs with the yellow flowers; I could no longer see our white tents, and all around me lay a dry livid wilderness of sand, closed in by smooth rocks, upright as the walls of a well, so gloomy that the clear light of the warm Eastern morning lost its radiance there and died away to a cheerless sadness. I recollected desolate pictures of the kind, with a long-bearded hermit pondering over a folio near a skull. But there was no hermit there mortifying his flesh in heroic penitence. Only in the center of the mournful place, isolated with the pride of some rare relic, as though the rocks had piled themselves there to form its shrine, stood a tree of an appearance so repulsive that it made the melancholy ballad die away upon my lips. Its trunk was short and stunted, without twisted roots, like an enormous stake planted in the sand; its smooth bark had the oily brightness of a black skin, and from its swollen head, of the hue of a burnt log, sprang, like long spider's legs, eight branches (for I counted them) black and soft, wooly, sticky and set with thorns.

After looking at the monster for a moment in silence, I slowly took off my helmet and murmured: "I salute you." For the tree in front of me was certainly illustrious. Such a branch, the ninth perhaps, arranged of old in the form of a crown by a Roman centurion of the garrison of Jerusalem, had sarcastically adorned on that supreme day the head of the condemned carpenter of Galilee; condemned for having gone about the quiet villages and the holy courts of the Temple declaring that he was the Son of David and the Son of God, and preaching against the established religion and ancient institutions, ancient order, ancient precepts. And the branch for having touched those rebel locks, had become divine and received a place on the altars, and as it passed, carried aloft in procession, the devout multitudes fell prostrate before it.

In the College of the Isidoros every Tuesday and Saturday, greasy Padre Soares would say, as he picked his teeth: "There was in the region of Judea [it was here] a tree, which, so writers say, was truly horrible." This was the tree! Before my frivolous eyes stood the most holy Tree of Thorns. And straightway an idea crossed my mind like an inspiration from Heaven. To take Auntie one of those branches, the wooliest, the thorniest, as a relic fruitful in miracles, to which she could devote her piety and confidently pray for celestial boons. "If you think that you owe me anything for what I have done for you, then bring me from the holy places a holy relic." So had Dona Patrocinio das Neves spoken on the eve of my pious journey, as she sat enthroned in red damask in the presence of the Bench and the Church, letting a tear escape from under her austere spectacles. And what more sacred, more affecting, more efficacious could I offer her than a branch of the Tree of Thorns plucked in the Valley of Jordan on a clear rosy holy morning?

But suddenly a bitter doubt beset me. What if that trunk possessed some magic virtue? What if Auntie began to mend of her complaints, and grow young as soon as I had placed in her oratory among lights and flowers one of those boughs bristling with thorns? Oh, miserable deception! I and none other would bring her the miraculous source of health and make her strong and indestructible, unburiable, with all G. Godinho's fortune clasped in her avaricious hand! I! I who would only begin to live when she began to die!

Walking round the Tree of Thorns, I therefore questioned it with hoarse and gloomy words: "Come, monster, tell me, are you a divine relic with supernatural powers? Or are you merely a grotesque shrub with a Latin name, duly classified by Linnæus? Speak! Have you, as He whose head you crowned in mockery, the gift of healing? Consider well: if I take you with me to a pretty Portuguese oratory, delivering you from the torture of solitude and the cheerless dark, and give you the comforts of an altar, the living incense of roses, the flattering flame of candles, the respect of hands joined in supplication, and all the sweetness of prayer, it is not in order that you should indulgently prolong a cumbersome existence and so deprive me of a speedy inheritance and of the pleasures due to my youth. Consider: if your contact with the Gospel has imbued you with puerile inclinations to charity and mercy and you go with the intention of curing Auntie, then you shall remain here among these rocks, lashed by the dust of the desert, defiled by birds of prey, wearied by the unbroken silence. But if you promise to remain deaf to Auntie's prayers and behave as a poor withered bough without influence and do not interrupt the desired decay of her body, then you shall have in Lisbon the comfortable softness of a chapel lined with damask, the warmth of devout kisses and all the pleasures of an idol: I will surround you with so much adoration that you will feel no envy towards the God whom your thorns wounded. Speak, monster."

The monster remained dumb, but suddenly I felt within my soul, like the consoling freshness of a summer breeze, the soothing presentiment that Auntie would soon die and molder in her grave. The Tree of Thorns, through the general communication of Nature, sent from its sap into my blood that sweet announcement of Dona Patrocinio's death, as a sufficient promise that none of its branches, when transferred to the oratory, would prevent the horrible old lady's liver from being the death of her.

We came in the desert to this silent, solemn and deadly pact. But was it really the Tree of Thorns? The quickness with which it had agreed to my conditions made me suspect the excellence of its divinity. I decided to consult the solid learning of Topsius. I hurried to the Fountain of Elijah, where he was searching for stones, refuse, splinters, fragments of the city of the palm-trees. From afar I could see the distinguished historian crouching by a well examining through his patient glasses a piece of a black column half buried in the mud. At his side a donkey, forgetting the tender grass, was contemplating in philosophic sadness the passionate endeavor of the learned man upon his knees on the ground searching for the Baths of Herod.

I told Topsius of my find and of my uncertainty. He at once rose, serviceable, eager, ever ready to cope with the problems of learning. "A shrub of thorns?" he murmured, wiping his brow. "It must be the Nabka, very common throughout Syria. Hasselquist, the botanist, considers that it was from it that was made the Crown of Thorns. It has delightful little green leaves, heart-shaped like those of ivy. No? Well, then it is the Lycium Spinosum, which, according to the Latin tradition, was used for the Crown. In my opinion the tradition is absurd, and Hasselquist ignorant, infinitely ignorant. But I will go and make the matter clear, Dom Raposo, make it irrefutably clear once for all."

Off we went. In the desert, before the dreadful tree, Topsius gave it a magisterial look, retired for an instant into the inner stores of his learning, and then declared that I could take my pious Aunt nothing more precious. The proof he gave was brilliant and convincing. All the instruments of the Crucifixion, he said, waving his sunshade, the nails, the sponge, the reed, for a moment made divine as having contributed to the divine tragedy, had gradually, owing to the requirements of civilization, entered into the material uses of life. The nail had not remained for ever idle on the altars, in memory of the sacred wounds: Catholic commercial humanity was gradually constrained to make use of it in other ways, and, having pierced the hands of the Messiah, it now, modest and industrious, fastens the tops of boxes far from holy; the most reverent members of the Brotherhood of Nosso Senhor dos Passos use the reed to fish with; it goes to make festive rockets, and the State itself, so scrupulous in matters of religion, thus makes use of it on merry nights celebrating a new Constitution or in festivities for the marriage of princes. The sponge, once sarcastically dipped in vinegar and offered on a spear, is now employed in the profane ceremonies of the bath. Even the cross, the supreme form of the cross, has lost its divine significance among men. Christianity, after using it as a standard, now uses it as an ornament; it is a brooch, a trinket, it hangs on necklaces and tinkles on bracelets, it is sealed in wax and engraved on cuff-links, and in this proud age really belongs more to the art of the goldsmith than to religion. "But the Crown of Thorns, Dom Raposo, has never been used for anything."

Yes, the Church received it from the hands of a Roman proconsul and it remained isolated for all eternity in the Church, in memory of the great outrage. In all this varied Universe it can only find a place in the gloom of chapels; its only use is to persuade to repentance. No jeweller has ever imitated it in gold set with rubies to adorn a fair lady's hair; it is exclusively the instrument of martyrdom and, stained with blood on the curly hair of images, is a ceaseless source of tears. The shrewdest merchant, after turning it over in his hands, would restore it to the altar as being useless to life and commerce and civilization; it is but an attribute of the Passion, a refuge for the sad and an object of tenderness to the weak. It alone, of all the accessories, sincerely provokes to prayer. Who, however anxious to adore, would bow down, with a stream of paternosters, before a sponge in a tub or before a reed at the edge of a stream? But to the Crown of Thorns the hands of the faithful are continually raised, and the echo of its cruelty is felt in the sad Misereres. What greater marvel could I take to Auntie?

"Yes, my excellent Topsius; what you say is pure gold; but the other one, the true one, the one really used, was it taken from here, from this trunk? What say you, my friend?"

The learned Topsius slowly unfolded his check handkerchief, and declared, in contradiction of the Latin tradition and the most ignorant Hasselquist, that the Crown of Thorns was taken from a thin and flexible bush which abounds in the valleys of Jerusalem, serves as fuel and to make hedges, and has a sad little red flower without scent.

I murmured in dismay: "What a pity! Auntie would have been so pleased that it should have come from here, Topsius; and Auntie is so rich."

Then the sagacious philosopher understood that there can be reasons of family as there are reasons of State, and was sublime. He extended his hand over the tree, covering it generously with the assurance of his learning, and spoke these memorable words: "Dom Raposo, we have been good friends. You may, then, assure your aunt, on the authority of a man to whom Germany listens on matters of critical archaeology, that the bough you take her from this tree in the shape of a crown was. . . ." "Was?" I cried eagerly. "Was the very crown which tore the brow of the Rabbi Jeschoua Natzarieh, whom the Latins call Jesus of Nazareth and others also call Christ."

The lofty science of Germany had spoken. I pulled out my Sevil-

lian knife and cut off one of the boughs; and while Topsius returned to search among the damp grass for the fortress of Cypron
and other stones of Herod, I went back to the tents in triumph with
my precious prize.

The amiable Potte was seated on a saddle, grinding coffee. "A
splendid bough," he cried. "Arranged in the form of a crown, it will
be an object of the greatest devotion." And forthwith the merry man
with his deft fingers bound the rough branch in the form of a holy
cross, so like, so touchingly like! "It only requires a few drops of
blood," I murmured with emotion. "Heavens, how delighted Auntie
will be!" But how were we to take these difficult thorns to Jerusalem over the hills of Judah? Having assumed the form they took in
the Passion, they seemed eager to rend innocent flesh. But the gay
Potte recognized no difficulties: he took from the depths of his well
stocked saddle-bags a soft cloud of cottonwool, wrapped the impious crown in it delicately like a fragile jewel, and with a piece of
brown paper and scarlet string made a light round solid parcel of it.
And I, smiling, as I rolled a cigarette, thought of that other parcel of
violet-scented laces and ribands which had remained at Jerusalem,
awaiting my return and my kisses. Potte, Potte, I cried radiantly; you
do not know how large a sum that little branch in that little parcel
means to me.

When Topsius returned from the sacred Fountain of Elijah, I produced one of the bottles of champagne with its golden top from
Potte's saddle-bag in order to celebrate the providential discovery
of the Great Relic. Topsius drank to Science. I drank to Religion; and
generously the froth of Möèt et Chandon watered the wilderness
of Canaan. At night we festively lit a bonfire and the Arab women
of Jericho came to dance before our tents. We went to bed late,
as a thin sickle of moon appeared above Moab in the direction of
Makeros, like the golden scimitar which had severed the fervent
head of Jokanan. The parcel containing the Crown of Thorns was
by the side of my bed. The fire had gone out and our camp slept in
the infinite silence of this scriptural valley. Happy and serene, I also
went to sleep.

Three

I must have lain asleep two hours stretched dully on my bed, when I seemed to behold a tremulous light like that of a smoking torch entering the tent, and through it a voice called to me in a melancholy tone of lamentation: Teodorico, Teodorico, rise and go to Jerusalem. I threw aside the blanket in fear and beheld the most learned Topsius: in the dim light of a candle which flickered from a table on which stood the bottles of champagne, he was rapidly fastening on his foot an ancient iron spur. It was he who had awakened me eagerly, fervently: Up, Teodorico, up! The mares are saddled. Tomorrow is Easter Day, and at dawn we must be at the gates of Jerusalem. Smoothing back my hair, I considered with astonishment the prudent sensible Doctor: "O Topsius, are we to start in this abrupt way without our saddlebags and leaving our tents plunged in sleep as men who flee in fear?"

The learned man raised his gold glasses which shone with an unusual irresistible intelligence. A white cloak which I had never seen him wear wrapped his learned thinness in the grave austere folds of a Latin toga, and slowly, silently opening his arms, he said (and his lips seemed molded in the classic marble): "Dom Raposo, this dawn about to appear and to touch the peaks of Hebron, is that of the fifteenth day of the month of Nizzam, and in all the history of Israel, from the time when the tribes returned from Babylonia to the day when Titus shall come and besiege the Temple for the last time, there has not been a more interesting day. I must be in Jerusalem to see this page of the Gospel living and sounding before my eyes. Let us therefore go and keep Easter in the house of Gamaliel, who is a friend of Hillel and mine, with a knowledge of Greek letters, a strong patriot and member of the Sanhedrin. It was he who said: In order to escape from the torture of doubt, impose upon yourself an authority. So up with you, Dom Raposo."

Thus murmured my friend, tall and motionless. And I obediently, as at a divine command, began in silence to put on my great riding-boots. As soon as I had wrapped a cloak round me, he pushed me impatiently out of the tent without even allowing me to take my watch and Sevillian knife which I kept cautiously every night under my pillow.

The light of the candle was dying down, red and smoky. It must have been midnight. Two dogs were barking in the distance dully as from between the leafy walls of a garden. The soft desert air was scented with garden roses and orange flower. The sky of Israel gleamed with unusual splendor, and above Mount Nebo a beautiful white star of a divine radiance was looking towards me, twinkling eagerly, as though, impotent in its dumbness, it strove to convey some secret to my soul.

The mares were waiting, motionless under their long manes. I mounted, and as Topsius was with difficulty arranging his stirrups, I saw in the direction of the fountain a marvelous sight which filled me with surpassing dread. The white wall of a new-built city seemed to rise beneath the diamond glitter of the stars of Syria. The fronts of temples gleamed palely from the depths of sacred woods, and the slender arches of an aqueduct stalked away to the distant hills. A flame smoked on the top of a tower, and moving below it shone the tips of spears; the slow sound of a bugle died away in the shadow; and sheltered against the bastions of the city wall a village slept among palm-trees.

Topsius, in the saddle, ready to start, plunged his hand in the mane of his mare. That whiteness yonder? I murmured with emotion. He answered with a single word: Jericho. He set off at a gallop. I know not how long I followed in silence the noble historian of the Herods, along a straight road made of great blocks of basalt. Ah, how different from the rough way by which we had come down to Canaan, that gleaming lime-colored way through the hills where the sparse whin seemed in the moonlight a mold produced by old age and neglect! And everything round me seemed also different, the shape of the rocks, the smell of the warm earth, the twinkling of the stars. What change had occurred in me, what change had occurred in the Universe?

Occasionally a harsh spark flashed from the shoes of the mares. And ceaselessly, clinging to the mane, Topsius galloped, the two folds of his white cloak beating like two flags behind him. But suddenly we halted. We were near a square house among trees, dark and silent. On its top it had a flagstaff, and on this strangely, as though cut out of a sheet of iron, stood a stork. A fire smoldered at the entrance. I stirred the logs, and in the brief flame that sprang from them I saw that it was an ancient inn by the side of an ancient road. Beneath the stork and above the narrow nail-studded door gleamed a Latin sign on a white stone: *Ad Gruem Majorem*, and at its side, covering part of the front of the house, ran an inscription roughly carved in the stone.

The inscription, which I with difficulty deciphered, said that Apollo promised health to the guest, and Septimus the innkeeper assured him a ready welcome, a restoring bath, strong wine of Campania, the clear wine of Engaddi and all the comforts of Rome. "Of Rome," I murmured distrustfully. What strange ways was I then treading? What strange men, different from me in speech and dress, drank there, under the protection of other gods, wine in jars of the time of Horace?

But again Topsius set off, like a thin phantom in the night. The road of sounding basalt had ended and we were now ascending by a steep path scooped out among rocks; great stones fell echoing beneath our mares as in a torrent bed parched by a sluggish August. The learned doctor, shaken in his saddle, was cursing hoarsely; he cursed the Sanhedrin and the rigid Judaic law, unbendingly opposed to any civilized work the Proconsul wished to undertake. The Pharisee even looked with rancor on the Roman aqueduct which brought him water, on the Roman road which took him to the cities, on the Roman baths which cured his skin diseases. Accused Pharisees! Sleepily recollecting ancient imprecations of the Gospel, I muttered, wrapped in my cloak: Accursed Pharisees, whited sepulchres!

It was the silent hour when the wolves come down from the

mountains to drink. I shut my eyes, the stars grew faint in heaven. Brief are the soft nights of Nizzam, when the white paschal lamb is eaten at Jerusalem; and soon the sky was whitening over Moab.

I awoke; the flocks were bleating on the hills and the air had a fresh scent of rosemary. Then I saw, wandering along the heights above the path, a man of strange and wild aspect, dressed in sheepskins, who reminded me of Elijah and Scriptural wrath; his breast and legs seemed made of red granite; between his hair and beard, rough and shaggy as a ferocious mane, his eyes gleamed in frenzy. He caught sight of us and, extending his arms as one who throws stones, he poured upon us all the curses of the Lord. He called us pagans, he called us dogs; he cried: Cursed be your mothers, dry be the breasts that bare you! Cruel and ill-omened sounded his cries from the tops of the rocks, and as his mare went slowly forward, Topsius cowered beneath his cloak as under an incessant shower of hail. At last I lost patience and, turning in my saddle, I called him drunkard and other foul names, and under the savage flame of his eyes I could see his black and noisy mouth twist and foam in devout fury.

But issuing from the ravine, we came upon the broad and paved Roman road to Sichem, and as we trotted along it we felt the relief of at last reaching a cultivated friendly humane and law-abiding region. There was abundance of water; new forts stood on the hills, sacred boundary-stones divided the fields; in the white threshing-floors oxen decked with anemones were treading out the corn of the Easter harvest, and in orchards where the fig-tree was already in leaf, the slave in his whitewashed tower, singing with a stick in his hand, frightening away the wild pigeons. Sometimes we would see a man standing by his vineyard or at the edge of an irrigation canal, upright, with the edge of his cloak thrown over his head and downcast eyes, saying the holy prayer of the Sachema. A potter, prodding his ass laden with jars of yellow clay, shouted to us: "Blessed be your mothers. A happy Easter." And a leper, resting in the shade of the olives, asked us, as he moaned and showed his sores, who was the

Rabbi who healed at Jerusalem and where he might find the root of baraz.

We were now approaching Bethlehem. We stopped for our mares to drink at a beautiful spring in the shadow of a cedar; and the learned Topsius, arranging one of his stirrups, was wondering that we had not met the caravan which comes up from Galilee to celebrate Easter at Jerusalem, when a slow sound of marching men came from farther down the road; and to my amazement I saw Roman soldiers such as I had often cursed in pictures of the Passion. Bearded, burnt by the Syrian sun, they marched solidly in cadence with an ox-like tread, as the iron soles of their sandals rang on the paved way. They all carried their shields on their backs enveloped in canvas sacks, and each had on his shoulder an iron-tipped staff from which hung corded bundles, bronze plates, implements and bunches of dates. In some of the files they went bare-headed and carried their helmets like buckets, others brandished a short spear in their hands. The decurion, stout and fair, followed by a tame gazelle decked with corals, was dozing on his slow-paced mare, wrapped in a cloak of scarlet. Behind, by the side of the mules laden with sacks of corn and bundles of wood, the muleteers were singing to the music of a clay pipe played by a half-naked Negro, who had the number of the legion marked on his breast in red figures.

I had retreated into the shadow of the cedar; but Topsius, like a servile German, had dismounted and almost knelt in the dust before the arms of Rome, and could not refrain from crying, as he waved his arms and cloak: Long life to Caius Tiberius, thrice Consul, Illyrius, Pannonicus, Germanicus, Emperor, Pacifier, Augustus! Some of the legionaries laughed dully; and they passed in close formation with a sound of iron, while a shepherd afar off, shouting to his goats, fled to the tops of the hills.

Once more we started at a gallop. The road of basalt came to an end, and we passed through a fresh and fertile country between woods and scented orchards. Oh, how different were those ways, those hills, from those I had previously seen around the sacred city,

dried by the parching wind and white like bones! Everything now
was green, well watered, and refreshed with murmuring shade. The
very atmosphere seemed to have lost that sad stricken look that I had
noticed over Jerusalem; and the branches were unfurling their April
leaves in a soft blue air, young and hopeful as they. My eyes kept
turning to those Scriptural orchards of olive, fig and vine, in which
grew wild and more splendid even than King Solomon the red lilies
of the field.

Charmed and humming a tune, I trotted along a hedge intertwined with roses. Topsius called to me to stop and showed me
high on a hill against a dark background of cypresses and cedars a
house with its white porch facing the Eastern light. It belonged, he
said, to a Roman, a relation of Valerius Gratus, formerly Imperial
Legate in Syria, and everything about it seemed full of Latin charm
and pleasant peace. A green carpet of smooth grass descended the
hill to a plot of lilies, and in its center, in scarlet flowers on the
green, showed the initials of Valerius Gratus; all around, in plots
of roses and lilies bordered with myrtle, gleamed noble vases of
Corinthian marble round which twined flowers of acanthus; a slave
in a grey hood was clipping a yew-tree in the shape of an urn, by the
side of a tall box-tree already made into a lyre; hens were pecking
the ground strewn with scarlet sand, in an alley of planes between
whose trunks ivy festooned as in the adornment of a temple; the
branches of the bay-trees threw their shade over the bare statues;
and in a pergola of vines, to the sound of water singing slowly in a
bronzen basin, an old man, serene, smiling, happy, read a long scroll
of parchment as he sat by a statue of Aesculapius, and a girl with a
golden arrow in her hair and dressed all in white linen was making
a garland of the flowers in her lap. At the sound of our horses she
raised her clear eyes. Topsius cried: O salve, pulcherrima! I cried: Viva la
gracia! The thrushes were singing in the flowering pomegranates.

Farther on, the learned Topsius again made me pause to point
out a country-house, dark and austere among cypresses; he told me
in a low voice that it belonged to Osanias, a rich Sadducee of Jeru-

salem, of the priestly family of the Beothos, and a member of the
Sanhedrin. No pagan ornament profaned his walls: square, stiff and
inaccessible, it reproduced the severity of the law. But the large gra-
naries roofed with thatch, the ovens, the vineyards told of wealth
accumulated by harsh tributes; in the court ten slaves scarcely sufficed to guard the sacks of corn, the wineskins, the lambs branded
in red which had been received in payment of tithes this Easter day.
Near the road, in ostentatious piety, freshly whitewashed, a private
tomb gleamed in the sun amid rose-trees.

Thus advancing, we came to Bethphage among its palms, and by
a green short cut known to Topsius we began to ascend the Mount
of Olives to the Winepress of the Moabite, where the caravans halt
on that interminable ancient road which comes from Egypt and
goes on to Damascus the well watered. And suddenly we found the
whole Mount, in the olive-trees down its side as far as the brook
Cedron, in the orchards of the valley as far as Siloe, amid the new
tombs of the Sacrificers, and even in the direction of the dusty road
of Hebron, covered with the noisy awakening of an encamped
people. Black tents of the desert made of sheepskins and surrounded
by stones; huts of canvas belonging to the Idumeans, white in the
sun among the green leaves; booths built of branches to give shelter
to the shepherds of Ascalon; awnings formed of carpets which the
pilgrims from Naphtali hang from stakes of cedar-wood: all Judea
was there at the gates of Jerusalem for the celebration of holy Easter.
There too, round a building where legionaries were on guard, were
Greek merchants of Decapola, Phoenician weavers from Tiberias,
and the pagans who come through Samaria from the direction of
Caesarea and the sea.

We advanced slowly and cautiously. In the shade of the olives,
camels freed from their loads were ruminating peaceably, and
hobbled mares of Perea hung their heads beneath their long thick
manes. Near the tents, open to show us the gleam of arms hung up
or some great enamelled plate, girls whose arms flashed with bracelets were grinding rye between two stones; others were milking the

goats; everywhere fires shone brightly, and holding their children by the hand and their slender pitchers on their shoulders, a file of women went down singing to the spring of Siloe.

Our mounts caught their feet in the intricate cords of the tents of Idumeans or paused before carpets spread on the ground, on which a merchant from Caesarea, in a bright Carthaginian cloak embroidered with flowers, set out pieces of linen of Egypt and silks of Cos and gleaming damascened arms; or with a bottle in the palm of either hand praised the perfection of nard of Assyria and the sweet oils of Parthia. The men standing round gazed at us with soft haughty eyes as they drew aside; sometimes they murmured a dull insult, or a mocking laughter provoked by the learned Topsius' spectacles showed the sharp teeth of wild animals in their black unkempt beards.

Under the trees, against the walls, rows of beggars whined, showing the shard with which they scraped their sores. In front of a hut built of branches of bay, a stout old man, ruddy as Silenus, was crying fresh wine of Sichem and the new April beans. The dark men of the desert crowded round the baskets of fruit. A shepherd of Ascalon on stilts in the midst of his flock of white lambs was blowing a horn to summon the devout to buy the unblemished paschal lamb. And among the crowd, in which sticks were constantly being raised in sudden brawls, went Roman soldiers in pairs, a twig of olive in their helmets, in friendly protection. Thus we arrived near two tall branching cedars so thickly covered with fluttering white doves that they seemed two great apple-trees in spring, with a wind scattering their flowers.

Suddenly Topsius halted, opening his arms, as I did also; and with beating hearts we stood there motionless, gazing in awe at Jerusalem that lay gleaming before us there below, magnificently bathed in sunlight. A proud austere wall, furnished with strong towers and with doors of which the masonry was adorned with work in gold, rose above the steep banks of the brook Cedron, now parched by the heat of the month of Nizzam, and continued, girdling Zion, towards Hinnon and the hills of Gareb. And inside, opposite the

cedars under whose shade we stood, the Temple, rising from its imperishable foundations, seemed to dominate all Judea, proud and
splendid, walled with polished granite, protected by bastions of
marble, like the gleaming fortress of a God.

Bending forward in his saddle, the wise Topsius pointed out to
me the first court, called the Court of the Gentiles, vast enough to
contain all the tribes of Israel, and all the pagans; its polished floor
shone like the tranquil surface of a pool; and at its side the columns
of Parian marble which formed the cool deep Porch of Solomon,
were thicker than the trunks of the palm-trees of Jericho. In this
space, filled with air and light, rose on glistening flights of steps
that seemed of alabaster, with doors encrusted in silver, arcades and
turrets with flights of doves, a noble terrace, only accessible to the
faithful, to the Chosen People of God, the proud Court of Israel.

Above it again by more bright stairs rose another white terrace,
the Court of the Priests. Black against its brightness stood a huge
altar of rough stone, from each corner of which rose a gloomy horn
of bronze and at its side two long straight lines of smoke ascended
slowly and were lost in the blue sky, serene symbols of unceasing
prayer. And beyond, higher still, dazzling with its white marbles
and scales of gold, snow-white and tawny, as though fashioned
of pure gold and pure snow, casting reflections of its marvelous
brightness on the surrounding hills, appeared the Hieron, the Holy
of Holies, the dwelling of Jehovah. Over its door hung the mystic veil, woven in Babylonia, of the hue of fire and the hues of the
sea; along its walls climbed a vine made of pearls, with bunches
of grapes wrought of other precious stones; from its cupola radi-
ated spears of gold which illuminated it as with rays of the sun;
thus radiant, triumphant, precious, august, it towered towards that
festive paschal sky, offering itself without reserve as the fairest, the
rarest gift of earth.

But at the side of the Temple and even higher, with the severe
look of a haughty master, Topsius showed me the Antonia Tower,
the black solid impenetrable citadel of the Roman troops. Armed
men moved about the terrace between the battlements; on a bastion

a stalwart figure in the red cloak of a centurion stood with arm outstretched; and slow trumpet-calls seemed to speak and give commands to other towers in the distance, blue in the clear air, which
enchained the holy city; Caesar seemed to me to be stronger than
Jehovah.

And he showed me too, beyond the Antonia Tower, the ancient
town of David. It was a dense cluster of houses, newly whitewashed
under the blue sky, which descended like a herd of goats into the
valley still in shadow to an ancient square surrounded by arcades;
thence it mounted in cracks of crooked streets and spread itself over
the opposite hill of Acra, rich with palaces and rounded cisterns that
shone in the light like shields of steel.

Farther away still, beyond the old ruinous walls, was the new
quarter of Bezetha, in course of construction. Here were the round
arches of the Circus of Herod, and the gardens of Herod extended
over a last hill to the tomb of Helena and lay fresh in the sun, watered
with sweet water of Enrogel. "Ah, Topsius, what a city!" I murmured
in amazement. "Rabbi Eliezer," answered Topsius, "says that he has
not seen a fair city who has not beheld Jerusalem."

But at our side gay folk were passing, running towards the grass
road that comes up from Bethany; and an old man hurriedly pulling forward his ass, laden with bundles of palms, shouted to us that
the caravan of Galilee had been seen and was arriving. In our curiosity we trotted to a hill near a hedge of cactus where was a crowd
of women with children on their necks: they were shaking their
bright veils and uttering words of blessing and welcome.

Then we saw, in a cloud of dust golden in the sun, the dense file
of the pilgrims who are the last to reach Jerusalem, coming from
afar, from Upper Galilee, from Gescala and the mountains. A glad
sound of chanting filled the road; round a green standard waved
palm branches and boughs of flowering almond; and large bundles
on the backs of camels swayed rhythmically among the crowd of
white turbans advancing. Six horsemen of the Babylonian Guard of
Herod Antipas, Tetrarch of Galilee, had escorted the caravan from

Tiberias. They wore skin caps, their long beards were plaited, and their legs swathed in yellow leather; they rode in front, prancing and cracking their whips of cord with one hand, and with the other throwing into the air and catching their gleaming scimitars. Behind them came a college of Levites, stepping out as they leaned on staffs decked with flowers, the scrolls of the law pressed against their breasts, and loudly chanting the praises of Zion. And by their side strong youths with full red cheeks blew fiercely into curved bronzen trumpets.

But a shout arose from the crowd at the roadside. An old man, his hair bound by no turban, was turning and dancing in frenzy; from his hairy hands came a sound of castanets as he waved them in the air; he threw up now one leg, now the other, and his face, bearded as that of King David, shone with a light of inspiration. Behind him girls, leaping in cadence on their light sandal-tips, plaintively struck small harps; others whirled round and round, beating their tambourines above their heads, and their silver anklets shone in the dust as they raised their feet under the whirling circle of their tunics. Then the crowd fervently began to sing the ancient chant of ritual journeyings and the psalms of pilgrimage. "All my steps go to thee, Jerusalem. Thou art perfect. He who loves thee knows abundance." And I too shouted enthusiastically: "Thou art the palace of the Lord, O Jerusalem, and the solace of my heart."

The noisy caravan passed slowly. The women of the Levites, wrapped up and veiled on their donkeys, resembled large soft sacks; the poorest, walking, carried in the folds of their cloaks a store of fruit and oats. Some had already provided themselves with their offering for the Lord and dragged along a white lamb tied to their waist. The stronger carried the sick on their backs, who held on with their hands and turned thin cheeks and wide-open eyes eagerly towards the walls of the holy city where all ills are healed. Noisy fervent blessings passed between the pilgrims and the gay multitude which welcomed them; some asked after neighbors and the crops and the old people who had remained in the village in the shade of the vines; and one old man at my side, bearded as Abraham, on hearing that his millstone had been stolen, threw himself on the ground, tearing his face and rending his tunic.

But now, closing the march, the mules were passing with tinkling bells, laden with fire-wood and skins of oil; and behind them came a crowd of fanatics who on the outskirts, at Bethphage and Rephrain, had joined the caravan and were now throwing to the side of the road empty wine jars and brandishing their knives and calling for the blood of the Samaritans and threatening all pagans. Then, following Topsius, I trotted again across the Mount to the cedars covered with the white flight of doves; and at the very moment the pilgrims, coming up from the road, came in view of Jerusalem gleaming there below, white and beautiful in the light, and flamed into a sacred tumultuous frenzy. Falling prostrate, they beat their faces against the hard earth; a clamor of prayer ascended to the cloudless sky amid the noise of the multitude; and mothers held up their children in their arms, offering them enthusiastically to the Lord. Some remained motionless in amazement before the splendors of Zion; and warm tears of faith and pious love rolled down their rough unkempt beards.

The old men pointed with their finger to the terraces of the Temple, the ancient streets, the sacred places of the history of Israel: "Yonder is the gate of Ephraim, there the tower of the Furnaces; those white stones beyond are the tomb of Rachel." And those who crowded round them to listen clapped their hands and cried: Blessed be thou, O Zion. Others ran madly with belt unfastened, tripping over the tent-ropes and baskets of fruit, to change their Roman money and buy the sacrificial lamb. Sometimes from among the trees a hymn arose clear, delicate and pure, and remained trembling in the air: for an instant earth seemed to listen as the heavens listened; Zion lay serenely bright below, and from the Temple the two lines of smoke ascended like an unbroken prayer. Then the hymn died away, and again blessings broke forth noisily: the soul of all Judah was plunged in the splendor of the sanctuary, and thin arms were extended in frenzy towards Jehovah.

Suddenly Topsius seized the reins of my mare, and almost at my side a man in a saffron-colored tunic came like a phantom from behind an olive-tree, brandishing a sword; he leaped on to a stone and shouted in despair: "To the rescue, men of Galilee, and you men of Naphtali." Pilgrims ran up, waving their sticks, and pale women came from the tents, pressing their children to their breasts. The man's sword trembled in the air, the whole man trembled, and again he cried disconsolately: "Men of Galilee, Rabbi Jeschoua has been arrested. Rabbi Jeschoua has been taken to the house of Hannan, men of Naphtali." "Dom Raposo," then said Topsius, with flaming eyes, "the Man has been taken and has appeared before the Sanhedrin. Quick, quick, my friend, to Jerusalem, to the house of Gamaliel!" And at the hour when in the Temple the scent-offering was being made, and the sun was already high over Hebron, Topsius and I slowly entered, by the Gate of the Fishmarket, a street of ancient Jerusalem.

It was steep, crooked and dusty, with low poor houses of brick; above the doors, closed by a leathern thong, above the narrow barred windows, plants and palms were intertwined in Easter decoration. On the terraces surrounded by balustrades women were diligently beating carpets or winnowing corn; others gossiped as they hung up rows of clay lamps for the customary illuminations. At our side walked wearily an Egyptian harp-player, a scarlet plume stuck in his hair, a white loin-cloth round his slender waist, his arms heavy with bracelets, and the harp on his back, the harp curved as a sickle and carved with flowers of lotus. Topsius asked him if he came from Alexandria, and if the songs of the battle of Actium were still sung in the taverns of Eunotus. Straightway the man, showing his long teeth in a sad smile, placed his harp on the ground and began to strike the strings.

We spurred on our mares and frightened two women in yellow veils who carried doves in the fold of their cloaks and were evidently hastening to the Temple, upright and graceful; the bells of their sandals tinkled as they went. Here and there a housewife had lit her fire in the middle of the street, and from saucepans on tripods came a penetrating smell of garlic. Fat children rolled in the dust as they greedily gnawed the rind of raw pumpkins; they gazed after us with their large bleary eyes covered with flies. Before a forge a shaggy group of shepherds of Moab were waiting, while inside, in a shower of sparks, the blacksmiths were placing new iron points on their lances. A Negro, with a sun-shaped comb in his curly hair, was crying strangely fashioned rye-cakes in a mournful chant.

Silently we crossed a bright paved square which was being re-paired. At the farther end stood a modern building, Roman warm baths, with an air of luxury and idleness in the long arcade of its granite portico; in the inner court, cool under plane-trees, from whose branches hung an awning of white linen, ran naked slaves shining with sweat, carrying bottles of scent and armfuls of flowers; through the open gratings in the pavement came a soft hothouse air scented with roses. And under the columns of the porch, where an onyx stone indicated the women's entrance, motionless, offering herself to men's admiration like an idol, stood a marvelous crea-ture. Above her face, white as a full moon, with thick lips, red and healthy, was set the yellow cap of the prostitutes of Babylonia; from her strong shoulders, over her splendid breasts, fell in hard folds of brocade a black cloak magnificently embroidered with a pattern of gold. In her hand she held a cactus flower, and her heavy eyelids and thick eyelashes opened and closed rhythmically as the fan rose and fell in the hands of a black slave who sang as she crouched at her feet. When her eyes closed, all around seemed to grow dark; and when she raised the black curtain of her lashes, a light fell from those large eyes, an influence as from the sun at midday in the desert, burning and filling with a vague sadness. And thus she offered herself, mag-nificent with her great marble limbs, her tawny cap recalling the rites of Astarte and Adonis.

Turning pale, I touched the arm of Topsius and murmured: "Caramba, I am off to the baths." Dry and stiff in his white cloak, he answered me roughly: "Gamaliel is awaiting us, the son of Simeon. And the wisdom of the Rabbis has taught us that women are the way of perdition." And he turned sharply into a dark narrow street all arched over. The hoofs of our mares, as they struck the pavement, called down upon us the howls of dogs and the curses of beggars huddled together in the dark. We issued by a gap in the ancient wall of Ezekiah, and passed an old dry cistern where the lizards lay asleep; and, trotting through the soft dust of a long street between gleaming whitewashed walls and doors covered with pitch, we stopped in front of a house of nobler build, with an arch and low wire grating to keep out the scorpions.

It was the house of Gamaliel. In the center of a vast court paved with brick and baking in the sun, the transparent water of a pond lay in the shade of a lemon-tree. Around it, on columns of green marble, ran a veranda, cool and silent, from which hung here and there a carpet of Assyria embroidered with flowers. The cloudless blue sky shone above, and in a corner, tied by cords like an animal to a wooden beam, weighed down with irons, covered with scars, a Negro in a shed made the great millstone of the private mill slowly groan and turn.

In the shadow of a door appeared a fat bearded man, almost as yellow as the soft tunic that enveloped him; he held an ivory wand in his hand, and seemed scarce able to raise his slack eyelids. Your master? shouted Topsius, dismounting. Enter, said the man in a faint voice like the hiss of a snake. We went up a rich stairway of black granite and came to a landing on which rested two candelabra, straight as the shrubs whose leafless trunks they reproduced in bronze, and between them stood before us Gamaliel, the son of Simeon. He was very tall, very thin, and his long, glistening, scented beard covered his chest, on which hung a bright coral seal on a scarlet riband. His white turban, interlaced with strings of pearls, revealed a piece of parchment clinging to his forehead and covered with sacred texts; and under the whiteness his deep-sunk eyes had a cold hard gleam. A long blue tunic fell to his sandals and was edged with a long fringe that trailed upon the floor; sewn on the sleeves and rolled round his wrists were more pieces of parchment black with the texts of Scripture. Topsius saluted him in the fashion of Egypt, letting his hand fall slowly to his knee. Gamaliel held out his arms and murmured rhythmically: Enter, be welcome, eat and enjoy yourselves.

We followed Gamaliel over an echoing floor of mosaic into a room in which there were three men. One of them, who turned from the window to greet us, was splendidly handsome, with long chestnut hair hanging in soft curls on his strong neck, smooth and white as marble; in the black sash round his tunic the golden handle of a short sword gleamed with precious stones. The second man, stout and bald, with a flabby face without eyebrows and so livid that it seemed covered with flour, had remained with arms crossed, wrapped in his wine-colored cloak on a sofa formed of straps of leather, a purple cushion under either arm, and his manner of welcome was more absent and disdainful than that of a man tossing an alms to a stranger. But Topsius, falling almost prostrate, kissed his rounded shoes of yellow leather fastened with gold laces; for this was the venerable Osanias, of the priestly family of the Beothos, of the royal blood of Aristobulus. The third man we did not salute nor did he see us; he was crouched in a corner, his face buried in the hood of a tunic whiter than new-fallen snow, as one wrapped in prayer; only occasionally he moved to wipe his hands on a fine towel white as his tunic which hung from a cord fastened tightly round his waist, thick and full of knots such as the monks wear.

Meanwhile, taking of my gloves, I examined the ceiling of the room, all of cedar, worked in scarlet. The smooth shining blue of the walls seemed a continuation of the warm clear Eastern sky which gleamed through the window, where in the full light a solitary branch of honeysuckle hung from the wall. On a tripod inlaid with mother-of-pearl, the smoke of an aromatic gum rose from a bronzen censer. But Gamaliel approached and, after letting his hard look rest on my riding-boots, said slowly: "The journey from the Jordan is a long one, you must be hungry." I politely said: "No," and he gravely, as if he were reciting a text: "The midday hour is the most pleasing to the Lord. Joseph said to Benjamin: 'Thou shalt eat with me at midday.' But the pleasure of the guest is also dear to the

Most High and Powerful. You are weak, you shall eat, so that your soul may bless me."

He clapped his hands. A slave, his hair bound by a metal diadem, entered carrying a jar filled with warm water smelling of roses, in which I cleansed my hands; another offered me cakes of honey on large vine leaves; another poured out a strong black wine of Emmaus. And that his guest might not eat alone, Gamaliel cut a slice of pomegranate and with closed eyes raised to his lips a bowl in which pieces of ice floated among orange-flowers. "Now," I said as I licked my fingers, "I can carry on till midday." "May your soul rejoice," he said.

I lit a cigar and went to stand at the window. Gamaliel's house was in a high part of the city, evidently on the hill of Ophel behind the Temple; the air there was so soft and sweet that its caress sufficed to fill one's heart with peace. Below ran the new wall built by Herod the Great, and beyond flourished gardens and orchards which gave shade to the Valley of the Fountain and ascended a hill on which cool and white glistened the village of Siloe. Through a crack between the Mount of Offence and the Hill of Tumults I could see the gleam of the Dead Sea like a band of silver; then came the undulating soft mountains of Moab, their blue scarce darker than that of the sky, and a white spot which seemed to tremble in the shimmering light must be the fortress of Makeros on its rock, on the borders of Idumea.

On the grassy terrace of the house, at the foot of the city walls, a motionless figure, protected by a tall sunshade fringed with bells, was also looking towards distant Arabia, and at its side a light graceful girl with bare arms raised was calling to a flight of pigeons fluttering near. Her tunic was open to display her charming breast, and she was so pretty, brown and golden from the sun, that I was about to kiss my hand to her in the silent air when I was checked by hearing Gamaliel say, like the saffron-cloaked man on the Mount of Olives: "Yes, last night, in Bethany, Rabbi Jeschoua was arrested." Then he added slowly, with eyes half closed, as he stroked the long hairs of his beard between his fingers: "But Pontius was seized with a scruple; he was unwilling to judge a man of Galilee who is a subject of Herod Antipas; and as the Tetrarch is in Jerusalem for Easter, Pontius sent the Rabbi to him at his house at Bethesda."

Topsius' learned spectacles shone in amazement. "Strange!" he exclaimed, opening his thin arms; "Pontius seized with scruples and formalities! And since when does Pontius show this respect for the Tetrarch's jurisidiction? How many poor Galileans did he not have killed without the permission of the Tetrarch, in the Aqueduct revolt, when Roman swords by his orders mingled the blood of the men of Naphtali with that of the sacrificial bulls in the courts of the Temple?"

Gamaliel murmured gloomily: "The Roman is cruel, but he is a slave of the law."

Then Osanias, the son of Beothos, said with his soft toothless smile, as he slightly moved his hands glittering with rings on the purple cushions: "Or maybe the wife of Pontius protects the Rabbi."

Gamaliel muttered a curse on the Roman matron's immodesty; and as Topsius' spectacles questioned the venerable Osanias, he expressed surprise that the Doctor should be ignorant of what was common knowledge in the Temple and even among the shepherds of Idumea who came to sell their lambs for the sacrifice. Whenever the Rabbi preached in the Porch of Solomon by the Susa gate, Claudia came to look at him from the high terrace of the Antonia Tower, alone, wrapped in a black veil. Menahem, who during the month of Tebeth was on guard on the stair of the Gentiles, had seen the wife of Pontius wave her veil to the Rabbi. Possibly Claudia, weary of the drivers of the Circus and all the actors of Saburra and of playing with the singer Accius, wished on coming to Syria to taste the kisses of a prophet of Galilee.

The man dressed in white linen suddenly raised his face, shaking back the hood from his disheveled hair; the glance of his large blue eyes flashed through the room like lightning and was then extinguished beneath the austere humility of lowered lashes. Then he murmured, slowly and severely: "Osanias, the Rabbi is chaste."

The old man laughed heavily. The Rabbi! What of the Galilean woman of Magdala who lived in the Bezetha quarter and used to mingle with the Greek prostitutes at the doors of the theatre of Herod? And Joanna, the wife of Khosna, one of the cooks of Antipas? And another, of Ephraim, who one night, at the bidding of the Rabbi, at a mere sign of his desire, had left her loom, and left her children, and with the family savings hidden in her cloak, had followed him to Caesarea?

"O Osanias," cried, joyfully clapping his hands, the handsome man with the jewelled sword, "O son of Beothos, how well you know the details of the Galilean Rabbi's sin, the son of the grass of the field and needier than it! He might be Elius Lamma, our Imperial Legate, a curse upon him!"

The eyes of Osanias, tiny as two beads of black glass, shone in a malicious subtlety: "O Manasses, it is in order that you patriots, the true heirs of Judas of Galaunitida, should not always be able to accuse us Sadducees of only knowing what happens in the Hall of the Priests and the threshing-floors of the house of Hannan." A hoarse cough checked him for a little, choking beneath the edge of his cloak in which he had swiftly wrapped himself. Then he added more quietly, with patches of red in his flour-hued face: "And indeed it was in the house of Hannan that we heard Menahem say this as we walked beneath the vines. He even told us that this Rabbi of Galilee carries his immodesty so far as to touch pagan women and others more unclean than pigs. A Levite saw him on the road to Sichem rise suddenly from behind the border of a well with a woman of Samaria."

The man dressed in white linen sprang up erect and trembling; and in the cry which escaped from him there was the horror of one who has witnessed the desecration of an altar. But Gamaliel with dry authority fixed his hard eyes upon him: "O Gad, the Rabbi is thirty and unmarried. What is his occupation? Where is the field he ploughs? Has anyone ever seen his vineyard? He wanders along the roads and lives on what he receives from dissolute women. What else do the beardless boys of Sybaris and Lesbos who spend their days in the Via Judiciaria and whom you Essenians loathe so that you run to wash your garments in a cistern if one of them touches you as he passes? You heard what Osanias, the son of Beothos said; only Jehovah is great, and verily I say to you that when Rabbi Jeschoua, despising the law, bestows on the adulterous a pardon which enchants the simple, he is acting out of the weakness of his morals, not out of the abundance of his mercy."

Waving his arms in the air, with burning face Gad cried: "But the Rabbi works miracles!"

And it was the celebrated Manasses who in calm disdain answered the Essenian: "Calm yourself, Gad. Others have wrought miracles. Simon of Samaria works miracles, so did Apollonius, and Gabbienus. And what are the wonders of your Galilean compared with those of the daughters of the High Priest Anius and those of the learned Rabbi Chekina?"

And Osanias scoffed at Gad's simplicity: "What verily do you Essenians learn in your oasis of Engaddi? Miracles! The very pagans work miracles. Go to Alexandria, to the right of the harbor of Eunotus, where stands the papyrus factory, and you will see the magi working miracles for a drachma, which is a workman's daily wage. If miracles are a proof of divinity, then is the fish Oannes divine, whose scales are of mother of pearl and who preaches on the banks of the Euphrates in nights of the full moon."

Gad's smile was proud and gentle. His anger had died away under the immensity of his disdain. He slowly took a step forward, then another, and considering in pity those dull, hard-hearted mocking men, he said: "You talk and your talk is empty as the buzz of flies. You talk without having heard him. In green and fertile Galilee when he spoke it seemed as if a fountain of milk was flowing through a parched and famished land; even the light seemed a blessing of new worth. The waters of the lake of Tiberias grew calm to listen, and the eyes of the children around him became grave with a sure faith. He spoke, and as doves opening their wings in flight from the door of a sanctuary, we saw all manner of noble holy things come from his lips to fly over the nations of the earth: Charity, Fraternity, Justice,

Mercy and new forms of Love, divinely fair." His face shone, raised heavenward as though to follow the flight of this love divine.

But already Gamaliel, the Doctor of Law, was contradicting him with harsh authority: "What is there original or individual in those ideas, man? Do you think the Rabbi drew them out of the abundance of his heart? If you wish to hear about Love and Charity and Equality, read the Book of Jesus, the son of Sidrach. All that was preached by Hillel, all that was spoken by Schemaia. These excellent precepts are to be found in the books of the pagans, which compared with ours, are as the mud beneath the pure water of Siloe. You Essenians yourselves have better precepts. The Rabbis of Babylonia, of Alexandria, have always taught the pure law of Justice and Equality. And your friend Jokanan taught them: he whom you call the Baptist and who came to a miserable end in a dungeon at Makeros."

"Jokanan!" cried Gad, shuddering, as though roughly awakened from a pleasant dream. His gleaming eyes became moist. Thrice bowing towards the ground with open arms, he repeated the name of Jokanan, as though evoking the dead. Then, as two tears rolled down his beard, he said very low, as if it were a secret that filled him with terror and faith: "It was I who went up to Makeros to fetch the Baptist's head; and as I came down the path with the head wrapped in my cloak, she, Herodias, like a lascivious tigress, bent over the wall and howled and shouted insults at me. Three days and nights I went along the roads of Galilee, holding his head hanging by the hair. Sometimes an angel all in black would appear from behind a rock and open its wings and begin to walk at my side." Again his head was bowed, his knees sounded on the pavement, and he remained prostrate, praying eagerly, his arms extended in the form of a cross.

Then Gamaliel went up to the learned Topsius and, standing straight as a column of the Temple, his elbows close against his waist and the palms of his thin hands raised, he said: "We have a law, and our law is clear. It is the word of the Lord, and the Lord said: I am Jehovah, the everlasting, the first and the last, who transfers to

others neither His name nor His glory; before Me there was no God,
with Me there is no other God, and there shall be no God after Me.
That is the word of the Lord. And the Lord said also: If therefore a
prophet or seer arise among you working miracles and attempting
to introduce another God and call the simple to worship him, that
prophet or that seer shall die. That is the law, that is the word of the
Lord. Now the Rabbi of Nazareth proclaimed himself God in Galilee
in the synagogues, in the streets of Jerusalem, in the holy courts of
the Temple. The Rabbi must die."

But the celebrated Manasses, whose languid eyes had grown dark
as a thundery sky, placed himself between the Doctor of the Law
and the historian of the Herods, and nobly repelled the cruel letter
of the law: "No, no. What matters it if the lamp on a tomb declares
that it is the sun? What matter if a man open his arms and cry that
he is a god? Our laws are mild, and for such a trifle one need not
fetch the executioner from his den in Gareb." In my charity I was
about to praise Manasses, but already he was shouting with violent
fervor: "Yet must that Rabbi of Galilee assuredly die, for he is a bad
citizen and a bad Jew. Did we not hear him advising us to pay tribute to Caesar? The Rabbi extends his hand to Rome and does not
regard the Roman as his enemy. He has been preaching for three
years and no one has heard him proclaim the sacred duty of expel-
ling the foreigner. We wait for a Messiah to come with a sword to
free Israel, and this man, full of foolish words, tells us that he brings
us the bread of truth. When there is a Roman Praetor in Jerusalem,
and Roman spears on guard at the doors of the Temple of our God,
what is the use of this visionary talking of the bread of heaven and
the wine of truth? The only useful truth is that there must be no
Romans in Jerusalem."

Osanias was restlessly looking towards the glowing window
whence sounded the fiery threats of Manasses. Gamaliel was smiling
coldly, and the fervent disciple of Judas of Gamala shouted with
passionate enthusiasm: "O verily I say to you that to beguile men's
souls with the hope of heaven is to make them forget their certain duty in the kingdom of earth, in this land of Israel in chains

which weeps and will not be comforted. The Rabbi is a traitor to his country. The Rabbi must die." Trembling, he had seized his sword; a gleam of rebellion filled his eyes, in eagerness for battle and the endurance of torture.

Then Osanias arose, learning on his cane with its knob of gold. A sorrow seemed now to cloud his gay old age, and he began to speak, gently and sadly, as one who in the presence of enthusiasm and the law points to the ineluctable decree of necessity: "Certainly, certainly it matters little that a visionary should call himself the Messiah and the Son of God and threaten to destroy the Law and the Temple. Law and Temple can afford to smile and forgive, certain that they are eternal. But, O Manasses, our laws are mild, and I do not think that one should go to call the executioner in Gareb because a Rabbi of Galilee, mindful of the sons of Judas of Gamala nailed to the cross, advises a malicious prudence in our relations with the Roman. Strong are your hands, O Manasses, but can they divert the stream of Jordan from the land of Canaan into the land of Trakaunitida? No. Nor can you prevent the legions of Caesar, which overran the cities of Greece, from overrunning Judah. Wise and strong was Judas the Maccabean, yet he made peace with Rome. For Rome on the earth is like a mighty wind. When it blows, the foolish man opposes his breast and is overthrown, but the wise man retires quietly to his house. Unconquerable seemed Galatia; Philip and Perseus had great armies in the plain; Antiochus the Great commanded one hundred and twenty elephants, and war chariots innumerable. Rome passed, and where are they? Slaves are they, paying tribute."

He bent forward heavily, as an ox beneath the yoke; then fixing upon us his small eyes, from which darted a cold inexorable gleam, he continued in the same faint gentle manner: "But verily I tell you that this Rabbi of Galilee must die. It is the duty of one who owns earthly goods and crops to stamp out with his sandal on the stones of his threshing-floor the spark which threatens to set fire to his corn. With the Roman in Jerusalem, anyone proclaiming himself Messiah as he of Galilee is harmful and dangerous to Israel. The Roman does not understand his promise of the kingdom of heaven, but sees that these sermons, this divine exaltation, moves the people darkly in the porticoes of the Temple, and he says: Truly this Temple, with its gold and its zealous crowds, is a danger to the authority of Caesar in Judea; and he proceeds gradually to diminish the strength of the Temple by diminishing its riches and the privileges of the priesthood. Already to our shame the priestly vestments are kept in the treasury of the Antonia Tower; soon it will be the golden candelabra. The Praetor, in order to impoverish us, has already appropriated the money of Corban; soon he will take the tithes of the crops, of the flocks, of the offerings, the tribute, all the taxes, all the possessions of the priesthood, of the trumpets, even the meat of the sacrifice will cease to belong to us. And we shall be left with our staffs to go as beggars along the roads of Samaria in wait for the rich merchants of Decapola. Verily I say to you that if we wish to retain the honors and treasures which are ours by the ancient law and are the splendor of Israel, we must display to the Roman who is watching us a quiet well-ordered submissive contented Temple, without too much zeal and without Messiahs. The Rabbi must die." Thus before me spoke Osanias, the son of Beothos, member of the Sanhedrin.

Then the thin historian of the Herods, reverently crossing his hands upon his breast, saluted thrice those eloquent men. Gad was praying, motionless. In the blue square of the window a honey-colored bee was buzzing about the honeysuckle. And Topsius said pompously: "Men who have bidden me welcome, truth abounds in your spirits as grapes upon the vine. You are three towers guarding Israel among the nations: one defends the unity of religion, another maintains the enthusiasm of patriotism, the third, even thou, venerable son of Beothos, cautious and flexible as the serpent beloved of Solomon, protects something even more precious — namely, Order. You are three towers, and against each the Rabbi raises his arms and throws the first stone. But you guard Israel and its God and its possessions and will not suffer yourselves to be overthrown. Verily, I now realize, Jesus and Judaism could never live together."

And Gamaliel, with the gesture of one who breaks a fragile wand, said, showing his white teeth: "That is why we crucify him." The words were like a knife of steel buried gleaming and hissing in my breast. Anxiously I seized the sleeve of the learned historian: "Topsius, Topsius, who is this Rabbi who preached in Israel and works miracles and is to be crucified?" The learned doctor opened his eyes in as much astonishment as though I had asked him what was the luminary that brings the light of day from behind the mountains, and answered dryly: "Rabbi Jeschoua bar Josepha who came from Nazareth in Galilee, whom some call Jesus and others also Christ." "Ours!" I cried, swaying as a man stunned. And my Catholic knees nearly fell upon the floor, in the impulse to remain there enveloped in my fear, praying desperately and for ever. But straightway the desire surged through me to run to meet Him and set my mortal eyes on the person of my Lord, on His real human body, dressed in linen as other men, covered with the dust that rises from the ways of men. And at the same time, more tremulous than a leaf in a harsh wind, my soul was filled with a dread fear, the fear of the careless servant before the just master.

Was I sufficiently cleansed by fasts and prayers to dare to look upon the radiant countenance of my God? No. O mean and bitter slackness of my devotion! I had never kissed with sufficient love the red wounded foot in the Graça church. Alas, on how many Sundays, in that unregenerate time when Adelia, the sun of my existence, was waiting for me smoking cigarettes in the Travessa dos Caldas, had I not cursed the slowness of the Mass and the monotony of the service? And being thus a crust of sin from head to heel, how could my body fail to fall reprobate and condemned when the two globes of the eyes of the Lord, like the two halves of heaven, turned slowly upon me? And yet to *see* Jesus! To see the color of His hair, and how His tunic was fastened, and what happened upon earth when His lips opened! Beyond those terraces where women were scattering grain for the doves, in one of those streets from which sounded clearly the rhythmic cry of the sellers of unleavened bread, perhaps Jesus my Savior was passing at this terrible moment between grave bearded Roman soldiers, His hands bound with a cord. The slow breeze which swayed the honeysuckle at the window, bringing out its scent, had perhaps just touched the forehead of my God, already pierced with thorns. I had only to push open that cedar door and cross the court where the mill-wheel of the private mill was groaning, in order to see in the street the bodily presence of my God as really and well as St. John and St. Matthew had seen it. I would follow His sacred shadow on the white wall, on which my shadow would also lie. In the dust I trod I would kiss His recent footsteps. And, smothering with both hands the beating of my heart, I would surprise on His divine lips a groan, a sob, a complaint, a promise. I should thus know a new word of Christ unwritten in the Gospels, and I alone would have the priestly privilege of repeating it to the prostrate multitudes. My authority would arise in the Church like a Newest Testament. I would be an unpublished proof of the Passion. I would become St. Theodoric the Evangelist. Then, with a desperate eagerness which amazed those quiet-mannered Orientals, I cried: "Where can I see Him? Where is Jesus of Nazareth, my Lord?"

At this instant a slave, running lightly on the tips of his sandals, fell prostrate on the pavement at the feet of Gamaliel; he kissed the fringe of his tunic as his thin ribs heaved; at last he murmured in exhaustion: "Master, the Rabbi is in the Praetorium." Gad left his praying and, with the leap of a wild beast, tightened the cord of knots round his waist and set off at a fierce run, his hood thrown back, his fair disheveled locks flying wild about him. Topsius had donned his white cloak folded like a Latin toga in which he resembled a marble statue, and, having compared the hospitality of Gamaliel to that of Abraham, he shouted to me triumphantly: "To the Praetorium!"

For long I followed Topsius breathlessly through old Jerusalem, wrapped in my tumultuous thoughts. We passed by a garden of roses of the time of the Prophets, splendid and silent, guarded by two Levites with gilt spears. Then came a cool street scented by the shops of the perfumers with their signs in the shape of flowers and mortars; an awning of fine mats shaded the doors; the floor was

watered and strewn with fresh grass and flowers of anemone; and
in the shade lolled languid youths with carefully trimmed locks and
paint around their eyes, scarcely able to raise in their hands, heavy
with rings, their flowing silken tunics of cherry or gold.

Beyond this lazy street was a square baking in the sun, in which
our feet sank in a thick white dust; in its center an ancient solitary palm-tree towered beneath its tuft of branches, motionless as
if cut in bronze; and at the further end gleamed the black columns
of granite of the ancient palace of Herod. This was the Praetorium.
In front of the entrance arch, where two legionaries of Syria were
on guard, with black plumes in their shining helmets, a band of
girls with roses in their ears and baskets of esparto grass in their
laps were crying their loaves of unleavened bread. Under an enormous sunshade of feathers fixed in the ground, men in felt caps
with boards on their knees and scales were exchanging Roman
money; and the water-sellers with their shaggy water-skins cried
their tremulous cry.

We went in, and terror at once overcame me. The bright court
was open to the blue sky, and paved with marble. On either side rose
a terrace with balustrade supported on an arcade cool and echoing,
like the cloister of a convent. From the arcade at the farther end, surmounted by the austere front of the palace, stretched a scarlet awning fringed with gold, forming a sharp square of shadow and sustained by two stakes of sycamore tipped with lotus-flowers. Here
was a dense knot of people; one could see the tunics of Pharisees,
edged with blue, the rough serge smocks of workmen, bound with
a leather girdle, the huge grey and white striped cloaks of the men
of Galilee, and the crimson cape with its large hoods of the merchants of Tiberias; a few women, outside the shadow thrown by the
awning, were standing on the tips of their yellow shoes, holding a
fold of their light cloaks over their faces against the sun; and from
the crowd came a warm smell of sweat and myrrh.

Beyond, above the serried white turbans, gleamed the tips of
spears; and at the farther end, on a throne, a man, a magistrate,

wrapped in the noble folds of the toga and motionless as marble, was leaning his thick grey beard on his strong hand; his deep-sunk eyes seemed indolently asleep; his hair was bound by a scarlet riband; and behind him, on a pedestal which formed a back to his curule chair, the bronze figure of the Roman Wolf wryly opened its voracious maw.

I asked Topsius the name of the melancholy magistrate. "A certain Pontius, called Pilate, who was Prefect of Batavia." I walked slowly about the court, striving as in a temple to muffle the sound of my footsteps. A deep silence fell from the gleaming sky; only at times, from one of the gardens, came the harsh sad cry of the peacocks. Lying on the ground by the parapet of the cloister, naked Negroes slumbered face upwards in the sun; an old woman was counting her copper coins, crouching over her basket of fruit. On scaffolding placed against a column, men were at work mending the roof; and children in a corner were playing with iron disks which clinked faintly on the flags.

Suddenly a familiar figured touched the historian of the Herods on the shoulder. It was the handsome Manasses, and with him was a splendid old man, noble as a high priest, the sleeve of whose jacket, embroidered with green vine-leaves, Topsius reverently kissed. A snowy beard, shining with oil, fell to the sash at his waist, and his broad shoulders disappeared beneath the careless abundance of his white hair, which fell from beneath his turban like a stream of royal ermine. One of his hands, covered with rings, rested on a strong cane of ivory; by the other he led a pale child whose eyes were fairer than the stars and who at the old man's side seemed a lily in the shade of a cedar-tree.

"Go up to the gallery," said Manasses; "you will find it cool and restful."

We followed the patriot, and I secretly inquired of Topsius who was the old man of the fine presence. "Rabbi Robam," whispered my learned friend respectfully; "one of the lights of the Sanhedrin, learned and subtle exceedingly and a confidante of Caiaphas." Reverently I thrice saluted Rabbi Robam, who had seated himself on a marble bench and was pensively fondling on his patriarchal breast the child's head, yellow as maize of Joppa.

We went slowly along the bright sounding gallery; at its farther end shone a sumptuous door of cedar-wood encrusted with silver; a sleepy Praetorian of Caesarea was on guard before it, resting on his tall wicker shield. Eagerly I went to the balustrade, and straightway my mortal eyes saw there below my God in human form. But, oh, surprising changes of man's soul, I felt neither ecstasy nor fear. It seemed as if suddenly the long weary centuries of history and religion had dropped from my mind.

It did not occur to me that that spare dark man was the Redeemer of mankind. I became strangely anterior in time. I was no longer Teodorico Raposo, a Christian Bachelor of Law; my identity had fallen from me like a cloak as we hurried from the house of Gamaliel. The antiquity of the things around me had infused into me a new being, and I too had become one of the ancients. I was Theodoricus, a Lusitanian, who had come from the sounding shores of the Great Promontory and was travelling in the reign of Tiberius through lands tributary to Rome. And the man before me was not Jesus nor Christ nor the Messiah, but a young man of Galilee who, filled with a great dream, had come down from his green village to transform the world and renew the kingdom of heaven; and an elder of the Temple had bound him and sent him to the Praetor on an audience day, between a thief who had robbed on the Sichem road and another who had used his knife in a quarrel at Emath.

In a space paved with mosaics, in front of the Praetor's curule chair under the Roman Wolf, stood Jesus with His hands crossed and lightly bound by a cord which fell to the ground. An ample cloak of coarse wool, striped in brown and edged with a fringe of blue, fell to His feet, and He wore sandals worn by the ways of the desert and tied with thongs of leather. His brow was not pierced by that inhuman crown of thorns of which I had read in the Gospels; it was covered with a white turban formed of a long roll of linen, the ends of which fell over either shoulder; he was bound by a cord under his pointed curly beard. His unanointed hair, brushed back behind his ears, fell in curls on his back; and in his thin sunburnt face, under the long continuous line of the thick eyebrows, his black eyes gleamed with infinite depth and splendor. He did not move, but stood strong and calm before the Praetor. Only a tremor of His bound hands betrayed the tumult of His heart, and at times He drew a deep breath as though His breast, accustomed to the clear free air of the hills and lakes of Galilee, was stifled among those marbles, under that heavy Roman awning and by the narrow formalism of the law.

At one side Sareas, a member of the Sanhedrin, having set his cloak and gilt stick on the ground, was unrolling and reading a dark scroll of parchment in a sleepy rhythmic murmur. Seated on a bench, the Roman assessor, stifled by the strong heat of the month of Nizzam, was cooling with a fan of dry ivy-leaves his clean-shaven face, white as plaster; at a stone table covered with tablets and iron rulers, a scribe, old and stout, was carefully sharpening his pens; and between the two the interpreter, a beardless Phoenician, smiled as he looked up, both hands in his girdle, and bent forward his chest, on the linen jacket of which was painted a red parrot. Doves kept flying about the awning. It was thus that I saw Jesus of Galilee bound before the Roman Praetor.

Meanwhile Sareas, having rolled the dark parchment round its iron stick, saluted Pilate, kissed the ring on his finger to impress on his lips the seal of truth, and immediately began a harangue in Greek, full of verbose flattery and quotation of texts. He spoke of the Tetrarch of Galilee, the noble Antipas, praised his prudence, exalted his father, the great Herod, restorer of the Temple. The glory of Herod filled the earth; he was terrible and ever faithful to the Caesars; his son Antipas was subtle and strong. Recognizing his wisdom, he wondered that the Tetrarch should have refused to confirm the sentence of the Sanhedrin condemning Jesus to death. Was not that sentence based on the laws of the Lord? The just Hannan had questioned the Rabbi, who had maintained an insulting silence. Was that the way to answer the learned, the noble, the pious Hannan? In his zeal a man had been unable to restrain himself and had slapped the Rabbi in the face. Where was the respect of former times, and the reverence for the priesthood?

His great hollow voice echoed incessantly. I was yawning with weariness. Beneath us two men squatting on the pavement were eating dates of Bathabara and drinking from a flask. Pilate, his chin resting in his hand, was looking sleepily at his scarlet boots sprinkled with stars of gold. Sareas was now proclaiming the rights of the Temple. It was the pride of the nation, the chosen abode of the Lord. Caesar Augustus had presented it with shields and vessels of gold. How had the Rabbi respected the Temple? He had threatened to destroy it! "I will overthrow the Temple of Jehovah and build it again in three days." Pure witnesses, hearing that fierce profanity, had covered their heads with ashes to ward off the wrath of the Lord. Blasphemy against the Sanctuary affected the very person of God.

Under the awning the Pharisees and Scribes, the Nethenins of the Temple, sordid slaves, were whispering together like wild shrubs moved by the wind. And Jesus continued motionless, absent and indifferent, with closed eyes, as though the better to isolate his constant lovely dream from the harsh vain things that defiled it.

Then the Roman assessor rose, laid on his desk his fan of leaves, skillfully arranged his blue-edged gown, thrice saluted the Praetor, and his delicate hand began to wave in the air, so that the jewel on it flashed.

"What does he say?"

"Exceedingly clever things," murmured Topsius. "He is a pedant, but he is right. He says that the Praetor is not a Jew, knows nothing about Jehovah, and cares nothing about the prophets who rise against Jehovah; and that the sword of Caesar does not avenge gods who do not protect Caesar. The Roman is ingenious."

Out of breath, the assessor fell back languidly in his chair, and Sareas at once began to speak, shaking his arms towards the crowd of Pharisees as though calling for their protests and taking refuge in their strength. More loudly now he accused Jesus, not of His revolt against Jehovah and the Temple, but for His pretensions as a prince of the House of David. All the inhabitants of Jerusalem had seen Him four days ago enter by the Golden Gate, in a stolen triumph amid green palm branches, surrounded by a crowd of Galileans crying: "Hosanna to the Son of David! Hosanna to the King of Israel!" "He is the Son of David, come to make us better!" cried, afar off, the voice of Gad, full of enthusiasm and love.

But of a sudden the fringed sleeves of Sareas remained glued to his sides, and he became dumb and stiff as the shaft of a spear; the stout Roman scribe, standing up, with his hands resting on the table, reverently bent his neck forward; the assessor smiled respectfully. The Praetor was about to question the Rabbi, and, trembling, I saw a legionary push Jesus, who raised His head. Slightly leaning towards the Rabbi, with hands open as though to let fall from them all interest in this ritual case of argumentative ruffians, Pontius murmured, bored and doubtful: "Art thou, then, the king of the Jews? Those of thy nation bring thee before me. What hast thou done? Where is thy kingdom?" The interpreter, self-satisfied, standing by the marble throne, repeated these words very loud in the ancient Hebraic language of the Holy Books; and as the Rabbi remained silent, he shouted them in the Chaldaic tongue spoken in Galilee.

Then Jesus made a step forward. I heard His voice. It was clear, assured, authoritative, serene: "My kingdom is not here. If it were the will of My Father that I should be king in Israel, I should not be standing before thee with hands bound. But My kingdom is not of this world."

A shout broke forth fiercely: Then take him from this world. And forthwith, as wood ready to be set afire by a spark, the fury of the Pharisees and of the servants of the Temple burst forth, crackling in a clamor of impatience: Crucify him, crucify him!

Pompously the interpreter translated the cries into Greek for the Praetor's benefit, the tumultuous cries uttered in the Syriac language spoken by the people of Judea. Pontius beat his boot against the marble. The two lictors raised into the air their staffs surmounted by the Roman eagle; the scribe shouted the name of Tiberius Caesar;

and straightway the frenzied arms were lowered and a terror seemed to reign before the majesty of the Roman People.

Again Pilate spoke, slow and hesitating: "Thou sayest thou art a king. And what dost thou here?"

Jesus made another step forward towards the Praetor. His sandal rested strongly on the pavement, as though it had taken possession of the earth. And the words that came from His trembling lips seemed to live and shine in the air, like the splendor which came from His black eyes, "I came into this world to bear witness to the truth. He who desires the truth, he who wishes to belong to the truth, must listen to My voice."

Pilate considered for a moment thoughtfully; then, shrugging his shoulders, he said: "But man, what is the truth?"

Jesus of Nazareth was silent, and through the Praetorium a silence spread as though all hearts had stopped beating, suddenly filled with doubt. Then, slowly gathering up his immense toga, Pilate descended the four bronze steps and, preceded by the lictors and followed by the assessor, penetrated into the palace amid the sound of arms as the legionaries saluted him by beating their iron spearheads against their bronze shields.

Immediately from all sides of the court arose a harsh fervent buzzing as of irritated bees. Sareas was finishing his speech, brandishing his stick amid Pharisees who were clasping their hands in dismay. Others whispered gloomily apart. A tall old man, with floating black cloak, ran anxiously through the Praetorium among those who lay sleeping in the sun and among the sellers of unleavened bread, crying: Israel is lost! And I saw fanatical Levites tear the tassels from their tunics as for some public calamity.

Gad appeared before us, raising triumphant arms: The Praetor is just and will set the Rabbi free. And with face aglow he told us his sweet hopes. The Rabbi, as soon as freed, would leave Jerusalem where the stones were not so hard as the hearts of men; his friends, armed, were awaiting him in Bethany, and they would start as the moon rose for the oasis of Engaddi. There dwelt those who loved him. Was not Jesus the brother of the Essenians? Like them the Rabbi preached contempt for earthly possessions, compassion for the poor, and the incomparable beauty of the kingdom of God.

I was rejoicing credulously, when the gallery, which a slave was watering, was invaded in tumult by a dark band of Pharisees hastening to the stone seat on which Rabbi Robam was conversing with Manasses, while his fingers gently stroked the child's hair, yellower than maize. Topsius and I ran towards the crowd of fanatics. Sareas in their midst, bowing the firmness of a command, was already saying: Rabbi Robam, it is necessary that you should go to speak to the Praetor and save our law. And at once from all sides arose an anxious supplication: Rabbi, speak to the Praetor. Rabbi, save Israel. Slowly the old man rose, majestic as Moses; and before him a Levite, very pale, murmured, trembling, with bending knees: "Rabbi, you are just, learned, perfect and strong before the Lord."

Rabbi Robam raised both hands palm upwards to heaven, and all bowed themselves as though the spirit of Jehovah, in answer to that silent invocation, had descended to fill the heart of that just man. Then, with the child's hand in his, he moved away, and after him sounded the sandals of the crowd as they passed along the marble pavement.

We came to a stop all together before the door of cedar-wood, where the Praetorian had set down his spear, after beating upon the rings of silver. A tribune of the palace came with a long vine-branch in his hand; within was a cold room, badly lighted and austere, with dark stucco covering the walls. In the center stood a pale statue of Augustus, its pedestal strewn with wreaths of bay and votive boughs; two great torch-holders of bronze gleamed in shadow in the corner of the room. None of the Jews entered, since to tread on pagan soil upon a paschal day was an unclean act before the Lord.

Sareas announced haughtily to the tribune that certain men of the nation of Israel at the door of the palace of their fathers awaited the Praetor. A nervous silence followed. But now two lictors advanced, and immediately behind them, coming forward with long steps, his immense toga folded on his breast, appeared Pilate. All the turbans bowed saluting the Procurator of Judea. He paused by the statue of Augustus, and as though in imitation of the noble gesture of the marble figure, extended his hand which held a roll of parchment and said: "May peace be with you and with your words. Speak."

Sareas, secretary of the Sanhedrin, came forward and declared that their hearts were indeed full of peace, but that as the Praetor had left the Praetorium without confirming or annulling the sentence of the Sanhedrin on Jesus the son of Joseph, they were as men who see grapes on a vine which neither wither nor ripen. Pontius seemed to me all equity and mercy. "I questioned your prisoner," he said, "and found in him no fault for the Procurator of Judea to punish. Herod Antipas, who is prudent and strong, who observes your law and prays in your Temple, also questioned him and found no fault in him. He merely makes incoherent remarks as they who speak in a dream. His hands are innocent of blood, nor do I know that he has trespassed upon his neighbor's land. Caesar is no merciless master. The man is simply a visionary."

Then, with a gloomy murmur, all fell back, leaving Rabbi Robam alone on the threshold of the Roman hall. A jewel gleamed trembling on the top of his tiara; his white hair, falling over his great shoulders, crowned him with majesty, as snows crown a mountain; the blue fringe of his ample cloak swept the pavement. Slowly, calmly, as if he were explaining the law to his disciples, he raised his hand and spoke: "Official of Caesar, Pontius, most just and wise. The man you call a visionary has for years offended all our laws and blasphemed against our God. But when did we arrest him, when did we bring him before you? Only when we saw him enter in triumph by the Golden Gate, acclaimed as the King of Judea. For Judea has no king but Tiberias, and when a rebel proclaims himself openly against Caesar we hasten to punish him. Thus we act who have no orders from Caesar and receive nothing from his treasury; and are you, Caesar's official, unwilling that a rebel against your master should be punished?"

Blood mounted in a flash to the long face of Pilate, usually soft and sleepy. That duplicity of the Jews who execrated Rome and now affirmed their fierce zeal for Caesar in order to be able, under cover of his authority, to satisfy their priestly hate, revolted his Roman rectitude, and the audacious admonishment was intolerable to his pride. Haughtily he exclaimed, with a gesture as though shaking them from him: "Stay. The procurators of Caesar do not come to learn their duties towards Caesar from a barbarous colony in Asia."

Manasses, who was pulling his beard impatiently at my side, strode away in indignation. I trembled; but the proud Rabbi continued, more indifferent to Pilate's anger than to the bleating of a lamb dragged to the altar: "What would Caesar's procurator in Alexandria do if a visionary were to descend from Bubastes and proclaim himself King of Egypt? That which you are unwilling to do in this barbarous land of Asia. Your master gives you a vineyard to guard, and will you allow men to enter it and take the grapes? Why, then, are you in Judea? Why is the Sixth Legion in the Antonia Tower? But our mind is clear, and our voice clear and loud enough, Pontius, to reach Caesar's ears."

Pontius took a step slowly towards the door; and with flashing eyes fastened upon those Jews who were so astutely enmeshing him in the subtle coils of their religious rancor, he murmured hoarsely: "I do not fear your intrigues. Elius Lamma is my friend, and Caesar knows me well."

"You see what is not in our hearts," said Rabbi Robam, as calm as though he were conversing in the shade of his orchard, "but we see clearly what is in yours, Pontius. What matters to you the life or the death of a Galilean vagabond? If, as you say, you are unwilling to avenge a god whose divinity you do not respect, how can you be willing to save a prophet whose prophecies you do not believe? Your device is of a different kind, O Roman: you wish for the destruction of Judah."

A shudder of anger, of pious passion, ran through the Pharisees; some felt the breasts of their tunics as if in search of a weapon. And Rabbi Robam continued to denounce the Praetor, slowly and serenely: "You wish to allow to go unpunished a man who preached revolt and proclaimed himself king in a province of Caesar in order by his impunity to incite other stronger ambitions and encourage another Judas of Gamala to attack the garrisons of Samaria. Thus do you prepare a pretext to bring down the imperial sword upon us and utterly extinguish the national life of Judea. You desire to have a revolt to crush out in blood and then to present yourself to Caesar as a victorious soldier, a wise administrator, worthy of a proconsulship or a command in Italy. Is this what you call Roman faith? I was never in Italy but I know that there it is called Punic faith. But do not think that we are as simple as a shepherd of Idumea. We are at peace with Caesar and perform our duty in condemning a man who rebelled against Caesar. You are unwilling to perform yours by confirming our sentence? Very well, we will send messengers to Rome with our sentence and your refusal, and, having denied our responsibility, we will show Caesar how the representative of the law of the Empire proceeds in Judea. And now, Praetor, you may return to the Praetorium."

"And remember the votive shields," cried Sareas; "perhaps once more you will find Caesar's approval fall in an unexpected quarter."

Pontius lowered his face in confusion. Certainly he must have been imagining he saw far away, on a bright terrace by the sea of Caprea, Sejanus, Cesonius, all his enemies, speaking in Caesar's ear and pointing to the messengers from the Temple. Caesar, always restless and distrustful, would at once suspect a conspiracy between him and this King of the Jews to cause the rebellion of a rich imperial province. And thus his justice and pride in maintaining it might cost him the procuratorship of Judea. Pride and justice then became in his weak spirit as waves which, after racing high for an instant, fall and melt away.

He came to the threshold of the door, slowly, opening his arms, as though impelled by a magnanimous desire of conciliation, his face as white as his toga: "I have governed Judea for seven years. Have you ever found me unjust or unfaithful to my sworn promise? Your threats have no power over me: Caesar knows me well. But for Caesar's sake there must be no dissension between me and you; I have always been ready to make concessions; I have respected your laws more than any other procurator since Coponius. When the two men of Samaria defiled your Temple, did I not have them executed? Between us there must be no disagreement or bitter words." He hesitated an instant, then slowly rubbing his hands and shaking them as though wet with unclean water, he added: "Do you desire the life of this visionary? What matter is it to me? Take it. Are you not satisfied with his scourging but wish the cross also? Crucify him. But it is not I who shed his blood."

The thin Levite cried passionately: "It is we, his blood be upon our heads." And some shivered at his words, in their belief that all words possess a supernatural power and can give a real life to thoughts. Pontius had left the hall; the decurion, after saluting, closed the door of cedar-wood. Then Rabbi Robam turned round, and calm, with the radiant look of the just as he advanced among the Pharisees, who stooped to kiss the fringe of his tunic, he murmured, grave and gentle: "It is better that one man should suffer than a whole nation."

Wiping the drops of sweat from my brow, I fell trembling upon a seat; and in my weariness I indistinctly perceived in the Praetorium two legionaries with belts unbuckled drinking from a great iron bowl which a Negro kept filling from a skin hanging from his shoulder; farther on, a strong handsome woman was sitting in the sun, her children at her breast; and farther on still stood a shepherd wrapped in skins, who was laughing and showing the bloodstains on his arm. Then I closed my eyes; for an instant I thought of the candle which I had left burning, red and smoky, by my bed in the tent, and then a light sleep overcame me.

When I awoke, the curule chair was still empty, with in front of it on the marble the purple cushion trampled by the Praetor's feet, and an even denser crowd filled the ancient court of the Herods with the rumor of an armed camp. There were rough men in short serge capes so dusty that they seemed to have been used as mats on the flags of a public square. Some held scales in their hands and doves in cages; and thin sordid women who followed them cursed the

Rabbi from afar with trembling arms. Others, meanwhile, walking on the tips of their sandals, were crying in a low voice small things of worth for sale, wrapped in the folds of their cloaks: grains of roast barley, pots of ointment, corals, bracelets of filigree of Sidron.

I inquired of Topsius, and my learned friend, wiping his spectacles, explained that these must be the merchants against whom, on Easter Eve, Jesus with raised stick had insisted on the fulfillment of the law which forbids profane sellers in the Temple outside the Portico of Solomon. "Another imprudence of the Rabbi, Dom Raposo," ironically murmured the acute historian.

Meanwhile, as the sixth hour of the Jews had come and work was over, workmen came in, stained with scarlet or blue, from the neighboring dye-works; scribes of the synagogues arrived with their tablets under their arms; gardeners with sickles round their necks and sprays of myrtle in their turbans; tailors with long iron needles hanging from their ears; Phoenician musicians in a corner were tuning their harps and drawing wails from their clay flutes; and in front of us two Greek prostitutes from Tiberias, with yellow wigs, were showing the tips of their tongues and puffing out their skirts, from which came a scent of marjoram.

The legionaries, their spears across their breasts, formed a circle of iron round Jesus, and I could now only with difficulty distinguish the Rabbi in the midst of the murmuring crowd, in which the harsh accents of Moab and the desert sounded amid the grave soft Chaldean tongue. Under the gallery a melancholy bell was tinkling. It was a gardener who in a basket of esparto grass on vine-leaves was offering for sale bursting figs of Bethphage. Weak from past emotion, I bent over the balustrade and asked him the price of that choice fruit of the orchards praised in the Gospel. And the man, laughing, stretched out his arms as though he had found the long-desired: "Between me and thee, O creature of abundance from beyond the sea, what are a few figs? Jehovah bids brothers exchange presents and blessings. This fruit I gathered one by one in the hour when the day rises on Hebron; sweet are they and refreshing, worthy indeed of Hannan's table. But what need of words between me and thee if our hearts understand one another? Take these figs, the best in all Syria, and the Lord load thy mother with every blessing."

I knew that this offer was the consecrated form of politeness in buying and selling since the time of the Patriarchs, and I fulfilled my part of the formality and declared that Jehovah, the most Mighty, ordered me to pay for the fruits of the earth with money coined by the princes; then the gardener bowed his head, accepting the divine command, and, setting his basket on the ground and taking a fig in each of his black earthy hands, he exclaimed: "Verily Jehovah is the most Mighty. If He orders, I must put a price on this fruit of His bounty; sweeter than the lips of a Bride. It is just, therefore, O man of abundance, that for these two figs, so fresh and scented, that fill my palms, you should give me one good traphik."

Magnificent God of Judea! The eloquent Hebrew was asking for each fig a sixpence of my native money. "Avaunt, thief!" I shouted, and then, tempted by greed, I offered him a drachma for all the figs that could be contained in a turban. The man raised his hands to the breast of his tunic as though to rend it in his infinite humiliation, and was about to invoke Jehovah and Elias and all the prophets to protect him when the wise Topsius intervened with abrupt annoy-ance, showing him a small disk of iron coined with an open lily: "Truly great is Jehovah, and you are noisy and empty as a wineskin full of wind. For the figs of your basket I will give you this *meah*, and if you refuse it I know the way to the gardens as well as that to the Temple, I know where the sweet waters of Enrogel bathe the fairest orchards. Go."

The man at once, eagerly climbing on to the balustrade of marble in angry dignity, filled with figs the fold of the cloak that I had stretched out; and then, showing his white teeth, he murmured, smiling, that we were more bountiful than the dews of Carmel.

Of a rare excellence seemed to me that meal of figs from Beth-phage in the palace of Herod. But we had hardly sat down to it with the fruit in our lap when I noticed below a thin old man humbly gazing at us with his misty eyes full of complaint and weariness.

In pity I was about to throw him some figs and a silver coin of the Ptolemies, when he plunged his trembling hand into the rags which partially covered his hairy chest and, with a sad smile, showed me a gleaming stone. It was an oval piece of alabaster engraved with an image of the Temple. While Topsius learnedly examined it, he pulled forth other stones of marble, jasper, onyx, with pictures of the Tabernacle in the wilderness and the names of the Tribes and confused figures in relief representing the battles of the Maccabeans. Then he stood with arms crossed and a light of eagerness on his careworn face as though to us alone he looked for mercy and relief.

Topsius was of opinion that he was one of the Guebri who worship fire and are skilled in the arts and go barefoot all the way to Egypt to sprinkle on the Sphinx the blood of a black cock. But the old man denied this in horror and told us his sad story. He was a mason of Naim who had worked in the Temple and the buildings constructed by Herod Antipas at Bezetha. The whips of the overseers had torn his flesh, and then an illness had taken away his strength as a frost withers an apple-tree. And now, without work and with his daughter's children to maintain, he searched for rare stones in the mountains and engraved on them the holy names and holy places to sell them to the faithful in the Temple. But on the eve of Easter a Rabbi of Galilee had come in anger and had taken away his livelihood. "He!" he muttered with feeling, shaking his hand towards Jesus.

I protested. How could injustice and sorrow have come from that Rabbi whose heart was divine and who was the best friend of the poor?

"Then you sold in the Temple?" asked the laconic historian of the Herods.

"Yes," sighed the old man; "it was there on the feast days that I earned the bread of many months. On those days I went up to the Temple, offered my prayer to the Lord, and by the Susa Gate, in front of the Portico of the King, laid my mat and set out my stones gleaming in the sun. Certainly I had no right to sell there; but how was I to pay for a yard of the Temple's pavement in order to sell the work of my hands? All those who offer their wares in the shade under the Portico on planks of cedar-wood are rich merchants who can afford the money: some even pay in gold; I could not, with two children at home in need of bread. Thus I remained in a corner outside the Portico, in the worst place. There I crouched, timid and silent, without complaining even when hard-hearted men shoved me aside or hit me on the head with their sticks. Near me were others, poor likewise, Eboim of Joppa who sold an oil to make the hair grow, and Oseas of Ramah who sold clay flutes. The soldiers of the Antonia Tower on their rounds pretended not to see us, even Menahem, who was always on guard at Easter, said to us: 'It is well, you may remain, but do not cry your wares too loud.' For they all knew that we were too poor to pay for the yard of pavement we needed and that we had famished children at home. At Easter and for the Feast of the Tabernacles, pilgrims come from distant lands to Jerusalem, and all bought an image of the Temple to show in their village or one of the moonstones which frighten away the devil. Sometimes at the end of the day I had made as much as three drachmas, and, filling my smock with lentils, would go home gaily to my hovel, singing praises to the Lord."

In my pity I forgot my meal, and the old man continued to sigh out his long complaint: "But now a few days ago that Rabbi of Galilee appears in the Temple and with words of anger raises his stick and drives us out, crying that it was his father's house and that we were defiling it. And he scattered all my stones, which I never set eyes on again, my livelihood! He broke on the pavement the oil jars of Eboim of Joppa, who did not even cry out, such was his amazement. The guards of the Temple ran up; Menahem also came and even said indignantly to the Rabbi: 'You are very harsh to the poor. What is your authority?' And the Rabbi spoke of his father and invoked against us the severe law of the Temple. Menahem bowed his head; and we were obliged to flee, followed by the insults of the rich merchants, who, comfortably installed on their carpets of Babylonia on the space of pavement for which they had paid, were clapping applause of the Rabbi. Ah, against them the Rabbi was powerless:

they were rich, they had paid! And now I am here. My daughter is ill and a widow, and cannot work, but sits wrapped in rags in a corner; my daughter's little children are hungry and look to me and see me so sad and do not even cry. And what had I done? I was ever humble, I keep the Sabbath, I go to the synagogue of my native Naim, and if any crumbs remained over from my food I gave them to those who have not even crumbs. What harm was I doing in selling? What offence to the Lord? Before extending my mat I always kissed the pavement of the Temple; and every stone was purified with lustral water. Truly Jehovah is great and knows; but I was expelled by the Rabbi simply because I am poor."

He paused and his thin hands trembled as he wiped away his flowing tears. I beat my breast in despair; and my sorrow was that Jesus should be unaware of this misfortune which, in the keenness of His spirit, His merciful hands had involuntarily wrought, as the beneficent rain sometimes, in giving life to the seed, breaks and kills an isolated flower. And so, that there might be nothing imperfect in his life and that there should be no complaint of Him on earth, I paid His debt (and may His Father pardon mine!) and threw into the old man's smock many coins, gold coins of Greek Philip and Roman Augustus, and even a large Cyrenaic coin which I admired on account of its head of Zeus Ammon which resembled mine. Topsius added to this treasure a copper lepta which in Judea is worth a grain of maize. The old mason of Naim turned pale from emotion; then, pressing the money against his breast in a fold of his smock, he murmured timidly and devoutly, raising his tear-dimmed eyes to heaven: "Father which art in heaven, remember the countenance of this man, who has given me sustenance for many days." And, sobbing, he was lost among the crowd, which now was surging noisily forward from every side towards the supports of the awning.

The scribe appeared, redder in the face and wiping his lips. By the side of the Rabbi and the Temple guards, Sareas had taken his place, leaning on his stick. Then, amid a gleam of arms, appeared the white staffs of the lictors, and once more Pontius, pale and heavy, in his huge toga, went up the bronze steps and sat in the curule chair. A silence fell so deep that one could hear the bugles sounding afar off in the Marian Tower. Sareas unrolled his dark parchment, and laid it on the stone table among the tablets; and I saw the slow fat hands of the scribe sign and seal a few red lines which were the death sentence of Jesus of Galilee, my Lord. Then Pontius Pilate, in indolent dignity, slightly raising his bare arm, confirmed in the name of Caesar "the sentence of the Sanhedrin, which judges in Jerusalem."

Immediately Sareas placed an edge of his cloak over his turban and prayed, with his palms raised towards heaven. And the Pharisees were triumphant; close to us, two of them, very old men with white beards, kissed one another; others threw their sticks into the air or sarcastically uttered the legal formula of the Romans: "*Bene et belle; non potest melius.*"

But suddenly the interpreter appeared on a bench, the gaudy parrot clear upon his breast. The crowd grew silent in surprise. The Phoenician, after consulting the scribe, smiled and cried in Chaldean, extending his arms adorned with coral bracelets: "Listen. In this your Feast of Easter it is the wont of the Praetor of Jerusalem, since Valerius Gratus so ordained and with the consent of Caesar, to pardon a criminal. The Praetor proposes to you that he should pardon this man. Listen further: you have the right to choose among the condemned criminals. The Praetor has in his power, in Herod's prison, another man condemned to death."

He hesitated and, leaning from the bench, again questioned the scribe, who was searching feverishly among the tablets and papyrus. Sareas, shaking away the corner of his cloak, which hid his prayer, was gazing at the Praetor in amazement with his palms extended.

But now the interpreter, with smiling face, was crying: "One of the condemned is Rabbi Jeschoua, who stands before you and calls himself the son of David. This is the man proposed by the Praetor. The other is a hardened criminal, arrested for having treacherously killed a legionary in a quarrel at the foot of Xistus. His name is Bar Abbas. Choose."

A sharp hoarse cry came from the Pharisees: Bar Abbas. Here and there through the court the name of Bar Abbas echoed confusedly; and a slave of the Temple in a yellow smock, leaping to the steps of the throne, began to yell in Pilate's face, as he slapped his thighs in frenzy: "Bar Abbas, you hear. The people will have none but Bar Abbas." With the shaft of his spear a legionary knocked him on to the pavement; but now the whole multitude, more easily inflamed than straw in a rick, was shouting for Bar Abbas, some in fury beating with their sandals and iron-pointed sticks as though they would demolish the Praetorium, others afar off lying in the sun and indolently raising a finger. The sellers of the Temple, rancorously shaking their iron scales and ringing their small bells, were shrieking, with curses on the Rabbi: "Bar Abbas is the better man;" and even the prostitutes of Tiberias, smeared with red paint like idols, hissed out Bar Abbas, Bar Abbas. Few were they who knew Bar Abbas, and many had no hatred for the Rabbi; but all quickly swelled the tumult, feeling that in their cry for a prisoner who had attacked legionaries there was an outrage against the Roman Praetor who sat there so augustly in his toga on his judgment seat.

Pontius meanwhile, indifferent, was writing on a huge sheet of parchment lying on his knees; and all around fell the cries regularly in cadence, as flails on a threshing-floor: Bar Abbas, Bar Abbas, Bar Abbas. Then Jesus slowly turned toward that harsh uproarious crowd that condemned him, and in the soft gleam of His eyes, in the momentary trembling of His lips, there shone for an instant a sorrowful pity for the dull folly of men, who were thus driving to death man's best friend. With His bound hands He wiped His brow, then remained before the Praetor tranquil and serene, as though He no longer belonged to earth.

The scribe, beating with an iron ruler on the stone table, thrice called the name of Caesar. The furious tumult subsided. Pilate rose, and gravely, without betraying anger or impatience, waved his hand and gave the final order: Go and crucify him. Then he went down the steps, while the crowd clapped ferociously. Eight soldiers of the Syrian cohort appeared in marching order, with their shields covered with canvas, their bundles of implements and measures of mead. Sareas, member of the Sanhedrin, touched Jesus on the shoulder and handed Him over to the decurion; a soldier unbound His cords, another took off His woollen cloak; and I saw the gentle Rabbi take the first step towards His death.

Hurriedly, rolling a cigarette, we left the palace of Herod by a passage known to Topsius, dark and damp, with barred cracks through which came the sad chant of imprisoned slaves. We came out on a terrace sheltered by the wall of a garden planted with cypresses. Two dromedaries lying in the dust were ruminating near a heap of cut leaves. The renowned historian was about to go towards the Temple, when under the ruins of an ivy-covered arch we saw a dense group round an Essenian, whose white linen sleeves were floating in the air like the wings of an irritated bird. It was Gad, hoarse with indignation, and inveighing against a thin man with sparse tawny beard and great gold ear-rings, who was trembling and muttering: "It was not I, it was not I."

"It was you," shouted the Essenian, stamping with his sandalled foot; "I know you well. Your mother is a wool-carder in Capernaum, and cursed be she for having borne you."

The man shrank with bowed head, like an animal brought to bay: "It was not I. I am Rephrahim, the son of Eliesar, of Ramah. I have always been known to all as strong and healthy as a young palm-tree."

"Twisted and useless were you like a shrivelled vine-twig, dog and son of a dog," cried Gad; "I saw you; it was at Capernaum, in the street with the fountain near the synagogue; there you appeared before Jesus, the Rabbi of Nazareth, and kissed his sandals and said: Rabbi, heal me; Rabbi, see this hand unable to work. And you showed your hand, the right hand, dry, shrivelled and black as a withered bough on a tree. It was on the Sabbath, and three elders of the synagogue were there, and Elzear and Simeon; and all looked towards Jesus to see if he would dare heal upon the Lord's Day. And you went, grovelling on the ground. Did the Rabbi repel you? Did he bid you go search for healing roots? Ah, dog and son of a dog, the Rabbi, heedless of the accusations of the Synagogue and listening only to the voice of his mercy, said to you: Stretch forth thy hand.

He touched it, and it became as a green plant watered with the dew of heaven, whole, strong, healthy; and you moved first one finger, then another, in trembling astonishment."

A rapturous murmur ran through the crowd in marvel at the sweet miracle; and the Essenian exclaimed, as his arms trembled in the air: "Even so was the Rabbi's charity. Did he extend a fold of his cloak, as do the Rabbis of Jerusalem, for you to throw in a silver coin? No. He bade his friends share with you their supply of lentils, and you went off running down the road towards your house crying: Mother, Mother, I am healed. And it was you just now, swine and son of a swine, who in the Praetorium were calling for the Rabbi to be crucified and shouting for Bar Abbas. Your vile lips need not deny it: I heard you, I was behind you and saw the veins of your neck swell with the fury of your ingratitude."

Some of the crowd were crying, scandalized: Accursed, accursed! An old man, in austere justice, picked up two large stones; and the man of Capernaum, shrinking, overcome, still kept muttering dully: "It was not I, it was not I; I am from Ramah."

Gad, in a frenzy, seized him by the beard: "On that arm, when you bared it before the Rabbi, we all saw two curved scars like the wounds of a sickle; and you will show them now, dog and son of a dog."

He tore open the sleeve of his new tunic and pulled him round in the iron clutch of his hands like a stubborn goat; he pointed out the two scars livid on the tawny skin and shoved him disdainfully among the crowd, which took dust from the road and pursued the man of Capernaum with hoots and stones.

We went up to Gad smiling and praised him for his loyalty to Jesus. Calming down, he had stretched out his hands to a water-seller, who was cleansing them with the flowing water from his shaggy leathern bag; and as he dried them on the linen towel hanging from his waist, he said: "Listen, Joseph of Arimathea has asked for the body of the Rabbi, and the Praetor has granted his request. Wait for me at the ninth hour in the court of Gamaliel's house. Where are you going now?"

Topsius confessed that we were going to the Temple for reasons of artistic and archaeological interest.

"Foolish is he who admires stones," murmured the lofty idealist, and went his way, drawing his hood about his face, amid the blessings of the people, which loves and believes in the Essenians.

In order to avoid the long walk through the Tyropeum and over the bridge of the Xistus, we took two litters, which a freedman, Pontius by name, had for hire near the Praetorium, after the fashion of Rome. Tired, I threw myself, with my hands behind my head, on the layer of dry leaves smelling of myrtle, and gradually over my spirit a strange obstinate disquiet came, which I had felt slightly in the Praetorium like the dread wing of a bird of ill omen: Was I going to remain for ever in this strong city of the Jews? Had I irrevocably lost my identity as Raposo, a Catholic Bachelor of Law, contemporary of gas and the *Times*, and become a man of classical antiquity, of the time of Tiberius? And, granted this wonderful retrogression in time, what should I find by that fair river were I to return to my country? I should certainly find a Roman colony there: the pro-consul's house on the coolest hill; by its side, a little temple covered with glazed tiles and sacred to Apollo or Mars; above, the entrenched camp of the legionaries, and, scattered around, the Lusitanian town, with its rustic ways, its hovels of loose stones, sheds for the cattle and stakes in the mud to which rafts are moored. Thus should I find my country.

And what would I do there, poor and lonely? Should I be a shepherd on the hills? Or sweep the steps of the temple and cleave wood for the cohorts so that the Romans might pay me a daily wage? Oh, misery of miseries! Yet, if I remained in Jerusalem, what career could be mine in this gloomy devout city of Asia? Should I become a Jew and pray the Schema and keep the Sabbath and anoint my beard with nard, idling away the time in the courts of the Temple, attending the lectures of a Rabbi, and walking of an afternoon with gilt stick in the gardens of Gareb among the tombs? Such an existence seemed to me equally terrible. No, if I must remain a prisoner of the ancient world with the most learned Topsius, we must gallop away that very night, when the moon rose, to Joppa; embark there in some Phoenician trireme bound for Italy, and live in Rome, even though it were in one of the obscure streets of the Velabrum, in one of those smoky garrets reached up by two hundred steps of stairs, reeking of tripe and garlic and scarcely surviving two months without falling down or catching fire.

Such thoughts were mine, when the litter stopped. I opened its curtain and saw before me the huge granite mass of the wall of the Temple. We entered beneath the arch of the door of Huldah and were delayed while the guards of the Temple were snatching from the hands of a rough and obstinate shepherd the nail-studded club with which he wished to go through the sanctuary. The rolling distant uproar of the courts, like that of a forest or a great angry sea, already made me tremble. And when at length we emerged from the narrow archway, I seized the thin arm of the historian of the Herods in my intense awe and astonishment. A brightness of snow and gold glimmered profusely in the soft air, lit by the shining marbles, the polished granites, the fretted work of precious metals bathed in the divine sun of the month of Nizzam.

The smooth courts which I had seen deserted in the morning, clear as the sleeping water of a lake, now disappeared beneath a gaily dressed throng of people. The pungent smell of dyed stuffs, aromatic gums, and fat frying on braziers was overwhelming. Above the continual noise sounded the hoarse lowing of oxen; and the smoke of sacrifice went up unceasing to the resplendent sky. "*Caramba*," I said timidly, "this is truly magnificent."

We entered the Portico of Solomon, where the profane tumult of a market-place prevailed. Behind great cases with bars of iron sat the money-changers, a gold coin hanging from their ear in unkempt locks, exchanging the priestly money of the Temple for the pagan coins of every age and region, from the massive disks of old Latium, heavy as shields, to the engraved bricks which circulate as notes in the fairs of Assyria. Farther on gleamed the freshness and abundance of an orchard: the pomegranates, ripe to bursting, overflowed from the baskets; gardeners with a twig of almond-flower in their caps selling garlands of anemones or bitter herbs for Easter; jars of pure milk rested on sacks of lentils; and thirsty lambs lying on the pavement with their feet tied to the columns, bleating sadly.

But it was especially round the jewels and silks that the crowd gathered with sighs of desire. Merchants from the Phoenician colonies, from the isles of Greece, from Tardis, Mesopotamia and Tadmor, some in splendid coats of embroidered wool, others in rough capes of painted leather, were unfolding blue cloths of Tyre which reflect the glowing brilliancy of Eastern skies, the wanton silks of Sheba, of a green transparency, floating in the breeze, and the solemn stuffs of Babylonia, black and fascinating with their great flame-colored flowers. In coffers of cedar-wood, set out on mats from Galacia, shone silver mirrors resembling the moon and its beams; seals of tourmalin which the Jews wear on their breasts, bracelets of precious stones strung on the horns of an antelope, diadems of rock salt with which bridegrooms deck themselves; and, guarded with greater care, talismans and amulets that seemed to me childish, pieces of root, black stones, stained leather and bones inscribed with letters.

Topsius also paused among the shops of the perfumers to admire a magnificent stick of Tylos made of a rare wood mottled like a tiger-skin; but we soon fled from the penetrating smell that came from the resins and gums from the lands of the Negroes, from the bundles of ostrich feathers, myrrh of Orontes, wax of Cyrenaica, rose-colored oils of Cyzicus, and great pouches of hippopotamus hide filled with dried violets and leaves of scented plants.

We then entered what was known as the Royal Gallery, set apart for doctrine and the law. Here daily rage rancorous controversies between Sadducees, Scribes, Sophorins, Pharisees, Followers of the Schemaia, followers of Hillel, Jurists, grammarians and fanatics of all the land of Judea. Near the marble columns, the masters of the Law installed themselves on high seats with a metal plate at their side for the offerings of the faithful; and around them, squatting on the ground, with their sandals round their necks and skins covered with red letters on their knees, their disciples, beardless or decrepit, chanted their sentences with a slow rhythmic movement of the shoulders.

Here and there, amid the rapt attention of the devout, two doctors were disputing with angry looks as to daring points of doctrine: Is it lawful to eat an egg laid on the Sabbath? With what part of the spinal cord does the Resurrection begin? The philosophical Topsius was concealing his laughter in a fold of his cloak; as for me, I trembled when the thin and bearded doctors threatened one another and cried Raca, Raca, and plunged their hands into the breasts of their tunics in search of a hidden weapon.

Pharisees passed by continually; sounding and hollow as drums, coming to the Temple to display their piety, some with bent backs bowed by the weight of men's sins, others stumbling and feeling their way with closed eyes so as not to look upon the impure shape of woman, a few covered with ashes and groaning, with their hands crossed in front of them in sign of their severe fasting. Then Topsius pointed out to me a Rabbi interpreter of dreams: the sunken eyes gleamed in his livid withered face with the gloom of two lamps on a tomb, and, seated on sacks of wool, he extended over each devotee who knelt at his naked feet the edge of his huge black cloak with signs painted on it in white.

In my curiosity I was thinking of consulting him, when we heard cries of affliction echo through the court. We ran to see, and found Levites with cords and canes furiously lashing a leper who in his uncleanness had entered the Court of Israel. The blood sprinkled the pavement; around him children were laughing.

It was not the sixth hour, the hour most pleasing to the Lord, when the sun in its march towards the sea pauses over Jerusalem and contemplates it passionately; and in order to reach the Court of Israel, we made our way with difficulty through the crowd which surged there from every land, cultured and barbarous. The rough coat of skins worn by shepherds of Idumea brushed against the short chlamys of the Greeks of shaven face whiter than marble. There were solemn men from the plain of Babylonia with their beards in blue sacks bound by a chain of silver to their caps of painted leather, and there were tawny Gauls with moustaches hanging like the reeds of their lakes, laughing and chattering and devouring, unpeeled, sweet lemons of Syria. Sometimes a Roman in his toga passed, as grave as if he had just stepped down from a pedestal. Men of Dacia and Mysia, with their legs swathed in leather, were stumbling, blinded by the brightness of the marbles. And it was strange indeed that I, Teodorico Raposo, should be there in my riding-boots behind a priest of Moloch, sensual and huge in his purple cloak, who, in the midst of merchants of Serepta, disdained this temple without images or trees and noisier than a Phoenician fair.

Thus slowly we advanced to the "Beautiful Gate" which gave entrance to the sacred Court of Israel. Beautiful indeed, precious and triumphant, above the fourteen steps of green marble of Numidia flecked with yellow; its great leaves, embossed in silver, gleamed like the folding doors of a reliquary, and the two lintels, resembling great bundles of palm leaves, supported a round white tower adorned with shields captured from the enemies of Judah, shining in the sun as a glorious collar on the strong neck of a hero.

Beyond this marvelous entrance rose a severe pillar surmounted by a black tablet on which in letters of gold was written this threat in Greek and Latin, Aramaic and Chaldean: "Let no foreigner enter on pain of death."

Fortunately we caught sight of the thin form of Gamaliel advancing towards the holy court, barefoot, with a sheaf of corn for an offering upon his breast; with him was a stout cheerful man whose face was red as poppies who was crowned by an enormous mitre of black wool adorned with strings of coral. Bowing to the pavement, we greeted the austere Doctor of the Law. He chanted with eyes closed: "Be welcome. This is the best hour to receive the blessing of the Lord. The Lord said: 'Come forth from your houses, bring me your first-fruits and I will bless you in all the works of your hands.' You today belong by a miracle to Israel. Come up into the house of the Eternal. This man at my side is Eliezer of Silo, kindly and wise above all men in things appertaining to Nature."

He gave us two ears of corn, and behind him our Gentile feet trod the forbidden court of Judah. Walking by my side, Eliezer of Silo, courteous and affable, inquired if my country was distant and the ways dangerous. I muttered, with vague respect: "Yes, we come from Jericho." "And how is the balsam crop there?" he asked. "It is excellent," I assured him fervently; "thanks be to the Eternal, the balsam in this year of grace is most abundant." He appeared delighted. He then told me that he was one of the doctors of the Temple, where the priests and sacrificers continually suffer from internal complaints due to treading barefoot, when heated, the cold flags of the courts. That is why, he said with a merry twinkle in his kindly eye, the people of Zion calls us the tripe doctors. I shook with delighted laughter at this jest whispered in the austere dwelling of the Eternal; then, remembering my internal complaints at Jericho brought on by my great love for the divine and treacherous melons of Syria, I asked the amiable physician whether in such cases he advised bismuth. The master cautiously shook his great mitre; then, extending a finger in the air, he whispered this most excellent recipe: "Take gum of Alexandria, garden saffron, an onion of Persia and black wine of Emmaus. Mix it, boil it, set it to cool in a silver dish; place yourself at a crossroads at sunrise. . . ." But he ceased abruptly, with outstretched arms and face upon the flags: we had entered the superb court known as the Court of the Women; and at that moment the blessings were ending, given by a priest at the sixth hour from above the Gate of Nicanor. Through this severe gate of bronze one could see at the farther end the gold, snow and precious stones of the sanctuary serenely gleaming. On the long steps, brighter than alabaster, were stationed two colleges of Levites kneeling, dressed in white, some with curved trumpets, others with their fingers on the mute strings of their lyres; and between these two wings of prostrate men a tall emaciated old man was coming slowly down the steps, a golden censer in his hands. The hem of his close-fitting linen tunic was adorned with pine-cones of pearls, alternating with bells that tinkled softly; his feet, bare of sandals and stained with henna, seemed made of coral, and in the middle of the sash around his thin body shone a great gold-embroidered sun.

The faithful, kneeling motionless without a sound, almost touched the pavement with their heads, hidden under cloaks and veils, and their gay colors, chiefly the red of anemones and the green of fig-leaves, seemed to strew the court with leaves and flowers as though it awaited the passage of Solomon on a triumphal morning. With his hard pointed beard raised to heaven, the old man waved incense towards the sands on the East and then to the seas on the West, and such was the devout silence that one could hear the lowing of the oxen in the sanctuary. He came still farther down the steps, raised his mitre set with gems and swung the censer gleaming in the sun; and in the white smoke, thin and scented, came rolling over Israel the blessing of the Almighty.

Then the Levites together struck the strings of their lyres, a bronzen cry came from the curved trumpets, and all the people, rising, with arms stretched heavenwards, sang the psalm which celebrates the eternity of Judah. And suddenly all was quiet; the Levites retired down the marble stair barefooted, silent; Eliezar of Silo and the rigid Gamaliel had disappeared in the porticoes, and the white court shone magnificently and was filled with women. The ornamentation of alabaster was so bright that Topsius contemplated in it as in a mirror the noble folds of his cloak; all the fruits of Asia and the flowers of its gardens were worked in silver embroidery on the doors of the ceremonial chambers in which the oil is scented, the wood consecrated and leprosy purified; between the columns hung in festoons great threads of pearls and onyx beads more numerous than on the breast of a bride; and in the vessels of bronze, shaped like huge war-trumpets lying on the pavement, shone inscriptions in gold relief calling for offerings, and rhythmical as verses of chants: Burn ye nard and incense; offer ye doves and pigeons.

But the sacred court blazed with women, and my eyes soon left the metals and marbles to become the prisoners of those daughters of Jerusalem, fair and brown as the tents of Kedar. In the Temple the faces of all were uncovered, or a soft veil, of muslin light as air, was Roman-fashion wound delicately about the turban and gave the face a foam-like whiteness, in which the eyes gleamed more softly between the thick eye-lashes artificially lengthened with dye of cypress-wood. The barbaric display of gold and jewels enveloped them in a trembling radiance from their strong breasts to their hair more curly than the wool of goats of Galaad. Their sandals, adorned with bells and chains, fell upon the flags in a silver melody: so graceful and harmonious were their grave and rhythmic movements; and the embroidered stuffs, the cottons of Galactia, the delicate colored linen in which they were dressed, drenched with amber and other strong scents, filled the air with fragrance and penetrated the souls of men.

The richest were solemnly escorted by slaves in yellow cloth, carrying their sunshade of peacock's feathers, the devout scrolls on which the Law is written, sacks of sweet dates and light silver mirrors. The poor, dressed in a simple many-colored shirt of striped cotton, and wearing for all jewels a rough coral talisman, ran and chattered, showing their bare arms and necks of the hue of ripening arbutus berries. And my desire hovered among them as a bee hesitating between flowers equally sweet.

"O Topsius, Topsius," I muttered, "what women! I shall die, my distinguished friend."

The learned man affirmed with disdain that they had not more intellect than the peacocks of the gardens of Antipas, and that certainly not one of them had read Aristotle or Sophocles!

I shrugged my shoulders. Splendor of heaven! For which of these women who had not read Sophocles would not I, were I Caesar, give a city of Italy or all Iberia! Some of them overwhelmed me by the slender and delicate grace of their pious maidenhood, lived continually in the gloom of rooms of cedar-wood, their bodies drenched with scent, their souls subdued with prayer. Others dazzled me by the solid, substantial splendor of their beauty. What long dark eyes, like those of idols; what bright smooth marble limbs! What shadowy softness, what magnificent forms when by their beds they unrolled their heavy hair and gently shed the veils and linens of Galacia!

Topsius was obliged to drag me by the cloak to the stair of Nicanor, and, even so, I paused on every step, turning my eyes agleam and breathing like a bull in May pastures: O daughters of Zion, how you rob the wits of men! At a tug from the learned historian I turned round and knocked my face against a white lamb which an old man was carrying on his back, tied by its feet and adorned with roses. Opposite ran a long balustrade of wrought cedar-wood, in which an open lattice of solid silver, open and weak on its hinges, was swinging to and fro in silence, gleaming.

"It is here," said the learned Topsius, "that bitter waters are given to adulterous women to drink. And now, Dom Raposo, you see Israel adoring its God."

We were at last in the Court of the Priests. I looked with emotion on this gigantic and splendid sanctuary. In the center of the vast bright terrace rose the altar of burst sacrifices, built of enormous black stones; at its corners stood four bronzen horns: from one of them hung garlands of flowers; from others strings of coral; from one, blood was dripping. From the large grating of the altar slowly ascended a thick reddish smoke, and around it crowded the sacrificers, barefoot: all in white, with bronze forks in their pale hands, and silver spits and knives stuck in their sky-blue sashes. With the constant austere mutter of the sacred ceremonial mingled the bleating of lambs, the tinkling of silver plates, the crackling of wood, the dull thud of wooden hammers, the slow trickling of water into marble vessels and the blare of trumpets. Despite the aromatic gums kept burning and the long fans of palms leaves which the attendants were waving in the air, I put my handkerchief to my face, overcome by the enervating smell of raw flesh, blood, frying fat and saffron which the Lord required of Moses as the best gift of earth.

At the farther end, oxen decked with flowers and white calves with gilt horns, were lowing and butting as they jerked at the cords which bound them to stout bronze rings; beyond, on marble tables, among blocks of ice, were great pieces of meat, red and raw, above which Levites brandished their feathered fans to ward off the bluebottles. From columns ending in gleaming globes of crystal hung dead lambs, which Netenins, protected by leathern aprons covered with sacred texts, were flaying with silver knives, while the sacrificers carried at arm's length vessels down the sides of which the entrails overflowed. Crowned with round metal caps, Idumean slaves were continually washing the pavement with sponges; some bowed under bundles of wood, others crouched to blow the fire in the stoves of stone. At every instant some old sacrificer advanced barefoot to the altar, carrying round his neck a young lamb which did not bleat, happy in the warmth of his bare arms. A player on the lyre went before him, and behind came Levites carrying jars of aromatic oils. Before the altar, surrounded by the acolytes, the sacrificer threw on the lamb a handful of salt, and then with muttered chant cut off a little wool between its horns. The trumpets sounded, the cry of a wounded animal was lost in the sacred din; above the white tiaras two raised red hands sprinkled blood in the air, and in the altar grating a flame of joy and offering shot up from the oils and fat, and slowly the reddened smoke ascended serenely to the blue sky, carrying in its coils the savor that delights the Eternal.

"A butcher's shop!" I murmured in confusion; "a real butcher's shop! O Doctor Topsius, let us return to the women!"

The learned man looked at the sun, then, gravely placing his friendly hand on my shoulder, said: "It is well-nigh the ninth hour, Dom Raposo; and we have to go outside the Gate of Judgment, beyond Gareb, to a desolate spot called Calvary."

I turned pale. I saw no spiritual advantage to my soul, no unexpected addition to the wealth of Topsius' learning to be derived from going to see, on the top of a hill, in the heather, Jesus bound to a cross and suffering; it would only be a torture to our sensitive nerves. But submissively I followed my wise friend down the Stair of the Waters, which leads to the square, paved with basalt, where the first houses of Acra stand.

Close to the Sanctuary and inhabited by priests, they profusely displayed their Easter devotion in a profusion of palms and lamps and carpets hung from the roof-tops, and the lintels of some of the doors were sprinkled with the fresh blood of a lamb. Before entering an untidy sordid street winding beneath old awnings of esparto grass, I turned towards the Temple; I could now see only the immense wall of granite surmounted with bastions, dark and unconquerable; and the arrogance of its strength and durability filled my heart with anger. While on the hill of death, destined for slaves, the Man of Galilee, the incomparable friend of man, was dying on His cross and that voice of love and of the joys of the spirit was being extinguished for ever, there stood the Temple which caused His death, gleaming triumphantly with the bleating of its lambs, the clamor of its sophisms, the usury beneath the porticoes, the blood on the altars, the iniquity of its harsh pride and its importunate incense for ever ascending. Then with clenched teeth I shook my fist at Jehovah and at his fortress and shouted: May you be razed to the ground!

I did not again open my dry lips until we reached the narrow door in the wall of Hezekiah, which the Romans called the Gate of Judgment. There I shuddered at the sight of a parchment pasted upon a stone pillar, on which three death sentences were written: that of the thief of Battebara, that of the assassin of Emath, and that of Jesus of Galilee. The scribe of the Sanhedrin, who, as the law commanded, had watched there till the condemned men passed in order to receive any unexpected witness to their innocence, was about to depart, his tablets under his arm, after marking a thick red line above each sentence. And that last mark, blood-red, hurriedly made by a scribe who was returning gladly home to eat his paschal lamb, moved me more than all the sadness of the Scriptures.

The road was bordered by cactus hedges in flower, and beyond were green hills of gardens divided by walls of loose stones covered with wild roses. Everything was bright, gay and peaceful. In the shade of the fig-trees, under the props of the vines, women squatting on mats were weaving flax or tying bunches of basil and marjoram for Easter offerings; and near them children with coral amulets round their necks were swinging themselves or shooting arrows. A line of slow dromedaries came down the road, laden with wares from Joppa; two stalwart men were returning from the chase, their tall red boots thick with dust, each with a quiver rattling against his side and a net over his back, while their arms were full of partridges and vultures tied by the feet. In front of us a poor old beggar walked slowly, leaning on the shoulder of the child who acted as his guide; he had a long beard, and bound at his waist the bard carried his Greek five-stringed lyre; on his forehead was a garland of bay-leaves. Beneath a wall, shaded by the boughs of almond-trees, in front of a door painted red, two slaves were waiting, seated on a fallen tree-trunk, with downcast eyes and hands upon their knees.

Topsius paused and pulled me by the cloak: "This is the garden of Joseph of Arimathea, a friend of Jesus and member of the Sanhedrin, a man of restless spirit, inclined towards the Essenians. And look, here comes Gad."

From the end of the garden, along a path of myrtle and roses, Gad was running down with a linen bundle and a wicker basket hanging from a stick. We stopped. "The Rabbi?" cried the illustrious historian, passing through the door. The Essenian gave to one of the slaves the bundle and the basket, which was full of myrrh and scented herbs; and he remained before us for a moment trembling with emotion, his hand pressed to his heart as though to stay its beating.

"He suffered greatly," he murmured at last. "He suffered when they pierced his hands, and even more when the cross was raised. And at first he refused the wine of mercy which would have dulled his senses. The Rabbi wished to enter with a clear mind into the death for which he had called. But Joseph of Arimathea, and Nicodemus, were there watching and reminded him of promises made one night in Bethany; then the Rabbi took the bowl from the hands of the woman of Rosmophin and drank."

And the Essenian, fixing his eyes on Topsius as though to imprint on his soul a supreme injunction, and standing back a step, said in slow grave accents: "To-night, after supper, in the terrace of Gamaliel's house." Then he disappeared in the cool path of myrtle and roses.

Topsius then left the Joppa road, and hastening by a short cut, in which my long cloak caught in the thorns of the aloes, explained to me as he went that the wine of mercy was a strong wine of Tharses, containing juice of poppies and spices, supplied by a sisterhood of pious women to deaden the pain of those condemned to death. But I scarcely heeded his abundant flow of knowledge. On the top of a rough hill, all rocks and heather, I had caught sight of a crowd of people stationary, standing out distinctly against the clear blue of the cloudless sky, and in their midst rose three thick points of wood, and among them the polished helmets of legionaries flashed in the sun. Overcome, I sat down by the side of the path on a white stone heated by the sun; but, seeing Topsius go forward in the wise serenity of one who considers death a cleansing and freeing from imperfect forms, I did not wish to be less spiritual than he, and, throwing off my stifling cloak, I climbed intrepidly up the awful hill.

On one side lay the Valley of Hinnom, sunburnt and livid, without grass or shade and strewn with bones and carcasses and ashes. And in front of us the hill went up, stained with a leprosy of black whin and pierced here and there by the point of a rock white and smooth as a bone. The path, from which our footsteps were frightening the lizards, ended in a ruined brick hovel; two almond-trees, more melancholy than plants growing from the crack of a grave, spread at its side their thin and flowerless branches, in which cicadas sang harshly; and in their scant shade four barefoot disheveled women with their poor tunics rent in mourning were weeping as at a funeral.

One of them, motionless and stiff against the trunk of one of the trees, was moaning dully beneath a fold of her black cloak; another, having exhausted all her tears, lay on a stone, her head fallen upon her knees and her magnificent fair hair trailing carelessly upon the ground. But the other two, torn and bleeding, were raving and bleating their breasts in despair and covering their faces with earth; then, raising their bare arms to heaven, they filled the hill with their cries: O my delight, my treasure, my sun! And a hound, sniffing among the ruins, gave a sinister howl.

In fear I pulled the learned Topsius by the cloak, and we cut across the heather to the top of the hill, where, gazing and shouting, stood a crowd of workmen from the factories of Gareb, servants of the Temple, hucksters, and some of those wretched priests in rags who live by necromancy and alms. At sight of Topsius' white toga, two moneychangers, with gold coins in their ears, stood back, muttering servile blessings. A rope of esparto grass held us back; it was tied to stakes fixed in the ground so as to isolate the top of the hill, and, where we had stopped, it was wound round an old olive-tree on the branches of which hung shields of legionaries and a red cloak.

Then anxiously I raised my eyes. I raised them to the tallest cross, fixed by means of wedges in a crack of rock. The Rabbi was at point of death. And that body, which was neither of marble nor of silver but hot, living, heaving, bound and nailed to the cross, with an old cloth round the waist and a bar between His legs, filled me with terror and dismay. The blood which had stained the new wood was clotted round the nails and blackened His hands: His feet nearly touched the ground, bound by a thick cord, red and twisted in pain. His head, now flushed, now white as marble, lolled gently from side to side, and between His disheveled hair, bathed in sweat, His sunken eyes were glazed and dull; and with their light seemed to die all the light and hope of earth.

The centurion, without his cloak, his arms crossed on his scaled cuirass, was pacing gravely to and fro near the Rabbi's cross, and at times stared harshly at the people of the Temple, all noise and laughter. And in front, near the rope, Topsius showed me a man whose yellow melancholy face was almost hidden by the two long locks of black hair that fell upon his breast, who was impatiently opening and rolling up a piece of parchment, watching the slow march of the sun or speaking low to a slave at his side.

"That is Joseph of Arimathea," whispered the learned historian. "Let us go to him and learn what it behoves us to know."

But at that instant, among the sordid group of servants of the Temple and ragged priests who are fed with the remains of the burnt offerings, broke out a louder murmur, like the cawing of crows on a hill; and one of them, a huge squalid man with thin misshapen beard, stretched out his arms towards the cross of the Rabbi and shouted in a drunken voice: "You who are strong and wished to destroy the Temple and its walls, why do you not break the wood of that cross?" Foolish laughter rang out; and another, beating his hands on his breast and bowing with infinite mockery, saluted the Rabbi: "Thou heir of David, my prince, how dost thou like thy throne?" "Son of God, call to thy father; see if He will come to save thee," muttered at my side a lean old man who trembled and shook his beard as he leaned upon his staff. Some brutal hucksters took up dry clods of earth and spat on them, meaning to throw them at the Rabbi; a stone echoed hollowly on the wood of the cross. But the centurion ran up angrily; the blade of his long sword flashed in the air, and the crowd retreated, cursing, while some wrapped in a fold of their smocks their bleeding fingers.

We went up to Joseph of Arimathea. But the gloomy man abruptly made off, escaping from the importunate learning of Topsius; and, hurt by his rudeness, we remained there by the trunk of a withered olive, opposite the other crosses. The two criminals had awakened from their first swoon in the coolness of the afternoon breeze. One, large and hairy, with prominent eyes, strained chest, and ribs heaving as if in desperate endeavor to tear themselves from the cross, was howling without ceasing, terribly; blood dripped slowly from his black feet and cracked hands; deserted, without any to pity or sorrow for him, he was like a wounded wolf howling and dying in a lonely thicket. The other, thin and fair-haired, hung without a groan, like the stalk of a broken plant. In front of him a lean woman in rags, continually pressing her knee against the rope, held out in her arms a naked child and cried hoarsely: "Look again, look." The livid eyelids remained motionless; a Negro, who was packing up the implements of the crucifixion, gently pushed her away; she was silent now and desperately hugged her son that they might not take him too, gnashing her teeth and trembling all over; the child in the rags turned to her thin breast.

Soldiers seated on the ground were unfolding the tunics of the dead; others, each with his helmet hanging from his arm, were wiping their brows, or from iron bowls slowly taking a drink of mead. And below, on the dusty road, in the less intense heat of the sun, people were coming back peacefully from the fields and gardens. An old man was goading on his cows towards the Genath Gate; women came singing with a load of wood; a horseman trotted along, wrapped in a white cloak.

Sometimes those who crossed the road or were returning from the orchards of Gareb caught sight of the three crosses on high and gathered their tunics about them and went up the hill through the heather. The inscription on the cross of the Rabbi, written in Greek and Latin, astonished them: "The King of Jews." Who was he? Two patrician youths, Sadducees, with pearl earrings and boots embroidered with gold, called out, scandalized, to the centurion: Why had the Praetor written: "King of the Jews"? Was the man nailed to the cross Caius Tiberius? Only Tiberius was King of Judea. The Praetor had meant to offend Israel but in reality had only insulted Caesar.

The centurion went on speaking impassively to two legionaries who were moving large bars of iron on the ground; and the woman with the Sadducees, a small dark Roman, with purple ribands in her blue-powdered hair, gently considered the Rabbi and sniffed at her scent-bottle, no doubt lamenting the fate of that young vanquished barbarian king who had met the death of a slave.

Weary, I sat down by the side of Topsius on a stone. It was near the eighth hour of the Jews; the sun, calm as an aged hero, was setting over the sea above the palm-trees of Bethany. Before us spread green Gareb, covered with gardens; near the city walls, in the new quarter of Bezetha, large red and blue cloths were hanging to dry on cords at the doors of the dye-shops; a light glowed red in the depths of a forge; children were running at play about the edge of a pool. Farther on, at the top of the Hippica Tower, the shadow of which already reached the valley of Hinnom, infantry soldiers on the battlements were aiming their arrows at the vultures flying in the blue; and farther still, among trees, fresh and rose-colored in the evening, stood the terraces of the palace of Herod.

With sad thoughts at random I remembered Egypt and our tents and the candle which I had left burning, red and smoky, when I saw slowly coming up the hill, leaning on the shoulder of the child who led him, the old man we had passed on the Joppa road, with his lyre bound at his waist. His steps were now slower and more uncertain, tired out by his long day; his bright flowing beard fell sadly on his breast, and beneath the wine-colored cloak that covered his head the bay leaves of his garland hung few and withered.

Topsius called to him: "Hey, rhapsodist!"; and when he had felt his way through the heather to our side, the learned historian asked him if he had brought some new song from the fair isles of the sea. The old man raised his sad countenance, and murmured very nobly that in the ancient songs of Greece smiles an imperishable youth. Then, setting his sandalled foot on a stone, he took the lyre between his trembling hands; the child, standing upright, with lowered eyelashes, put the reed pipe to his lips; and in the splendor of the evening that shed its gold over Zion, the rhapsodist sang his tremulous song, full of glory and adoration, as though he stood before some temple altar on an Ionian shore.

I perceived that he sang of the gods and their beauty and heroic deeds. He told of the Delphian god, beardless, golden-hued, who raised the thoughts of man by the rhythmic notes of his lyre; of Athene, armed and active, who guided the hands of men over the loom; of Zeus, ancestral and serene, who gave beauty to the race of men and order to cities; and above them all, shapeless and vague, was Destiny, stronger than any.

But of a sudden a cry pierced the sky on the hill-top, a supreme and fervent cry as of deliverance. The old man's weak fingers became silent on the metal strings; with his head fallen forward and the crown of epic bay half shorn of leaves, he seemed to mourn the Greek lyre which henceforth for long ages was to be useless and silent. At his side the child, taking the flute from his lips, raised his clear eyes to the black crosses, his eyes in which appeared a look of curiosity and desire for a new world.

Topsius asked the old man his story, and he told it bitterly. He had

come from Samnos to Caesarea, and played the harp by the Temple
of Hercules. But the people were abandoning the pure cult of the
heroes, and all the feasts and offerings were for the Good Goddess
of Syria. He had then accompanied some merchants to Tiberias;
there men showed no respect for old age, and their hearts were mer-
cenary as the hearts of slaves. Thence he had gone along the high-
ways, stopping at Roman posts, where the soldiers came to hear him
play; in the villages of Samaria he knocked at the door of the wine-
presses, and to earn a crust of bread he had played the Greek harp at
the funerals of barbarians. Now he was wandering here in this city
with its great Temple and ferocious god, without definite shape,
who hated the heathen.

His desire was to return to Miletus, his home, and hear the soft
murmur of the Meander and touch the sacred marbles of the temple
of Phoebus, to which as a child he had carried, singing, a basket containing the first locks of his hair. The tears ran down his face, melancholy as rain on a ruined wall. Great was my pity for this rhapsodist
from the isles of Greece, lost like myself in this unfriendly city of
the Jews and surrounded by the sinister influence of an alien god.
I gave him my last silver coin. He went down the hill, leaning on
the child's shoulder, bowed and tottering, with the ragged hem of
his cloak fluttering about his legs and the heroic five-stringed lyre
dumb and insecure at his waist.

Meanwhile a growing sound of protest came from the hill-top,
around the crosses. We found the people of the Temple, with their
hands in the air, pointing to the sun, which was descending like a
golden shield towards the Tyrian Sea, and bidding the centurion
take down the criminals from the cross before the holy hour of
Easter struck. The most devout demanded that the crucified, if still
alive, should have their legs broken Roman-fashion with bars of
iron and that they should then be hurled into the ravine of Hinnom.

The impassive attitude of the centurion exasperated their pious
zeal. Would he dare defile the Sabbath by leaving a corpse hanging
in the air? Some were gathering up the folds of their cloaks to run
to Acra to warn the Praetor. "The sun is setting, the sun is leaving

Hebron," cried a Levite from the top of a rock, in dismay. "Make an end of them, an end of them." And at our side a handsome youth exclaimed, as he rolled his eyes and moved his arms covered with gold bracelets: "Throw the Rabbi to the crows; give the birds of prey their Easter feast."

The centurion, who was watching the Mariana Tower, on which the suspended shields shone in the last rays of the run, slowly made a sign with his sword; and two legionaries, heavily taking the iron bars on their shoulders, marched with them towards the crosses. Horrified, I grasped Topsius' arm; but before the cross of Jesus the centurion paused, raising his hand. The white strong body of the Rabbi lay calm, as one asleep; His dusty feet, which a moment before had been twisted with pain within the cords, now hung straight towards the ground as though about to tread it; His face could not be seen, for it rested slackly on one of the arms of the cross, turned towards the sky, in which He had set His desire and His kingdom. I too looked at the sky: it shone without a shadow, smooth, clear and silent, very lofty and impassive.

"Who demanded the body of this man?" asked the centurion, looking towards the people.

"I, who loved him in life," answered Joseph of Arimathea, holding out his parchment above the rope.

The slave waiting by his side then set the linen bundle on the ground and ran towards the ruined hut where the women were weeping by the almond-trees. Behind us a crowd of Pharisees and Sadducees acidly expressed their astonishment that Joseph of Arimathea, a member of the Sanhedrin, should ask for the body of the Rabbi in order to cover it with scents and accompany it with funeral flutes and lamentation. One of them, a hunchback with thin locks shining with oil, asserted that he had always known that Joseph of Arimathea to be inclined to all innovating and seditious persons; more than once he had seen him speak with that Rabbi near the Dyers' Field; and with them Nicodemus, a rich man who possessed many flocks and vines and all the houses on either side of the Synagogue of Cyrenaica.

Another, red-faced and flabby, moaned: "What will become of the nation if men in the highest position join those who flatter the poor and teach them that the fruits of the earth must be evenly divided between all?"

"Race of Messiah," shouted the younger of them in fury; "race of Messiah, ruin of Israel."

But the Sadducee of the oily locks slowly raised his hand, swathed in sacred bands: "Calm yourself; great is Jehovah, and in truth he determines everything for the best. In the Temple and Council Chamber, there will never be a lack of strong men to defend the old order, and happily crosses will always be raised on the top of hills of Calvary." And all murmured Amen.

Meanwhile the centurion, with the soldiers behind him carrying the iron bars on their shoulders, went towards the other crosses, on which the condemned men, still alive and in agony, were asking for water, one hanging moaning, the other twisted with torn hands, roaring terribly. Topsius, smiling coldly, whispered: "It is time for us to go." My eyes filled with bitter tears and, stumbling over the stones, I went down the Hill of Sacrifice by the side of the learned critic. And I felt a great sadness darken my spirit as I thought of those future crosses announced by the Conservative of the oily locks. Thus would it come to pass, O misery! Henceforth through all the ages would be renewed, round fires and in cold dungeons and on the gallows-step, the scandalous spectacle of priests and patricians, magistrates, soldiers, doctors and merchants gathering together to give a cruel death on a hill-top to the just man who, filled with the splendor of God, teaches men to worship in spirit, or, filled with love for men, proclaims the reign of equality.

With these thoughts I returned to Jerusalem, while the birds, happier than man, sang in the cedars of Gareb. It was growing dark and near the hour of the paschal supper when we arrived at the house of Gamaliel; tied to a ring in the court stood the ass with trappings of black cloth which had brought the amiable physician Eliezer of Silo. In the blue room with ceiling of cedar and scented with spices, the austere doctor was expecting us, lying on the sofa of white leather.

His feet were bare, and his sleeves turned back and fastened at the shoulders; by his side lay a staff, scrip and water-flask, ritual emblems of the exodus from Egypt. In front of him, on a table inlaid with mother of pearl, between clay vessels adorned with painted flowers, stood bowls of silver filigree overflowing with fruit and glittering pieces of ice, and a candelabra shaped like a shrub, with a faint blue flame at the end of every branch.

With his eyes shining vaguely and tremulously, and his hands crossed in front of him, Eliezer, the kindly "tripe doctor," was smiling beatifically as he leant back on cushions of red leather. Near him two seats, covered with carpets of Assyria, were awaiting me and the sagacious historian.

"Be welcome," murmured Gamaliel; "great are the wonders of Zion; you must be famished."

He clapped his hands gently; two slaves, treading silently in their felt sandals, and preceded majestically by the stout man in the yellow tunic, entered, carrying aloft large smoking copper dishes. At one side, to cleanse our fingers, we had a ball of white flour, delicate and soft as a linen napkin; on the other a large dish bordered with pearls, in which, black amid parsley leaves, rose a mound of fried cicadas. On the floor stood jars of rose-water. We performed the customary ablutions, and Gamaliel, having purified his mouth with a piece of ice, murmured the ritual prayer over the huge silver tray on which was a roast kid in overflowing sauce of saffron and pickles.

Topsius, well acquainted with Oriental ways, politely hiccoughed loudly in sign of abundance and enjoyment; then, with a piece of lamb in his fingers, he assured the doctor that he had found Jerusalem magnificent, bright and beautiful, and blessed among the cities.

Eliezer of Silo replied with eyes closed joyfully as under a caress: "This city is a gem finer than the diamond, and the Lord set it in the center of the earth that it might illumine it in all directions with its brilliance."

In the center of the earth! murmured the historian, in learned amazement.

Yes, and dipping a piece of bread in the saffron sauce, the profound doctor explained the earth.

It was flat and rounder than a disk; in its center stood Jerusalem the holy, a heart filled with the love of the Highest; Judea, rich in balsam and palms, encircles it with shade and scent; beyond Judea live the pagans in harsh regions where both honey and milk are scarce; after that come the seas enveloped in darkness; and above all is the sounding, solid sky.

Solid! muttered my wise friend in his astonishment.

The slaves were handing round yellow beer of Media in silver cups. Gamaliel with careful attention advised me that in order to give it a savor I should take a bite of fried cicada. And Rabbi Eliezer, wise more than other men in the things appertaining to Nature, revealed to Topsius the divine construction of the sky.

It is made of seven hard wonderful gleaming layers of crystal; above these continually roll the great waters, and on the waters the spirit of Jehovah floats and gleams. These crystal layers, pierced like a sieve, glide over one another with a sweet music which the most favored prophets sometimes hear. He himself one night, as he prayed on the terrace of his house at Silo, had, by a rare grace of the Highest, heard that harmony; so piercing sweet that the tears fell one by one upon his open hands. In the months of Kisleu and Tebeth the holes in the heavenly sheets coincide, and through them drops of the eternal waters fall upon the earth and cause the crops to grow.

"The rain?" asked Topsius reverently.

"The rain," answered Eliezer calmly.

Topsius, restraining his laughter, turned towards Gamaliel his gold spectacles that flashed with learned irony; but the countenance of the devout son of Simeon, emaciated by study of the Law, preserved an impenetrable gravity. Then the historian, as his fingers fumbled among the olives, asked the enlightened physician why the crystals of the sky were of that fascinating blue color. Eliezer of Silo enlightened him: A great blue mountain, as yet invisible to men, stands in the East, and when the sun beats upon it, its reflection bathes the crystal of heaven with blue. It is perhaps on that mountain that dwell the souls of the just. Gamaliel coughed slightly and murmured: Let us drink, praising the Lord. He raised his glass filled with the wine of Sichem, pronounced a blessing over it, and handed it to me, calling down peace upon my heart. I muttered: "To yours, and many of them;" and Topsius, reverently receiving the cup, drank to the prosperity of Israel, to its strength and learning.

Then the slaves, preceded by the stout man in the yellow tunic, who pompously beat on the pavement his rod of ivory, brought in the most devout part of the paschal feast: the bitter herbs. A great tray was filled with lettuce, agrimony, chicory and endive, with vinegar and rough lumps of salt. Gamaliel munched them solemnly, as one performing a rite; they stood for the bitter sorrows of Israel in the captivity of Egypt. And Eliezer, sucking his fingers, declared them delicious, both invigorating and spiritually most edifying. But Topsius remembered, on the authority of the Greek authors, that all vegetables diminish man's virility, deaden his eloquence and weaken his heroism; and in a flood of erudition he quoted Theophrastus, Eubulus, Nicander in the second part of his Dictionary, Phenias in his "Treatise on Plants," Diphilus and Epicharmus.

Gamaliel dryly condemned the vanity of their learning, for Hecateus of Miletus, in the first book of his "Description of Asia" alone, is guilty of fifty-five errors, fourteen blasphemies and a hundred and nine omissions. For instance, the scatter-brained Greek affirmed that the date, that marvelous gift of the Highest, weakens the intellect.

"But," exclaimed Topsius fervently, "Xenophon, in the second book of the 'Anabasis,' is of the same opinion, and Xenophon. . . ."

But Gamaliel rejected the authority of Xenophon. Then Topsius, red in the face, beating with a gold spoon on the edge of the table, exalted the eloquence of Xenophon, the strong nobility of his character, his tender affection for Socrates; and while I helped myself to a pie of Commagenia, the two learned doctors embarked on a vehement discussion about Socrates.

Gamaliel asserted that the secret voices heard by Socrates and which guided him with such pure divinity were distant murmurs derived from Judea, miraculous echoes of the voice of the Lord. Topsius jumped in his seat, shrugging his shoulders in desperate sarcasm. Socrates inspired by Jehovah! Nonsense! Yet it was certain, insisted Gamaliel, whose face had become livid, that the heathen were emerging from their darkness, attracted by the strong pure light shed by Jerusalem; reverence for the gods appeared in Aeschylus, a profound reverence based in fear; in Sophocles it became serene and charming; in Euripides superficial and undermined by doubt. Thus each of these dramatists had made a great step forward towards the true God.

"O Gamaliel, son of Simeon," murmured Eliezer of Silo, "why do you, who possess the truth, admit the pagans to your intelligence?"

Gamaliel answered: "So that I may the better despise them in my mind."

Tired of so classical a controversy, I pushed the bowl of honey of Hebron towards Eliezer and told him how delighted I had been with the road of Gareb and its gardens. He agreed that Jerusalem surrounded with orchards was fair to view as a bride crowned with anemones. He then expressed surprise that I should have chosen for my pleasure the neighborhood of Gihon, full of butchers' shops, and near the bald hill where the crosses were raised. I would have found the fragrant orchards of Siloeh pleasanter.

"I went to see Jesus," I interrupted severely; "I went to see Jesus, crucified this afternoon by order of the Sanhedrin."

Eliezer with Oriental politeness beat his breast in sign of sorrow; and he wished to know if this Jesus was of my blood or had shared the bread of peace with me to account for my attending at his slave's death. I looked at him in astonishment: "He is the Messiah." And Eliezer considered me with even greater astonishment, while a stream of honey ran down his beard. Wonderful to relate, Eliezer, the doctor of the Temple, the physician of the Sanhedrin, knew nothing of Jesus of Galilee. Busied with the sick, who fill Jerusalem at Easter, he confessed to me that he had not gone to the Xistus nor to the shop of the perfumer Cleos nor to the terraces of

Hannan, where gossip flies abroad more frequent than the doves; and thus he had not heard of the appearance of a Messiah. But indeed, he added, it could not be the Messiah. The Messiah would be called Manahem the Comforter, since he would bring consolation to Israel. And there would be two Messiahs: the first, of the tribe of Joseph, would be vanquished by Gog; the second, the son of David, and full of strength, would vanquish Magog. Before his birth would occur seven years of miracles, during which seas would evaporate, stars would fall from heaven, and there would be famines and also such abundance that the very rocks would bring forth fruit. In the last year there would be war among the nations; then a mighty voice would sound, and with a sword of fire the Messiah would appear. These strange things he said as he broke open a fig; then he added with a sigh: "And none of these marvels, my son, has as yet announced the Consolation." And he plunged his teeth into the fig.

Then I, Teodorico, an Iberian, from a remote Roman town, told this physician of Jerusalem, who had grown up among the marbles of the Temple, the life of the Lord. I told him of the pleasant things and the mighty things: the three bright stars over His cradle, His words calming the waves of Galilee, the hearts of the simple turning to Him, the kingdom of heaven which He had promised, His serene countenance shining before the Praetor of Rome. . . . Then the elders and patricians and rich men crucified Him.

Doctor Eliezer, his fingers again in the basket of figs, murmured thoughtfully: "Very sad, indeed; and yet, my son, the Sanhedrin is merciful: in the seven years that I have served it, it has only signed three death sentences. Yes, the world has much need of words of love and justice, but Israel has suffered so much from innovators and prophets. Certainly one should never shed a man's blood, and certainly these figs of Bethany are not worth mine at Silo."

I rolled a cigarette in silence; and at this instant Topsius, still discussing with Gamaliel on the subject of Hellenism and the Socratic schools, with an exalted air, his spectacles on the tip of his nose, gave utterance to this clear summary: "Socrates is the seed, Plato the flower, Aristotle the fruit; and on this complete tree the human

spirit has fed." But Gamaliel rose abruptly, and Doctor Eliezer followed his example, hiccoughing courteously. They both took their
staffs and cried: Alleluia, praise the Lord, who brought us out of the
land of Egypt.

The paschal supper was over. The enlightened historian, wiping
his brow after the controversy, looked keenly at his watch and asked
permission of Gamaliel to go up to the terrace to refresh himself
in the soft air of Opel. The Doctor of the Law conducted us to the
veranda, faintly lit with lamps of mica; he pointed out the steep
stair of ebony that led to the terrace; and, invoking upon us the
blessing of the Lord, he entered with Eliezer into a room partitioned
off with curtains of Mesopotamia, from which came scent and a
delicate sound of laughter and the slow notes of a lyre.

How soft was the air on the terrace! And how gay that Easter
night in Jerusalem! In the sky, silent and dark as a palace in mourning, there was no star; but the town of David and the hill of Acra in
their ritual illuminations seemed sprinkled with gold. On every terrace, vessels with wicks in oil cast a flickering red flame. Here and
there, on some taller house, the strings of lights against the dark wall
shone like a necklace of jewels on the neck of a Negress. The sighs of
flutes, the plaintive twanging of the strings of a harp, fell softly on
the air; and in streets lit up by great fires of wood we could see the
bright short tunics fly as Greeks danced the *callabida*. Only the towers,
seeming larger in the night, the Roman towers, remained dark; and
the hoarse rough blare of their bugles sounded from time to time as
a threat over the holy festal city.

But beyond the city walls the joy of the paschal night broke out
afresh. There were lights in Siloe; in the encampments on the Mount
of Olives, bright fires burned; and as the city gates remained open,
lines of torches smoked along the ways amid the sound of singing.
Only one hill, beyond Gareb, remained in darkness. At that hour,
below it, in a rocky ravine, whitened two mangled bodies, in which
the beaks of vultures, with a dry sound as of iron tools clashing,
were engaged on their paschal supper. At least one body, the precious shell of a perfect spirit, lay safe in a new tomb, wrapped in

linen, anointed, perfumed with cinnamon and nard. Thus on this holiest night of Israel, it had been left by those who loved it and who would henceforth love it ever more passionately; thus it had been left, with a smooth stone above it; and now among the houses of Jerusalem, so full of lights and song, in one, dark and locked, fell tears that knew no comfort. The hearth was fireless and cold, a sad lamp burnt dimly on the shelf, the water-jar was empty, for no one had gone to the fountain, and seated on a mat, their hair fallen about them, the women who had followed Him from Galilee spoke of Him and their early hopes, and the parables told among the corn-fields, and the pleasant times at the border of the lake.

Thus I thought as I bent over the wall, looking at Jerusalem, when silently on the terrace appeared a form wrapped in white linen and spreading a scent of cinnamon and nard. A brightness seemed to come from it, its feet seemed scarcely to touch the pavement, and my heart trembled. But a blessing, grave and familiar, came from the white clothes; "Peace be with you." O what a relief! It was Gad. "Peace be with thee," we answered.

The Essenian stopped before us in silence and I felt his eyes search the depths of my spirit in order to gauge its worth and strength. At last he murmured, motionless as a funeral image in his long white robes: "The moon is about to rise; all the expected things are coming to pass; do you feel your hearts strong enough to accompany Jesus, to protect him as far as the oasis of Engaddi?" I rose, extending my arms in terror. To accompany the Rabbi! Was he not lying dead, bound and scented, under the stone in the garden of Gareb? He was alive! When the moon rose, he was to start with his friends for Engaddi! I anxiously seized Topsius by the shoulder, sheltering myself behind his great learning and authority. My learned friend appeared embarrassed by a weight of uncertainty: "Yes, perhaps. Our hearts are stout, but . . . besides, we have no arms." "Come with me," replied Gad fervently; "come with me: we will pass by the house of one who will tell us what it behoves us to know and who will give you arms." Still trembling, still seeking the protection of the wise historian, I made bold to murmur: "And Jesus? Where is He?" "In the house of Joseph of Arimathea," whispered Gad, looking round like a miser when he speaks of his treasure. "In order that the people of the Temple might suspect nothing, we placed the Rabbi in their presence in the new tomb in Joseph's garden. Thrice the women wailed upon the stone, which, according to the ritual, as you know did not completely close the tomb but left a large crack through which we could see the Rabbi's face. Some servants of the Temple looked in and said: It is well; and each went to his own house. I entered the city by the Genath Gate and saw nothing further; but as soon as night fell, Joseph and another man of proved loyalty were to go to fetch the body of Jesus, and by means of the recipes in the book of Solomon revive him from the swoon into which the drugged wine and suffering had thrown him. Come then, ye who likewise love and believe in him."

Impressed and decided, Topsius wrapped his ample cloak about him, and we descended in cautious silence a stair which led from the terrace to a gravel path close to the new wall of Herod. For a long time we walked on in darkness, guided by the white form of the Essene. Sometimes from ruined huts dogs leapt up howling; on the tall battlements dull lanterns passed as the soldiers went their rounds. A shadow, coughing, rose from under a tree, soft and melancholy as if it had emerged from a tomb; it touched my arm and pulled Topsius by the cloak and with groans and a smell of garlic besought us to go with it to its bed scented with nard.

At last we stopped in front of a wall, the entrance to which was closed by a large mat of esparto grass. A passage in which water dripped led us to a court surrounded by a veranda supported on rough beams of wood; the ground, soft with mud, deadened the sound of our footsteps. Gad thrice at intervals uttered the cry of the jackal. We waited in the center of the court, at the edge of a well covered over with planks; the sky above was dark, hard and impenetrable as bronze. At length in a corner under the veranda appeared the bright light of a lamp showing the black beard of the man who carried it; over his head he had thrown a corner of his brown Galilean cloak. But the light was blown out sharply, and the man came slowly in the darkness towards us. Gad broke the melancholy silence: "Peace be with you, brother; we are ready." The man slowly placed the lamp on the top of the well and said: "All is finished." Gad shuddered and said: "The Rabbi?" The man put out his hand to repress the cry of the Essene. Then, after searching the surrounding shadows with his restless eyes, which gleamed like those of an animal in the desert, he said: "These are matters higher than we can understand. Everything seemed to go well. The drugged wine was prepared by the woman of Rosmaphim, who is skilled and knows the ingredients. I had spoken to the centurion, a comrade whose life I saved in Germany, in the campaign of Publius. And when we rolled the stone on the tomb of Joseph of Arimathea, the body of the Rabbi was still warm."

He paused, and as though the closed court under the black sky was not safe and secret enough, he touched Gad on the shoulder and without a sound of his bare feet retired to the intenser darkness under the veranda close to the stones of the wall. Near him we waited in silence, trembling with anxiety; and I felt myself in the presence of a supreme and marvelous revelation which would throw light on great mysteries. "At nightfall," he whispered, in a sad murmur, as of water flowing in shadow, "we returned to the tomb. We looked through the crack: the face of the Rabbi was still there, serene and full of majesty. We rolled away the stone and took out the body. It seemed to be asleep, fair and divine in its cerements. Joseph carried a lantern, and we bore it along Gareb, running through the wood. At the fountain we met soldiers of the Auxiliary Cohort going their rounds. We said: 'A man of Joppa has fallen ill, and we are taking him to the synagogue.' They answered: 'Pass.' In Joseph's house was Simeon the Essene who has lived in Alexandria and knows the nature of plants and everything was prepared, including various roots. We laid Jesus on the mat; we gave him cordials to drink, we called him and waited and prayed; but alas, we felt his body grow cold beneath our hands. One instant he slowly opened his eyes, and a sentence fell from his lips. So indistinct it was that we could not understand; he seemed to call to his father and complain of abandonment. Then he shuddered; a little blood appeared at the corner of his mouth, and with his head on the breast of Nicodemus the Rabbi died."

Gad fell heavily on his knees, sobbing; and the man, as if everything had been said, made a step forward to fetch his lamp from the well. Topsius retained him eagerly: "Listen, I must know the whole truth. What did you do then?" The man stopped near one of the wooden pillars. Then, extending his arms in the darkness and standing so near that I could feel his warm breath in our faces, he said: "It was necessary, for the good of the earth, that the prophecies should be fulfilled. For two hours Joseph of Arimathea prayed, lying prostrate. I know not if the Lord spoke to him in secret, but when he rose his face shone and he cried: 'Elias has come, Elias has come; the time has arrived.' Then by his order we buried the Rabbi in a cave that he possesses, cut in the rock, behind the mill."

He crossed the court, took his lamp, and was retiring slowly without a sound, when Gad, raising his face, called to him through his sobs: "Listen! Verily great is the Lord! And the other tomb, where the women left him bound and wrapped in linen cloths, with aloes and with nard?"

The man, without stopping, murmured as he disappeared in shadow: "It remained open, empty."

Then Topsius dragged me by the arm so eagerly that we stumbled against the pillars of the veranda. A door at the farther end opened, with a sharp sound of drawn bolts; and I saw a square surrounded by pale arches, sad and cold; grass grew in the cracks of its uneven flags, as in a deserted city. Topsius came to a stand, his spectacles flashing: "Teodorico, the night is near an end; we are about to start for Jerusalem. Our journey into the Past is over. The legend in which Christianity begins is come to pass, and the ancient world is ending."

I considered the learned historian in fear and astonishment. His hair waved, shaken by a wind of inspiration; and the words that came lightly from his delicate lips fell with tremendous weight upon my heart: "The day after tomorrow, when the Sabbath ends, the women will return to the tomb of Joseph of Arimathea, where they left Jesus buried; and they find it open, they find it empty. 'He has gone hence, He is not here.' Then Mary of Magdala in her fervent faith will go crying through Jerusalem: 'He is risen, He is risen.' And thus a woman's love changes the face of the world and gives a new religion to humanity."

And, throwing his arms into the air, he ran across the square, and its marble pillars began to fall, softly and silently. Breathlessly we arrived at the door of Gamaliel. A slave, having still round his wrists the remains of riven fetters, was holding our horses. We mounted. With a roar as of stones hurled down by a torrent, we shot through the Gate of Gold and galloped towards Jericho along the Roman road of Sichem, so swiftly that we could not hear our horses' hooves strike the black slabs of basalt. In front of me Topsius' white cloak whirled in a furious blast of wind, the mountains rushed past us, like bundles on the backs of camels in the pilgrimage of a people. The nostrils of my mare flashed forth a reddened smoke, and I clung to her mane dully, as though I were rolling through clouds.

Suddenly we came in sight of the plain of Canaan stretching away to the mountain-ranges of Moab. Our camp lay white by the smoldering embers of the fire. Our horses stopped, trembling. We ran towards the tents. On the table the candle which Topsius had lit to dress by eighteen hundred years ago was dying down in a spluttering white flame. Tired by the immense journey, I threw myself on to the bed, without even taking off my boots covered with dust. Immediately it seemed to me that a smoking torch had entered the tent, shedding a golden brilliance. I rose in fear. In a broad ray of sunlight coming from the mountains of Moab, the jocund Potte was entering in his shirt-sleeves with my boots in his hand. I threw aside my rug, and brushed back my hair, the better to see the terrible change wrought in the world since yesterday. On the table lay the bottles of the champagne which we had drunk to Science and Religion. The parcel containing the crown of thorns stood at the side of my bed. Topsius, upon his bed, in his vest and with a handkerchief bound round his forehead, was yawning as he placed his gold spectacles on his nose. And the merry Potte, reprimanding our idleness, wished to know if we preferred tapioca or coffee this morning. I sighed, a noisy comforting sigh of delight, and in the joy and triumph of having recovered my individuality and re-entered my own age, I leapt over the mattress and, my shirt flying loose in the wind, cried "Tapioca, O Potte, sweet and soft, to remind me of Portugal!"

Four

ext day, a radiant Sunday, we struck our tents in Jericho, and journeying with the sun towards the West, through the valley of Cherith, began our pilgrimage into Galilee. But whether because the consoling spring of admiration had dried within me or because my spirit, after being carried away for a moment to the high peaks of history and then beaten upon by rough blasts of emotion, could no longer find delight in the quiet and desolate ways of Syria, I was always tired and indifferent, even from the land of Ephraim to the land of Zebulon.

When we encamped that night at Bethel, the full moon was appearing from behind the black mountains of Gilead. The festive Potte pointed out to me the sacred spot where the shepherd Jacob, having fallen asleep on a rock, had seen a gleaming ladder which ended at his feet and leaned against the stars and by which he saw ascending and descending between earth and heaven a procession of silent angels with folded wings. I yawned formidably and muttered: "Very nice." And, thus muttering and yawning, I traversed the land of miracles. I found the charm of its valleys as tedious as the holiness of its ruins. At Jacob's well, sitting on the very stones where Jesus, tired, like me, by the heat of those roads, and drinking, like me, from the pitcher of a woman of Samaria, had taught a new pure way of worship; on the side of Mount Carmel in the cell of a convent, listening to the clashing of the boughs of cedars which had sheltered Elias and to the moaning of the waters below, which owed fealty to Hiram, King of Tyre; galloping with cloak flying in the wind over the plain of Esdralon; gently rowing on the Lake of Gennesareth, full of light and silence: tedium stood ever at my side, a faithful companion hugging me to its soft breast under its grey cloak.

Sometimes nevertheless a delicate pleasant longing from a remote past faintly raised my spirit as a slow breeze raises a heavy curtain; and then, as I smoked before my tent or trotted along a dry torrent-bed, I saw again to my delight disconnected fragments of that antiquity which had absorbed my interest: the Roman baths where a marvelous creature in a yellow cap majestically offered her charms; the handsome Manasses placing his hand on his jeweled sword; merchants in the Temple unfolding brocades of Babylon; the death sentence of the Rabbi with its red mark on the stone pillar at the Gate of Judgment; the illuminated streets and the Greeks dancing; and an eager desire would come over me to plunge again into that world irremediably lost. Laughable indeed: I, Raposo, Bachelor of Law, enjoying all the comforts of civilization, felt a longing for that barbarous Jerusalem where I had spent one day of the month of Nizzam, when Pontius Pilate was Procurator of Judea!

Then these memories died down like a fire without wood; in my soul only ashes remained and before the ruins of Mount Ebal or in the orchards which scent Sichem of the Levites I started yawning afresh. When we arrived at Nazareth, which appears in the wilderness of Palestine like flowers on a tomb, I felt no interest even in the fair Jewesses for whom the heart of St. Antonine was bathed in tenderness. With their red pitchers on their shoulders, they went up among sycamores to the fountain where Mary, the Mother of Jesus, was wont to go of an afternoon, singing as they sang, dressed like they in white.

The jovial Potte, twirling his moustache, addressed them with murmured madrigals; they smiled, lowering their soft heavy eyelashes. It was this modesty that made St. Antonine sigh, as he leaned on his staff and shook his long beard: "O noble virtues inherited from Mary full of grace;" for my part, I muttered dryly: "Hypocrites."

Through narrow streets in which vines and fig-trees shelter the houses, humble as befits the sweet village of Him who taught humility, we went up to the hill of Nazareth, ever blown upon by the great wind which comes from Idumea. There Topsius doffed his cap, saluting those distant plains which Jesus must have come to contemplate, conceiving in their light and charm the incomparable beauty of the kingdom of God. The finger of the learned historian pointed out to me all the holy places with sounding names that impress one like a solemn prophecy or the roar of battle: Esdralon, Endor, Sulam, Tabor. I gazed as I rolled a cigarette. A whiteness of snow lay smiling on Mount Carmel; the plains of Perea glittered in a rolling cloud of golden dust; the gulf of Caipha gleamed blue; gloom hung above the mountains of Samaria in the distance, and great eagles were planing above the valleys. "A pretty view," I muttered with a yawn.

One morning at length we began to descend to Jerusalem. From Samaria to Ramah we were drenched by those dense black downpours of Syria which send the torrents foaming down the rocks beneath the flowering oleanders. But near the hill of Gibeah, where of old David in his garden, amid bay and cypress, played upon his harp as he gazed at Zion, the air everywhere was clear and blue. Then a doubt came into my mind, like a melancholy wind in a ruin: I was about to see Jerusalem, but which Jerusalem? Would it be that which I had seen one day gleaming magnificently in the sun of Nizzam, with its strong towers, its Temple of the hues of gold and snow, the hill of Acra covered with palaces and Bezetha watered by the streams of Enrogel?

"El-kurds, El-kurds!" shouted the old Bedouin, raising his lance aloft, announcing by its Muslim name the city of the Lord. I galloped forward in trembling eagerness; and I saw it below, near the ravine of Cedron, gloomy, crowded with convents and crouched in its crumbling walls, like a poor woman covered with fleas who wraps herself in her ragged cloak in order to die in a corner. Soon we had entered the Damascus Gate, and the hooves of our horses were thundering down the paved Street of the Christians; near the wall a stout priest with his breviary and cotton sunshade under his arm was taking a great pinch of snuff. We dismounted at the Hotel of the Mediterranean; in its narrow hall, beneath an advertisement for Holloway Pills, an Englishman, with a monocle stuck in his clear eye and his feet on the sofa, was reading the *Times*; at the back of an open veranda on which some dingy underclothes were hung to dry, a discordant voice was singing: "*C'est le beau Nicolas, holá.*" Ah, this indeed was Catholic Jerusalem. When we entered our room, bright and cheerful with blue-patterned wall-paper, I thought for an instant of a certain hall containing golden candelabra and a statue of Augustus in which a man in a toga stretched out his arm and said: "Caesar knows me well."

I went to the window to breathe in the atmosphere of modern Zion. There was the convent with its green blinds down and the gutters now silent in this soft sunny afternoon; in the winding steps among garden terraces passed sandalled Franciscans and lean unkempt Jews. And how cool and resting would be our convent cell after the blazing roads of Samaria! I went to feel the soft bed; I opened the mahogany cupboard; I lightly caressed Mary's parcel as it lay tied with red string, round and charming, among my socks.

At this moment the jovial Potte entered, carrying the precious parcel of the Crown of Thorns, round and firm, tied with red string, and gaily told me the news of Jerusalem. He had learnt news of importance in the barber's shop in the Via Dolorosa. From Constantinople had come a firman banishing the Greek Patriarch, a poor evangelical old man who suffered from the liver and was kind to the poor. The consul Damiani had asserted, as he stamped his foot in the relic shop of Armenia Street, that in consequence of the quarrel in which the Franciscans and the Protestant Mission had come to blows, Italy would declare war on Germany before the Day of Kings. At Bethlehem in the church of the Nativity, a Latin priest, in a squabble as the wafers were being blessed, had broken a Coptic priest's head with a wax candle. Finally, a more welcome item, near the Gate of Herod which looks over the valley of Jehoshaphat, there has opened for the joy of Zion a café with billiards called the Retreat of Sinai.

Suddenly the sorrowful regret for the past, the ashes that lay thick on my spirit, were brushed aside by a fresh breath of youth and modernity. I bounded on the sounding brick floor, crying: "Hurrah for the fair Retreat. Good food and billiards that is what I needed; and then the women. Put the crown here, my fine Potte. It means a fortune to me. Heavens, how pleased Auntie will be! Put it on the chest of drawers, between the candlesticks. And as soon as we have had a meal, my good Potte, we will be off to the Retreat of Sinai."

But the learned Topsius came in excitedly with a fine piece of historical news. During our pilgrimage to Galilee, the Commission for Biblical Excavations had discovered in some ancient rubbish one of the marble tablets which, according to Josephus and Philon and the Talmud, were placed on the Temple near the Beautiful Gate forbidding the Gentiles to enter. And he insisted that we should go, as soon as we had swallowed our soup, to gaze at this marvel. For a moment in my memory flashed a gate beautiful indeed, precious and triumphant above the fourteen steps of green marble of Numidia. But I shook my arms roughly in revolt: "I will not go; I have had enough," I shouted. "Once for all, I tell you, Topsius, solemnly, that from today I will not look at a single stone or holy place. I have had my dose, Doctor, and a pretty strong one too."

The learned man went off timidly with his coat-tail between his legs.

I spent that week in classifying and packing the smaller relics destined for Aunt Patrocinio. Many and precious they were, such as would give a most pious brilliance to the treasures of the proudest cathedral. Besides the articles which Zion imports in cases from Marseilles, rosaries, medals and images; besides those which are sold at the Holy Sepulchre by the hucksters, bottles of water of Jordan, pebbles from the Via Dolorosa, olives from the Mount of Olives, shells from the Lake of Gennesareth, I had others, rare, wonderful and unknown. I had a small plank planed by St. Joseph, two straws from the manger where the Lord was born, a piece of the pitcher which the Virgin was wont to carry to the fountain, a shoe of the ass on which the Holy Family had fled into the land of Egypt, and a crooked rusty nail. These treasures, wrapped in colored paper, tied with silk ribands and adorned with touching inscriptions, were arranged in a strong case which I prudently had bound with iron.

Then I turned my thoughts to the chief relic, the Crown of Thorns, a source of heavenly blessings for Auntie and of good ringing coin for me, her knight and pilgrim. I desired to pack it in some famous holy wood. Topsius advised me to choose cedar of Lebanon, which was so beautiful that for its sake Solomon had made an alliance with Hiram, King of Tyre. The jocund Potte, however, who had less archaeology, suggested honest Flanders pine blessed by the Patriarch of Jerusalem. I might tell Auntie that the nails used had belonged to Noah's ark, that a hermit had found them by a miracle on Mt. Ararat, and that the rust left upon them by the primeval mud when dissolved in holy water was a cure for colds.

We settled these important matters as we drank beer in the Sinai. During this busy week the parcel containing the Crown of Thorns had remained on the chest of drawers between the two glass candlesticks; it was only on the eve of our departure from Jerusalem that I packed it carefully. I lined the wood with blue cloth bought in the Via Dolorosa; at the bottom I placed a soft layer of cotton-wool whiter than the snow on Carmel, and, without opening it, placed inside the venerable parcel just as Potte had made it up in its brown paper and red string, for the very paper folded at Jericho and the knot ties by the river Jordan would have a special savor of piety for Dona Patrocinio.

The slender Topsius watched my devout preparations as he smoked his porcelain pipe. "O Topsius," I said, "what a pile of money this means to me! But tell me, my good friend, you are sure that I may affirm to Auntie that this Crown of Thorns is the same that. . . ."

The most learned man, in a little cloud of smoke, gave utterance to a weighty maxim: "Relics, Dom Raposo, derive their value not from their authenticity but from the faith which they inspire. You may tell your aunt that it is the same."

"My blessing on you, Doctor," said I.

On that afternoon the learned man had gone with the Commission of Excavations to the Tombs of the Kings. I went alone to the Mount of Olives, because nowhere else near Jerusalem was there a place of such pleasant shade in which to spend a fine afternoon lazily smoking. I went out by the Gate of St. Stephen, I trotted over the bridge across the Cedron, climbed the short cut between aloes to the low wall, the rustic whitewashed wall which encloses the Garden of Gethsemane. I pushed open the small green door freshly painted with its copper knocker and entered the orchard where Jesus knelt and groaned beneath the olive-trees. They are still alive, those sacred trees which soothingly swayed their branches above His world-weary head. There are eight of them, black decrepit trees propped up with wooden stakes, in dull forgetfulness of that night of Nizzam when the angels came silently flying to watch between their branches the human sorrows of the Son of God. In their hollow trunks are kept mattocks and pruning-hooks; on the tips of their branches a few fragile leaves of sapless green tremble and faint like the smiles of a dying man. Around them is a small garden well watered and carefully tended. In plots with privet hedges were planted rows of cool green lettuce; not a withered leaf spoils the immaculate neatness of the sand paths between; near the walls, in which in twelve niches gleam the twelve Apostles in porcelain, drills of onion and carrots are bordered with sweet-scented musk. Why was not there so fair a kitchen-garden here in the time of Jesus? Perhaps those useful vegetables in their placid orderliness might have calmed the torments of His heart.

I sat down under the oldest olive-tree. The guardian monk, a smiling saint with an interminable beard, was watering, with habit tucked up, his pots of ranunculus. It was an afternoon of a melancholy splendor. Filling my pipe, I smiled thoughtfully. Yes, next day I would leave that ashen-grey city, crouching there below, its funeral walls like a widow who will not be comforted; and one day, borne over the blue waves, I would come in sight of the cool Serra de Sintra; my native gulls would come to cry me a welcome, swerving about the masts; and gradually Lisbon with her white walls and grass-grown roofs would appear soft and indolent before my eyes. Crying "Auntie, Auntie!" I would run up the stone steps of our house at Sant'Anna, and Auntie with wide-open mouth would start trembling before the great relic which I humbly offered her. Then in the presence of celestial witnesses, of St. Peter and Our Lady of the Patrocinio, of St. Casimiro and St. Joseph, she would call me her son, her heir. And on the day following she would turn yellow and groan and die.

Delicious thought! On the wall among the honeysuckle a bird sang faintly; more joyous than its song was the hope singing in my heart. Auntie was in bed, a black kerchief tied round her head, her hands clutching anxiously at the folds of the sheet about her, her chest heaving in fear of the devil. Auntie was growing stiff in the death agony. One warm May day they placed her cold corpse in a coffin carefully nailed down and, with cabs following behind, she went off to her last home. Then the seal of her will was broken in the damask room, where I had placed cakes and port-wine for the notary Justino. In deep mourning, leaning on the marble table, I hid the scandalous radiance of my face in the crumpled folds of my handkerchief; and from between the official documents, I heard rolling with a tinkling of gold, rolling with a murmur of cornfields, rolling, rolling towards me the thousands of G. Godinho. What ecstasy!

The holy man had set down his watering-can and was walking to and fro with open breviary on a path hedged with myrtle. What should I do in my house in Sant'Anna as soon as they had carried away the horrible old woman dressed in the habit of the Virgin? My first act would be one of justice: I would run to the oratory, put out the lights, scatter the flowers, and leave the saints in moldy darkness. Yes, I, Raposo, a Liberal, needed my revenge for having prostrated myself before their painted images like a sordid sacristan, for having implored their mercy day by day like a painted slave. I had served the saints to serve Auntie; but, now, ineffable delight, she was moldering in her grave; those eyes in which there had never shone a tear of charity were now the prey of worms; and between her decaying lips at last appeared smilingly those decayed teeth of hers which had never known a smile. The thousands of G. Godinho were mine; and, freed from the disgusting lady, I no longer owed her saints either prayers or roses. And after fulfilling this philosophic act of justice I would be off to Paris, to enjoy myself.

The good friar, smiling in his snow-white beard, touched me on the shoulder, called me his son, and reminded me that it was closing-time and that my alms would be received with pleasure. I gave him sixpence and went back happily to Jerusalem, slowly along the valley of Jehoshaphat, humming a soft ballad. Next afternoon, as the bell of the Church of the Flagellation was ringing to a special service, our caravan formed up at the door of the Hotel of the Mediterranean to leave Jerusalem. The boxes of relics were on the mule among the bundles. The Bedouin, whose cold had grown worse, had wrapped himself in a sordid scarf like a sacristan. Topsius rode a grave and leisurely mare. And I, who in my joy had set a red rose in my buttonhole, muttered as we trod the Via Dolorosa for the last time: "Adieu, cesspool of Zion!"

We were close to the Damascus Gate when a cry echoed along the street by the corner of the convent of the Abyssinians: "Friend Potte, Doctor, gentlemen, a parcel, you have forgotten a parcel." It was the Negro from the hotel, hatless, waving a parcel which I at once recognized by the brown paper and red string—Mary's parcel! And I remembered now that in packing I had not seen it in the cupboard, nestling among the socks. Breathlessly the slave told us that after our departure, as he was sweeping out the room, he had discovered the parcel in dust and cobwebs behind the cupboard; he had carefully cleaned it and, as he had always been anxious to serve the Portuguese nobleman, he had come running after us without even staying to put on his coat.

"All right," I muttered dryly and severely, and I gave him the coppers that weighed down my pockets. I wondered how it had rolled behind the cupboard. Perhaps the Negro, in tidying, had taken it from its place among the socks. I would rather that it had remained among the dust and cobwebs; for in truth this parcel was now terribly inconvenient. Certainly I loved Mary; I felt delight at the thought of being soon once more in the land of Egypt, enfolded in her plump arms. But as I kept her image faithfully in my heart, I had the less need to carry her night-dress perpetually at my saddlebow. What right, then, had this piece of linen to run after me through the streets of Jerusalem and insist on being included in my luggage and accompanying me home?

It was the thought of my country that tormented me as we rode away from the walls of the Holy City. How could I ever enter the sacerdotal house of my Aunt Patrocinio with this scandalous parcel? Auntie was continually rummaging in my room, furnished as she was with false keys, harsh and eager, searching in the corners among my letters and linen. How green with rage she would become if one evening she came upon this beloved and sinful parcel of lace with its written dedication: "To my valiant little Portuguese." "If I heard that on this holy journey you had been running after women, I would drive you out like a dog." Thus had Auntie spoken, before the Church and the Bench, on the eve of my pilgrimage. For the mere sentimental desire to preserve the relic of a gloveseller, was I to lose the friendship of the old woman which had cost me so dear to win, by means of prayers and drops of holy water and acts humiliating to my Liberal reason? Never! And if I did not forthwith drown the fatal parcel in the water of a pool as we passed the huts of Kolonieh, it was from a desire not to betray to the penetrating Topsius the cowardice of my heart. But I determined that as soon as we had entered at nightfall the mountains of Judah, I would linger behind and, far from Topsius' spectacles and the kindly attentions of Potte, I would hurl into a ravine Mary's terribly incriminating parcel which might wreck my fortunes. And I prayed that it might soon be rent asunder by jackals or decay beneath rain sent by the Lord.

We had already passed the tomb of Samuel behind the rocks of Emmaus, and Jerusalem had disappeared for ever from my sight, when Topsius' mare, seeing a fountain in a hollow by the road, deserted caravan and duty and trotted towards the water with imprudent eagerness. I stopped indignant: "Pull the rein, Doctor. What a shameless animal; it has only just drunk; do not give in to it; pull; do not use the whip."

But in vain the philosopher, with elbows projecting and stiff legs, pulled at bridle and mane. The mare went off with the philosopher. I too went to the fountain, so as not to abandon the valuable man in the wilderness. Near it whitened the bones of a great dromedary, and the branches of a solitary mimosa had been burnt by the fire of a caravan. Afar off, a shepherd on the bare steep hill-side, and black against the opal sky, was moving slowly among his sheep, a lance upon his shoulder. And in the gloomy silence the fountain wept. That ravine was so deserted that I determined to leave there Mary's parcel to rot away like the bones of the dromedary.

The historian's mare was drinking leisurely, and I was searching about for a gap or pool, when mingled with the fountain's lamentation I thought I heard the sound of human weeping. I went round a rock which jutted out as proudly as the prow of a galley and found crouching among the stones and thistles a woman weeping with a baby in her lap; her curly hair was spread over her arms and shoulders that her rags barely covered, and over the child asleep against her warm breast her tears fell more constantly, more sadly than the water of the fountain, as if they could have no ending. I cried to the jovial Potte.

When he trotted up showing the silver of his pistol, I begged him to inquire of the woman the reason of her much weeping. But she seemed rendered foolish with grief; she murmured something about a burnt hut and the passage of Turkish horsemen and milk failing; then she pressed the child against her face and, overcome, with disheveled hair, began to weep afresh. The festive Potte gave her a silver coin; Topsius took a note of her misfortune to serve for a severe lecture on Muslim Judea; and I began to search in my pocket for coppers, when I remembered that I had given them all to the Negro of the Hotel of the Mediterranean. But I had a fortunate inspiration: I threw her my dangerous parcel, and bade Potte explain to the unhappy woman that any of the women who dwell by the Tower of David, fat Fatme or Palmira the Samaritan, would give her two golden piastres for the luxurious civilized article of clothing.

We trotted on to the road again; behind us the woman, between sobs and kisses to the child, showered upon us the blessings of her heart. Our caravan resumed its march, while the muleteer in front, sitting on the top of the luggage, sang to the new-risen star of Venus the harsh slow plaining song of Syria, telling of love and Allah and a battle of spears and the roses of Damascus.

When we dismounted next morning at the Hotel of Jehoshaphat in ancient Joppa, great was my surprise to see, pensively sitting in the hall, in a great white turban, the melancholy Alpedrinha. My eager embrace nearly broke his bones; and when Topsius and the jocund Potte had departed under the sunshade to inquire about the steamer which was to take us to the land of Egypt, Alpedrinha told me his story while he brushed my cloak.

Sadness had driven him away from dear Alexandria. The Hotel of the Pyramids and its luggage had filled his soul with an infinite weariness, and our departure on the Shark for Jerusalem had inspired him with a longing for the sea and historical cities and unknown multitudes. A Jew of Kesham, who was about to found an inn, with billiards, at Bagdad, had hired him as marker; and he, placing in a sack the piastres saved in the bitterness of Egypt, was going to make trial of this adventure of Progress by the sluggish waters of the Euphrates in the land of Babylonia. But first, being tired of carrying other persons' bundles, he was going to Jerusalem, insensibly perhaps carried thither by the spirit, like the Apostle, meaning to have a rest, with empty hands, at a corner of the Via Dolorosa.

"And has the gentleman received any newspapers from our Lisbon? I should be glad to learn how things are going there."

While he thus babbled sadly and with his turban awry, I thought happily of the hot land of Egypt, of the bright Street of the Two Sisters, the little chapel under plane-trees, the poppies of Mary's hat. And my wish for my fair gloveseller grew more intense. What a passionate cry would spring to her lips when one afternoon, strong and burnt by the sun of Syria, I appeared before her counter, frightening away the white cat! And the night-dress? Well, I could tell her that one night by a fountain Turkish horsemen with spears had robbed me of it.

"Tell me, Alpedrinha; have you seen Mary? How is she? Plump and well, eh?"

He bent his face, and a strange red appeared in his withered cheeks: "She is not there; she has gone to Thebes."

"To Thebes? To the ruins? Why, that is in Upper Egypt; that is in Nubia. Well, I never! What has she gone there for?"

"To embellish the pictures," murmured Alpedrinha disconsolately.

To embellish the pictures! I only understood when my fellow-countryman informed me that the ungrateful rose of York, the pride of Alexandria, had been carried off by a long-haired Italian who was going to Thebes to photograph the ruins of the palaces in which had dwelt, facing one another, Rameses, King of men, and Ammon, King of the gods. And Mary had gone in order to lend a charm to the views by appearing in them in the shadow of the sacred granite with her modern parasol and hat garnished with poppies.

"Shameless woman!" I cried in my grief. "With an Italian? Out of love for him or merely as a matter of business, In love with him?"

"Passionately," murmured Alpedrinha. And his sigh sounded through the Hotel of Jehoshaphat.

At this cry of passion and despair, an abominable suspicion flashed through my mind. "Alpedrinha," I said, "that sigh: there is some treachery here, Alpedrinha."

He bowed his head in such contrition that the loose turban fell on to the brick floor; and before he could pick it up I had furiously seized his flabby arm: "Alpedrinha, the truth: you too and Mary, eh?" My bearded face flashed; but Alpedrinha was of the South, of our chattering land of vainglory and wine, and, fear yielding to vanity, he turned upon me the whites of his eyes and murmured: "I too."

I shook his arm away in fury and disgust. She too! and he: O earth, earth, what is it but a heap of rottenness rolling through space with the brightness of a star? "And tell me, Alpedrinha, did she also give you a present?"

"Yes, a small present." To him too! I laughed bitterly, my hands on my thighs. "And tell me, did she call you her valiant little Portuguese?"

"As I was serving with Turks, she used to call me her nice little Moor."

I was about to roll on the sofa, and tear it with my nails in ceaseless laughter, despair and disdain, when Topsius and the merry Potte appeared all smiles. Well? Yes, a steamer had arrived from Smyrna and would weigh anchor this afternoon for Egypt, and it was none other than our beloved *Shark*. "Good," I cried, stamping on the brick floor. "Good indeed, for I have had enough of the East. I have had nothing but sunstrokes and treachery and fearful dreams and kicks. I have had enough."

Thus did I shout in fury; but that afternoon on the shore, near the dark boat which was to take us on board the *Shark*, I was filled with regret for Palestine and our tents beneath the glittering stars and our caravan marching amid song through the ruins with fine-sounding names. My lip trembled when Potte sadly held out to me his pouch of tobacco of Aleppo: "Dom Raposo, it is the last cigarette from the merry Potte." And my tears fell when Alpedrinha, without a word, stretched out his lean arms. From the boat, squatting on the cases of relics, I could see him on the beach waving his melancholy check hankerchief, by the side of Potte, who was waving kisses, his great boots touching the water. And as I leant over the side of the *Shark*, I could still see him motionless on the stone pier holding on to his huge white turban with his hands against the sea breeze.

Unhappy Alpedrinha! Truly I alone understood your greatness! You were the last of the Lusiads, of the race of the Castros and Albuquerques, the strong men who went in the fleets to India! The same divine thirst for the unknown will take you, like them, to that land of the East from which spring stars that spread light abroad from heaven and gods who unfold the Law. Only as you have not, like those Portuguese of old, heroic beliefs giving birth to heroic enterprises, you do not go, like them, with a great sword and a great rosary to impose on foreign peoples your king and your God. You have no God to fight for, Alpedrinha; you have no king to explore for, Alpedrinha! Therefore among the Eastern peoples you follow the only professions compatible with the faith and ideal and courage of the modern Lusiads: to stand idly at a street corner or sadly carry the bundles of others.

The wheels of the *Shark* churned the water. Topsius raised his silk cap and cried gravely in the direction of Jaffa, which was growing dark in the pale afternoon beneath its gloomy rocks and amid its dark-green orchards: "Farewell, farewell for ever, land of Palestine." I likewise waved my helmet: "Good-bye, good-bye, religion." I was going slowly away, when the long black robe of a nun brushed against me and, beneath the modest shadow of the hood which was turned slightly towards me, a gleam of black eyes sought my powerful beard.

Wonderful! It was the same holy sister who had borne on her chaste knees, over those Scriptural waves, Mary's unhallowed parcel. The same! Why had fate once more placed beside me, on the narrow deck of the *Shark*, this church lily, this withered bud? Who knows? Perhaps it was in order that before the hot breath of my desire she should grow green and flower and not remain for ever barren and useless, prostrate at the dead feet of a God!

And she was not now accompanied by the other sister, the plump sister in spectacles. Fate gave her to me defenceless, like a dove in the desert. Then was I invaded by a bright hope of a nun's love stronger than the fear of God, of a breast worn by sackcloth and penitence, falling trembling and vanquished in my valiant arms. I determined to whisper to her forthwith: "O my little sister, I am dying of love for you"; and all on fire, twirling my moustache, I went towards the gentle sister, who had taken refuge on a seat and was passing the beads of her rosary through her white fingers.

But suddenly the deck of the *Shark* failed beneath my triumphant feet. I stopped in dismay. O miserable humiliation: it was a wave bringing sea-sickness in its train. I ran to the side, I defiled the blue sea of Tyre and slunk away to my cabin, nor did I raise my pale face from the mattress until I felt the *Shark* enter those calm waters where of old, fleeing from Actium, the galleys of Cleopatra had hastily cast their gilded anchors. And again worn out and disheveled, I saw the low land of Egypt, hot and tawny as a lion. Round the delicate minarets the doves calmly fluttered. The languid palace slept at the water's edge among palm-trees. Topsius, holding my hatbox, made a most learned harangue on the subject of the ancient Pharol. The pale nun had already left the *Shark*, the dove of the desert had escaped from the kite, because the kite in mid flight had folded its wings in sordid sea-sickness.

On that very afternoon, in the Hotel of the Pyramids, I learnt to my joy that a steamer with a cargo of cattle would leave early next morning for the blessed land of Portugal. In the carriage, alone with the learned Topsius, I went for a last drive through the scented shade of Mamoudieh; and I spent the brief night in a delicious street. O my fellow-countrymen, go thither if you wish to know the fierce delights of the East! The unprotected gas-jets flicker and whistle in the wind; the low wooden houses are only closed to the street by white curtains through which light shines; there is a smell of sandalwood and garlic everywhere. Women seated on mats, with flowers in their hair, murmur softly: Eh, Mossiu, eh, Milord.

I returned late, tired out. In passing up the Street of the Two Sisters, above the door of a closed shop, I caught sight of the wooden hand, painted red, which had taken my heart prisoner. I hit at it with my stick. That was my last feat on this long journey.

In the morning the faithful learned Topsius came with me in galoshes to the Customs shed. I held him in a long embrace: Good-bye, fellow-traveller, good-bye. Write to me, Campo de Sant'Anna. He murmured in my arms: That six pounds, I will send it. I clasped him to my generous heart, to drown his money explanation; then, with one foot on the prow which was to take me to the *Cid Campeador*, I said: Then I may tell Auntie that the little Crown of Thorns is the same. . . . He raised his hands, solemn as a high priest of learning: You may tell her on my authority that it is the very same, thorn for thorn. He lowered his stork's beak adorned with spectacles and we kissed as brothers.

The Negroes fell to their rowing. On my knees lay the case containing the mighty relic. But when my boat was sailing through the blue waters, it passed close to a boat which was being slowly rowed towards the palace asleep among the palms; and suddenly I saw the black habit, the lowered hood. My beard felt for the last time a long eager look, and, standing up, I cried: "O my dear little woman!" But the wind carried me on; she in her rowing-boat contritely bowed her face, and on her heaving breast the jealous iron cross pressed more heavily.

I remained desolate. Who knows? Possibly in the whole vast earth that was the only heart in which I might find peace and a sure refuge. But alas, she was but a nun and I was but a nephew. She was going to her God, I was going to my Aunt. And when our hearts crossed upon these waters and beat silently in mutual sympathy, my boat was sailing merrily towards the West and her black boat was being slowly rowed toward the East. So do kindred souls ever fail to meet in this world of eternal aspiration and eternal imperfection.

Five

Two weeks later I was rolling in Pingalho's cab along the Campo de Sant'Anna, the door open and my boot upon the step as I caught sight of the dark door of Auntie's house among the trees. Inside the cab I shone more splendidly than a stout Caesar crowned with a garland of gold on his triumphal car after vanquishing gods and peoples. Partly it was the joy to see again, under that delicate blue January sky, my Lisbon with its quiet streets of dull-washed houses, and here and there a green blind drawn at the windows like eyebrows weighed down with weariness and sleep.

But especially it was the glorious change in my domestic fortunes and social influence. Hitherto I had been in the house of Dona Patrocinio simply Master Teodorico, who for all his Bachelor's degree and Raposo beard could not order the mare to be saddled in order to go and have his hair cut in the lower city without asking Auntie's permission. And now? Now I was our Doctor Teodorico, who by holy contact with the places of the Gospel had attained an almost pontifical authority. How had I figured in the Chiado hitherto among my fellow-citizens? Simply as the young Raposo, who owned a horse. And now? Now I was the great Raposo who had made a poetical pilgrimage through the Holy Land like Chateaubriand and, in view of the remote inns at which I had stayed and the plump Circassian women I had kissed, might speak with authority in the Geographical Society or in a certain house directed by Benta.

Pingalho drew up his horses. I jumped out, with the case of the relic pressed against my heart. And at the farther end of the gloomy court, paved with small stones, I saw Dona Patrocinio das Neves, dressed in black silk, a black lace kerchief on her head, baring her teeth in her face, livid under her smoked spectacles, in a smile of welcome.

"O Auntie."

"O child."

I set down the holy parcel and fell upon her withered breast; and the smell of snuff, chapel and ants was, as it were, the spirit of the house enveloping me and leading me back into the pious routine of the home.

"How sunburnt you are!"

"Auntie, I have many messages for you from the Lord."

"Oh, give them to me all, all." And, pressing me against her hard breast, she touched my beard with her cold lips as reverently as if it were the wooden beard of the image of St. Theodoric.

At her side Vicencia was wiping her eyes with the edge of her new apron. Pingalho had set down my leather trunk; and, taking up the precious case of holy Flanders pine, I murmured with unctuous modesty: "Here it is, Auntie, here it is; here I present you with your divine relic which formerly belonged to the Lord."

The livid emaciated hands of the horrible old lady trembled as they touched that wood which contained the miraculous source of her health and a refuge from her afflictions. Stiff and silent, eagerly hugging the parcel, she ran up the stone steps, passed through the room of Our Lady of the Seven Sorrows, and made for the oratory. Behind her, I, resplendent in my helmet, kept murmuring: How are you? How are you? to toothless Eusebia and the cook who bowed in the passage as at the passing of the Host.

In the oratory, before the altar strewn with white camellias, I was magnificent. I did not kneel or make the sign of the cross, but from afar off with two fingers familiarly greeted the golden Jesus nailed on His cross and gave Him a look of smiling intimacy, as to an old friend with whom one shares old secrets. Auntie perceived this intimacy with the Lord, and when she knelt on the carpet, leaving the cushion of green velvet for me, her hands were raised in adoration of her nephew as much as of her Savior.

When the paternosters to return thanks for my return were finished, she said humbly, still on her knees: "It would be well, my son, if I knew what the relic is, so as to place candles and prepare what is suitable."

I answered, as I brushed my knees: "You will see it later. At night-fall the relics will be unpacked, according to the recommendation made to me by the Patriarch of Jerusalem. But in any case you might light four more candles, for even the wood of the box is holy."

She lit them in humble submission; she then with devout care placed the case on the altar, gave it a long noisy kiss, and covered it with a splendid lace cloth. Then I, with two fingers, episcopally, traced above the cloth a blessing in the form of a cross. She waited with her black spectacles, gazing at me tenderly.

"And now, my son, and now?"

"Now dinner, Auntie, for I am ravenously hungry."

Dona Patrocinio at once gathered up her skirts and ran to hurry Vicencia. I went to my room to unstrap my portmanteau. Auntie had covered the floor with new matting; the muslin curtains swelled out, stiff with starch; a bunch of violets scented the chest of drawers. Our meal lasted many hours; the tray of sweet rice was adorned with my initials under a heart and a cross designed in cin-namon by Auntie. And I without ceasing related my holy journey.

I told her of the devout days of Egypt, spent in kissing one by one the tracks made by the Holy Family in their flight; I told her of the landing of Jaffa with my friend Topsius, a learned German, Doctor of Theology, and of the delicious Mass which we had heard there; I told her of the hills of Judah covered with scenes of the Nativity, at which I, holding my mare by the reins, knelt and gave the images and monstrances the messages of my Aunt Patrocinio. I told her of Jerusalem, stone by stone. And Auntie, eating nothing, clasping her hands, sighed an ecstasy of devotion: "Oh how holy, how holy it is to listen to such things! Heavens, it even makes one feel glad inside."

I smiled humbly. And as I furtively considered her, it seemed to me more and more that she was different. Those harsh black spec-tacles which used to gleam so harshly now appeared ever moist and dim with tenderness. Her voice had lost its sharpness and changed to a soft sighing caress in a nasal tone. She had grown thinner, but her dry bones seemed at last to harbor a warmth of human kindness. And I thought to myself: "I shall have her as soft as velvet." And unrestrainedly I continued to shower proofs of my intimacy with Heaven. I would say: "One afternoon, on the Mount of Olives, as I was praying, suddenly an angel went by;" and I would say: "I threw aside these cares, went to the tomb of Our Lord, opened the top of the tomb and called out. . . ."

Her head hung, she was overcome by these prodigious favors, only comparable to those of St. Anthony and St. Bras. Then I recounted my tremendous prayers and terrific fasts.

At Nazareth, by the fountain where Our Lady was wont to draw water, I had prayed a thousand Ave Marias kneeling in the rain. In the wilderness where St. John had lived, I had sustained myself, like him, on locusts. And Auntie, with wide-open mouth, said: "Oh, how touching, how touching! What a joy for our dear St. John! How pleased he must have been! And tell me, did they agree with you?"

"Why, I even grew fat, Auntie. And, as I said to my German friend, since such an opportunity had come one's way one must take full advantage for the salvation of one's soul."

She turned to Vicencia, who was smiling in happy amazement in her traditional place between the two windows, under the portrait of Pio Nono and the old telescope of Comendador Godinho: "Ah, Vicencia, he has come back full of virtue, chock-full of virtue."

"I think Our Lord was not displeased with me," I murmured as I helped myself to the quince jelly. And the odious old lady contemplated all my movements, even as I sipped my soup, with a reverence due to the holy actions of a saint. Then with a sigh she said: "And another thing: have you brought back some prayers, good prayers taught you by the friars and patriarchs?"

"I have brought some first-rate ones, Auntie." And many of them too, copied from the pocket-books of saints, efficacious for all complaints. I had prayers for coughs, prayers for when the drawers of cupboards refused to open, prayers for the eve of lotteries.

"And have you any for the cramp? Sometimes at night. . . ."

"I have an infallible one for the cramp. It was given to me by a friend of mine, a monk to whom the Child Jesus is wont to appear," I spoke, and lit a cigarette.

I had never dared to smoke before Auntie. She had always hated tobacco more than any other manifestation of sin; but now she eagerly drew up her chair to mine, as towards a miraculous coffer full of prayers which prevail against the hostility of things and vanquish illnesses and make the lives of old women endless upon earth.

"You must give it to me, my dear. It will be a charitable act."

"Of course, Auntie, of course. All of them. And tell me, how are your complaints?"

She gave a groan of infinite discouragement. She was ill, very ill; every day she felt weaker, as though she were literally falling to pieces. At all events, she would not die without the pleasure of having sent me to Jerusalem to pay a visit to the Lord, and she hoped that He would take it into account, as also the expense and the grief of separation. But she was ill, very ill.

I turned my face away to hide the scandalously bright flash of joy that had lit it up. Then I encouraged her generously. What had she to fear? Could she not count now, against the law of natural decay, on the support of that relic of Our Lord?

"And tell me, Auntie, how are our friends?"

She told me a sad piece of news. The best and dearest of them, the delightful Casimiro, had gone home last Sunday with swollen legs. The doctors declared that it was a dropsy. She was afraid it was due to the curse of a Galician porter. "Whatever the cause, there he is. And I miss him, miss him terribly; you can't imagine how I miss him. Fortunately for me, his nephew, Padre Negrão. . . ."

"Negrão?" I murmured, ignorant of the name.

"Ah," she said, "you do not know him."

Padre Negrão lived near Torres and never came to Lisbon, the dissoluteness of which disgusted him. Only on her account and to help her in her affairs had the saint vouchsafed to leave his village. "And he is so refined and serviceable. A perfect treasure. You can't think how much good he has done me. His prayers alone, asking that God might protect you in the land of the Turks! And the way he keeps me company! Every day I have him to dine. Today he would not come; he said a very nice thing: 'I do not wish to spoil a scene of family affection.' He speaks so well and so touchingly. There is no one like him. A real comfort, I assure you. A most desirable man."

I shook the ash from my cigarette in annoyance. Why did this priest from Torres come to dine every day with Auntie against his usual habits? I muttered authoritatively: "In Jerusalem priests and patriarchs only dine out on Sundays. It has greater effect."

It had grown dark. Vicencia lit the gas in the passage, and as our friends, summoned by Auntie to salute the pilgrim, would soon be arriving, I retired to my room to put on my black evening coat. There, as I considered my sunburnt face in the glass, I smiled triumphantly and thought: Teodorico, you have conquered.

Yes I had conquered. What a welcome Auntie had given me! How reverent and devoted! And she was ill, very ill. Soon, with a heart full of joy I would hear her being nailed into her coffin. And nothing could now oust me from Dona Patrocinio's will. In her eyes I had become St. Teodorico. The horrible old woman was at length convinced that to leave her gold to me was the same as to leave it to Christ and the Apostles and the Holy Mother Church.

But the door creaked and Auntie entered. And, strange to say, she seemed to me to be the Dona Patrocinio das Neves of old, green-hued, stiff and severe, hating all love with disgust and casting from her for ever those who ran after women. Her spectacles once more gleamed dryly and were fixed distrustfully on my trunk. Good heavens, it was the old Dona Patrocinio! Her curved livid hands, crossed on her shawl, were fumbling at its fringe, eager to examine my clothes. I trembled, but was straightway inspired by the Lord. In front of my trunk I opened my arms candidly and said: "Here, you see, is my trunk which went to Jerusalem. Here it is open for all the world to see that it is the trunk of a religious man. For as my German friend, who knew everything, said: 'Raposo, my saintly one, if a man has sinned on a journey and has given himself up to dissolute ways and run after women, there are always the proofs of this in his trunk. Hide them as he may, destroy them as he may, he is sure to forget something that will betray him.' This he said to me many times, and even once in the presence of the Patriarch. And the Patriarch signified his approval. And so here is my open trunk: I have no fears; anyone may search and examine it. Look, Auntie, look: here are my underclothes; and I must have some, for it is considered a sin to go naked. And all the rest is holy, my rosary, my prayer-book, my images, all of the best, straight from the Holy Sepulchre."

"There are some parcels there," muttered the vile old lady, stretching out a great bony finger.

I opened them at once eagerly. They were two sealed bottles of water of Jordan. And with grave dignity I stood before Dona Patrocinio with a bottle of the holy liquid in either hand. Then she, her spectacles again grown dim, penitently kissed the bottles, slobbering over my nails; and at the door, yielding with a sigh, she said: "See, my dear, I am all atremble. So many joys coming together."

She went out, and I remained stroking my chin. Yes, there was one circumstance that might exclude me from Auntie's will, and that was if she obtained tangible material proof of my behavior. But how could she in this logical world? All my past frailties were like the vanished smoke of an extinguished fire which no effort can again condense. And how could my last sin, afar off in the land of Egypt, ever come to Auntie's ears? No human combination could succeed in bringing to Sant'Anna the only two witnesses of it: the glove-seller now busy leaning the poppies on her hat against the granite of Rameses at Thebes, and a doctor hidden away in some scholastic street in the shadow of a German University, piecing together the historic rubbish of the history of the Herods. And apart from that flower of corruption and that pillar of learning, nobody on earth knew of my sinful delight in the amorous city of the Lagidae. Besides, the terrible proof of my affair with the sordid Mary, her violet-scented night-dress, was now covering the languid waist of some Circassian woman in Zion or the bronze breasts of a Nubian of Kosboro; the compromising dedication "To my valiant little Portuguese" must have been unpinned and burnt in a brazier;

the lace was becoming worn with use, and soon, old, torn and dirty, it would be thrown into the dustbins of Jerusalem. Yes, nothing could come between my justifiable impatience and the green velvet purse of Auntie. Nothing, unless her aged flesh, inhabited by a stubborn vital flame, refused to be extinguished. Oh, fate most terrible: if Auntie, obstinate and contumacious, were to live till next year's carnations were aflower! I lifted up my heart in a desperate cry, prompted by the keenness of my desire: "O Holy Virgin Mary, make her soon give up the ghost!"

At this instant the great bell of the court sounded; and it was pleasant, after so long a separation, to recognize the two swift timid knocks of our modest Justino; and even more pleasant to hear, immediately afterwards, the majestic knock of Dr. Margaride. Auntie then pushed open my door in nervous eagerness: "Listen, Teodorico; I have been thinking, it seems to me best to wait before opening the relic until Justino and Dr. Margaride have left. They are great friends of mine and very virtuous persons, but I think that for a ceremony of this kind it is best if only persons belonging to the Church are present." She considered that she herself by her devout piety belonged to the Church; me after my journey she considered almost to belong to heaven.

"No, Auntie: the Patriarch of Jerusalem recommended that it should be in the presence of all the friends of the house, in the chapel, with candles burning. It adds to the solemnity. And will you tell Vicencia to come to fetch my boots to clean?"

"Oh, I will take them; are these they? Yes, they need cleaning. You shall have them again in an instant." And Dona Patrocinio took the boots. Dona Patrocinio went out with my boots in her hand! Yes, she was changed, changed.

And before the glass, as I fixed a Malta cross of coral in my tie, I considered that from that day forth I should reign there in Sant'Anna from the height of my holiness, and perhaps, in order to hasten the slow march of death, I would end by beating the old woman.

Pleasant it was, on entering the room, to find my cherished friends, dressed with all solemnity, standing up and extending towards me their welcoming arms. Auntie sat upon the sofa in festal satins and jewels, stiff and filled with pride. At her side a very lean priest was bowing with his hands pressed against his breast, and displaying in his thin face his sharp and hungry teeth. It was Negrão. I dryly held out two fingers: "I am glad to see you."

"A very great honor for your humble servant," he whispered, pressing my fingers to his heart. Then, with bowed servile back, he ran to raise the shade of the lamp, so that the full light might beat upon my face and they might read the effect of my pilgrimage in my altered looks.

Padre Pinheiro decided, with the smile of a sick man: "He is thinner." Justino stammered, cracking his fingers: "More sunburnt." And Margaride added, affectionately: "More of a man." The flexible Padre Negrão turned himself round and bowed before Auntie as to a sacrament in its circle of lights: "And with an air that inspires respect. Most worthy to be the nephew of the most virtuous Dona Patrocinio!"

Meanwhile there was an uproar of friendly curiosity. And your health? And Jerusalem? And the food? But Auntie beat with her fan upon her knee, afraid that so familiar a tumult might displease St. Teodorico; and Padre Negrão intervened with honeyed accents: "Method, gentlemen, method; there can be no pleasure if all ask at once. It is better if we allow our interesting Teodorico to speak."

I hated that "our" and detested that priest. Why were his words so honeyed? Why had he the privilege of a place on the sofa, his sordid knee brushing against the chaste satins of Auntie? But Dr. Margaride, opening his snuff-box, agreed that method would be the best plan. "We will all sit round him here and our Teodorico will tell us in due order all the marvels that he saw."

The lean Padre Negrão, with a scandalous familiarity, ran out to fetch a glass of sugar and water to moisten my throat. I spread my handkerchief on my knee; I coughed, and began to sketch my wonderful journey. I told them of the luxury on board the *Malaga*, of Gibraltar and its cloud-capped hill, of the number of tables with puddings and soda-water.

"Everything on a large scale, French-fashion," sighed Padre Pinheiro, with a greedy gleam in his dull eyes; "but, naturally, all very indigestible."

"Yes, Padre Pinheiro, everything on a large scale, but wholesome things, Padre Pinheiro: excellent roast beef, excellent mutton."

"Which were certainly not so good as your minced chicken, most excellent lady," interrupted the unctuous Negrão close to Auntie's bony shoulder.

I loathed that priest. And as I stirred the sugar I made up my mind that as soon as I had begun to rule Sant'Anna with a rod of iron, there would be no more minced chicken for the flattering throat of that man of God. Meanwhile the worthy Justino, pulling at his collar, smiled at me eagerly. How, he asked, did I spend my nights at Alexandria? Was there a club there or recreation room? Was I acquainted with any serious family with whom I could have a cup of tea?

"Let me tell you, Justino. I did know some, but, to say the truth, I did not like to go to house of Turks. People, you know, who only believe in Mahomet. Do you know how I used to spend the evenings? After dinner I would go to a church of our own beautiful religion, in which there were no strange rites and the Host looked most inviting. There I said my prayers and then went to meet my German friend the Professor in a great square which the inhabitants of Alexandria claim to be finer than the Rossio. And in mere brute size it may exceed it, but it is not beautiful as our Rossio with its mosaic pavement, its trees, its statue and theatre. To my taste, at least, the Rossio is pleasanter for a summer evening, and I told the Turks so."

"And it well became you to stand up for the things of Portugal," observed Dr. Margaride, very pleased and beating on his snuff-box; "I will even say it was the act of a patriot. Worthy of the Gamas and the Albuquerques."

"Well, as I was saying, I used to meet the German, and then for a little amusement, for one must have some amusement when one is travelling, we went to have some coffee. And in the matter of coffee the Turks are really excellent."

"Good coffee, eh?" said Padre Pinheiro, pulling his chair towards me with eager interest; "strong, very strong and scented?"

"Yes, Padre Pinheiro, delicious. We had our coffee and came back to the hotel, and there, in our room, with the holy Gospels set ourselves to study the divine places of Judea where we must go to pray. And as the German professor knew everything, I learnt continually. He even said to me: 'You, Raposo, with these long nights of study, will become a walking dictionary.' And, indeed, as to the holy things and the story of Christ, I do know everything. Well, thus we spent the evening by the light of the lamp till ten or eleven, and then tea and prayers and to bed."

"Most enjoyable, well-spent nights," declared the estimable Dr. Margaride, smiling, to Auntie.

"Ah, it has given him much virtue," sighed the hateful lady; "it is as if he had been for a short time in heaven. Even his very words have a good smell, a smell of holiness."

I slowly lowered my eyelids with great modesty. But Negrão perfidiously insinuated that it would be more unctuous and profitable for our souls to hear of feasts and miracles and acts of penitence.

"I am following my itinerary, Padre Negrão," I replied with asperity.

"Like Chateaubriand and all the celebrated authors," chimed in Margaride with approval.

And it was with my eyes turned to him, as to the most learned person there, that I related our departure from Alexandria one afternoon during a thunderstorm, of the touching moment when a sister of charity, who had been in Lisbon and heard of Auntie's virtue, saved from the salt waves a parcel in which I was carrying earth of Egypt trodden by the Holy Family; our arrival at Jaffa and how by a miracle no sooner had I gone on deck in top-hat and thinking of Auntie than the city was crowned with the sun's rays.

"Magnificent!" exclaimed Dr. Margaride; "and tell me, my Teodorico, had you no learned guide with you to point you out the ruins and tell you about them?"

"Of course we had, Dr. Margaride; we had a great Latin scholar,

Padre Potte." I moistened my lips, and told them of the emotions of that glorious night when we encamped at Ramleh, with the moon illuminating the religious scene: Bedouins, lance on shoulder, guarding our tents and, all round, the lions roaring.

"What a scene!" shouted Dr. Margaride, starting up in enthusiasm; "what a splendid scene! Would that I had been there! It is like one of those grand passages in the Bible or in Eurico. Most inspiring. Had I seen it, I could not have restrained myself. No, I could not have restrained myself, I would have written a sublime ode."

But Negrão pulled at the coat of the eloquent magistrate: "It will be better to let our Teodorico talk, that we may all have the pleasure."

Margaride, annoyed, frowned with his tremendous eyebrows blacker than ebony: "No one in this room, Padre Negrão, relishes what is grand more than I do."

And Auntie, insatiable, beating with her fan, said: "It is well, very well; but go on, my dear, tell us more; tell us more; tell us something that happened to you in close relation with the Lord, something affecting."

They all became reverently silent. Then I told them of our journey to Jerusalem, with two stars going before us to be our guides, as happens to all pilgrims of good education and good family; of the tears I shed when, one rainy morning, I saw for the first time the walls of Jerusalem, and of my visit to the Holy Sepulchre, in top-hat, with Padre Potte, and the words I had murmured through my sobs and in presence of the acolytes: "O Christ, my Lord, here I am, here I come from Auntie."

And the terrible lady said with emotion: "How truly affecting! Before the dear tomb!"

Then I passed my handkerchief over my excited face and said: "That night I returned to the hotel to pray. And now comes a disagreeable incident." And I confessed contritely that, constrained by religion and the honor of the Raposos and the dignity of Portugal, I had had a conflict with a great bearded Englishman.

"A quarrel!" perversely exclaimed the villainous Negrão, anxious to diminish the brilliance of the holiness with which I was amazing Auntie; "a quarrel in the city of Jesus Christ! Oh, how irreverent!"

With teeth clenched, I turned upon the vile priest: "Yes, sir, a squabble. But understand once for all that the Patriarch of Jerusalem said that I was justified; he even patted me on the shoulder and said: 'My congratulations, Teodorico; you behaved nobly.' What have you to object to now?"

Negrão bowed his head, showing the livid blue of his tonsure, like a moon in a pestilence: "If his Eminence approved. . . ."

"Yes, sir. And now, Auntie, hear the cause of the quarrel. In the room next to mine there was an Englishwoman, a heretic, and whenever I began to pray she began to play the piano, singing ballads and nonsense and immoral songs from the play of Bluebeard. Now imagine, Auntie, a person on his knees saying fervently: 'O Santa Maria of the Patrocinio, give my good Auntie many years of life,' and then from behind the partition wall hearing an excommunicated voice yelling: 'I am the great Bluebeard, a widower to be feared.' Outrageous! And one night in despair I restrained myself no longer, I ran into the passage; I hit the door with my fist and shouted: 'Will you kindly be quiet? For here is a Christian who wishes to say his prayers.'"

"And you were perfectly right," affirmed Dr. Margaride; "you had the law on your side."

"That is what the Patriarch said. Well, as I was saying, I shouted this out to the woman and was about to retire gravely to my room when out comes her father, a great bearded fellow with a stick in his hand. I behaved prudently, I folded my arms and courteously informed him that I wished for no quarrel near the tomb of Our Lord and only desired to pray in peace. And what does he answer? That he. . . . I can really not repeat what he said, indecently insulting the tomb of Our Lord. And the blood went to my head, Auntie; I took him by the scruff of the neck. . . ."

"And did you hurt him?"

"I knocked him senseless."

They all acclaimed my fierceness. Padre Pinheiro quoted canonical laws authorizing Fate to knock out Impiety. Justino, leaping up, was delighted at the thought of this John Bull laid low by a solid Lusitanian fist. And I, excited by these praises, as by bugles calling to battle, stood up and shouted tremendously: "Impious remarks in my presence is what I will not admit. I smash everything to smithereens. In matters of religion I am ferocious." And I took advantage of my holy rage to brandish my hairy formidable fist in front of Padre Negrão's sunken chin as a warning. The thin fragile man of God drew back.

At this moment Vicencia came in with the tea, served in the silver plate of G. Godinho. Then my cherished friends, toast in hand, broke forth into ardent applause: What an instructive journey! As good as attending a course of lectures. And what a pleasant evening we have spent! Sao Carlos is nothing to it. This is real enjoyment. And how well he tells his story! What a memory!

Gradually the good Justino, his tea-cup in his hand with biscuits in its saucer, had approached the window as though to examine the starry sky; and between the fringe of the curtains his gleaming greedy eyes called to me secretly. I went to him, humming a tune from a sacred opera, we both plunged into the shadow of the damask, and the virtuous notary, brushing my beard with his lips, murmured: "And the women, my dear friend?" I could trust Justino and whispered into his collar: "My dear Justino, most ravishing!" His eyes gleamed like those of a cat in January, the tea-cup shook in his hand.

I returned to the lighted room, and said thoughtfully: "Yes, a fine night; but they are not those holy stars that we used to see by the Jordan."

Then Padre Pinheiro, cautiously drinking his tea, came and tapped lightly on my shoulder: "Did you remember in those holy places my little bottle of water of Jordan?"

"O Padre Pinheiro, of course I did. I have brought everything: the branch from the Mount of Olives for our Justino, the photograph of the Tomb for our Dr. Margaride, everything." I ran to my room to fetch the presents from Palestine. And as I returned, holding by its

four corners a handkerchief full of devout treasures, I paused behind the curtain on hearing my name, and had the pleasure of hearing the priceless Dr. Margaride assuring Auntie, with all the weight
of his authority: "I did not like to say so in his presence, but he is
now more than a nephew and a gentleman to you: you now have in
your house and at your board an intimate friend of Our Lord."

I coughed and went in. But Dona Patrocinio was still troubled
by a doubt: it did not seem to her polite to Our Lord or to herself
that the smaller relics should be distributed before she, the aunt and
mistress of the house, had received in the chapel the great one.

"For know, my friends," she announced, and her flat chest heaved
with satisfaction, "that my Teodorico has brought me a holy relic
which will be a support in my afflictions and cure me of all my ills."

"Well done," cried the impetuous Dr. Margaride; "so you followed my advice, Teodorico? You searched among the tombs? Well
done indeed, and like a generous pilgrim."

"Like a nephew such as there are none left in Portugal," added
Padre Pinheiro, near a looking-glass in which he was studying his
white tongue.

"Like a son, like a son," proclaimed Justino, rising on the tips of
his boots.

Then Negrão, showing his hungry teeth, muttered this vile in-
sinuation: "It remains to be seen, gentlemen, what the relic is."

I thirsted eagerly for that priest's blood. My eyes went through
him sharper and more glowing than two red-hot spits: "Possibly, if
you are a real priest, you will fall with your face upon the floor to
pray when the marvel appears," I said. And I turned to Dona Patrocinio with the impatience of a noble spirit that requires reparation
for an insult: "We will go to the oratory at once, Auntie. The effect
will be amazing. As my German friend said to me: This relic, when
opened, is enough to stun a whole family."

In her emotion Auntie had risen, with clasped hands. I ran to
fetch a hammer. When I returned, Dr. Margaride was gravely drawing on his black gloves. And behind Dona Patrocinio, whose satins
brushed along the floor with the sound of a prelate's vestments, we

passed into the passage where the great gas-jet was noisily burning in its dark glass. At the farther end, Vicencia and the cook watched us, rosary in hand.

The oratory was resplendent. The ancient silver plates, lit up by the flames of the wax candles, gave to the back of the altar a white heavenly radiance. On the glowing white lace, among the fresh snow of the camellias, the tunics of the saints in their shining red and blue silk, seemed to be new and specially made in heaven for that solemn festal night. Sometimes the rim of an aureole trembled and shone as though through the wood of the images ran a shiver of rejoicing. And on his cross of black wood the Christ, rich and solid, all of gold, gold sweat, gold wounds, gleamed preciously.

"Everything in excellent taste. How divine a scene!" murmured Dr. Margaride, delighted in his love of the grandiose.

With pious care I placed the case on the velvet cushion; bowing, I muttered over it an Ave Maria; then I took off the cloth that covered it and, holding it in my arms, solemnly cleared my throat and said: "Auntie, gentlemen, I would not reveal the nature of this relic because so the Patriarch recommended. But now I will tell you. But first of all I think I should say that everything about this relic, paper, string, box, nails, everything is holy. The nails, for instance, are from Noah's Ark. You may look, you may touch them. Padre Negrão: they are from the Ark, with the rust still on them. And all of the best, and full of sanctity. Moreover, I wish to state before you all that this relic belongs to Auntie and that I have brought it to prove to her that in Jerusalem I thought only of her and of what Our Lord suffered and of obtaining for her this special grace."

"You may count on me, always, my son," stammered the horrible lady ecstatically. I kissed her hand to seal the compact before the Bench and the Church as true witnesses.

"And now, in order that each of you may be prepared and may say the prayers you deem most suitable, I must tell you what the relic is." I coughed and shut my eyes: "It is the Crown of Thorns."

Overcome, with a hoarse groan, Auntie fell forward on the case, embracing it in her tremulous arms. But Margaride was thoughtfully stroking his austere chin, Justino's face had disappeared in his tall collar, and the wily Negrão opened his black mouth wide and looked at me in astonishment and indignation. Good heaven! Both magistrates and priests were displaying an incredulity which would be fatal to my fortunes. I sweated and trembled until Padre Pinheiro, with serious conviction, bent down and pressed Auntie's hand to congratulate her on the religious eminence to which the possession of that relic entitled her. Then, yielding to Padre Pinheiro's high authority in liturgical matters, they all, one after the other, in silent congratulation, pressed the fingers of the delighted lady. I was saved. Rapidly I knelt down, introduced the chisel beneath the lid and raised the hammer in triumph.

"Teodorico, my dear!" cried Auntie in horror, as though I were about to hammer on the living body of the Lord.

"You need not be afraid, Auntie: I learnt at Jerusalem how to handle these holy things."

The slender cover having been unfixed, a layer of white cotton-wool appeared. I raised this gently and reverently, and before their ecstatic eyes lay the most holy parcel of brown paper tied with red string.

"Oh, what a scent; oh, I shall die," sighed Auntie, overcome with devout joy, the whites of her eyes showing above her dark spectacles.

"It is for my dear Aunt and for her only, owing to her great virtue, to unwrap the parcel."

Awaking from her languor, pale and trembling, but with the gravity of a high priest, Auntie took the parcel, made obeisance to the saints, and placed it on the altar. Then devoutly she untied the knot of red string, and carefully, as one anxious not to injure a body which was divine, she undid one by one the folds of the brown paper. A whiteness of linen appeared. Auntie held it in her finger-tips and suddenly shook it, and on to the altar, among the saints, over the camellias, at the foot of the cross fell in its ribands

and laces, Mary's night-dress. Mary's night-dress! In all its shameless luxury, fold on fold. And pinned upon it, clear in the light of
the candles, was the paper offering it to me in a round hand: "To my
Teodorico, my valiant little Portuguese, in memory of our past joy."
Two initials signed it: M.M. I scarcely know what happened in the
flowered oratory. I found myself all in a swoon in the green curtain,
with my legs hanging down. Crackling like logs thrown into a fur-
nace I could hear the accusations hurled against me by Padre Negrão
into Auntie's ear: "Dissolute ways. A mockery. The night-dress of a
prostitute. An insult to Dona Patrocinio." A profanation of the oratory. I saw his boot furiously propelling the white rag into the passage. I saw my friends pass out one by one like long shadows in a
raging wind. The wicks of the candles flickered in affliction. And,
bathed in sweat amid the folds of the curtain, I saw Auntie coming
towards me, slow and stiff, livid, frightful. She paused. Her cold
ferocious spectacles went through me; and through clenched teeth
she uttered but one word: "Swine," and went out.

I tottered to my room, fell upon the bed, shattered. A sound of
scandal ran through the austere house. Vicencia timidly, her white
apron in her hand, stood before me: "Mr. Teodorico, the mistress
bids you depart immediately into the street, for she will not have
you another instant in the house. And she says you may take your
linen with you and all your filthy belongings."

Expelled! I raised my face gently from the lace pillow. And Vicencia added dully, twisting her apron: "O Mr. Teodorico, if you do not
go at once, the mistress says she will send for a policeman."

Kicked out! I lowered my feet uncertainly to the floor. I shoved
a toothbrush into my pocket; stumbling against the furniture, I
looked for my slippers and packed them in a copy of the Nação. I
took up at random from among the trunks an iron-bound box and
on tiptoe descended Auntie's stairs, shrinking timidly like a mangy
dog ashamed of its mange. As soon as I had crossed the court Vicencia, obeying Auntie's fierce commands, banged the iron-studded
door behind me, contemptuously and for ever.

I was alone in the street, alone in life. In the cold starlight I counted my money in my hand. I had two pounds, about ten shillings in change, a Spanish *duro* and some coppers. I then discovered that the box which I had taken up anyhow among the trunks was that of the lesser relics. Most complicated irony of fate! To cover my shelterless body I had nothing but planks of St. Joseph and pieces of the Virgin's pitcher. I put the parcel containing the slippers in my pocket and, without casting a look of my troubled eyes at the house of my aunt, went off on foot with the box on my back through the silent starry night to the lower city, to the Hotel of the Golden Dove.

Next day, pale and listless at the dinner-table of the Dove, I was stirring a dark soup of chickpeas and turnips, when a gentleman with a coat-collar of black velvet took the seat opposite, by a bottle of Vidago water, a box of pills and a copy of the *Nação*. The great veins traversed his forehead, vast and domed like the front of a chapel; and beneath his large nostrils, blackened with snuff, his moustache was a short bush of grey hairs hard as the hairs of a brush. The Galician waiter, handing him the soup of chickpea and turnip, muttered with respect: "Welcome back, Senhor Lino."

After the soup this gentleman, setting aside the *Nação*, in which he had carefully examined the advertisements, turned his dull bilious yellow eyes upon me and remarked that since Epiphany we had had very pleasant weather.

"Perfect," I murmured reservedly.

Senhor Lino dug his napkin farther into his soft collar and said: "If it is not an impertinent question, have you come from the provinces of the North?"

I ran my fingers slowly through my hair. "No, sir; I come from Jerusalem."

In his astonishment Senhor Lino let the rice drop from his fork; and, after silently revolving his emotion, confessed to me that all the holy places held great interest for him, because he was a religious man, thank God. And he was employed, thank God, on the Patriarch's staff.

"Ah, on the Patriarch's staff," I said in my turn. "Very respectable. I knew the Patriarch of Jerusalem very well. A very nice, very holy gentleman. We were on terms of great familiarity."

Senhor Lino offered me some of his Vidago water, and we began to talk about the Gospel land.

"What were the shops like at Jerusalem?" he asked.

"What, fashion shops?"

"No, no," interrupted Senhor Lino, "I mean the shops of holy relics and things divine."

"Yes. Precisely. There is Damiani on the Via Dolorosa, who has everything, even martyrs' bones. But it is best to search and dig. I brought back marvels."

A flame of strange greed lit up the yellow pupils of Senhor Lino's eyes, and suddenly with an inspired thought he called out: "Andrés, a drop of port-wine; today is a special occasion."

When the waiter had brought the bottle, with its date written in manuscript on an old cardboard label, Senhor Lino offered me a glassful: To your health, by the grace of the Lord. — To yours.

Out of courtesy, when we had eaten our cheese, I invited him, a religious man thank God, to come into my room and admire my photographs of Jerusalem. He accepted joyfully, but as soon as he was inside the door he ran eagerly without ceremony to my bed, on which lay scattered some of the relics which I had unpacked that morning. "You like them?" I asked, unrolling a view of Jerusalem and thinking of offering him a rosary. He was examining in silence, turning it about in his fat hands with ragged nails, a bottle of water from Jordan. Then he smelt it, weighed it, shook it. Then, very serious, with the veins swelling on his vast forehead, he asked: "Is it guaranteed?"

I held out the certificate of the Franciscan friar, guaranteeing that it was authentic unadulterated water from the baptismal river. Delighted with this venerable piece of paper, he cried with enthusiasm: "I give you seven and sixpence for the bottle."

It was as if in my Bachelor's mind a window had been opened and the sun had entered. In its clear light I unexpectedly beheld the real character of these medals and images and water and fragments and pebbles and straws, which I had hitherto considered as ecclesiastical rubbish forgotten by the broom of Philosophy. The relics were money! And therefore all-powerful: one gave á piece of clay and received a golden coin. And, thus enlightened, I began to smile, my hands resting on the table as on a shop-counter.

"Seven and six for pure Jordan water! Really, you do not seem to think highly of our St. John the Baptist. Seven and six! It is almost impious. Do you imagine that Jordan water is as plentiful as that of the Arsenal? Why, by this very bed this morning I refused fifteen shillings offered by a priest of Santa Justa."

He balanced the bottle in his fat palm, considering, calculating: "I will give you eighteen shillings," he said.

"Well, as we are both living at the Dove."

And when Senhor Lino left my room with the bottle of Jordan water in a copy of the *Nação*, I, Teodorico Raposo, found myself fatally, providentially turned into a seller of relics. On them I lived and smoked and loved during two months, quietly and happily at the Golden Dove. Almost every morning Senhor Lino appeared in my room in slippers, chose a fragment of the Virgin's pitcher or a straw from the Manger, packed it up in the *Nação*, paid for it, and went off whistling a *De Profundis*. And evidently the worthy man sold my treasures at a good profit, for very soon a gold watch-chain shone on his black velvet waistcoat.

Meanwhile, very diplomatically, I had not attempted, either by supplication or explanation or the assistance of others, to mollify Auntie's devout wrath and recover her esteem. I contented myself with going to the church of Sant'Anna dressed in black and carrying a prayer-book. Auntie now attended Mass in her own oratory, said every morning by Padre Negrão; but I bowed myself and contritely beat my breast and sighed, knowing that through Melchior the sacristan she would hear of my unfailing devotion.

Very discreetly, too, I had not sought out Auntie's friends, obliged as they were to share her passions in order to figure in her will. I thus spared those worthy members of the Bench and the Church some anxious moments. Whenever I met Padre Pinheiro or Dr. Margaride, I crossed my hands inside my sleeves, lowered my eyes, showing repentance and humility. And this discretion was certainly pleasing to my friends, for one night, when I chanced to meet Justino near the house of Benta, the worthy man whispered to me, after assuring himself that the street was empty: "That is the way, my friend. We shall find a means. At present she is perfectly ferocious. Oh, the devil, there are people coming." And he made off.

Meanwhile through Lino I went on selling relics. Soon, however, mindful of my text-books of Political Economy, I reflected that my profits would increase if I were to eliminate Lino and deal directly with the devout consumers. I thereupon wrote to noble ladies, slaves of the Senhor dos Passos, letters giving lists and prices of relics. I sent proposals of bones of martyrs to churches in the provinces. I treated sacristans to glasses of brandy in order that they might whisper to old women with complaints: "For relics there is no one like Dr. Raposo, who has just returned from Jerusalem." And luck favored me.

My specialty was water of Jordan in zinc bottles sealed and stamped with a heart in flames. I sold this water for baptisms, for drink, for baths, and for a time there was a second Jordan, more abundant and transparent than that of Palestine, flowing in Lisbon, with its source in a room of the Golden Dove. Being gifted with imagination, I invented profitable and poetical novelties. I successfully placed on the market a small piece of the pitcher that the Virgin carried to the fountain; I introduced to the piety of my countrymen one of the shoes of the ass on which the Holy Family fled into Egypt. And now, when Lino in slippers came to knock at the door of my room, in which heaps of straws from the Manger alternated with piles of planks of St. Joseph, I only opened a crack of the door grudgingly and whispered: "My stock is exhausted, but next week I am expecting a case from the Holy Land." The veins on the great man's forehead swelled with the indignation of a cheated middleman.

All my relics were received with much fervor as coming from

Raposo just back from Jerusalem. The other relic-sellers had not the splendid guarantee of a journey to the Holy Land. Only I, Raposo, had personal knowledge of that unfailing source of holy articles; and only I could plausibly write on the greasy label which guaranteed the relic the signature of the Patriarch of Jerusalem with all its flourishes.

But I soon found that this profusion of relics was becoming too much for the devotion of my country. Being now crammed full of relics, this Catholic Portugal could swallow no more, not even one of those withered bunches of flowers of Nazareth which I offered for half a crown. Disturbed by this fact, I disconsolately lowered my prices. I scattered tempting advertisements in the *Diário de Notícias*: "Treasures from the Holy Land. Moderate prices. Apply to Rego's Tobacco Shop." Often of a morning, in an ecclesiastical coat and a silk scarf hiding my beard, I accosted devout old women at the door of churches; I offered them pieces of the tunic of the Virgin Mary, strings of the sandals of St. Peter, and I muttered anxiously close to their kerchiefs and mantillas: "Very cheap, my lady, very cheap, and excellent for colds."

I already owed a large account at the Golden Dove; I came downstairs furtively to avoid the proprietor; I addressed Andrés the Galician waiter humbly and affectionately. All my hope was now in a renewal of faith. Any notice of a church festival delighted me as a sign of increasing devotion among the people. I fiercely hated the Republicans and philosophers who undermine Catholicism and thereby diminish the value of its relics. I wrote articles for the *Nação* protesting that "if you do not cling to the bones of the Martyrs, how can you expect the country to prosper?" In the Café Montanha I rained blows upon the table: "We must have religion, *caramba*; without religion even a beefsteak is unpalatable." In the house of Benta I threatened the girls that unless they wore their relics I would transfer my attentions to the house of Adelaide.

My uncertainty as to my daily bread became so alarming that I again sought the intervention of Lino, a man with numerous ecclesiastical acquaintances and relatives among the convent chaplains.

Once more I showed him my bed littered with relics; once more I said, rubbing my hands: "Let us do more business together, my friend; I have here a new consignment fresh from Zion." But the worthy member of the Patriarch's staff was now nothing but bitter recrimination. "That story will not hold water, sir," he cried, as the veins stood out in anger on his flaming forehead. "It is you who have ruined the market. It is so overstocked that one cannot even sell a single bib of the Child Jesus, a relic so much in demand. Your traffic in horseshoes is perfectly indecent. Perfectly indecent, sir. That is what a chaplain, my cousin, said to me the other day: 'Too many horseshoes for so small a country.' Fourteen horseshoes! It is scandalous. Do you know how many nails, those which nailed Christ on the cross, you have fobbed off, with guarantee of their authenticity? Seventy-five! I need not say another word. Seventy-five!" And he went out, slamming the door and leaving me annihilated.

Fortunately that night I met Rinchão in the house of Benta and he gave me an important order for relics. Rinchão was engaged to a Miss Nogueira, daughter of Senhora Nogueira, a rich and devout lady of Beja, a rich owner of pigs, and he wished to give a nice present to the superstitious old dame, things of religion and the Holy Sepulchre. I made up a fine box of relics for him (I included in it my seventy-sixth nail) and adorned it with the best withered flowers of Galilee. With the sum generously paid me by Rinchão, I settled my bill at the Golden Dove, and prudently took a room at Pitta's lodging-house in the Travessa da Palha.

Thus did my prosperity diminish. My room was now high upon a fifth floor, with an iron bedstead and an ancient mattress, the evil-smelling tow of which kept protruding through the ragged cover. For all ornament hung over the chest of drawers in a case adorned with tassels, a colored lithograph of Christ Crucified; dark storm-clouds rolled at His feet, and His clear wide-open eyes followed and watched my every movement, even when I cut my corns. I had been installed here a week, running about Lisbon in pursuit of my daily bread, with worn-out shoes, when one morning Andrés of the Golden Dove brought me a letter which had been left there the evening before marked "Urgent." The paper had a black edge, it was sealed with black wax. I opened it trembling, and saw Justino's signature.

"My dear Friend," it ran; "it is my sad duty, which I perform tearfully, to inform you that your respectable aunt has succumbed. . . ." *Caramba!* The old woman had given up the ghost. Eagerly I caught a detail here and there: "Congestion of the lungs." "Received the Sacraments." "All in tears." "Our Negrão," and at the very end I came, pale and sweating, to this fearful sentence: "By her will the virtuous lady leaves to her nephew Teodorico the telescope hanging in the dining-room."

Disinherited! I took my hat, and ran blindly to Justino's office at S. Paulo. I found him at his desk, wearing a black tie, pen behind his ear, and eating slices of veal on an old copy of the *Diário de Notícias*.

"So, the telescope?" I muttered breathlessly, leaning against the corner of a bookshelf.

"Yes, the telescope," he murmured with his mouth full.

I fell almost senseless upon the leather sofa. He offered me wine of Bucellas. I drank a glass, and, passing my tremulous hand over my livid face, said: "Tell me, tell me everything, good Justino."

Justino sighed. The holy lady, poor woman, had left him four hundred pounds. For the rest, the riches of G. Godinho had been distributed in the most perverse and incoherent manner. The house in the Campo de Sant'Anna and £8000 had gone to the Senhor dos Passos. Her shares in the gas company, the best plate and the house at Linda a Pastora were for Casimiro, who was past caring, being at death's door. Padre Pinheiro received a house in the Rua do Arsenal. The delicious Mosteiro house with its picturesque porch on which one could still see the arms of the Condes de Lindoso, her investments in the public funds, the furniture of the house in the Campo de Sant'Anna and the gold Christ had gone to Padre Negrão. Vicencia had received the bed linen and I the telescope. "So as to be able to consider the rest of the fortune from afar," philosophically observed Justino, cracking his fingers.

I returned to the Travessa da Palha, and during hours, in slippers, with flaming eyes, I nursed a desperate desire to insult Auntie's corpse, to spit in her livid face and dig my walking-stick into her body. I called down the wrath of all Nature upon her. I prayed the trees to refuse their shade to her grave. I prayed the winds to blow over her all the refuse of the earth; I invoked the devil: "I will give you my soul if you torture the old woman continually." I cried with arms raised to heaven: "O God, if there is a heaven, drive her out." I determined to throw stones at her mausoleum. I decided to write to the papers, saying that every afternoon in the drawing-room, in petticoat and black spectacles, she received the visit of a Galician porter. Exhausted with hatred, I fell asleep.

I was awakened at dusk by the entrance of Pitta carrying a long parcel. It was the telescope. Justino had sent it, with a few friendly words: "Here is your modest inheritance." I lit a candle and with the utmost bitterness took the telescope, opened and looked through it as from the deck of ship lost in mid-ocean. Yes, Justino had very sagaciously remarked that the vile Patrocinio had left the telescope to me in sarcastic rancor, that I might gaze through it at the rest of the inheritance. And though the night was dark, I could see with perfect distinctness the Senhor dos Passos pocketing the bundles of notes in his red tunic, and Casimiro fingering with dying hands the silver plate set out upon his bed, and the vile Negrão in cotton jacket and galoshes walking happily by the edge of the water beneath the elms of the Mosteiro.

And I here with the telescope! And I here for ever in the Travessa da Palha, the possessor, for the battle of life, of the sum of half a crown in the pocket of my baggy trousers! With a yell I hurled away the telescope, which went rolling to the hat-box in which I kept the helmet of my journey through the Holy Land. There they were together, the telescope and the helmet, emblems of my two lives, that of splendor and that of penury. A few months ago, with that helmet on my head, I was the triumphant Raposo, heir of Dona Patrocinio das Neves, with gold in my pocket and around me, waiting for me to pluck them, all the scented flowers of civilization. And now, with the telescope, I was the penniless Raposo, with gap-

ing boots and all the black thistles of life around me waiting to
wound me. And why? Because one day in an inn of a city of Asia
two brown paper parcels had been confused. Never had there been
such a mockery of fate. To a devout aunt who hated love as a thing
accursed and was only waiting, in order to make me heir to her
houses and silver, that I, disdaining all women, should bring her a
relic from Jerusalem, I had taken a gloveseller's night-dress; and in
a moment of charity intended to win heaven, as rich alms to a poor
woman in rags, with a starving child at her breast, I had thrown a
branch of thorns.

O God, tell me, O devil, tell me how came about this change in
the parcels which has ruined my life? They were alike in paper, size
and string. The one lay in the dark depths of a cupboard, the other
stood in honor on a chest of drawers between two candlesticks.
And no one touched them, not the jovial Potte nor the learned Topsius nor I myself. Who had moved them, then? Evidently someone
with invisible hands. Yes, someone incorporeal, almighty, had out of
hatred miraculously changed the thorns into lace that Auntie might
disinherit me and I become for ever outcast.

And even as I thus cried, disheveled, I found coldly fixed upon
me and wide open as though rejoicing in the ruin of my life, the
clear eyes of the crucified Christ in its case adorned with tassels.
"It was you," I cried, suddenly enlightened and understanding the
miracle; "it was you, it was you." And with clenched fists I complained to it from my injured heart: "Yes, it was you who before
Auntie's eyes transformed your traditional Crown of Thorns into
Mary's night-dress. And why? What had I done to you? Fickle and
ungrateful god! When and where have you ever received a more
perfect devotion than mine? Did I not go every Sunday dressed in
black to hear the best Masses Lisbon could offer? Did I not every
Friday devour codfish and oil to please you? Did I not spend whole
days in Auntie's oratory with aching knees muttering your favorite
prayers? What prayers were there that I failed to learn by heart for
your sake? In what gardens were there flowers that I did not take to
deck your altars?"

And eagerly, with disheveled hair, pulling my beard, I cried, so near the image that the breath of my anger dimmed its glass case: "Look at me: do you not remember to have seen this face, this hair, centuries ago in a marble hall beneath an awning, where the Roman Praetor sat in judgment? Perhaps you may not remember, for a victorious god upon his altar is very different from a provincial rabbi bound with cords. Well, on that day of Nizzam, when as yet you had no comfortable places in heaven to offer to the faithful; on that day when as yet no one had found in you a source of wealth or a prop of power; on that day when Auntie and all those who now prostrate themselves at your feet would have hooted at you as did the sellers of the Temple, the Pharisees and the rabble of Acra; on that day when the soldiers, who now accompany you with bands, the magistrates who now imprison anyone who insults or denies you, the proprietors who now lavish on you gold and feasts of the church, would all have joined forces, with their arms and codes and purses in order to secure your death as a revolutionary, an enemy of order, a danger to property; on that day when you were merely a creative Intelligence and an active Goodness and therefore considered by man as a peril to society, there was one heart in Jerusalem which, without thought of heaven or fear of hell, loved you. And that heart was mine. And now you persecute me. Why?"

Suddenly, oh, miracle, from the rough frame with its tassels shot trembling rays of light of the color of snow and gold. The glass opened with a gleam and crash like that of a door of heaven. And from within, the Christ on His wooden cross, without unfastening His arms, began to move towards me, and as He moved He grew till He touched the stuccoed ceiling, fairer in brightness and majesty than the sun when it stands upon the mountain tops. With a cry I fell upon my knees and beat my frightened forehead on the floor; and then through the room I heard, like a light breeze wandering among jasmine flowers, a soft calm voice: "When you used to kiss the foot of an image, it was in order to tell Auntie with servile compunction of your piety; for there was never a prayer on your lips or a humble look in your eyes that was not intended to please Auntie's devout fervor. The god before whom you prostrated yourself was the money of G. Godinho, and the heaven to which you raised your trembling hands was Auntie's will; in order to secure the best place in it, you pretended to be devout when you were impious, and chaste when you were wanton, and charitable when you were mean; you pretended to be tender as a son when you were merely eager to be her heir. You were the hypocrite personified: you had two existences, the one ostentatiously before Auntie, all rosaries and fasts and services; the other out of Auntie's sight, all greed and Adelia and Benta. You lied continually, and were only sincere to earth and heaven; you prayed to Christ and the Virgin that Auntie might quickly give up the ghost. Then you concentrated this laborious deceit of a whole lifetime in a parcel in which you had placed a branch which was as false as your heart, and by its means you intended definitively to pocket the houses and silver of Dona Patrocinio. But in another parcel you were bringing back from Palestine with its lace and ribands the irrefutable proof of your deceit. And it justly came about that the parcel which you gave to Auntie and which Auntie opened was precisely the one which must reveal to her your duplicity. And this, Teodorico, has proved to you how useless is all hypocrisy."

I was moaning on the floor, and the voice whispered, growing stronger, as an afternoon wind among the branches: "I do not know who made that malicious and terrible exchange of parcels. Perhaps nobody; perhaps you yourself. Your penniless plight comes not from the transformation of the thorns into lace but from your double life, your true life of iniquity and your false life of holiness. Being in this contradiction, half pious Raposo, half obscene Raposo, it was impossible that you should continue long at Auntie's side and show only the one side, the one in Sunday black, shining with virtue; the day must fatally arrive in which she would behold to her horror the other side with its black stains of vice. And that is why, Teodorico, I observe to you how useless is all hypocrisy."

At full length on the floor, I abjectly sought to kiss the feet of Christ, hanging transparent in the air, with a tremulous radiance of jewels flashing from the nails that pierced them. And the voice passed over me, full and powerful as the blast which bends the cypresses: "You say that I persecute you. No. The telescope and what you allude to as your outcast state are the work of your hands, not mine. I do not construct the episodes of your life; I attend them and judge them serenely; without any action of mine or supernatural influence, you may yet descend to the darkest misery or ascend to profitable earthly paradises and become the manager of a bank. This depends entirely on you and on your work as a man. Listen: you asked just now if I did not remember your face, and I ask if you do not remember my voice. I am not Jesus of Nazareth, or any other god created by man. I am before the gods that come and go; in me they are transformed and perish, and I remain around them and superior to them, creating them and destroying them perpetually, in ceaseless effort to realize outside me the absolute god that I feel within. My name is Conscience; at this moment I am your own conscience reflected outside you, in the air and the light, and taking before your eyes the familiar form in which you, badly educated and unphilosophical as you are, are accustomed to understand me. You have but to rise and look me in the face for the splendid image to vanish."

And, indeed, no sooner had I raised my eyes than everything disappeared. Then in a transport before this proof of the supernatural I raised my arms to heaven and cried: "O Lord Christ, God and Son of God, who took on human flesh and suffered for us. . . ." But I grew suddenly dumb; for that ineffable voice still sounded in my soul: showing me the uselessness of all hypocrisy. I consulted my conscience, which had returned to me, and, quite sure now that I did not believe that Jesus was the son of God and of a married woman of Galilee, as Hercules was the son of Jupiter and a married woman of Argolis, I rejected from my lips, now sealed by truth, the remainder of my useless prayer.

Next day I chanced to enter the gardens of S. Pedro de Alcantara, where I had not been since the time when I was studying Latin, and I had taken but a few steps among the flower-plots when I met my old friend Crispim, the son of Telles, Crispim & Co., with a linen factory at Pampulha, a fellow-student whom I had not seen since I took my Bachelor's degree. This was the fair-haired Crispim whom I mentioned in the college of the Isidoros.

The old Crispim was dead, Telles, rich and stout, had become Visconde de S. Telles; and my Crispim was now the Firm. After a noisy embrace, Crispim & Co. noticed thoughtfully that I appeared very much pulled down. Then he spoke of his envy of my journey to the Holy Land, which he knew about through the *Jornal das Novedades*, and referred with friendly pleasure to the large sum which I must have received in my Aunt's will. Bitterly I showed him my gaping boots. We sat down on a bench near a climbing rose; and there in the scent and the silence I told him of the fatal night-dress and the relic in the parcel and the disaster in the oratory; of the telescope and my wretched room in the Travessa da Palha. "So that you see, my dear Crispim, that I have not even a crust of bread."

Crispim & Co., much impressed, murmured, as he twirled his fair moustache, that in Portugal, thanks to religion and the Constitution, everyone had a crust of bread, although some lacked cheese. "But I can provide you with the cheese," gaily added the Firm, slapping me on the knee. One of the staff at Pampulha had taken to writing verses and running after actresses. "A great Republican too, always mocking at holy things. Quite disgusting, in fact, and I got rid of him. Now your handwriting used to be good, and you must be able to add up a sum. There is the man's place, take it; it is five pounds a month and will always provide the cheese."

With tears in my eyes I embraced Crispim & Co. The Firm murmured again, as one who has a bitter taste in his mouth: "You seem very much pulled down."

I then began to serve with devotion in the linen factory at Pampulha, and every morning at my desk, pulling on my office sleeves, I copied letters in my fine bold hand and added up figures in a great account book. The Firm had taught me the rule of three and other accomplishments. And as from seeds carried by a stray wind to an unoccupied plot of soil useful plants unexpectedly spring up and prosper, so lessons of the Firm developed in the barren intellect of a Bachelor of Law a considerable aptitude for the linen business. Already the Firm, in the club-room of the Carmo, would say with conviction: "Raposo, despite the University of Coimbra and the textbooks they made him swallow, is capable of serious work."

One Saturday afternoon in August, as I was about to close the account book, Crispim & Co. stopped in front of my desk, smiling and lighting a cigar: "Tell me, Raposo, what Mass do you usually attend?"

In silence I took off my office sleeves.

"I ask you," went on the Firm, "because tomorrow I am going with my sister to a country-house of ours across the Tagus; and if you are not especially attached to any Mass, you would come to that in the Santos church at nine; we would then go and have luncheon at the Hotel Central and we would afterwards cross the river to Cacilhas. I should like you to become acquainted with my sister."

Crispim & Co. was a religious gentleman who considered religion necessary to his health and commercial prosperity and to the maintenance of order in the country. With sincere devotion he visited the Senhor dos Passos and he belonged to the Brotherhood of St. Joseph. The chief reason why the man whose place I had taken had become intolerable to him was that he wrote in The Future, a Republican sheet, articles in which he praised Renan and insulted the Eucharist.

I was on the point of telling Crispim & Co. that I was so much attached to the Mass at the Church of the Conceição Velha that I could not attend any other, but I remembered the austere and salutary voice of the Travessa da Palha and said, pale but firm: "The truth is, Crispim, I never go to Mass. It is all nonsense. I cannot believe that the body of God is present on Sundays in a wafer made of flour. God has no body and never had. All that is idolatry and superstition. I say this to you openly, and now you can do what you like to me. I cannot help it."

The Firm considered me for a moment, biting his lips, and then he said: "Well, Raposo, I like such frankness. I like people to be straightforward. That other knave who sat here at this desk used to say in my presence: 'A great man, the Pope,' and go off to the masonic lodges and play ducks and drakes with the Holy Father. Never mind: you are not religious, but you are a gentleman. In any case, ten o'clock at the Hotel Central, and then a sail across the river."

Thus I made the acquaintance of the sister of the Firm. Her name was Jesuina, she was thirty-two and squint-eyed; yet ever since that Sunday on the river and in the country, the wealth of her brown hair as that of Eve, her solid substantial breast, her skin the hue of ripe apples and the healthy laughter of her bright teeth rendered me thoughtful of an afternoon as, smoking my cigar, I returned from the office, looking at the masts of the sailing-boats. She had been brought up in the Salesian convent; she knew geography and all the rivers of China; she knew history and all the kings of France; and she called me Teodorico Coeur de Lion because I had gone to Palestine. On Sundays now I dined at Pampulha; Dona Jesuina would make a special dish of eggs, and her squinting eye rested with pleasure on my strong bearded face.

One evening, as we were drinking our coffee, Crispim & Co. praised the Royal Family and its constitutional moderation and the charming charity of the Queen. Then we went into the garden; and as Dona Jesuina watered the flowers and I rolled a cigarette, I sighed and murmured in her ear: "It is your Excellency that would make a delightful queen if poor Raposo were king." She colored and gave me the last rose of summer.

On Christmas Eve, Crispim & Co. came to my desk, gaily placed his hat on the page of the account book which I was blackening with figures, and said, as he crossed his arms, with a friendly laugh: "So, a queen if poor Raposo were king? Now tell me, Mr. Raposo: is there in your heart a sincere love for my sister Jesuina?"

Crispim & Co. was an idealist and liked passion. I was on the point of saying that I adored Dona Jesuina as a distant star; but I remembered the pure lofty voice of the Travessa da Palha; I forced back the sentimental lie that was already on my lips, and said bravely: "Love? Not love. But I think her a fine woman, I like her dowry, and I would make her a good husband."

"Give me your honest hand!" cried the Firm.

I married. I am a father. I have a carriage, am esteemed in my district, and am a Comendador of the Order of Christ. And Dr. Margaride, who dines ceremoniously with me every Sunday, considers that for my culture, my important travels and my patriotism the State owes me the title of Baron of Mosteiro. For I have bought the Mosteiro.

The worthy magistrate, one afternoon at table, informed me that the horrible Negrão, wishing to round off his property at Torres, had decided to sell the ancestral house of the Counts of Lindoso. "Now those trees, Teodorico," the excellent man reminded me, "gave their shade to your mother; indeed, I may say that the same trees sheltered your most respectable father, Teodorico; if I had the honor of being a Raposo, I could not restrain myself, I would buy the Mosteiro and build a house with tower and battlements."

Crispim & Co. set down his glass and said: "Buy it; it is right that you should, as it belongs to the family."

So one Easter Eve, in Justino's office, in the presence of Negrão's solicitor, I signed the document which, after so many hopes and fears, at last made me master of the Mosteiro. "What is that knave Negrão doing now?" I asked the good Justino as soon as the sordid priest's solicitor had left.

My good and faithful friend cracked his fingers. Negrão was in clover. He had inherited everything from Padre Casimiro, whose body was now underground and his soul in the bosom of Abraham; and now he was the intimate friend of Padre Pinheiro, who had no heirs and whom he had carried off to Torres, in order to cure him! Pinheiro lived there now, feasting at Negrão's tremendous dinners and putting out his tongue before every looking-glass; and the poor man would not last long. So that, with the exception of what had gone to the Senhor dos Passos, who could not die again, Negrão would unite the greater part of G. Godinho's fortune.

I turned pale and muttered: "What a brute."

"You may well call him a brute, my friend," said Justino; "he has a carriage, a house in Lisbon, and Adelia. . . ."

"What Adelia?"

"One who was with Eleuterio, and afterwards in secret with some simpleton, a Bachelor, I know not who."

"It was I."

"Well, that one. Negrão maintains her luxuriously; she has a carpet on the stairs, damask curtains, everything. He has grown stouter. I saw him yesterday; he was coming from preaching, at least he told me that he came from the church of St. Roque quite worn out by the amiable things he had been obliged to say about some devil of a saint. He is sometimes witty; and he has good friends, a ready flow of words, and influence at Torres. We shall see him a bishop yet."

I returned home thoughtfully. All that I had hoped for and admired, even Adelia, was now the legitimate possession of the horrible Negrão. A tremendous loss. And it was not due to the confusion between two parcels, nor to my mistaken hypocrisy. Now that I was a father, a Comendador, a proprietor, I had a more material perception of life, and I realized that I had been done out of the fortune of G. Godinho simply because for an instant in Auntie's oratory I had not had the courage to affirm. Yes, when in place of the martyr's crown appeared the wicked night-dress, I should have shouted without blenching: "This is the relic. I wished it to be a surprise. It is not the Crown of Thorns. It is better still. It is the night-dress of St. Mary Magdalene. She gave it to me in the desert." And I would prove my assertion by means of the paper written in so clear a hand: "To my valiant little Portuguese, in memory of our past joy." It was the letter which the saint had written when she gave me the night-dress. There were her initials M. M., and there was the convincing confession: our past joy, the great joy that I had experienced when the saint wafted my prayers to heaven and the great joy of the saint in receiving my prayers.

And who would dare to doubt it? Do not the holy missionaries of Braga in their sermons display notes from the Virgin, sent down from heaven without a stamp? And does not the *Nação* guarantee the divine authenticity of these notes, which preserve in their folds a scent of Paradise? The two priests, Pinheiro and Negrão, aware of their duty and in their natural eagerness to prop up a tottering faith, would at once acclaim in the night-dress, the letter and the initials a miraculous triumph of the Church. Aunt Patrocinio would have fallen upon my breast, calling me her son and heir. And I would have been rich. And holy. My portrait would have hung in the sacristy of the Cathedral; the Pope would have sent me his apostolic blessing by telegraph. Thus my social ambitions would have been satisfied.

And who knows? Perhaps the intellectual ambitions which I had caught from Topsius would also have been realized. Science, perhaps, envious of this triumph of Faith, would have claimed for itself the night-dress of Mary Magdalene as an archaeological document. It might illustrate obscure points of contemporary dress in the New Testament; the fashion of night-dresses in Judea in the first century, the industry of Syrian lace under the Roman administration, the hemstitch of the Semitic races. And my name in Europe would rank with that of the Champollions and the Topsiuses and the Lepsiuses and other sagacious reconstructors of the past. The Academy would throw open its doors to Raposo; Renan, the sentimental heresiarch, would refer to his dear colleague Raposo. Straightway books would be written about Mary's night-dress, learned ponderous books in German, with maps of my pilgrimage through Galilee.

Thus, cherished by the Church, admired by the universities, with my corner assured to me in eternal blessedness and likewise a page in history, I could peacefully grow fat on the fortune of G. Godinho. And all that I had lost. Why? Because for an instant I had lacked that shameless heroism of affirmation which stamps its foot vigorously on the earth or gently raises its eyes to heaven, and amid the universal illusion founds new sciences and religions.

THE END

Other Titles in the Adamastor Series

Chaos and Splendor & Other Essays
  Eduardo Lourenço
  Edited by Carlos Veloso

Producing Presences:
  Branching Out from
  Gumbrecht's Work
  Edited by Victor K. Mendes
  and João Cezar de Castro
  Rocha

Sonnets and Other Poems
  Luís de Camões
  Translated by Richard Zenith

The Traveling Eye:
  Retrospection, Vision, and Prophecy
  in the Portuguese Renaissance
  Fernando Gil and
  Helder Macedo
  Translated by K. David
  Jackson, Anna M. Klobucka,
  Kenneth Krabbenhoft,
  Richard Zenith

The Sermon of Saint Anthony
  to the Fish and Other Texts
  António Vieira
  Translated by Gregory Rabassa

The Correspondence of Fradique Mendes
  José Maria de Eça
  de Queirós
  Translated by Gregory Rabassa

Maiden and Modest:
  A Renaissance Pastoral Romance
  Bernardim Ribeiro
  Translated by Gregory Rabassa